Morgan

'Full of romance and sparkle'
—*Lovereading*

'Morgan is a magician with words.'
—*RT Book Reviews*

'Sarah Morgan continues to hang out on my autobuy list and
each book of hers that I discover is a treat.'
—*Smart Bitches, Trashy Books*

'Morgan's brilliant talent never ceases to amaze.'
—*RT Book Reviews*

'Dear Ms Morgan, I'm always on the lookout for
a new book by you…'
—*Dear Author* blog

Sarah Morgan is the bestselling author of *Sleigh Bells in the Snow*. As a child Sarah dreamed of being a writer and, although she took a few interesting detours on the way, she is now living that dream. With her writing career she has successfully combined business with pleasure and she firmly believes that reading romance is one of the most satisfying and fat-free escapist pleasures available. Her stories are unashamedly optimistic and she is always pleased when she receives letters from readers saying that her books have helped them through hard times.

Sarah lives near London with her husband and two children, who innocently provide an endless supply of authentic dialogue. When she isn't writing or reading Sarah enjoys music, movies and any activity that takes her outdoors.

Readers can find out more about Sarah and her books from her website: www.sarahmorgan.com. She can also be found on Facebook and Twitter.

Sarah Morgan

Suddenly Last Summer

Published in Great Britain 2014
by Mills & Boon, an imprint of Harlequin (UK) Limited,
Eton House, 18-24 Paradise Road, Richmond, Surrey, TW9 1SR

© 2014 Harlequin Books S.A.

ISBN: 978-0-263-24563-9

097-0714

Harlequin (UK) Limited's policy is to use papers that are natural, renewable and recyclable products and made from wood grown in sustainable forests. The logging and manufacturing processes conform to the legal environmental regulations of the country of origin.

Printed and bound by
CPI Group (UK) Ltd, Croydon, CR0 4YY

Dear Reader,

They say the way to a man's heart is through his stomach, so when fiery French chef Élise Bonnet meets supercool surgeon Sean O'Neil, there should be nothing standing in the way of true love. Except neither is interested in true love.

Like his two brothers, Sean grew up at the beautiful Snow Crystal Resort in Vermont, but he couldn't wait to get away, to pursue his career as a surgeon and enjoy life in a big city. Reluctant to make the sacrifices he believes come with a long-term relationship, he has stayed resolutely single. But when circumstances force him to return home, he finds himself confronting more than just his conflicted feelings about his family.

Writing this story was so much fun. I loved bringing together two characters determined to stay apart and I loved writing about Snow Crystal in the summer. It also made me hungry, because I was forced to spend hours drooling over Vermont cookery books (and quite a few bottles of pinot noir just might have been harmed during the research process, but we won't talk about that). Unfortunately, writing leaves me little or no time to shop, so sadly the chances of finding a delicious, freshly baked loaf of rosemary and sea-salt bread in my kitchen are about as likely as opening my front door to find Henry Cavill standing there wearing nothing but a towel. (Wait! Is that the doorbell…?)

Suddenly Last Summer is the second book in my O'Neil Brothers series, but you don't have to have read the first one for it to make sense (but just in case you want to, it's called *Sleigh Bells in the Snow*).

I'm thrilled you decided to pick up this story. I hope you enjoy it and, if you feel like letting me know your thoughts, then the best way to get in touch is to send me an e-mail via my website or find me on Twitter, @SarahMorgan_ (don't forget the underscore) or www.Facebook.com/Author SarahMorgan.

Have a happy summer!

Love,

Sarah

To Flo.
Behind every happy author is a brilliant editor.
I'm so lucky to have you.

CHAPTER ONE

"Phone call for you, Dr. O'Neil. She says it's an emergency."

Sean rolled his shoulders to ease the tension, his mind still in the operating room.

His patient was a promising soccer player. He'd torn the anterior cruciate ligament in his left knee, a common enough injury that had ended plenty of sports careers. Sean was determined it wasn't going to end this one. The procedure had gone well, although surgery was only the beginning. What followed would be a lengthy rehabilitation that would require dedication and determination from all involved.

Still thinking about how to manage expectations, he took the phone from the nurse. "Sean O'Neil."

"Sean? Where the hell were you last night?"

Braced for a different conversation, Sean frowned with irritation. "Veronica? You shouldn't be calling me here. I was told this was an emergency."

"It *is* an emergency!" Her voice rose along with her temper. "Next time you invite me to dinner, have the decency to show up."

Damn.

A nurse came out of the operating room and handed him a form.

"Veronica, I'm sorry." He tucked the phone between

his cheek and his shoulder and gestured for a pen. "I was called back to the hospital. A colleague had problems with a patient. I was operating."

"And you couldn't have called me? I waited in that restaurant for an hour. An hour, Sean! A man tried to pick me up."

Sean signed the form. "Was he nice?"

"*Do not joke about it.* It was the most embarrassing hour of my life. Don't ever, *ever* do that to me again."

He handed the form back to the nurse with a brief smile. "You'd rather I left a patient to bleed to death?"

"I'd rather you honored your commitments."

"I'm a surgeon. My first commitment is to my patients."

"So what you're saying is that if you had to choose between me and work, you'd pick work?"

"Yes." The fact that she'd asked that question showed how little she knew him. "That is what I'm saying."

"Damn you, Sean. I hate you." But there was a wobble in her voice. "Tell me honestly, is it just me or is it all women?"

"It's me. I'm bad at relationships, you know that. Right now my focus is my career."

"One of these days you're going to wake up alone in that fancy apartment of yours and regret all the time you spent working."

He decided not to point out that he woke up alone through choice. He never invited women back to his apartment. He was barely ever there himself. "My work is important to me. You knew that when you met me."

"No, important is being dedicated to what you do but still having a personal life. What work is to you, Sean O'Neil, is an obsession. You are single-minded and focused to the exclusion of everything else. That might make you a brilliant doctor but it makes you a lousy date. And here's a news flash—being charming and good in bed doesn't stop you being a selfish, workaholic bastard."

"Sean?" Another nurse appeared at his elbow, her pink cheeks and awkward demeanor suggesting she'd overheard that last sentence. "The team coach is waiting outside for news along with the boy's parents. Will you talk to them?"

"Are you even listening to me?" Veronica's voice came down the phone, shrill and irritated. "Are you having another conversation while you're talking to me?"

Hell.

Sean closed his eyes. "I've just come out of the operating room." He rubbed his fingers over his forehead. "I need to speak to the relatives."

"They can wait five minutes!"

"They're worried. If that was your kid in recovery, you'd want to know what was going on. I have to go. Goodbye, Veronica. I really *am* sorry about last night."

"No, wait! Don't go!" Her voice was urgent. "I love you, Sean. I really love you. Despite everything, I think we have something special. We can make this work. You just need to flex a little bit more."

Sweat pricked at the back of his neck. He saw the nurse's eyes widen.

How had he got himself in this situation?

For the first time in years he'd made a misjudgment. He'd thought Veronica was the sort of woman who was happy to live in the moment. Turned out he was wrong about that.

"I have to go, Veronica."

"All right, *I'll* flex. I'm sorry, I'm being a shrew. Let me cook you dinner tonight, I promise I won't complain if you're late. You can show up whenever. I'll—"

"Veronica—" he cut across her "—do *not* apologize to me when I'm the one who should be apologizing to you. You need to find a guy who will give you the attention you deserve."

There was a tense silence. "Are you saying it's over?"

As far as Sean was concerned it had never started. "Yeah, that's what I'm saying. There are hundreds of guys out there only too willing to flex. Go and find one of them." He hung up, aware that the nurse was still watching him.

He was so tired he couldn't even remember her name.

Ann? No, that wasn't right.

Angela. Yes, it was Angela.

Fatigue descended like a gray fog, slowing his thinking. He needed sleep.

He'd been called to an emergency in the night and had been on his feet operating since dawn. Soon the adrenaline would fade and when it did he knew he was going to crash big-time. Sean wanted to be somewhere near his bed when that happened. He had the use of a room at the hospital but he preferred to make it back to his waterside apartment where he could nurse a beer and watch life on the water.

"Dr. O'Neil? Sean? I'm so sorry. I wouldn't have put the call through if I'd known it was personal. She said she was a doctor." The look in her eyes told him she'd have no objection to being Veronica's replacement. Sean didn't think she'd be flattered to know he'd temporarily forgotten her existence.

"Not your fault. I'll talk to the relatives—" He was tempted to take a shower first, but then he remembered the white face of the boy's mother when she'd arrived at the hospital and decided the shower could wait. "I'll go and see them now."

"You've had a really long day. If you want to come by my place after work, I make a mac and cheese that is wicked good."

She was sweet, caring and pretty. Angela would come close to most men's idea of a perfect woman.

Not his.

His idea of a perfect woman was one who didn't want anything from him.

Relationships meant sacrifice and compromise. He wasn't prepared to do either of those things, which was why he had remained resolutely single.

"As you just witnessed, I am an appalling date." He managed what he hoped was a disarming smile. "I'd either be working and not show up at all, or so tired I'd fall asleep on your sofa. You can definitely do better."

"I think you're amazing, Dr. O'Neil. I work with loads of doctors, and you're easily the best. If I ever needed a surgeon, I'd want you to look after me. And I wouldn't care if you fell asleep on my sofa."

"Yes, you would." Eventually they always did. "I'll go and talk to the family now."

"That's kind of you. His mother is worried."

He saw the worry the moment he laid eyes on the woman.

She sat without moving, her hands gripping her skirt

as she tried to contain anxiety made worse by waiting. Her husband was on his feet, hands thrust in his pockets, shoulders hunched as he talked to the coach. Sean knew the coach vaguely. He'd found him to be ruthless and relentlessly pushy and it seemed that surgery on his star player hadn't softened his approach.

The guy wanted miracles and he wanted them yesterday. Sean knew this particular coach's priority wasn't the long-term welfare of the kid lying in the OR, but the future of his team. As a sports injury specialist he dealt with players and coaches all the time. Some were great. Others made him wish he'd chosen law instead of medicine.

The moment the boy's father saw Sean he sprang forward like a Rottweiler pouncing on an intruder.

"Well?"

The coach was drinking water from a plastic cup. "You fixed it?"

He made it sound like a hole in a roof, Sean thought. Slap a new shingle on and it will be as good as new. Change the tire and get the car back on the road.

"Surgery is only the beginning. It's going to be a long process."

"Maybe you should have got him into surgery sooner instead of waiting."

Maybe you should stop practicing armchair medicine.

Noticing the boy's mother digging her nails into her legs, Sean decided not to lock horns. "All the research shows that the outcome is better when surgery is carried out on a pain-free mobile joint." He'd told them the same thing a week before but neither the coach nor the father had wanted to listen then and they didn't want to listen now.

"How soon can he play again?"

Sean wondered what it must be like for the boy, growing up with these two on his back.

"It's too early to set a timetable for return. If you push too hard, he won't be playing at all. The focus now is on rehab. He has to take that seriously. So do you." This time his tone was as blunt as his words. He'd seen promising careers ruined by coaches who pushed too hard too soon, and by players without the patience to understand that the body didn't heal according to a sporting schedule.

"It's a competitive world, Dr. O'Neil. Staying at the top takes determination."

Sean wondered if the coach was talking about his player or himself. "It also takes a healthy body."

The boy's mother, silent until now, stood up. "Is he all right?" The question earned her a scowl from her husband.

"Hell, woman, I just asked him that! Try listening."

"You didn't ask." Her voice shook. "You asked if he'd play again. That's all you care about. He's a person, Jim, not a machine. He's our son."

"At his age I was—"

"I know what you were doing at his age and I tell you if you carry on like this you will destroy your relationship with him. He will hate you forever."

"He should be thanking me for pushing him. He has talent. Ambition. It needs to be nurtured."

"It's your ambition, Jim. This was *your* ambition and now you're trying to live all your dreams through your son. And what you're doing isn't nurturing. You put pressure on him and then layer more and more on until the boy is crushed under the weight of it." The words burst out of her and she paused for a moment as if she'd shocked herself. "I apologize, Dr. O'Neil."

"No need to apologize. I understand your concern."

Tension snapped his muscles tight. No one understood the pressures of family expectation better than he did. He'd been raised with it.

Do you know how it feels to be crushed by the weight of someone else's dreams? Do you know how that feels, Sean?

The voice in his head was so real he rocked on his feet and had to stop himself glancing over his shoulder to check his father wasn't standing there. He'd been dead two years, but sometimes it felt like yesterday.

He thrust the sudden wash of grief aside, uncomfortable with the sudden intrusion of the personal into his professional life.

He was more in need of sleep than he'd thought.

"Scott's doing fine, Mrs. Turner. Everything went smoothly. You'll be able to see him soon."

The tension left the woman's body. "Thank you, Doctor. I— You've been so good to him right from the start. And to me. When he starts playing—" she shot her husband a look "—how do we know the same thing won't happen again? He wasn't even near another player. He just crumpled."

"Eighty percent of ACL tears are non-contact." Sean ignored both the woman's husband and the coach and focused on her. He felt sorry for her, the referee in a game of ambition. "The anterior cruciate ligament connects your thigh to your shin. It doesn't do a whole lot if you're just going about your normal day, but it's an essential part of controlling the rotation forces developed during twisting actions."

She gave him a blank look. "Twisting actions?"

"Jumping, pivoting and abrupt changes of direction. It's an injury common among soccer players, basketball players and skiers."

"Your brother Tyler had the same, didn't he?" The coach butted in. "And it was all over for him. It killed his career as a ski racer. Hell of a blow for such a gifted athlete."

His brother's injury had been far more complicated than that, but Sean never talked about his famous brother. "Our aim with surgery is to return the knee joint to near-normal stability and function but it's a team effort and rehabilitation is a big part of that effort. Scott is young, fit and motivated. I'm confident he'll make a full recovery and be as strong as he was before the injury, providing you encourage him to attack rehab with the same degree of dedication he shows to the game." He hardened his tone because he needed them to pay attention. "Push too hard or too soon and that won't be the case."

The coach nodded. "So can we start rehabilitation right away?"

Sure, just throw him a ball while he's still unconscious.

"We generally find it helps for a patient to have come around from the anesthetic."

The man's cheeks turned dusky-red. "You think I'm pushy, but this kid just wants to play and it's my job to make sure he gets whatever he needs. Which is why we're here," he said gruffly. "People say you're the best.

Everyone I talked to gave me the same response. If it's a knee injury, you want Sean O'Neil. ACL reconstruction and sports injuries are your specialty. Didn't realize you were Tyler O'Neil's brother until a few weeks ago. How's he coping now he can't compete? That must be hard."

"He's doing just fine." The response was automatic. At the height of Tyler's skiing success the whole family had been bombarded by the media and they'd learned to deflect the intrusive questions, some about Tyler's breathtaking talent, others about his colorful personal life.

"I read somewhere he can only ski for recreation now." The coach pulled a face. "Must be hard for a guy like Tyler. I met him once."

Making a note to commiserate with his brother, Sean steered the conversation back on topic. "Let's focus on Scott." He went through it again, repeating words he'd already spoken.

Drumming the message home took another twenty minutes. By the time he'd showered, checked on a few of his patients and climbed into his car, two hours had passed.

Sean sat for a moment, summoning the energy to drive the distance to his waterfront home.

The weekend lay ahead, a stretch of time filled with infinite possibilities.

For the next forty-eight hours his time was his own and he was ready to savor every moment. But first he was going to sleep.

The phone he kept for his personal use rang and he cursed for a moment, assuming it was Veronica, and then frowned when the screen told him it was his twin brother, Jackson. Along with the name came the guilt. It festered inside him, buried deep but always there.

He wondered why his brother would be calling him late on a Friday.

A crisis at home?

Snow Crystal Resort had been in their family for four generations. It hadn't occurred to any of them that it might not be in the family for another four. The sudden death of his father had revealed the truth. The business had been in trouble for years. The discovery that their home was under threat had sent a ripple of shock through the whole family.

It was Jackson who had left a thriving business in Europe to return home to Vermont and save Snow Crystal from a disaster none of the three brothers had even known existed.

Sean stared at the phone in his hand.

Guilt crawled over his skin because he knew it wasn't the pressures of his job that kept him away.

Breathing deeply, he settled back in his seat, ready to catch up on news from home and promising himself that next time he was going to be the one who made the call. He was going to do better at staying in touch.

"Hey—" he answered the call with a smile "—you fell over, smashed your knee and now you need a decent surgeon?"

There was no answering banter and no small talk. "You need to get yourself back here. It's Gramps."

Running Snow Crystal Resort was a never-ending tug of war between Jackson and their grandfather. "What's he done this time? He wants you to knock down the lodges? Close the spa?"

"He collapsed. He's in the hospital and you need to come."

It took a moment for the words to sink in and when they did it was as if someone had sucked all the oxygen from the air.

Like all of them, he considered Walter O'Neil invincible. He was as strong as the mountains that had been home for all his life.

And he was eighty years of age.

"Collapsed?" Sean tightened his grip on the phone, remembering the number of times he'd said that the only way his grandfather would leave his beloved Snow Crystal would be if he was carried out in an ambulance. "What does that mean? Cardiac or neurological? Stroke or heart attack? Tell me in medical terms."

"I don't know the medical terms! It's his heart, they think. He had that pain last winter, remember? They're doing tests. He's alive, that's what counts. They didn't say much and I was focusing on Mom and Grams. You're the doctor, which is why I'm telling you to get your butt back here now so you can translate doctor-speak. I can handle the business but this is your domain. You need to come home, Sean."

Home?

Home was his apartment in Boston with his state-of-the-art sound system, not a lake set against a backdrop of mountains and surrounded by a forest that had their family history carved into the trees.

Sean leaned his head back and stared up at the perfect blue sky that formed a contrast to the dark emotions swirling inside him.

He imagined his grandfather, pale and helpless,

trapped in the sterile environment of a hospital, away from his precious Snow Crystal.

"Sean?" Jackson's voice came through the speaker. "Are you still there?"

"Yeah, I'm here." His other hand gripped the wheel of his car, knuckles white because there were things his brother didn't know. Things they hadn't talked about.

"Mom and Grams need you. You're the doctor in the family. I can handle the business but I can't handle this."

"Was someone with him when it happened? Grams?"

"Not Grams. He was with Élise. She acted very quickly. If she hadn't, we'd be having a different conversation."

Élise, the head chef at Snow Crystal.

Sean stared straight ahead, thinking about that single night the summer before. For a brief moment he was back there, breathing in her scent, remembering the wildness of it.

That was something else his brother knew nothing about.

He swore under his breath and then realized Jackson was still talking.

"How soon can you get here?"

Sean thought about his grandfather, lying pale and still in a hospital bed while their mother, the family glue, struggled to hold everything together and Jackson did more than could be expected of one man.

He was sure his grandfather wouldn't want him there, but the rest of his family needed him.

And as for Élise—it had been a single night, that was all. They weren't in a relationship and never would be so there was no reason to mention it to his brother.

He made some rapid mental calculations.

The journey would take him three and a half hours, and that was without counting the time it would take to drive home and pack a bag.

"I'll be with you as soon as I can. I'll call his doctors now and find out what's going on."

"Come straight to the hospital. And drive carefully. One member of the family in the hospital is enough." There was a brief pause. "It will be good to have you back at Snow Crystal, Sean."

The reply wedged itself in his throat.

He'd grown up by the lake, surrounded by lush forests and mountains. He couldn't identify the exact time he'd known it wasn't where he wanted to be. When the place had started to irritate and chafe everything from his skin to his ambitions. It wasn't something he'd been able to voice because to admit that there might be a place more perfect than Snow Crystal would have been heresy in the O'Neil family. Except to his father. Michael O'Neil had shared his conflicted emotions about the place. His father was the one person who would have understood.

Guilt dug deep, twisting in his ribs like a knife, because apart from the row with his grandfather and his wild fling with Élise, there was something else he'd never told his brother.

He'd never told him how much he hated coming home.

"I 'ave killed Walter! This is all my fault! I was so desperate to have the old boathouse finished in time for the party, I let an eighty-year-old man work on the deck." Élise paced across the deck of her pretty lakeside lodge, out of her mind with worry. "*Merde,* I am a bad person. Jackson should fire me."

"Snow Crystal is in enough trouble without Jackson firing his head chef. The restaurant is the one part of this business that is profitable. Oh, good news—" Kayla leaned on the railing next to the water, scanning a text "—according to the doctors, Walter is stable."

"*Comment?* What does this mean, 'stable'? You put a horse in a stable."

"It means you haven't killed him," Kayla said as she texted back swiftly. "You need to calm down or we'll be calling an ambulance for you next. Are all French people as dramatic as you?"

"I don't know. I cannot help it." Élise dragged her hand through her hair. "I am not good at 'iding my feelings. For a while I manage it, but then everything bursts out and I explode."

"I know. I've cleared up the mess after a few of your explosions. Fortunately your staff adore you. Go and make pizza dough or whatever it is you do when you want to reduce your stress levels. You're dropping your *h*'s and that is never a good sign." Kayla sent the text and read another one. "Jackson wants me to drive over to the hospital."

"I will come with you!"

"Only if you promise not to explode in my car."

"I want to see with my own eyes that Walter is alive."

"You think we're all lying to you?"

Her legs were shaking so Élise plopped onto the chair she'd placed by the water. "He is very important to me. I love him like a grandfather. Not like my real grandfather because he was a horrible person who refused to speak to my mother after she had me so I never actually met him, but how I think a grandfather should be in my dreams. I know you understand because your family, they were also rubbish."

Kayla gave a faint smile, but didn't argue. "I know how close you are to Walter. You don't have to explain to me."

"He is the nearest thing I have to family. And Jackson, of course. It makes me very happy to think he will marry you soon. And Elizabeth and dear Alice. And Tyler is like a brother to me, even though sometimes I want to punch him. It is normal for siblings to sometimes want to punch each other, I think. I love you all with every bone in my body." The dark side of Élise's life was carefully locked away in the past. Loneliness, fear and deep humiliation were a distant memory. She was safe here. Safe and loved.

"And Sean?" Kayla lifted an eyebrow. "Where does he fit into your adopted family? Presumably not as another brother."

"No." Just thinking about him made her heart race a little faster. "Not a brother."

"So you won't be telling him you love him? Aren't you worried he might feel a little left out?"

Élise frowned. "You are not funny."

"Is this a good time to warn you he's coming home?"

"Of course he is coming home. He is an O'Neil. The O'Neils always stick together when there is trouble and Sean hasn't been home for a while."

And she was worried that was her fault.

Was it because of what had happened between them?

"So it isn't going to feel awkward when he shows up?"

"Why would it feel awkward? Because of last summer? It was just one night. It's not so hard to understand, is it? Sean is *un beau mec.*"

"He's a *what?*"

"*Un beau mec.* A hot guy. Sean is very sexy. We are two adults who chose to spend a night together. We are both single. Why would it feel awkward?" It had been her idea of the perfect night. No ties. No complications. A decision she'd made with her head, not her heart. Never again would she allow her heart to be engaged.

No risks. No mistakes.

"So seeing him isn't going to bother you?"

"Not at all. And it isn't the first time. I saw him at Christmas."

"And neither of you exchanged a single look or word."

"Christmas is the busiest time of year for me. Do you know how many people I fed in the restaurant? I had more important things to worry about than Sean. And it is the same now. We probably won't even have time to say hello. All he thinks about is work and I am the same. It is only a week until the Boathouse Café opens and at the moment it doesn't have a deck."

"Look, I know how much this project means to you—to all of us—but it is no one's fault that Zach crashed his dirt bike."

Élise scowled. "He is their cousin. Family. He should have shown more responsibility."

"Distant cousin."

"So what? He should have finished my deck before he crashed!"

"I'm sure that's what he told the boulder that jumped into his path." Kayla gave a fatalistic shrug. "He has O'Neil DNA. Of coure he is going to indulge in dangerous sports and have accidents. Tyler says he's lethal on a snowboard."

"He should not have been indulging in anything lethal until my deck was finished!"

"So does that mean Zach has been struck off the list of people you love?"

"You make fun of me but it is important to tell people you love them." It wasn't just important to her, it was vital. Sadness seeped into her veins and she breathed deeply, trying to block the spread. Over the years she'd learned to control it. To keep it locked away so it didn't interfere with her life. "I should never have let Walter step in. It is because of me he is lying there all full of tubes and needles and—"

"Stop!" Kayla pulled a face. "Enough."

"It's just that I keep imagining—"

"Well, don't! Talk about something else?"

"We can talk about how I have ruined everything. The Boathouse Café is important for Snow Crystal. We have included the projected revenue in our forecasts. We have a party planned! And now it cannot happen."

Frustrated with herself, Élise stood up and gazed across the lake, searching for calm. The evening sun sent flashes of gold and silver over the still surface of the lake. It was rare that she saw the place at this time of day. Usually she was in the restaurant preparing for the evening. The only time she sat on her own deck was in the dark when she returned in the early hours, or immediately on rising when she made herself a cup of freshly brewed coffee and sipped it in the dawn silence.

Morning was her favorite time of day in the summer, when the forest was still bathed by early morning mist and the sleepy sun had yet to burn off the fine cobweb of white shrouding the trees. It made her think of the curtain in the theatre, hiding the thrill of the main event from an excited audience.

Heron Lodge was small, just one bedroom and an open plan living area, but the size didn't worry her. She'd grown up in Paris, in a tiny apartment on the Left Bank with a view over the rooftops and barely room to pirouette. At Snow Crystal she lived right on the lakeshore, her lodge sheltered by trees. At night in the summer she slept with the windows open. Even when it was too dark to see the view, there was beauty in the sounds. Water slapping gently against her deck, the whisper of a bird's wing as it flew overhead, the low hoot of an owl. On nights when she was unable to sleep she lay for hours breathing in the sweet scents of summer and listening to the call of the hermit thrush and the chattering of the black-capped chickadees.

If she'd slept with her window open in Paris she would have been constantly disturbed by a discordant symphony of car horns punctuated by Gallic swearing as drivers stopped in the street to yell abuse at each other. Paris was loud and busy. A city with the volume fixed on maximum while everyone rushed around trying to be somewhere yesterday.

Snow Crystal was muted and peaceful. Never, in the turmoil of her past, had she imagined one day living in a place like this.

She knew how close the O'Neil family had come to losing it. She knew things were still far from secure and that losing it was still a very real possibility. She was determined to do everything she could to make sure that didn't happen.

"Can you find me another carpenter? Are you sure you've tried everyone?"

"There is no one. Sorry." Looking tired, Kayla shook her head. "I already made some calls."

"In that case we are all doomed."

"No one is doomed, Élise!"

"We will have to delay the opening and cancel the party. You have invited so many important people. People who could spread the word and help grow the business. *Je suis désolée.* The Boathouse is my responsibility. Jackson asked me for an opening date and I gave him one. I anticipated a busy summer. Now if Snow Crystal has to close we will all lose our jobs and our home and it will be my fault."

"Don't worry, with your talent for drama you could easily get a job on Broadway." Kayla paced the deck, obviously thinking. "We could hold the party in the restaurant?"

"No. It was supposed to be a magical, outdoor evening that will showcase the charm of our new café. I have it all arranged—food, lights, dancing on the deck—the deck that isn't finished!" Frustrated and miserable, Élise walked into her little kitchen and picked up the bag of food she'd packed for the family. "Let's go. They've been at the hospital for hours. They will be hungry."

As they walked along the lake path to the car, Élise thought again what a good thing it was that Jackson had employed Kayla. She'd arrived at Snow Crystal only six months earlier, the week before Christmas, to put together a public relations campaign that would boost the resort's flagging fortunes. The intention had been that she would stay a week and then return to her

high-powered job in New York, but that had been before she'd fallen in love with Jackson O'Neil.

Élise felt a rush of emotion.

Calm, strong Jackson. He was the reason she was
here, living this wonderful life. He'd saved her. Res-
cued her from the ruins of her own life. He'd given her
a way out from a problem of her own making, and she'd
taken it. He was the only one who knew the truth about
her. She owed him everything.

The Boathouse Café was a way of repaying him.

Élise had always known that Snow Crystal needed
something more than the formal restaurant and the
small, cramped coffee shop that had been part of the
resort since it was built.

On her first stroll down to the lakeshore she'd seen
the derelict boathouse and envisaged a café right on
the water's edge. Now her dream was almost reality.
She'd worked with a local architect and together they'd
created something that matched her vision and satis-
fied the planners.

The new café had glass on three sides so that no part
of the view was lost to those dining indoors. During the
winter the doors would be kept closed, but in the summer months when the weather allowed, the glass walls
could be pulled back to allow guests to take maximum
advantage of the breathtaking position.

In the summer most of the tables would be set on the
wide deck, a sun-trap that stretched across the water.
The building should have been finished in June, but
bad weather had delayed essential work and then Zach
had crashed the bike.

Kayla slid behind the wheel and drove carefully out
of the resort. "How long do you think Sean will stay?"

"Not long."

And that suited her perfectly.

They probably wouldn't even have any time alone together and she wasn't going to worry about something that didn't represent a threat.

Sean was entertaining company, charming and yes, insanely sexy, but her emotions weren't engaged. And they never would be. Never again.

Memories slid into her, dark and oppressive and she gave a little shiver and stared hard at the forest, reminding herself that she was in Vermont, not Paris. This was her home now.

And it wasn't as if she was living without love.

She had the O'Neils. They were her family.

That thought stayed in her head as they arrived at the hospital and it was still in her head as Kayla walked into Jackson's arms.

She saw Kayla reach out her hand and curl her fingers into Jackson's. Saw her friend rise up on the balls of her feet and brush her lips over his in a kiss that somehow managed to be both discreet and intimate. In that moment she'd ceased to exist for either of them. Their emotions were definitely engaged.

Witnessing it robbed her of breath.

She felt a pang and looked away quickly.

She didn't want that.

"I will go and see Walter and drop off this food while you two catch up. Give me the keys, Kayla." She held out her hand. "You can go home with Jackson later. I will try to persuade Alice to come back with me now."

She didn't succeed. Walter looked pale and fragile and when she eventually left the room it was with the image of Alice, his wife of sixty years, sitting by his side with her hand on his, her knitting abandoned in her lap as if by holding hands they might prevent their life together from unraveling.

All Alice had talked about was Sean. Her belief in her grandson's ability to perform miracles was as touching as it was worrying.

Élise was on her way out of the hospital when she saw him.

He walked with confidence and authority, comfortable in the sterile atmosphere of the high-tech medical facility. The well-cut suit and pristine white shirt couldn't conceal the width of his shoulders or the leashed power of his body, and her heart gave a little dance in her chest.

Despite the air-conditioning, her skin heated.

It had been just one night, but it wasn't a night she was likely to forget and she doubted he would, either.

Like her, Sean had no interest in forming deep romantic relationships. His job demanded control and emotional detachment. The fact that he applied the same rules to his personal life had made everything simple.

She walked briskly across the foyer toward him, determined to prove to herself and anyone who happened to be watching that this meeting wasn't awkward. "Sean—" she rose on tiptoe, placed her hand on his shoulder and kissed him on both cheeks. "*Ça va?* I'm so sorry about Walter. You must be out of your mind worried."

It was fine. Not awkward at all. Maybe her English wasn't as fluent as usual, but that sometimes happened when she was tired or stressed.

As her cheek brushed against the roughness of his

jaw she was almost knocked flat by a rush of sexual chemistry. Rocked off-balance, she tightened her fingers on his shoulder, feeling the thickness of muscle through the fabric of his suit. If she moved slightly to the left she'd be kissing his mouth and it shocked her just how much she wanted to do that.

Sean's head turned slightly. His gaze met hers and for a moment she was mesmerized.

His eyes were the same startling blue as his twin brother's but she'd never felt anything this dangerously potent when dealing with Jackson. Some people might have waxed lyrical about blue skies or sapphires but for her those eyes were all about sex. For a moment she forgot the people around them, forgot everything except the sexual energy and memories of that one night. She hadn't closed her eyes and neither had he. Through the whole breath-stealing madness of it, they'd held that connection and it was all she could think of as she lowered her heels to the floor and stepped back.

Her heart was racing. Her mouth was dry. It took all her willpower to let go of his shoulder. "How was your journey?"

"I've had worse."

"Have you eaten? I brought food. Alice has the bag."

"I don't suppose that bag contains a good Pinot Noir?"

It was a typically Sean response.

Even in a crisis he projected calm. It washed over her, as welcoming as cool air in a heat wave and for the first time since that awful moment when Walter had collapsed at her feet she felt her mood lift slightly. It was as if someone had taken off some of the weight she'd been carrying.

"No Pinot Noir. But there is homemade lemonade."

"Oh, well, a guy can't have everything. If you made it, I'm sure it's good." He loosened his tie with long, strong fingers, cool and composed, and she wondered if he remembered it had been Pinot Noir they'd drunk that night. "Where is the rest of my family?"

"They're with your grandfather."

"How is he?" His voice was gruff, those thick dark lashes failing to conceal the concern in his eyes. "Any change?"

"He looks frail. I hope the doctors know what they're doing."

"It's a good hospital. And how are you?" He caught her chin in his fingers and turned her face to him. "You look like hell."

"Is that your medical opinion?"

"It's the opinion of a friend. If you're asking me as a doctor I'll have to bill you—" his hand dropped and he tilted his head as he calculated "—let's say, six hundred dollars. You're welcome."

Her heart rate slowly returned to normal. "You trained all those years to tell people they look like hell?"

"It's a vocation." He was smiling, too, and that smile made her heart kick hard against her ribs.

"And there I was congratulating myself on looking good in a crisis." She'd forgotten how easy it was to relax with him. He was easy to talk to and charming. And dangerously attractive.

"I have to go. I need to see Grams."

"She won't leave his side and she's exhausted. She thinks you're going to be able to perform a miracle."

"I'll go to her right now." His hard features softened

fractionally as he spoke of his grandmother. "You're driving back to Snow Crystal?"

"I just wanted to see him for a few minutes, keep Kayla company and bring food."

"You still haven't told me how you are." Sean's gaze didn't shift from her face. "You're very close to Gramps."

How was she?

The person she loved most in the world was in the hospital and the Boathouse still wasn't finished and wasn't going to open on time.

There would be no opening party. She'd let Jackson down.

She'd had bad days before, but this had been the king of bad days.

But Sean didn't need to hear that. Their relationship didn't involve cozy confidences.

"I'm fine," she lied. "It's different for me. I am not family. Although I'd also like you to perform a miracle if you have time."

"I think my grandfather would be the first to dispute that you're not family."

"Walter would dispute anything. You know how he loves to argue. He is my perfect man. I love him so much."

"Now you've broken my heart."

She knew he was joking. Sean was too busy with his career to be interested in a relationship, and that suited her just fine.

"I will see you soon."

"Are you safe to drive home?" He caught her wrist and pulled her back to him and just for a moment, standing toe-to-toe with him, she forgot the people around her.

"Of course." She was torn between being touched that he'd noticed how badly affected she was and appalled that she was so easy to read. Why couldn't she be cool and enigmatic like Kayla? "It has been a long day, that's all."

He gave her a long, searching look and then let go of her wrist. "Drive carefully."

As she walked to the car, she congratulated herself on how well she'd handled that encounter. No one watching would have guessed that they'd once generated enough heat to melt a frozen ice cap.

They had their feelings under control.

There was nothing about Sean O'Neil that threatened her life here.

When it came to love, she was invulnerable.

CHAPTER TWO

"THE PRODIGAL GRANDSON RETURNS." A familiar voice came from behind him and Sean turned to find Tyler standing there holding two cups of coffee.

He took one without invitation. "Didn't realize the whole family was here."

"They are now that you walked through the door and that's Jackson's coffee you're drinking. You look like a banker, not a doctor. What happened to the scrubs?"

"I wear those when I'm operating. The rest of the time I wear a suit."

"Why? So you can charge more?" The banter did nothing to disguise the tension in Tyler's shoulders and Sean felt a rush of concern.

"This may come as a surprise to you given your TV viewing preferences, but most people don't like doctors covered in blood." He took a sip of coffee, coughed and handed it straight back to his brother. "That is disgusting."

"Straight from the machine, the way you hate it. That's your punishment for stealing something that wasn't yours in the first place. Believe me, when you've been in this place all day it tastes like nectar."

"How's the leg?"

"Behaving. I never thought I'd say this, but it's good

to see you." Tyler gave a laugh. "Listen to me, getting all mushy on you."

"Yeah, suddenly I'm worried."

"Don't be. The only reason I'm pleased to see you is because now you can do the boring incomprehensible bit of talking to the doctors and I can focus my attention on more important things."

"Would those more important things be female?"

"They might be. Was that Élise I saw leaving? Did you know she was with Gramps when he collapsed?"

"Jackson told me. She didn't mention it." Which, now that he thought about it, was a little strange.

What had they talked about?

All he could remember was the brush of her cheek against his, the silk of her hair and the scent that had slid into his veins like a drug. And the chemistry. Always the chemistry, simmering in the background like a summer heat wave.

The doors to the nearest elevator opened and Sean saw Jackson standing there with Kayla.

"Élise texted me to tell me you were here. We weren't expecting you for another hour at least."

"I may have broken a few speed limits." Sean wondered how long it had been since his twin had slept. "Any change?"

"Not that I can tell, but I'm not the doctor. It's hard to get information from anyone. For all I know they might be useless at their jobs. You need to speak to them."

"I called from the car. This place has one of the highest heart attack survival rates in the country. They took him straight to the cath lab for balloon inflation and stenting. They had him out of the E.R. in seventeen minutes. That's impressive." It came as a relief to discover that even though he was affected personally, the doctor in him was still able to detach and analyze.

Jackson glanced at Tyler, who shrugged.

"Don't look at me. I never understand a word he says. It's all those books he reads. Don't suppose his patients understand him, either, but they're probably reassured by the expensive suit and the astronomical fees he charges."

It was a relief to relax with his brothers for five minutes. "You could wear a suit occasionally, Ty. If you tided yourself up you might even get laid."

"The reason I'm not getting laid is because my teenage daughter is living with me. I'm a shining example of parenthood."

Sean grinned. "It must be killing you."

Jackson intervened before the conversation could degenerate. "Can we focus on Gramps for a moment? Explain again, and this time use plain language."

"The artery was blocked, so they unblocked it by inflating a balloon against the artery wall and inserting a stent, like mesh, to hold it open—" Sean used his hands to demonstrate. "All the studies show that if they can do that within ninety minutes of the original attack, there is a better chance of survival and fewer complications. Time from the onset of symptoms to reperfusion is an important predictor of outcome."

Jackson pressed a button on the elevator and the doors closed. "I asked for plain language."

"That was plain language."

Tyler rolled his eyes. "If he ever gives us the complicated version I'm going to need a large drink."

Jackson was frowning. "So is that good news?"

Relatively speaking.

Sean decided they didn't need to know all the potential outcomes. "How did it start? Was Gramps sick? Did he have chest pain?"

"According to Élise, one minute he was standing up, the next minute he was on the ground." Jackson watched as the buttons illuminated one by one, stopping at what felt like every floor to let people in and out. "He was working on the deck of the old boathouse."

"Why?"

"We're converting it into a café." It was Jackson's turn to sound irritable. "Don't you read your emails?"

"I get a ton of emails. So why was Gramps doing the work?"

"Because there wasn't anyone else. We're stretched to the limit. Gramps wanted to help and I don't have the luxury of being able to stop him, even supposing I could. Everyone has been doing what they can to keep the place afloat."

Everyone except him.

Sean stared straight ahead, feeling the guilt cover him like sweat. He was the only one not doing anything to stop the family business from sinking.

He turned his head to speak to Jackson and wished he hadn't because his brother was kissing Kayla. A slow, lingering kiss that had as much eye contact as lip contact.

Immediately he thought of Élise. Of that single, hot night the summer before.

The night neither of them had ever mentioned.

He looked away. "Could you put each other down just for two minutes so we can focus here?"

"You're witnessing true love," Tyler drawled, "and it's a beautiful thing."

"Sorry, but it's been a tough day and we don't see that much of each other." Kayla rested her head on Jackson's shoulder. "But that's going to change soon. One more week!"

Sean frowned. "You've given up your job in New York?"

"Yes. I'm going to be working and living here full-time. You knew I was doing that." Kayla twisted the engagement ring on her finger. "I told you at Christmas."

At Christmas he'd been focused on surviving three days of living in close quarters with his family without revealing the rift with his grandfather. He'd given virtually no thought to the way anyone else was feeling.

"Right. I guess I lost track of time."

So Kayla was giving up her life to come and live here at Snow Crystal. Another person sacrificing everything for love. What the hell was he supposed to say to that?

Congratulations?

Have you thought this through?

What happens when you wake up and start resenting everything you gave up to live here?

"I hope you'll both be very happy."

"We are and we will be." Jackson looped his arm around Kayla's shoulders. "Ignore him. He's just jealous. He can't keep a woman long enough to learn her name, that's his problem."

"I'm not the one with the problem."

Commitment meant putting your own needs second and he was too selfish to make that sacrifice for anyone. He wanted to be able to work when he needed to without feeling the constant tug of duty and responsibility. He wanted to travel without always feeling there was another place he should be. He wanted freedom.

He didn't want to feel trapped and stifled in the same way his father had.

10,11,12—the elevator had to be the slowest ever. He felt like getting out and pushing.

"Tyler, you should go home." Jackson still had his arm around Kayla. "Gramps won't thank us if he comes home and finds the place neglected."

"He never thanks us, anyway," Tyler muttered and Sean slid his finger around his already loosened collar.

"I'm not expecting a warm welcome."

"You could come home more often," Jackson replied mildly. "That would help."

Tyler eyed his suit. "He doesn't have the right clothing. You can't walk around Snow Crystal in silk shirts and Armani."

"It's Brioni. I bought it when I was presenting at a medical conference in Milan." He didn't add that moving to Snow Crystal permanently would be one sacrifice he wouldn't be making anytime soon. "A good suit is an investment. I seem to remember you owning a decent suit once. Several, in fact. Of course, that was in the days before you let yourself go."

The exchange with his brothers was comfortable and familiar and kept him sane until the elevator finally stopped. He strode out before the doors were fully open, relieved to be out of the confined space, trapped with emotions he didn't want to confront.

Tyler was right on his heels. "I can't stand hospitals. All those white coats and beeping machines and people using incomprehensible words." His face was noticeably paler than usual. "It's like being on an alien spaceship."

Sean wondered if being here reminded his brother of his accident.

For him, hospitals were exciting places, centers for research, full of possibilities.

He felt completely at home and his brothers seemed to know that because Jackson slapped him on the shoulder.

"You know your way around this spaceship. Ready to kick some butt?"

"Do aliens have butts?"

Kayla rolled her eyes. "You sound like a bad movie."

"What sort of movie?" Jackson's eyes were on her mouth. "You mean like a porn movie? Because if you want to do bad things to me, that's fine."

Sean caught Tyler's eye. His brother shrugged.

"Like I said—true love. It will happen to you one day when you least expect it. And the next thing you know you'll be walking around with your lips glued to some chick making embarrassing noises like our beloved brother here."

And not long after that the sacrifices would start. *I* became *us* and along with *us* came a giant dollop of compromise and suddenly your life didn't look anything like the way you'd once wanted it to look. You stared into the mirror and asked yourself *how the hell did I end up here?*

There was no way, *no way,* that was ever going to happen to him.

"There's an ice machine at the end of the corridor." Sean glanced at the signs and found the direction he wanted. "You two should go sit in it while I talk to Gramps."

Élise spent the evening cooking. Combining flavors and textures was a way of occupying her mind and soothing her anxiety. She told herself it was work, that she needed new recipes for the café, but in truth it was distraction. Distraction from thoughts of Walter and that horrible moment when he'd collapsed at her feet.

It had been hours and she'd heard nothing. She'd texted Kayla twice and received no response. The next step would be to call the hospital and she was close to doing that.

It was almost midnight. Why hadn't Kayla called?

Dark fell over the lake.

An owl hooted.

Unable to contemplate sleep, she cooked and wrote notes on the laptop she kept permanently on the countertop in the kitchen. Some of the recipes would make it into her repertoire and would be used in the restaurant or the café. Others would never be used again.

She pulled a tray of savory mushroom pastries out of the oven and set them aside to cool, pleased with the result. Picking up a fork, she cut into one. The pastry was a pale golden-brown, crisp and buttery. It flaked in the mouth and melted on the tongue, blending perfectly with the creamy filling.

"Something smells good." Sean's voice came from behind her and she turned sharply, her pulse rate doubling.

He stood in the doorway, his broad shoulders blocking her view of the lake.

It was the first time he'd been to her lodge since she'd been living in it. The fact that he'd come in person could only mean bad news.

"Something has happened to Walter? Is he—?" The fear was brutal. Her head spun and her vision felt distant and strange.

She didn't see him move, but the next moment strong hands clamped her shoulders and she was being guided into the chair.

"Put your head down." His voice was calm and sure. "You're fine, sweetheart, you've just had a long day. Gramps is good. He's doing well."

She leaned forward, waiting for the world to stop spinning. "Is that the truth? You're not lying to me?"

"I never lie. Some women would say it's my biggest failing." He crouched down next to her and closed a hand over hers. "Better?"

"Yes."

She didn't say that his honesty was one of the things she liked best about him.

Lifting her head, she met his gaze. Her stomach tightened.

It didn't matter how much they tried to ignore it, the connection was always there.

Merde. And now she was leaning on him like a pathetic creature. And she didn't do that. She never did that.

"You scared me. I thought—" She couldn't even say what she'd thought. It was a relief to feel her heart thudding against her chest. For a moment she'd thought it had stopped. "Kayla didn't answer my texts. I was worried."

"Probably too busy kissing my brother to check her phone." He gave her hand another squeeze and stood up. "Do those two ever stop?"

She flexed her fingers, thinking that she should have been the one to pull her hand away.

"They're apart for a lot of the week so I suppose they

want to make the most of the time they're together. Tell me about your grandfather. How was he when you left?"

"Awake and talking. Scolding Grams for having stayed with him the whole time when she should have gone home to bed."

"Scolding? That sounds so much like him." The relief was so great it was almost physical. "I will *kill* Kayla for not texting me." She knew she should stand up but she didn't trust her legs so she stayed sitting on the pretty blue wooden chair she'd bought for her kitchen. "I'm shaking! I am a mess."

"From what I've heard you've had a hell of a day, so shaking is allowed. Here. Have a drink." Pulling a bottle of cognac from her shelf, he sloshed a generous measure into a glass and sniffed it with appreciation. "This is good stuff. If I'd known you were hiding this I would have been around sooner."

He handed her the glass and she took it, horrified to feel a hot ball of tears wedged in her throat.

"Sorry—"

"Are you apologizing for not sharing your cognac or for caring about my grandfather?"

"I'm apologizing for overreacting." And she was furious with herself for allowing her thoughts to wander into worst-case land. She sipped and felt the liquid burn her throat.

Sean watched her. "I'm the one who should be apologizing for showing up at your door without warning. It didn't occur to me that you might think I was the bearer of bad news. Women are usually pleased to see me." He obviously intended it as a joke, but she knew it was probably the truth.

"You have never come to my lodge before and I've

been worrying and when I couldn't reach Kayla I thought maybe—" her heart was still pounding "—I saw you there and I was so afraid—"

"If you were that afraid why didn't you call me?"

"I wouldn't do that."

"For God's sake Élise, we're not strangers. You ripped my clothes off. We had sex. If we can roll naked together, you can pick up the damn phone."

She felt the betraying color streak across her cheeks. "You ripped my clothes off, too, in case your memory is faulty."

But she'd started it.

She'd made the first move on that hot summer night with the scent of the forest around them and her blood on fire for him.

"Yeah, that's right. I did. There was plenty of mutual ripping that night. And my memory is working just fine, thanks." His smile was slow and sexy, his eyes a vivid intense blue. "How is yours?"

"I can barely remember it now."

The corners of his mouth flickered. "Because it wasn't a very memorable night, was it? Look," he said, as he took the glass from her, "I'm bad at relationships, I admit it. But that doesn't mean I'm going to pretend that night didn't happen. Next time you're worried about something, pick up the phone."

"I don't have your number and I don't want it." Their relationship had never been about numbers and phone calls. It had been about hot sex, and it was hot sex she was thinking of now and she knew he was, too.

"I'm not suggesting you call me while I'm operating to tell me you love me, but if you'd had my number you could have called me tonight instead of worrying."

"Do people do that? Call you while you're operating?"

"Sometimes." He leaned against her kitchen counter. "Women usually want more than I can give."

"I don't."

She knew she never would have called him. Calling was the first step on the path to a relationship and she'd never tread that path again, not even a little way. She'd done it before and it had been like walking over broken glass with bare feet. She still bore the scars and it was because of those scars her heart no longer had a say in any of the decisions in her life.

When it came to men, her head was in charge.

Sean held out his hand. "Give me your phone."

"There's no need."

"Give it to me or I'll wrestle it away from you and then things could get ugly." He kept his hand outstretched and, reluctantly, she dug it out of her pocket.

"This is ridiculous."

He leaned forward and prised it from her fingers with the determination of a man who knew what he wanted and went for it. "I love the way you roll your *r*'s. It's very sexy." Cool and collected, he accessed her contacts and keyed in his number. "Next time you're worried about something, call me."

"Fine. I'll call you twenty times a day when you're operating to tell you I love you, and if you don't answer I'll leave a message."

He laughed. "My team will enjoy each and every one of those calls."

"Maybe I will sell your number on eBay and make some money for Snow Crystal."

"What's the going rate for overworked surgeons? I'm

probably not worth much." Handing the phone back, he turned his attention back to the pastries. "Are those for eating?"

"No."

"You're cruel and heartless. I knew it the moment I met you. You used me for a night of scorching sex and then discarded me."

Flirting with him was like dancing with fire.

One wrong move and that heat would burn and leave permanent damage.

Not once had she ever questioned her decision to spend the night with him, but there was no way she would do it again.

"Tell me more about Walter."

"Feed me first. I haven't eaten a proper meal since breakfast and that wasn't a memorable experience." He eyed the tray of pastries. "They look almost too pretty to eat, but not quite."

"They're an experiment."

"I'm a doctor. I'm a believer in the importance of research in the pursuit of excellence and I'm happy to help you out. I'll even submit a paper to the *New England Journal of Medicine*. Relief of anxiety symptoms after ingestion of Élise's cooking. Don't make me beg."

"You don't need to beg." She slid her phone back into her pocket, resisting the temptation to delete his number. Just because it was in there, didn't mean she had to use it. "I'm still working on the menu for the café, even though there is no possibility of us opening on time."

"How much work is there to be done?"

"Not much. That's what makes it all the more frustrating. We were so nearly there. But it will open eventually and I'm devising a whole new menu. It will be a different dining experience."

A cool breeze blew in through the open door and she heard the call of a bird as it flew low over the lake. The stillness of the night added to the intimacy.

She told herself that she could control the chemistry, that she could either act on it or ignore it. Either way she would make the decision with her head, as she always did.

"This particular dining experience smells good. I predict I'll be a frequent guest."

"You live a four-hour drive from Snow Crystal."

"Tonight I did it in three."

"So you're going to be driving here for my food?" She reached for a plate but he had already helped himself to a pastry.

He bit into it and moaned deep in his throat. Élise turned away quickly, thinking that all the sophisticated tailoring in the world didn't disguise the raw physicality of the man.

"If you're still alive in five minutes, I'll assume they pass the test," she said lightly. "For the café the plan is to keep the menu simple and of course, we'll source as much locally as we already do for the restaurant. Vermont is the most beautiful place. We want to support local agriculture and do everything we can to give our guests locally grown food. Green Mountain ham, local cheeses, fruit from our orchard and salad from our gardens. And our own maple syrup, of course, or Walter would kill me. It's going to be about flavor and quality."

"And quantity, I hope. How many of these am I allowed to eat?" His hand hovered over another. "And before you decide I should tell you my last meal was over twelve hours ago and I spent most of the day in the operating room."

"You'll eat the next one the way it is supposed to be served, on a plate with salad. In France we believe food is something to be savored, not crammed into the mouth while standing up." It took her moments to combine various salad leaves and mix a dressing. She plated it up swiftly along with the warm pastry, added bread she'd made earlier in the day and handed it to him. "The bread is sea salt and rosemary. You can tell me what you think."

"I think I might marry you so that I can eat like this every day."

Her heart pumped a little harder.

Marriage.

The word alone had an almost visceral effect on her. Even after so many years it turned her cold and made her want to look over her shoulder.

"Then you'd be disappointed. I cook for a living. When I am at home on my own I sometimes just make myself a perfect omelette."

"When I'm operating I don't always have time to eat. I take fuel when I can."

She was conscious of the width and power of his shoulders, of his height in the small space and the shadow that darkened his lean jaw. His sex appeal was undeniable and suddenly Heron Lodge seemed smaller than ever. She was a physical person and she'd denied that part of herself for too long. Her stomach was tight with awareness, her nerve endings alive to the change in the atmosphere. Its chemistry spun a web around them, trapping them both. She wondered what he'd say if he knew she hadn't slept with a man since him.

"Let's go outside on the deck." She handed him the heaped plate. "It's a warm evening and after spending a day in the restaurant and the hospital I need fresh air. You can tell me about Walter."

Sean pulled out a chair next to the little wooden table she'd placed right by the water. Her deck was bathed by light spilling from the open door of the lodge. "I gather you were with him when it happened." He started to eat and she realized this was probably how life was for him. Snatching what time he could between the ferocious demands of his job.

"It was horrible. One minute he was teasing me about those 'terrible French pancakes' as he calls them. The next he was on the floor. My hands were shaking so badly I could hardly make the phone call. I thought I'd killed him."

"It wasn't your fault." He tore a chunk of bread. "There were no clues before that? No mentions of chest pains?"

"He said nothing to me. Elizabeth said he'd mentioned indigestion a few times, but nothing that rang any alarm bells. He has been helping me with the deck. I feel so guilty about that."

"Don't. This place is his passion and the physical demands of keeping it running are part of the reason he has stayed fit for so long."

"I should have thought of a way of involving him that didn't include him doing physical work."

"No one has ever been able to stop Gramps from doing physical work. In all the years I lived here I never saw him take a day off. He worked. We all worked." Sean finished the bread. "This is good. Sea salt and rosemary gets my vote."

As he ate, he updated her about his grandfather.

She envied his calm, and was reassured by it. "I am very worried for him. He's eighty." *Which was why she dared to love him.* He was the only man in possession of her heart, apart from Jackson, to whom she owed a debt she could never repay.

"There's no reason why he shouldn't make a full recovery."

Except that life was full of events that weren't reasonable and made no sense, she knew that.

Élise rubbed her fingers across her forehead, refusing to let her mind linger on that thought. "Did your mother come home with you?"

"Yes, I brought her back. But Grams won't leave his side. Tyler's there now and I'll go back later."

The O'Neil family stuck together in difficult times. It was one of the many things she loved about them. That was why Sean had driven straight here after a day of operating. No one from this family would ever find themselves alone and struggling. No one would find themselves sitting in a dark Paris room with the door barricaded and no one to turn to.

"You must be exhausted. You can't go back to the hospital tonight."

"We can't leave Grams there by herself and Tyler needs to get some rest. I'll grab a few hours before I go back." He lifted his broad shoulders in a dismissive shrug. "One of the advantages of medical training is that you learn to function on little sleep."

"Walter must have been very relieved to see you."

"He opened his eyes for long enough to tell me to get the hell back to Boston where I belonged." He finished his food and pushed the plate away. "That was delicious. Best thing I've tasted in months."

"He said that?" Shocked, Élise stared at him. "He didn't mean it."

"Yes, he did. Don't look so worried. I took it as a sign that at least part of him was functioning normally. If he'd welcomed me with hugs and balloons I would have been sending him for a brain scan." But Sean's smile was tired and Élise felt a flash of frustration that human relationships had to be so complicated.

"Is that why you don't come home more? Because he's difficult?"

"My home is Boston." His answer was smooth. "And I come home when my schedule allows."

Which was hardly ever. She'd assumed he was busy. Occasionally she'd wondered if his absence had something to do with her. Now she wondered if there was more to it. "Don't you miss Snow Crystal?"

"I like the city. I like having a choice of restaurants within two blocks and access to culture. Don't you ever miss Paris? I can't believe you don't sometimes feel trapped in a place like this."

Surrounded by lakes, forests, mountains and beauty, working in a job she loved with people who cared about her?

This wasn't trapped.

Something dark unfurled inside her.

She'd been trapped and it had felt nothing like this.

"I don't miss Paris." When she thought of Paris now, she thought not of strolling along the *Jardin des Tuileries* or of the light playing over the surface of the Seine, she thought of *him*. She thought of the ugly side of love and relationships. She lifted her hand to her short, styled hair and felt suddenly cold. "I love it here. Even though I wasn't born at Snow Crystal, I'm sure I love it as much as you do."

"Well, that's lucky for my family. You're an exceptional chef. Before you arrived our taste buds had never really lived. Whatever Jackson did to persuade you to come here, we're all grateful."

Jackson hadn't persuaded her. He'd offered her a lifeline. She'd messed up her life through a series of bad choices and Jackson had given her a way out. Without him—

She didn't want to think about that. But she was never going to let him regret his decision. She was going to make sure that Snow Crystal was known for its food as well as its other charms. She was determined to do her bit to make the place a success, but she was already failing, wasn't she? She'd promised the Boathouse Café would be open in time to make the most of the summer tourist traffic and now it wouldn't be. The delay would harm them, there was no doubt about that.

Frustrated and upset with herself, Élise stared at the glassy surface of the lake, barely visible in the darkness.

This place felt more like home than anywhere she'd ever lived.

Sean leaned back in his chair, watching her. "You look as if someone just killed your pet rabbit. Is this about my grandfather or is it something else?"

"It's nothing. I'm just tired."

"Don't lie to me. I'm a doctor. I spend my entire life talking to anxious patients. Tell me what's wrong."

She stared at the water and shrugged. "I am upset because I'm letting him down."

"Who? Gramps?"

"Jackson. He is working so hard to save Snow Crystal. The Boathouse Café is part of that. The launch wasn't just an excuse for a party, it was supposed to be a way of showing important people how far we've come. How much the place has to offer. I wanted to make it happen for him."

"So it will happen a bit late. No big deal."

"It is a big deal! I owe him so much." Seeing the question in his eyes, she realized she'd said too much. "I mean, I work for him and I love it here. It's in my interests that this place survives and thrives."

"Lucky Jackson, having staff as loyal as you." He was silent for a moment. "How did the two of you meet? I don't think I've ever asked either of you that."

"We met in Paris." She phrased her answer carefully. "He ate in the restaurant I once worked in."

"Chez Laroche? I know you worked for Pascal Laroche. I read that you were the only woman in his kitchen."

He knew that? Somehow, she kept the smile fixed on her face. "That's right."

"Major career achievement. I ate there once. He's brilliant."

And controlling, unscrupulous and, as it turned out, violent.

"He taught me a great deal."

It wasn't a lie. Pascal had taught her, not just how to make a perfect soufflé but that love was a gift that, once given, left a person exposed and vulnerable. He'd taught her that love could be obsessive, narcissistic and sometimes dangerous. He'd taught her that and more and the lessons had been well learned and never forgotten.

She'd graduated from his school of life with honors.

Pascal hadn't killed her belief in love. You only had to look at Walter and Alice or Jackson and Kayla to know love existed. No, he'd killed her belief in herself. Her belief in her ability to judge people, her ability to know where and when to trust. Passion had blinded her. Impaired her judgment. She wasn't going to let it happen again, no matter how attractive the man.

Wishing she hadn't started the conversation, Élise rose. "Would you like cheese?"

"No, thanks. How are you feeling? Dizziness gone?"

"Yes." All she was feeling was sick, but thinking about Pascal always did that to her. "It was a stressful day. Thank you for listening."

"Exercise is good for stress." Sean stood up. "I'd suggest sex, but I'm guessing you'd say no, so why don't we go for a walk instead?"

Distracted by the mention of sex, Élise stared at him. "Walk?"

"You'd prefer sex?" His lazy gaze was loaded with humor and she felt some of the tension ease.

"I should go to bed."

"You won't sleep with all that adrenaline rushing around your veins. Show me what you've done with the boathouse. Last time I saw the place it was nothing but splintered planks and cobwebs."

"Now? It's dark."

"I'll be fine if you hold my hand."

It was impossible not to smile. "All right."

Why not? Deciding that fresh forest air might stop her from thinking of Walter and her past, she walked back into her lodge and picked up a thin sweater and a flashlight.

It was just a walk. Just two people enjoying some fresh air.

Where was the harm in that?

CHAPTER THREE

HIS PLAN HAD been to give her a report on his grandfather and leave. What hadn't been part of his plan was lingering and eating a meal, but when he'd arrived she'd looked so shocked to see him he'd thought she was going to pass out at his feet.

There was no way he was leaving her on her own until he was sure she was all right.

"I'm ready, but I warn you it isn't finished so you'll need to be careful where you tread." Switching on the flashlight, she took the steps to the lake path that wound through trees to the almost finished café. "We're finishing off the interior over the next few days but opening will be delayed because of the deck."

He wondered why she was so agitated about it. "What difference does a few days make? It's a café, not a matter of life or death."

She turned, almost dazzling him with the beam of light. "It could mean life or death for Snow Crystal. Don't you *care?*" In the seconds before he was temporarily blinded, he saw the blaze of anger in her eyes.

It didn't surprise him.

Élise was emotional and passionate about everything. He'd witnessed the intensity of that passion once before, on that night when both of them had ceased to pretend their mutual attraction didn't exist.

"This place has been in my family for four genera-tions. Of course I care." His emotions were much more complex than that simple statement suggested, but he had no intention of sharing that.

The light wobbled. "But what we do here is not really important?"

"That's not what I'm saying."

"You are saying it has to be a person's life before it matters? Well let me tell you something, Sean O'Neil." She advanced on him, her green eyes the only color in her pale face. "This place is like a person to me. And the people who live and work here matter more than anything. And if Snow Crystal doesn't survive, then that will make a huge difference to people's lives. You might not want to be involved with what is going on here, but don't *ever* dismiss it as irrelevant."

She was wild. Furious. Uncontrolled. She'd also switched to French without realizing it.

He knew her exaggerated response was fallout from the intense emotion of the day. He saw the same thing happen all the time in his working life.

It made perfect sense.

What made less sense was the fact that he wanted to kiss her.

He wanted to slide his fingers into her hair, cover her mouth with his and kiss her until the fire in her eyes turned from anger to passion. He wanted to taste that passion again, feel it slide over his tongue and into his veins.

Disturbed by how badly he wanted to grab her, knowing that the last thing he needed in his life was a romantic entanglement, he stepped back. "I never said it was irrelevant. You're worried about opening late. I was trying to put it in perspective."

"Your perspective and mine are different." She turned and walked away, the beam from the flashlight bouncing angrily across the path.

While he was waiting for his vision to adjust, Sean breathed in the scent of the trees and the water and was immediately transported back to his childhood.

He was back in a place that made him feel as if he were being suffocated. And now, to complicate things, he was with a woman who made him think of nothing but sex.

A woman who had walked off with the flashlight.

He followed her down the path, making his way, barely able to see where he was going, cursing fluently as his feet crunched on twigs and sank into something soft and unidentifiable.

"That's a perfectly good pair of shoes ruined. I should have followed Gramps's orders and driven straight back to Boston."

She turned, almost blinding him with the beam of the flashlight. "So why didn't you?"

"Because I've had a long day." And because the sight of his grandmother's pale face had been enough to weld his feet to the floor. "And the food is pretty good around here. I'm planning on hanging around for a while."

"Good. Because whatever Walter says, your family needs you." She paused, her shoulders stiff. "I apologize for shouting. You made me angry."

"Yeah, I got that. Still, at least you didn't smack me over the head with the flashlight. I should probably be grateful for that. Any chance you could shine it at my feet so I can see what I'm stepping in?"

"It's a forest! How did you ever survive growing up here?"

"I didn't wear expensive shoes." He contemplated wiping them on something but decided it would make it worse. "We used to play down here when we were kids. Mom would send us out with a picnic and we played pirates on the lake and built a camp in the forest. We smeared ourselves with mud to camouflage ourselves and then hid when Gramps came looking for us."

She eyed his suit. "I cannot imagine you filthy and covered in mud."

"Take a closer look and you'll see it now." He cursed again as his foot slid. "These shoes are Italian." Giving up on his feet, he glanced up though leaves and branches. "Tyler fell out of this one. He never could keep quiet. He was wriggling, fell and broke his arm. That was the first time I saw what bone looked like. He screamed himself hoarse. Jackson was white and rushing around trying to remember the first aid we'd been taught while I stood there thinking, *it would be so cool to know how to fix that.* The following winter Jackson broke his arm snowboarding and that was when I knew for sure I wanted to be a doctor. I was seven years old." He grinned at her. "Of course, I also thought it would be a great way to pull women."

She glared at him. "You don't charm me. I'm still angry with you."

"There's no justice in the world."

"You think women are impressed by the fact you're a doctor?"

Plenty were, but he decided this wasn't a good moment to mention that. "Obviously you're not."

"Maybe you should have chosen something impressive like brain surgery."

"I could retrain. You think that would make a difference to my hit rate?"

Her scathing look told him she knew exactly how good his hit rate was. "If you're trying to pull women you should change the way you tell the story—less mention of bone and more heroics might help."

"You want heroics?"

"Every woman wants heroics."

"Really? I had no idea. It's a wonder I've scored at all in the past. So give me some help here—what do I have to do to impress you? Fight a moose? Wrestle a bear?"

"Wouldn't that ruin your suit?" She was softening, her anger a faint glow instead of an intense burn.

"I could ask the bear to wait while I hang my jacket on a tree." The scent of her hair made him dizzy. He was sure if a bear walked up now, he wouldn't notice it.

"You pretend to worry about your suit, but you are quite at home in the forest."

Sean's foot sank into mud again and he turned the air blue. "Trust me, I really am worried about my suit. It's done nothing to deserve this treatment."

"So it has to be intellectual heroism. Nothing physical."

"I have no problems with physical." He moved closer to her and saw her back away fractionally. "I just might remove my clothes first."

She backed away until she was pressed up against the tree. "Don't flirt with me."

"Why not? It's the perfect way to take our minds off a bad day." He planted his hand against the tree and smiled down at her, forcing himself not to kiss that mouth. *Not yet.*

She'd probably been on her feet for hours and yet she looked cool and elegant, a scarf knotted with artful simplicity around her throat. Her style was effortless and subtle, her hair glossy dark and cut in a sleek, geometric bob that brushed her jaw. She looked delicate and fragile but he knew she was neither of those things. She was strong, fit and driven by more passion and energy than anyone he'd ever met except perhaps his grandfather. She poured that passion and energy into everything she did, from cooking to—

His body hardened.

She pushed at his chest. "We're here because you wanted to see the boathouse, remember?"

"I confess I brought you here with nefarious intentions."

"Nefarious?" She rolled her tongue around the word and he tried to focus his mind sufficiently to provide a translation.

"Maléfique?"

"Wicked. Of course." She frowned, irritated with herself. "It's just not a word I have reason to use often at Snow Crystal."

"Maybe we should do something about that."

"I don't think so." Cool, back in control, she ducked under his arm. "You wanted to see what we've done, so come and see. I'm excited about this place. It's the first time I've been involved with something from the start."

He forced himself to focus on her words and not on the long, lean lines of her body.

"So I've told you why I wanted to be a doctor. Now it's your turn. Did you always want to be a chef?"

It occurred to him that it was the first personal question he'd asked her.

"From the age of four. I was making madeleines with my mother. She was a *pâtissière*. You call it pastry chef. She stood me on a stool so that I could reach the table and I helped her whisk the mixture. I still remember how it felt to pull the tray from the oven and know I'd made them. The aroma filled our little apartment. And so did my mother's smile when she tasted them. I decided that was what I wanted to do. Make people smile with my food." Her own smile faltered for a moment and he saw something in her face before she turned away and walked the last few strides to the boathouse, taking the flashlight with her.

He followed, walking on a carpet of pine needles, twigs crunching under his feet while wondering what the rest of her story was. Because there was more, he was sure of that.

She took the steps onto the half-finished deck. "Be careful not to trip. There are still some planks lying around and the railings aren't finished. You might end up in the water."

"Wouldn't be the first time. My shoes are already ruined so I might as well ruin the suit right along with it." He glanced around him, surprised by the progress. "You're closer to finished than I thought you'd be."

"That makes it worse. We so nearly made our deadline."

"Why this obsession with deadlines? Is my brother a tough boss or something? Do you need me to beat him up for you?"

Her eyes glinted in the semidarkness. "Jackson is

the best boss anyone could ever have. Do not ever say a single word against him or you'll make me angry."

"Hey, calm down. Jackson is a saint," Sean drawled. "I've always said it." But he wondered what it was about his brother that induced such loyalty from Élise.

Pondering that, dealing with the surprising flash of jealousy, he strolled across the half-completed deck and stared through the glass into darkness.

It was strange to see it renovated.

This place had been his hideout. Somewhere he could sit with his nose in a book and not be disturbed. Hell, he was pretty sure he'd carved mathematical algorithms into the time frame. He and his brothers had played on the old splintered planks and hidden when their grandfather had come looking for them. There had always been something that needed to be done at Snow Crystal. Trails to be cleared, logs to be chopped, trees to be tapped—the list of jobs was endless and his grandfather had applied himself tirelessly to the upkeep of the family home.

Sean remembered his tenth birthday when his grandfather had told him proudly that Snow Crystal would belong to the three boys one day. It was a legacy, he'd said, something that had to be preserved and protected for future generations.

Sean had kept his head down and sanded the planks of wood, thinking of the science books in his bag and wanting to ask his grandfather if "legacy" meant the same thing as "burden." He'd heard his father use the word *burden* a hundred times. Heard him talk about being trapped in a life he hadn't wanted.

Sean hadn't wanted it, either.

Instead, he dreamed of being a surgeon. And he

dreamed of doing it in a large, busy hospital far away from the lake and forests of Snow Crystal.

You didn't need to come. You should have stayed in Boston.

With his grandfather's voice ringing in his ears, Sean paced to the edge of the completed part of the deck. "I'm not used to seeing this place without daylight between the planks. So what is left to do apart from the deck?"

"Just finishing touches." Élise was looking through the glass into the empty shell. "The internal decoration was finished yesterday. I still have to take delivery of tables and chairs and I have a few final staff interviews to do. All that was supposed to be finished in time for the opening party."

"And when is that?"

"A week from today. I know Kayla sent you an invitation."

"I get a lot of emails."

"You weren't planning to come." She sounded baffled, as if she couldn't understand how a person with his heritage wouldn't want to spend every spare minute here. And he was used to that. He didn't expect her to understand.

"I was going to check my schedule."

The night air was still and quiet, the only sound the occasional call of an owl or a soft splash as a bird skimmed the surface of the lake.

"Whatever he said to you, however he acted, I know your grandfather would have been pleased and relieved to see you there tonight."

Pleased?

Sean bent to pick up a stone, wondering how he was

supposed to answer that. He could ignore the question, or he could just be honest. In the end he chose an answer halfway between the two. "Grams was relieved I was there."

If Élise noticed the omission she didn't comment. "Where are you staying tonight?"

Pushing away the past, he turned. "Is that an invitation?"

"No. Will you stay with your mother?"

"She already has Jess staying. It's simpler for everyone, at least while Gramps is still in the hospital and Tyler is coming and going." He sent the stone spinning across the water and it bounced, skimmed and vanished into the darkness. "I'll use Jackson's spare room."

"The whole family will feel much better having you here, even if it's only a night or two."

"And how will you feel?"

Her gaze skidded to his. "Of course, I am pleased, too. It is a very great stress having someone you love in the hospital and I love Walter."

"That wasn't what I was asking you." He'd often wondered. Wondered whether she thought of it. Thought of *him*. The fact that the night had held no emotional significance hadn't stopped it being unforgettable.

"I don't have a problem with you being here." Her voice was husky in the darkness. "It isn't awkward, if that's what you're asking me. But it must be a great pressure for you. You need to make sure you think of yourself, too."

"That's good advice." Taking it, he slid his hand behind her head and brought his mouth down on hers in a hard, demanding kiss that stirred up a raw hunger. A kaleidoscope of emotions ripped through him but the prime one was need. It spread through him, not slowly, but like wildfire burning everything in sight. Gripped by it, Sean powered her back against the railing and trapped her there.

Last time, she'd started it.

Now it was his turn.

He felt the softness of her body pressing through the thin fabric of his shirt, the erotic slide of her tongue against his, and desire escalated to a dangerous blaze. Her arms went around his neck and she purred deep in her throat like a thoroughly contented kitten.

His brain blurred.

No other woman had made him feel like this. No other woman had stirred this intense, desperate hunger that wiped all thoughts from his head.

Maybe it was because she didn't want anything from him but this, and knowing that meant he could relax and give in to it.

Rock-hard, he felt her tug his shirt out of his trousers and slide her hands over his skin, greedy to touch him. And he was equally greedy to touch her. His fingers were on her buttons, loosening them, giving him access to the smooth creamy skin revealed by the lace of her bra.

His body craved hers. It was a visceral, physical need that drove all thought from his brain.

And then she stilled, placed her hands on his chest and drew her mouth away from his.

Sensing the change in her he stopped himself from dragging her back. "What's wrong?"

"We shouldn't be doing this. It's been a tough day. Our judgment is impaired."

"My judgment is just fine." He held her hard against

his body, leaving her in no doubt that he wanted this as much as she did, but she eased away from him and buttoned her shirt.

"You're in the middle of a stressful experience."

"And I was managing my stress levels with physical contact."

"Sex should not be an emotional decision. You're tired. You need to get to Jackson's and get some sleep."

He wondered if it was worth pointing out there was no way he'd sleep. "Fine, but admit to me that that kiss was the best part of your day."

"It didn't have much competition. It was a very bad day." Her hand lingered on his chest as if she was still making up her mind whether to hold on or pull away. She pulled away. "Good night, Sean."

"Wait—" he caught her arm "—I'll walk you back to your lodge."

"I don't need your protection."

"I was planning on using you for protection. For my suit, you understand. You're the one with the flashlight. You go first. That way if something goes squelch, you step in it first."

"Such a gentleman." But he heard the smile in her voice.

"You said you wanted a man to perform heroics. I was planning on finding something heroic to do on the walk." He let go of her arm and adjusted his pace to match hers. "You might want to stick around. You're about to see a tough, macho man of the forest in action."

"Does a tough, macho man of the forest always choose to dress in a suit?"

"A bear tore my loincloth when we were wrestling."

"I can't imagine you in a loincloth."

"Mine are custom-made. I have them shipped from Milan."

They reached Heron Lodge and she took the steps two at a time, lithe and athletic. "Sleep well, Sean."

"Will you be all right tonight? Are you sure you want to sleep alone?" He had no idea why he'd asked that question. What would he do if she said no? Spending the whole night with a woman wasn't something he did.

"I sleep alone every night, Sean." She paused with her hand on the door, a quiet, wistful note to her voice. "And that's the way it's staying."

CHAPTER FOUR

ÉLISE ROSE AT dawn after a night where her only sleep had produced a nightmare in which Jackson told her Snow Crystal had been sold and the shock had killed Walter.

After splashing her face with cold water, she pulled on her shorts and running shoes, grabbed her water bottle and MP3 player and paused for a moment on the deck to breathe in the scent of the lake. The water was mirror-smooth, reflecting a perfect image of the trees crowding the shoreline. The air was fresh and clean. A cool breeze brushed over her bare arms, waking her up and driving out the dream.

It was her favorite time of day. In Paris she would have run along the banks of the Seine and through the *Jardin des Tuileries* in front of the Louvre, the accompanying sounds the noise of traffic and the cacophony of horns. She would have weaved through crowds of fractious tourists and breathed in air clogged by traffic fumes while her feet pounded pavements baked by the summer sun. Here, the air she breathed was fresh and clean and the only sounds came from the forest and the lake. Even days when it rained continuously didn't detract from her love of the place.

She ran along the forest path to the boathouse and the only sounds were her breathing, the crack of twigs underfoot and the call of the birds. A family of ducks swam lazily around the edge of the lake, diving in and out of the reeds.

As she took the steps to the boathouse, she glanced at the railing, half expecting to see a charred mark where Sean had kissed her, but the wood was smooth and perfect.

The forest had kept their secret for a year and it seemed it was willing to keep it a little longer.

Her friends were already waiting for her.

Brenna was warming up, performing a series of small lunges while Kayla was leaning against the trunk of a tree, using the time to catch up on work.

"You're late, Chef." She spoke without looking up from her phone. Scarily efficient, she lived her life with one eye on the clock. Right now her blond hair was pulled into a ponytail but later it would hang smooth and perfect to her shoulders as she attacked her working day.

Élise had seen the effort Kayla had put into building the Snow Crystal name and had nothing but respect for her. It wasn't just because of Jackson that the business was still alive and they all had jobs.

"Any news on Walter?" Brenna bent into a deep stretch. Supremely fit from her job running the Outdoor Center and sports program, she was the one who had suggested their daily morning run and they'd been doing it since the snow had melted. Today she was wearing a scoop-neck tank top in bright fuchsia-pink with a pair of minuscule black shorts.

Élise blinked. "Has Tyler ever seen you in those?"

"No idea. Why would I even care?"

Élise shared a brief glance with Kayla who shrugged and then went back to her phone.

Brenna's feelings for Tyler were something they'd both learned not to mention.

"You need to put that phone down and warm your muscles up, Kayla." Brenna carried on stretching. "One of these days you're going to have an injury."

"I just left Jackson in bed. I'm toasty warm, thank you very much." But she halfheartedly jogged on the spot while she finished dealing with her emails. "And Walter had a good night, according to Sean. He called Jackson from the hospital just before I left. Do we have to run today? Can't we just test the new coffee machine in the Boathouse? Élise makes great coffee."

"No." Brenna put her hands behind her head and squeezed her shoulder blades together. "Without me you'd turn into a couch potato."

"I would love to be a couch potato." Kayla smothered a yawn. "I didn't get enough sleep last night."

"Thanks for pointing out you're the only one of the three of us with a sex life."

"It isn't my sex life that's making me tired. It was Sean, crashing around at three in the morning to go to the hospital. He spent the night at our place. Why can't men ever tread softly? I thought a moose was walking through the living room."

"He's six-two. All that prime male muscle weighs some." Brenna winked at Kayla. "Not that I'd know, of course. I've never had his weight on me."

"Jackson told him we have a house rule about guests not walking around naked." Kayla looked up from her phone long enough to smile. "I told him that wasn't my house rule."

"Wouldn't be mine, either. Or Élise's, I'll guess." Brenna adjusted her running shoes and glanced slyly at Élise. "Now that Sean's home, your sex life might liven up."

Élise was lost in a pit of gloom over having to cancel the party. "Why would my sex life liven up?"

"You and Sean were pretty close last summer."

Élise was beginning to wish she hadn't told them what had happened. "It was one night. And if either of you mention it to Jackson I will kill you."

"Why only one night?"

"Because I felt like having sex and so did Sean." And she would never, ever risk more than one night. "Haven't you ever just had sex because a guy is seriously hot and makes you laugh?"

"No. I've never been any good at the one-night thing." Brenna pulled her dark hair into a ponytail. "Just about everyone I meet has known me since kindergarten. If I have a one-night stand with someone chances are I'll bump into them in the store the next day. I'd die."

"Why would that cause you to die?" Élise was curious. "Why would it matter if you bumped into them?"

"It would be *majorly* embarrassing."

"If it was something you both agreed to, why would it be embarrassing? You just say *bonjour* and smile or if the sex was really bad I suppose you might just smile a little less. Be a little cooler so that they don't think you want to do it again."

Brenna gave her a look of exasperation. "Are all French people like you?"

"*Je ne sais pas.* Kayla asked me the same question yesterday. I don't know all French people, only a few.

But I don't understand why sex between consenting adults is something to feel embarrassed about. It is certainly not a reason to die."

"So you don't feel embarrassed when you see Sean? It isn't at all uncomfortable? You don't look at him and think *shit* I wish I hadn't done that?"

"No, I look at him and think *Élise, this guy is super hot and you have impeccable taste in men.* It was great sex and why would I ever regret great sex?"

"So why not do it again?"

"My rule is one night."

"I had a rule of never having a relationship with someone at work." Kayla sent another email. "Look at me now."

"That doesn't count." Brenna flipped open the cap on her water bottle. "Technically speaking, you didn't work for Jackson."

"He was a client," Kayla said dryly. "I think that's probably worse. Shame Brett didn't just fire me for gross misconduct. Then I wouldn't have spent the last six months commuting backward and forward between New York and Snow Crystal."

"You could have left sooner."

"Yes, but we were in the middle of projects and I have too much pride in my work to abandon them."

"You mean you are a control freak."

"That, too." Kayla shrugged. "Hey, I admit it. And talking of control freaks, I need your plans for the winter program, Bren, so I can work up some promotional ideas."

"Sure. While Sean is home I'm going to pin him down and talk him into helping me design a pre-season conditioning program of strength training for the winter. He's an expert in sports medicine. I thought we'd offer a short program for the guests and also advice on avoiding ski injuries. Sean has a good reputation. He's a skier as well as a surgeon so he has a lot of respect around here."

"Better be quick about it." Kayla finally slipped her phone into her pocket. "I doubt he'll hang around for long."

"Maybe he'll stay because Élise is here," Brenna suggested.

"The principle behind one night is that it's just one night." Why did they have such trouble understanding that? "I cannot make this any plainer. The only reason I would want him to stay is for Walter."

But Walter had told him to go. Why? Was it pride? Was he worried about Sean's job? His stress levels?

"One night doesn't sound very romantic. You never want to fall in love and get married? What?" Brenna spread her hands as they both stared at her. "So I admit I'm a little old-fashioned. I believe in relationships and happy-ever-afters and maybe it's not cool to admit it, but I want all that one day. The whole package. I know there's a man out there for me somewhere. I just need time to leave this place so I can find him."

Élise suspected the right man might be closer than Brenna thought.

Kayla glanced at her and then shrugged, clearly thinking there was no point in broaching a subject Brenna refused to touch. "Give up, Bren. Does Élise really strike you as the nesting type?"

Élise slid her headphones into her ears. "Let's run."

They had no idea.

Once, she'd wanted all those things. She'd dreamed

of family and a love like the one Walter and Alice shared. A love that would last decades and weather the hailstones that life hurled down from time to time. She'd dreamed of all that and more, but then she'd learned that dreams could be dangerous and love was the most dangerous emotion of all.

It could destroy a person. Break them into pieces.

She ran hard and fast, using exercise to clear her head, overtaking even Brenna and arriving back first to the Boathouse.

She unlocked the door and opened up the glass front, allowing in light and air, feeling a rush of excitement as she saw the newly painted interior and the floor. Framed photographs of Snow Crystal taken in all four seasons hung on the walls. She'd chosen everything, from the chairs to the china and she was thrilled with the result.

It was going to be a success, she knew it.

The Inn at Snow Crystal, the main restaurant, was perfect for people looking for elegant fine dining. It was for special occasions—birthdays, anniversaries, the celebration of a vacation, but not everyone could afford that, or wanted that. Sometimes all people wanted was to enjoy a relaxed meal with their family with a view of the water. They wanted to enjoy fresh, simple food that wouldn't blow the holiday budget.

Élise had been experimenting with dishes for months. The Boathouse would serve fresh, seasonal food either on the pretty, sun-baked deck or indoors while summer rain drenched the roof. She'd worked hard on the children's menu, developing recipes that were varied, appealing and nutritious. There would be something for everyone.

She'd overseen everything from kitchen design to

the subtle outdoor lighting that would add a little romance for couples wanting to savor a special evening dining alfresco.

Breakfast by the water would be a highlight. There would be fluffy pancakes, both American and French *crêpes,* served with their own maple syrup. She'd perfected a homemade granola recipe and she intended to offer it with fresh blueberries and compote made from fruits picked from the orchard. She'd even considered making her own Snow Crystal apple juice.

For those who rose later in the day there would be a range of coffee options with freshly baked pastries. Lunch and dinner would be a bistro menu, with food from the grill. Casual, but still top-quality. All her food was purchased from local suppliers and she spent a part of every week visiting farmers and working to build long-term relationships with the local agricultural community. *Seasonal* and *sustainable* were the two words she drummed into the people who worked for her.

Everything was perfect, except the fact that they wouldn't open on time.

Brenna ran across the deck without pausing. "See you later."

Kayla arrived two minutes later, panting for breath. "You two are going to kill me. If I don't die on the way home, I'll email you that list and we can start making those calls to cancel the party."

Left alone with that dispiriting thought, Élise made coffee for herself but even her new coffee machine couldn't cheer her up. She ground the beans fresh, tamped the coffee and then timed the pour, taking comfort from the familiarity of the routine. Unfortunately it didn't take her mind off the fact that she'd failed Jackson. Nor did it take her mind off Sean.

It was a good job her friends hadn't chosen to go for a late-night run or they might have witnessed more than the flight of an owl.

And no doubt they would have read things into it that weren't there.

People did that, didn't they? To most people a kiss was never just a kiss, but always the prelude to something more.

Not for her.

Never for her.

With the sun shining and the aroma of fresh coffee rising from the cup, she started to relax.

She'd make the calls. Get it done.

There really wasn't a problem.

She'd reached the point of almost believing that when she turned her head and saw Sean standing on her almost finished deck.

HE'D BEEN WATCHING her for a full minute, standing in the quiet of the morning, breathing in the scent of lake and forest, tinged with the tantalizing aroma of freshly ground coffee.

After the fright he'd given her the night before he'd intended to make his presence known, but he'd been distracted first by the length of her legs in running shorts and then by his first proper look at the project he'd viewed in the dark the previous evening.

Bathed in sunlight, he could see just how much had been done and it took a minute for him to reconcile the sleek lines of the renovated boathouse with the wreck that had been his sanctuary growing up.

Before he could announce himself she'd turned, her hair swinging softly around her face and brushing her jaw. "Are you going to make a habit of showing up behind me without warning?"

"Sorry. I was just wondering what happened to all the splintered planks and spiders." Pushing aside the past in favor of the present, he stared at the cup in her hand. "I don't suppose you need more practice using that fancy new machine?"

"No, but if you'd like coffee I'll make you one. Jackson and Kayla not treating you well?"

"The only coffee I could find was instant. And they definitely need you to stock their kitchen." Sean walked across the half-finished deck, scanning the work that needed to be done. "So do you run every morning?"

"Yes. With Brenna and Kayla. You just missed them. We do a circuit of the lake." She reached for another cup. "Espresso? I don't have milk here yet. You'll have to drink it black."

"Black works for me. Double please. So this is how the place looks in daylight."

"We're expecting delivery of the tables today. Apart from that, the interior is almost finished."

"That coffee machine looks as if it could fly to the moon and back on its own." Polished chrome and levers stood proudly behind the counter that would no doubt stock an array of food once they opened. "Looks complicated."

"This from a man who operates on complex fractures?"

"Most of the time it's like doing a jigsaw. There's a certain rhythm to it." He watched as the coffee dripped into the cup, the rich, pungent smell mingling with the tang of varnish and fresh paint. The old boathouse was barely recognizable as the place he'd hidden out in his youth. The stained, splintered walls peppered by daylight no longer existed. In their place was creamy paintwork and polished floorboards. The eye was drawn, not to trees waving through gaps in the wood, but to large photographs of the lakes and mountains around Snow Crystal that now hung on the walls. Where cobwebs had once been strung floor to ceiling, there were tall elegant plants. It was stylish, and yet welcoming.

He couldn't fault it, nor was he sentimental, so it made no sense to feel a sense of loss for what had once been. "You've designed this place well. I never would have thought of developing it."

"It seemed like a good idea at the time. Today, I'm not so sure. At some point Kayla and I have to start calling a hundred and twenty people to tell them the party isn't happening."

"There's no way the deck will be finished on time?"

"Not unless the elves come in the night. I am angry with myself for not putting in place a contingency plan." She handed him the coffee, scooped up her own and took it outside. The half-finished deck was warmed by early morning sunshine. "I am lucky Jackson is too much of a gentleman to shout at me."

"Maybe he doesn't think there's a reason to shout." He followed her. "Seems to me you're angry enough without anyone else adding to it. Are you always this hard on yourself?"

"I don't like letting people down. I'm part of the team here." Her voice was fierce. "This party is important. We've invited people from the tourist office, from local business, Kayla even has journalists coming in from New York. And I've messed it up."

"I don't see why it's your fault. Sometimes things happen. Life happens. Believe me, I know. I clear up after life all the time. She has a habit of leaving her mess everywhere, often when people least expect it."

"I should have built in more time. But I chose the date because I wanted the Boathouse open so that we could make the most of the summer months. I was doing my best to boost our profits and get good publicity, but now it will backfire because we will look inefficient."

Her loyalty and devotion to a place with which she had no blood ties still puzzled him. "Do you always give your all to everything?"

"Of course. My passion is my biggest strength." She sipped her coffee and gave a wry shrug. "And my biggest failing."

He remembered how that passion had felt under his hands and mouth. "I don't see it as a failing."

Their eyes met briefly and he knew her mind was in the same place as his.

Then she turned away. "This is my favorite time of day, before I face the stress. When I see the mist on the lake, I think it's the most beautiful place in the world, don't you agree?"

He didn't, but he'd learned long ago to keep those feelings to himself so he stood still and let the silence wash over him.

"Sean?"

For a moment he'd forgotten she was standing there.

"This place is full of memories."

He turned his head and looked at what needed to be

done to finish the deck, but instead of seeing planks of wood he saw his grandfather, back curved like a bow as he hunched over, sawing wood and banging in nails, Jackson kneeling next to him, soaking it in.

It had been his grandfather who had taught all three boys about the forest, the lake and the wildlife. His love for Snow Crystal was deep and unwavering. He'd been born on O'Neil land and his wish was to die on it. Sean remembered his grandfather taking him into the forest when he was five years old and showing him the growth rings on a tree trunk that had split during a storm in the night. He remembered wondering if his grandfather had the same inside him. A ring for every year he'd spent at Snow Crystal. Walter O'Neil loved the place so deeply he wasn't able to comprehend that others might not share that devotion. That some people needed more than fresh air, beautiful scenery and a family so close there were days it had felt like being buried in an avalanche.

Sean had felt trapped and unable to breathe. Smothered by expectation.

Élise sighed. "It's so peaceful, isn't it? Unbelievably beautiful. You must miss it when you're in the city."

Miss it?

He forced himself to glance at the water and see what she was seeing. This time, instead of his grandfather, he saw trees reaching skyward, their shape reflected in the mirrored surface of the lake with perfect clarity. He saw light bounce and sparkle as the early rays of the sun kissed the surface of the water and realized that at some point in his life he'd started to see Snow Crystal as a pressure, not a place.

How often did he take the time to stand still and admire the beauty around him? His day was a series of obligations and commitments. He lived a life that barely allowed time to breathe and rarely allowed time for reflection. His job was about working fast and hard and getting things done, never about standing still.

"It's going to be a pretty day." It was the closest he could get to saying what she expected to hear.

"This is one of my favorite spots." Élise moved to the edge of the deck, stepping over the part that wasn't finished. "I went for a run on my first morning here and couldn't understand why it hadn't been developed along with the rest of the buildings."

"Snow Crystal has always been full of falling-down buildings. Restoring it is a labor of love." And he didn't feel the love. Just the pressure. He wasn't like Jackson, who had taken the old dilapidated barn and turned it into a stylish home. It was Jackson who had seen the potential for building log cabins in the forest for families to enjoy the outdoors. Sean was happy fixing bones, but not buildings. Left to him, the whole place would have all fallen down.

"It was an obvious site for a café. The building was already here and it had become a safety issue." She turned, her eyes glowing with pride as she looked at the Boathouse.

Sean remembered the shaft of light that had shone through the hole in the roof onto his textbooks.

Science had excited him the way a steep slope had excited Tyler. While his brother had been executing eye-wateringly difficult feats on the snow, Sean had been indulging his fascination in the development of surgery in prehistoric cultures. He'd learned about the *Edwin Smith Papyrus,* the earliest known surgical text, which showed that the Egyptians had had a scientific understanding of traumatic injuries. He'd greedily devoured everything he could find about the history of surgery, reading about the Greek Galen, the work of Ambroise Paré, a French barber surgeon, and studying Joseph Lister's contribution to reducing infection rates during surgery.

The potential of surgery to change and save lives excited him in a way that living a quiet life at Snow Crystal didn't.

At seven years old he'd known he wanted to be an orthopedic surgeon. It was a burning ambition inside him and he knew then he didn't want to die here with those rings inside him, showing how long he'd spent in the same place doing the same thing. He didn't want to spend his days mending leaking roofs and maintaining trails so that tourists could churn them up again. He wanted to fix people's bones and help them walk again. How cool was that?

"We spent a lot of time on this lake growing up."

"Jackson told me about the time you all sank the boat."

"That was Tyler. He was the one who sank the boat. We built it from scraps of wood lying around the place. It wasn't what you might call completely watertight. Tyler couldn't help standing up in the thing and rocking it. Jackson was yelling at him to sit down but Tyler never did anything anyone told him. Damn boat sank to the bottom of the lake and we all took a soaking."

Her eyes danced. "Growing up here must have been very special."

Special?

"It didn't look anything like this back then." He

leaned back against the railing, remembering. "This place was a wreck. Perfect for playing pirates. We used to scoop up spiders to take to Mom."

"Poor Elizabeth. It is a wonder she is sane."

"She's good with spiders. We taught her to be." Looking at the Boathouse, he saw that its position was perfect. Nestling in the sunshine on the edge of the lake, the wooden structure blended with the forest so that at a single glance you might not even notice it. It had been beautifully restored, the work in keeping with the original structure although hardly any of that remained. But the real charm was the wide deck that almost circled the Boathouse, allowing for alfresco eating. The wide deck that wasn't finished.

He dropped to his haunches and ran his hand over the planks, feeling the grain under his palm and hearing the gentle lap of the water beneath. "He's using marine grade wood. It's a nice job. Zach has improved since the days when we built your lodge."

"You built Heron Lodge? I didn't know that."

"The five of us, with the occasional intervention from Gramps." But never his father.

His father had vanished on one of his many trips and when he'd returned the job had been done. Sean frowned, wondering why of all the memories he'd banked, that was the one to come to mind.

"You three and Zach makes four. Who was the fifth?"

"Brenna." Sean straightened, pushing away thoughts of his father. "She pretty much did everything we did. I guess she was the little sister we didn't have. She climbed the same trees we climbed, scraped her knees right along with us and skied down everything we skied down. She and Tyler were inseparable. The two of them were so close it was impossible to find one without the other."

It seemed ironic to him that the one relationship that wouldn't have needed sacrifice and compromise had never happened. Tyler and Brenna both shared the same love of Snow Crystal and the land around it. They were both athletic, outdoor types, perfectly matched. Both of them had built a life around lakes and mountains.

There had been a time when they'd all assumed their relationship would naturally progress, but then Janet Carpenter had come along and all that had changed.

And now Tyler had Jess living with him, which narrowed his life choices more than his damaged knee. With a thirteen-year-old daughter, he'd had to give up his party lifestyle.

That had to be the ultimate compromise for love.

"So now that I know you all built Heron Lodge, I need to know if I should be nervous." Élise finished her coffee. "When I lie in my bed at night, should I worry that the lodge will collapse under me?"

"It's a sound structure. Tyler tested it out on the first night by kicking a football around the bedroom. We had to replace the window but the rest of it survived."

Smiling, she took his empty cup from him. "Thank you."

Distracted by the tiny dimple that appeared at the corner of her mouth, he lost focus. "For what?"

"For cheering me up. And now I need to go home and take a shower and then make those calls to cancel the party. I can't put it off any longer. *Merde*—" She ran her fingers through her hair, the sweet smile fading and the dimple disappearing. "I keep hoping for a miracle."

"Why can't you just fix another date?"

"Apart from the fact we'll have to pay cancellation fees to the band that we can't afford, the date was set months ago. It was my mistake." Her shoulders drooped and she looked utterly beaten.

His car was parked a few steps away. His keys were in his pocket. His plans didn't include hanging around Snow Crystal any longer than was necessary. His grandfather had made it clear he didn't want him here. He'd looked at the test results himself and could see he was making a good recovery.

His brothers seemed to have everything under control. There was nothing to keep him.

Nothing except his conscience and the look on Élise's face.

Sean tried to move, but his feet were glued to the deck. The part of the deck that was finished. The unfinished part of it glared at him accusingly.

"How is Walter?" Élise smoothed her hair behind her ear, making a visible effort to be cheerful. "Any change overnight?"

"He's doing well."

He tried to kill the idea forming in his mind.

No.

"So you'll be going back to Boston."

He opened his mouth to tell her the same thing he'd told Jackson. That he had work backing up and patients to see. That he had to take it a day at a time. *That this place made him think of his father and he wouldn't be hanging around a moment longer than was necessary.*

"I'll finish the deck for you." He couldn't quite believe he'd said it and clearly she couldn't either because she stared at him, as if checking the meaning of each word.

"You'll finish my deck? How? You're a surgeon, not a carpenter."

"I'm good with my hands."

Color streaked across her cheeks. "Is this a game you are playing or is it a serious offer?"

"It's a serious offer." He watched her mouth, hoping the dimple would reappear. "Never let it be said that I walk away from a maiden in distress. I have a free weekend. It's yours if you want it."

"What's your price?"

"We'll negotiate that later. So I assume that's a yes? You'd like me to do it?"

Suspicion was replaced by joy. "Yes, of course, yes!" She sprang at him and wrapped him in a tight hug that almost cut off his air and his blood supply. "Thank you. Oh, thank you. I will never again shout at you even when you say Snow Crystal isn't important."

The scent of her wrapped itself around him, making him dizzy. Her hair was soft and silky against his jaw. "I didn't say it wasn't important. Just that you don't need to have a nervous breakdown about the café opening late."

"Thanks to you it's not going to open late now. It's going to be on time. What about clothes?" She released him. "You cannot work on a deck in your suit."

"I have a pair of jeans in my car and I'll borrow everything else from Jackson."

"*Vraiment?* You would do that?" She stared at him for a moment as if she couldn't quite believe what he was saying and then her eyes filled. "Now I think you're a hero."

More used to being cast in the role of the bad guy, Sean felt a flash of unease. "Élise—"

"Zach's tools are locked inside." She smiled and the dimple peeped from the corner of her mouth. "I'll show you where. Then I need to take a shower and call Kayla to stop her canceling the party. She will be so happy. So will Jackson. It is very kind of you, I think."

Sean dragged his mind and his eyes from Élise's lips. He wasn't sure what his motivation was, but he was fairly confident kindness hadn't played any part in his decision making. "No problem."

CHAPTER FIVE

TWENTY-FOUR HOURS later Élise stood on the deck of the café and wondered why it hadn't occurred to her that accepting Sean's offer of help would mean he'd be working here, under her nose.

Why was she so impulsive?

Why did she never think anything through?

After her daily run around the lake, she'd spent the morning in the restaurant, working lunchtime service, discussing menus, meeting with her team. She'd met with two new local suppliers and interviewed a kitchen assistant. And if all that conspired to keep her away from the Boathouse, she told herself it was coincidence, nothing more. It was everything to do with pressure of work and nothing to do with the fact that Sean was working on her deck. And she told herself that pressure of work was also the reason she hadn't responded to frequent text updates from her new sous-chef, Poppy.

Hi boss, the view from the Boathouse is better than ever today.

And five minutes later.

It's scorchin' hot over here J

And now she was back at the Boathouse and could see it for herself.

Concentrating was impossible.

"What is it about a guy using power tools?" Poppy grinned as she balanced a stack of boxes in her arms on the way to the kitchen. "I just look at him and want him to nail me to the deck. He is insanely good-looking. I'm taking my lunch break outside today, Chef."

Élise gritted her teeth. "Did everything arrive?"

"One chair was damaged but they're replacing it. Oh, dear God, he's taken his shirt off. How does a man with an indoor job get muscles like that?" Eyeing Sean, Poppy almost dropped the boxes. "Sorry, but honestly you just have to look."

"I don't have time to look! We are snowed under with things to do before the party next weekend. Poppy—" Sensing she was losing her audience again, Élise sharpened her voice. "Focus!"

"Yes, Chef. Sorry." Poppy dragged her gaze from the deck to Élise. "I'm going to get these unpacked. I'm on it."

"Good!" Exasperated, she watched as Poppy wound her way through the newly arranged tables, bumping into at least two as she stole a final look at Sean.

Teeth clenched, Élise walked to the kitchen, grabbed a glass and jug of lemonade from the fridge and strode out onto the deck to see for herself what all the fuss was about.

Sean was doing something to a plank of wood. Something that required him to stretch forward, displaying his torso. Glancing over her shoulder, she saw all the female staff lined up in the doorway.

Catching her eye, they grinned and slunk back to their jobs.

"Sean!" Torn between exasperation and irritation, Élise thumped the jug of lemonade down on the table next to him.

He glanced up and rocked back on his heels, his smile slow and sure. "Is that for me? You're a lifesaver." Putting down the plank of wood, he stood up and took the glass from her.

She watched as he drank. Sweat glistened on his forehead and his wide shoulders. It reminded her of that night in the forest. She'd ripped at his clothes. He'd ripped at hers.

Thinking about it raised her temperature another notch and she gritted her teeth. "You need to put your shirt back on."

Raising his eyebrows, he lowered the glass slowly. "I beg your pardon?"

"Your shirt. You need to put it back on."

Blue eyes held hers.

Heat built inside her. Her insides melted.

"Care to tell me why?" His voice was soft and suddenly she wished she'd just let her staff carry on falling over tables. What were a few bruises compared to the effects of standing this close to Sean?

"You are distracting my workforce."

He glanced over her shoulder. "They seem to be working pretty hard to me."

"Now. But two minutes ago they were all staring at you. They can't concentrate while you're working out here half-naked."

"It's a hot day and I'm doing manual labor." He drained the glass and ran his hand over his mouth.

"That's why I brought you a cold drink. Are you done?" Everything about him was physical. Sexual.

"Why? Are you having trouble concentrating, too?"

"No." Why hadn't she sent Poppy out with the iced lemonade? "I couldn't care less if you're totally naked on my deck, but I have a deadline to meet and I can't have my staff distracted. Let me know if you need anything else." She took the glass from him and was about to walk away when his fingers closed around her wrist and he pulled her back to him.

Caught off guard, she lost her balance and fell against him. She put her free hand on his chest to steady herself, met his eyes and almost drowned in a flash of intense blue, heat and raw desire.

"Sean—"

"You asked me to let you know if there's anything else I need."

"I didn't mean—" She couldn't breathe properly. The attraction was so shockingly powerful it almost knocked her off her feet. "You promised you'd finish the deck."

"You'll get your damn deck." His voice was rough. "You think about it, don't you?"

"What?"

"You know what." His eyes were on her mouth. "Last summer. Us."

All the time. "Rarely."

He smiled. "Yeah, right."

"Arrogance isn't attractive."

"Neither is pigheadedness. Want me to remind you what happened? Who cracked first last time?"

Her heart was pounding. "I didn't crack."

"Honey, half of that shirt I was wearing is still lying

somewhere in the forest. We never did find it. Maybe next time we shouldn't let it build up."

"It's not building up. I make that sort of decision with my head, not my hormones."

"Really?" His eyes were back on her mouth. "In that case your head was in one hell of a hurry to get me naked."

"Having made the decision, I didn't see the point in hanging around."

"A decision I supported wholeheartedly. And would again."

The heat was intense. Suffocating.

There were people working around her, members of her team, no doubt trying to lip-read and probably reading too much into the fact that their boss was currently up close and very personal with the dangerously attractive Sean O'Neil.

"More than one night with the same woman, Sean? That doesn't sound like you. You should be running."

"Normally I would be." His mouth curved into a sinfully sexy smile. "But you don't want a relationship any more than I do, which makes you my perfect woman."

The words managed to snap the spell in a way that her fading willpower hadn't.

"I'm not anyone's perfect woman, Sean."

She wasn't the person he thought she was. She was deeply damaged, with secrets even Jackson didn't know. She'd put herself back together, piece by piece, and now she protected herself carefully.

Aware that her staff were probably watching and speculating, she extracted her wrist from his grip.

"Put the shirt on. That way there will be something to rip off should I ever decide to go down that route again."

TWO DAYS LATER, Sean drove Walter home from the hospital. His grandfather clutched the car seat and stared straight ahead.

"This car should be on a racetrack."

Sean drove gently, nursing the Porsche around the bends so that his grandfather didn't even shift in his seat. The car purred like a tame lion. "It's engineering perfection. There is no such thing as a bad day when you're driving this."

His grandfather grunted. "You could have bought a Corvette."

"I didn't want a Corvette."

"It doesn't even have cupholders."

Sean tried to imagine what would happen to a cup of coffee as he accelerated away and waltzed around corners. "But it does have a super sharp throttle response. You can't drive this car and not smile. If you ever want to give it a try, let me know."

"If I want to kill myself I'll just stand in the middle of the road."

Sean slowed down as he took a right and drove past the sign for Snow Crystal Resort and Spa.

Everyone was gathered, waiting to greet him, faces pressed to the kitchen window.

"Why is everyone in the kitchen?" Pale and shaking, his grandfather struggled to undo his seat belt. "Don't they have work to do?"

"They wanted to welcome you home. Élise and Mom

have been cooking. Wait there—I'll help you out of the car."

"I'm not an invalid! I'm capable of getting myself out of a car."

As his grandfather faltered in the doorway, Sean took his arm. "Let's get you inside so you can sit down, Gramps."

His grandfather shook him off. "I don't need to sit down and I can walk perfectly well. I don't need babying. And I don't need a doctor, either, so you can go back to the city now."

Sean held his temper. He didn't know whether to be relieved his grandfather sounded so much like himself, or concerned that he was getting upset when he'd promised himself he was going to stay calm.

"Walter O'Neil, that is no way to speak to your grandson!" His grandmother was by his side, coaxing him into his chair at the head of the table while Maple, Jackson's miniature poodle, sprang up and down with excitement. "He isn't a taxi service and he isn't going anywhere until you're well enough to be left."

"Well enough to be left? Of course I'm well enough to be left! Do I look as if I need a babysitter?" Walter's scowl was terrifying. "I'm out of the hospital, aren't I? We all know my grandson can't bear to be away from the city for more than ten minutes, so he can leave now as far as I'm concerned and get back to those bright lights he can't live without."

Five minutes together and they were on a collision course, Sean thought. He saw his mother's worried look as she placed two roasted chickens in the center of the table ready to be carved.

"How are you feeling, Walter?"

"Perfectly well," Walter snapped, "so people don't need to be hovering over me."

"Having Sean here makes me feel better. He drove all the way over here to be with you and he's not going back until you're well."

"I'm well now." But Walter's hand shook slightly as he held the edge of the table. "And you can all stop looking at me as if you're waiting for me to drop dead at any moment. And what use would Sean be, anyway? He's an orthopedic surgeon. I haven't broken my leg, have I?"

Tyler rolled his eyes to heaven and Élise calmly placed a bowl of potato salad next to the chicken.

"It's good to have you home, Walter."

Walter finally noticed her, but instead of smiling his scowl deepened. "You here, too? You should be running the restaurant, not standing in the kitchen fussing over me. What's happening to the Boathouse while you're in here? This is the reason Snow Crystal is in trouble. No one does their job when I'm not here to keep an eye on things. This whole place would fall apart without me."

His irritation mounting, Sean was about to spring to Élise's defense when she placed her hand on his grandfather's shoulder, her touch soothing and calming. If she was upset by the attack, she didn't show it.

"It is true we certainly need you here. We have missed you."

Jackson carved chicken onto a plate. "When you're feeling better I'll tell you what's been going on, but you should take it easy for a few days." His tone was mild and his grandmother sent him a grateful look.

"That's right, you are. You're spending tomorrow in bed, Walter O'Neil," Alice said firmly as she picked up her knitting. "No arguments."

"Bed?" Walter's jaw was rigid, his eyes bright as he went into full combat mode. Maple whined and shot under the table for protection. "I will not spend tomorrow in bed. Do you think I don't know how much there is to do here? Summer is a busy time. The place is heaving with tourists."

"Which is surprising when you think that no one does their jobs when you're not here," Tyler drawled and earned himself a fierce look from his grandfather.

"This place doesn't have enough staff to be able to afford to be a man down. I am not going to lie in bed so don't suggest it again. I'll be on that deck by nine o'clock, helping Élise. And now I'd like a beer, please."

Alice pursed her lips. "You're not drinking beer. And this place can run perfectly well without you for a few days."

"Life is for living." Walter thumped his fist down on the table. "What use is it being back home if a man can't enjoy a beer in his own kitchen?"

Concerned about the effect the stress was having on his grandfather's blood pressure, Sean smoothly steered the conversation toward the renovations of the boathouse and soon the whole family were gathered around the table talking and sharing food.

He'd spent half his childhood in this kitchen, arguing with his brothers, grabbing food on the run to some place more exciting. It had always been a place to gather, to argue and to eat. The only thing that had changed was that his father was missing.

Sean sat quietly, struggling with his own emotions, and then realized that his grandfather was unusually quiet, barely touching the food on his plate and not joining in the laughter.

He felt a flash of concern.

Had they discharged him too early?

Was he exhausted by the number of people around the table?

He wished now he'd put a stop to it, but trying to stop the O'Neil family from being there in a crisis would have been like trying to hold back an avalanche with a shovel.

It didn't help that the meal was disturbed twice by calls from his hospital. Each time he excused himself he earned a disapproving glare from his grandfather.

"We're not even allowed one meal with you undisturbed? If you spent a bit more time around here, you wouldn't need to ask your brothers what's been happening. The hospital can't carry on without you?"

"I left a few ends untied." It was an understatement. "I'm tying them off now."

His grandfather grunted. "If you're so important then perhaps you'd better just go back and save them the trouble of calling you. Work is all you think about."

Sean counted to ten. He'd hit twenty by the time he felt in control enough to reply. He'd pulled in a dozen favors in order to stay at Snow Crystal for a few more days and now he was wondering why he'd bothered when it was clear he wasn't wanted.

"They had an emergency."

"So go. We manage without you every other day. Today is no different."

Intercepting his mother's worried look, Sean clamped his jaws down on the words that hovered on his lips.

Driving Walter from the hospital had taken almost thirty minutes. It would have been the perfect time to clear the air. To talk about what had happened the day of the funeral. Instead, the tension between them had grown thicker.

Concerned about upsetting his grandfather at a time when he needed to be kept calm, Sean had decided not to tackle the subject of their row.

"Hell of a welcome, Gramps." Tyler leaned forward and helped himself to a chicken leg. "Is this supposed to be fatted calf? Because it's a weird shape."

"Walter O'Neil, you apologize right now." Alice glared at her husband. "Sean is not going anywhere. He's staying right here so I can get some sleep at night. And it's time you learned when to speak and when to be silent, otherwise I'll put you back in that hospital myself and if that happens something will certainly be broken!"

Sean decided there was no one more intimidating than his grandmother when she was angry.

His grandfather obviously felt the same way because he subsided slightly. "I'm just saying I can manage without him, that's all."

"You're home because of Sean." Alice slapped her knitting down on the table. "Those doctors let you out because they know he's here. He's a doctor and a good one at that. So if you send him away you're going straight back into that hospital bed and this time I won't be sitting with you."

"He doesn't want to be here."

"And whose fault is that?" his grandmother erupted in Sean's defense. "Life is about people, not places but all you think about is Snow Crystal. You push it down people's throats until they choke on it! It's a home, not a labor camp, and it's time you woke up and saw that.

Sometimes a man wants more in his life than a belly full of duty and obligation."

Sean had grown up amid the frequent explosions but he'd never heard his grandmother speak so directly. For the first time ever he wondered if his grandmother had known just how unhappy his father had been running this place. Did she know about the row at the funeral? He reached out and covered her hand with his, concerned by her outburst.

"Grams—"

"Don't you worry about me." Alice sniffed and patted Sean's hand. "You're a clever boy. Always were. You spent all those years with your head in a book so it's right and proper not to waste it. And I'm proud. Very proud. So is your grandfather even if he's too mule-headed to say it aloud."

No, he wasn't.

Sean stared across the table into blue eyes exactly like his own and felt the same way he had when he was six years old and his grandfather had found him with his head in a book instead of with his hand on a saw.

Walter O'Neil couldn't imagine why anyone would want a life that didn't involve Snow Crystal. He couldn't understand why anyone born and bred here would want something more. *Something different.*

Despite his grandmother's attempts to clear the air, the atmosphere was tense and it came as a relief when Alice pronounced she was tired and Walter dutifully offered to escort her home. With Kayla driving them the short distance, and his mother and Jess going to help them settle in, that left the three brothers alone.

"Holy shit." Tyler sprawled in the nearest chair and closed his eyes. "Well, that was relaxing. I'd forgotten how much I love family time. When I grow up I want six kids and a hundred grandkids, preferably all with different opinions and expressing them at the same time. Can't think of anything better."

Sean's phone buzzed again and he glanced at it in frustration and saw Veronica's name.

Already right on the edge of control, he closed his eyes. *Not now.*

"Is that the hospital again? Answer it, Oh, Great One." Tyler reached for his beer. "Heal the sick and don't mind us. We're cool with the whole God complex you've got going here, isn't that right, Jackson?"

"We'll just wait in line while you tend to the injured." Jackson's tone was light but his eyes were concerned and Sean knew he was worrying about their grandfather.

"It isn't the hospital. It's a woman."

And he didn't have the energy to deal with that particular woman right now. He had to decide what to do for the best. Staying here would be best for his grandmother, but his grandfather didn't want him here.

Tyler grinned. "Is she hot?"

"Body like Venus."

"Then either answer the goddamn phone or give it to me and I'll answer it."

"She thinks she's the one who will reform my workaholic ways. Last time we spoke she told me she loved me."

Tyler recoiled. "On second thoughts, switch your phone off."

"She's in love with you?" Jackson helped himself to another slice of chicken. "I didn't think you dated women long enough for that to happen. How many times did you go out with her?"

"Twice." Sean dropped his phone onto the table. "That turned out to be one time too many."

Tyler was helpless with laughter. "Twice and she was ready to have your babies? Where do you find these women?"

"There was a whole line of them when we were growing up," Jackson said irritably. "Mostly crying on my shirt. They wanted to know why Sean didn't love them back."

Tyler took another slug of his beer. "Didn't realize you turned down sex to be here. It explains why you're in a filthy mood."

Sean clenched his jaw and turned his phone off. "I'm not in a filthy mood."

"You are borderline dangerous. I recognize the signs." Tyler suppressed a yawn. "Instead of exploding, you simmer like a pot left on the heat. Same when we were growing up."

Jackson stood up and started stacking plates. "Listen, about Gramps—"

"Forget it. He doesn't want me here. Enough said." Sean pushed his food away untouched. "I'll finish the deck tomorrow morning and be back in Boston by dinnertime. That way everyone will be happy."

Including him.

What had he expected? That his grandfather would suddenly accept who he was and what he wanted? That they'd mend broken fences and sit around the table sharing a drink together?

Life wasn't that neat and tidy, was it?

Tyler tipped his chair back and stuck his feet up on the table. "So you're leaving again?"

"Looks that way." He felt something tug inside him. "I'm the black sheep. The one who got away."

"Not for long. No one escapes this place for long. There's a whole damn herd of black sheep here, munching his grass. But go ahead and leave tomorrow. I'll win a shit-load of money from Jackson."

"You had a bet going?" Despite the emotions churning inside him, Sean gave a faint smile. "How much?"

"Enough to make it worth goading you. Fortunately Gramps is doing my job for me. All I have to do is sit back, watch and wait."

It was almost worth staying, just to annoy his brother. Almost. "I guess you'll be in the money, then."

"Mom would feel better if you stuck around." Jackson shoved the remains of the chicken into the fridge. "And Grams."

"You saw the way he was. He was pushing his blood pressure up just thinking about me staying. The objective is for him to relax and recover, not blow a fuse. I bring out the worst in him. And anyway, your fridge is empty." He didn't want to talk about his relationship with Walter anymore. It left him with a bitter taste in his mouth and a sense of failure.

"Thanks to you my wardrobe is empty, too." Jackson closed the fridge and frowned at him. "Isn't that my shirt? Kayla bought it for me."

"That explains why I like it. She has good taste."

"Which is why I want it back." Jackson gave Tyler's legs a shove with his foot. "Those muscular thighs might do it for women but get them off the damn table."

Tyler cursed as he lost his balance and beer sloshed

onto his thigh. "You never used to be this fussy. I blame Kayla."

"It wouldn't kill you to clear up once in a while. You're responsible for a teenage daughter. What sort of example are you setting?"

"I'm a supercool dad. And the easiest way to clear up food is to eat it." Tyler heaped the remains of the potato salad onto his plate and Sean stood up.

"I need to get some air."

Tyler waved his fork. "Why not just lose your temper right here? That's what everyone else in this family does. Just let it out. Don't mind us."

Sean looked at his brothers. They didn't know the whole story.

They didn't know just how unhappy their father had been.

They didn't know about the rift that existed between him and his grandfather.

His head exploding with it, he strode to the door and scooped up his jacket. "I'll finish the deck before I leave tomorrow."

"Temper, temper." Tyler speared a potato with his fork. "You can pay up anytime you like, Jackson. Cash works for me."

CHAPTER SIX

SEAN BREATHED IN the night air, trying to walk off the anger. Anger that made no sense. Had he really expected everything to change just because his grandfather was ill and he'd dropped everything to rush to his side?

Had he really anticipated an emotional reunion, gratitude and a shift to a new level of mutual understanding?

No, but he'd hoped for it.

He wanted to heal the rift. His grandfather wanted him gone.

And he wanted to go. This whole damn place just made him think of his father.

Sean strode along the path to the lake, a hollow ache in his gut. Instead of turning left to go to Jackson's house, he turned right and walked toward the boathouse.

The sun was setting over the lake, sending flashes of dark gold over the still surface. An owl hooted in the darkness, a familiar sound from his childhood.

The sudden rush of emotion caught him low in the gut.

How many hours had he spent here? How many facts had he soaked up while listening to the beelike buzz of the blue-winged warbler in the trees nearby? There'd been no better place to learn about Galileo than here, sitting, looking up at the stars.

Sean bent to examine the unfinished section of the deck. If he started work at dawn he'd be finished by lunchtime. That way he could fulfill his promise to Élise, help Jackson and still be gone before his grandfather showed up.

Frustration overflowing, he picked up a stone and sent it skimming across the darkened surface of the water into the black of the night.

"You could jump in," a voice said from behind him. "That would cool you down."

He turned and saw Élise leaning against the boathouse, arms folded, watching him. "My brothers have thrown me in the lake often enough for me not to want to do it voluntarily. How long have you been there?"

"Long enough to see you boiling with anger." She pushed away from the side of the boathouse and walked toward him, her eyes glinting in the moonlight. "You are like a little boy, throwing things and having a tantrum because things aren't going your way. Instead of thinking of yourself, you need to think about your grandfather." Her accent was more pronounced than usual, her voice velvet-soft. "He is the one who is suffering."

Anger collided with exasperation. "What the hell do you think I'm doing here? I've done nothing but think about my grandfather. I dropped everything the moment I got Jackson's call. I've been wearing the same clothes for three days, pulled in a million favors from colleagues and slept in Jackson's spare room, and all I've done is made things worse. Gramps doesn't want me here. Fortunately that's easily fixed."

"What makes you think he doesn't want you here?"

"You were there. You heard him."

"I heard him snapping at everyone as he always does when he's stressed. I didn't hear anything that made me think he wanted you to leave."

"Then maybe you weren't concentrating. He told me to go. Ordered me. And if it's stress that caused his heart attack, then I'm adding to that stress by being here. The best way I can help him is by leaving."

Her foot tapped on the deck. "You are going back to Boston?"

"Tomorrow." He saw her eyes narrow dangerously and assumed she was worried about her party. "Don't worry. I'll finish your deck first."

"Putain." She spat out a swearword and those eyes blazed, her anger matching his. "So you'll leave them? When your family needs you most? That is not what O'Neils do!"

"Don't throw guilt on me. I'm already drowning in it." Sean came right back at her, his temper fueled by an evening of holding back. "I'm doing what Gramps wants."

"You are supposed to be so intelligent but sometimes I think you are a great big stupid person. Today I chopped liver that has more brain than you. It isn't because he doesn't want you here. The two of you, you are both so stubborn, neither of you will back down. I could smash your *stupide* heads together were it not for the fact that Walter is already enough injured."

"Injured enough."

"Are you correcting my English?" Élise's tone was dangerous but for some reason her words shattered the tension and made him want to smile.

"No."

"Yes, you were. Well let me tell you this, *Dr. O'Neil*—" it was clear that her emphasis on the Dr. wasn't supposed to be complimentary "—I may have my words the wrong way around, but my thinking is straight which is more than can be said for you."

"Gramps is recovering just fine. He doesn't need me here."

An owl hooted in the darkness but neither of them heard it.

"Look beneath the surface! Sometimes people don't always tell the truth about their feelings. You are a doctor! You should know that. And what about dear Alice? She 'as not slept since her beloved Walter was taken into hospital and now she will not sleep because he is at home and she is worried." Her accent grew thicker as her temper rose. "And what about your mother? She is worrying about Walter and Alice and now also she is worrying about you because she sees you are hurt by this rift with your grandfather and you are her baby."

Sean lifted his eyebrows. "Do I look like a baby?"

"I am not talking about your height or your muscles. To a mother, her child is always a baby. She is divided, no? She is being pulled by Walter and pulled by you and—" She gave up on English entirely and switched to French but he understood her perfectly so the change in language offered him no respite from the fierce burn of her temper. "And what about Jackson? He is working so hard already, you think he has time to watch over Walter, too, while you storm off in a sulk?"

"I am not sulking." Sean's own temper sparked. "And if Jackson wants me here, he can say so."

"But he won't. Because he is your brother and he

loves you and he knows how hard it is for you to be here." Muttering to herself, she turned away and paced across the finished portion of the deck and back again. "Think, Sean. *Think.* Ignore your bruised feelings and use your brain."

"This isn't about my feelings."

"You're hurt because you think your grandfather doesn't want you here, but that isn't what is going on!"

"You don't understand what is going on." His own emotions dangerously close to the surface, he dragged his hand through his hair. "There was a row. We had a row." It was the first time he'd told anyone and he saw her frown.

"With Walter there will always be rows. It is in his nature to provoke."

"This was different." His mouth was dry. *Why the hell was he telling her this?* "It was at my father's funeral. I said things—"

"What things?"

"It doesn't matter." Remembering it still made him feel sick. The ocean of grief, the agony of missing his father, the desperate need to wind back time and do things differently, and the blame. *Always the blame.* "But I can tell you that is the reason he doesn't want me here. He's angry with me. And he has reason to be." And he was still angry with his grandfather.

He knew he should let it go, but he couldn't.

It simmered. Festered. The surgeon in him wanted to cut it out but because that wasn't possible he'd learned to live with it.

Élise frowned and shook her head. "I am glad you told me because now I understand a little bit more, but the reason he wants you to leave has nothing to do with your argument."

"Of course it does."

She advanced on him and stabbed him in the chest with her finger. "One day, Sean O'Neil, I will roll you in poison ivy and maybe then you will wake up. You are—you are—" she said something in French and he raised his eyebrows.

"Are you calling me an idiot?" He decided this wasn't the moment to tell her she was sexy when she was angry.

"Yes, because you are. The reason your grandfather wants you to leave is not about you at all! It isn't because he is stubborn, or because he doesn't want you here, or because he is dwelling on the row you had, but because he is very afraid. *He is afraid.* And you would see that if you weren't so focused on your own feelings."

Silence settled between them.

The only sound in the night air was the soft slap of water against the deck.

"Afraid?" It was an explanation that hadn't occurred to him. He thought of his grandfather, the strongest person he knew, and shook his head. "You're wrong. Gramps is the toughest guy you will ever meet. I've never seen him afraid. Not when Tyler fell in the river as a toddler, not even when we came face-to-face with a bear in the middle of a trail on a camping trip in Wyoming when we were young."

She waved a hand dismissively. "None of that is scary compared to this."

"Compared to what exactly?"

"Sean, wake up! With a bear you can punch it on the nose or whatever, but with this—this heart attack, this silent scary thing that came at him from nowhere, this he cannot punch on the nose. Do you not understand that? He has no control over this. He cannot shout at it, hit it on the head or blind it with pepper spray. He cannot even see it." Palms raised, Élise looked at him with exasperation. "What has happened has *terrified* him. Snow Crystal is his life. He is afraid that this will slow him down and change things and what is the first thing that happens when he walks back through the door of his own home? Everyone is telling him to sit down and not do anything. For Walter that is like telling him to just be dead already. He isn't the sort of man who would relish living his life in a chair. He wants to be active. And so he is terrified. And the more terrified he is, the more aggressive and snappy he becomes."

Afraid?

"I deal with people who are afraid all the time. I know what fear looks like. He isn't behaving like a man who is afraid."

"You think because he doesn't say it he doesn't feel it? Maybe you are used to dealing with people who are afraid, but with Walter you switch off being a doctor and become his grandson. Instead of thinking about how you know so much because you're this great big important doctor, instead of feeling guilty about the row, you should think about him and what he needs."

"So if your theory is right and he's scared, why is he sending me away?"

Her eyes were bright with exasperation. "Because having you here makes him feel more vulnerable."

"*More* vulnerable? The idea of staying is that having me here will make him feel less vulnerable. It's supposed to reassure him."

"As far as Walter is concerned, you have been home once since Christmas and that was a fleeting visit. You do not spend chunks of time here."

Guilt stabbed. "That's true, but—"

"The fact is you don't usually do this and suddenly you are doing it. So for Walter, he thinks you are agreeing to stay because you are worried about him. Instead of reassuring him, he is taking the fact that you are staying as a sign that he is going to have another heart attack. That you think he is going to drop dead. That everyone is waiting for him to drop dead. They are all hovering like blackfly. He is very afraid. He needs everything to be normal."

Confronted by the very real possibility that he'd misread everything, Sean stood still. Why hadn't that interpretation occurred to him?

What the hell sort of doctor was he?

"It's possible that you're right."

"*I am right.* Now forget your stupid pride, admit that you messed up and let's move on for Walter's sake."

He pressed his fingers to the bridge of his nose. He'd been so busy managing his own complex emotions he hadn't analyzed the possible psychology behind his grandfather's response. "If you're right and my being here is making him more afraid, then I am in an impossible position. I should stay, but that will just make him worse." Battling with the options, Sean tilted his head back and stared up at the sky, wondering if Galileo had found physics easier than human relations. "So I have to find another reason to stay. A reason that doesn't involve him. A reason he'll believe."

She nodded approval. "Yes, so then he will not feel you are waiting for him to drop dead."

"I could say I'm staying to reassure Grams."

Élise rolled her eyes. "Then he will think you are ready to comfort her when he drops dead. That is not reassuring, as you would realize if you started thinking."

"I am thinking!" Sean clenched his jaw and cursed under his breath. "And no one is dropping dead."

"Good! So find a reason for staying that he will find plausible."

He paced across the completed part of the deck and then glanced down at his feet. "The deck." He wondered why it hadn't occurred to him before. "I will tell him I have to finish the deck before the party. It's essential for Snow Crystal. He will never argue with anything involving Snow Crystal."

"The deck is nearly completed."

"He doesn't know that. He hasn't seen it yet. I'll undo the work I've already done. I'll get here early, before he shows up, and rip it up. He'll never know. I'll make the job last all week."

Élise's eyes gleamed. "He'll tell you off for being slow."

"You wanted his life to be normal. That sounds normal to me." Sean tried to focus but the scent of her was dizzying. It smothered his brain and pumped itself through his veins until she was the only thing in his head. "I'll make it clear my being here has nothing to do with him, and I'll tell the rest of the family to stop hovering and back off. Does that work?"

"I think so." She relaxed slightly and stepped away from him. "Now that is solved, I can sleep."

"Wait a minute—" He caught her arm and pulled her back to him, his eyes on her mouth.

"Stop looking at me like that."

"How am I looking at you?"

"As if you want to strip me naked."

He felt the tension leave him. "Stripping you naked is just the beginning of what I want to do to you. Do you want to hear the rest?"

"No." But heat flared in her eyes. "You will not talk me around with sex if that is what you are thinking."

"Talking wasn't part of my plan."

"I am angry with you. I cannot kiss you when I'm angry with you."

"Fine. Then I'll kiss you." And he did. Except that the second he crushed her mouth under his, she was kissing him back. Her lips were soft and sweet, her response instant and it was as hot and crazy as every other time. They took hungrily, greedily, the kiss explicit and passionate to the point of violence. Her tongue was in his mouth and his in hers, tangling intimately. Moaning, she grabbed a handful of his shirt, pressed herself hard against him and then whimpered slightly as he switched positions and pushed her back against the railings, trapping her.

"You think you can soften my mood with kisses?" Her tone was thickened. "You're a good kisser but it won't work. I'm still angry."

"No, you're not." His hands tore at her shirt in his haste to get to her skin. "God, Élise, I want you—" The taste of her sent fire rushing through him. The chemistry was as sharp as a whip, biting into him. He felt her fingers dig hard into his shoulders.

"I will scratch you like a cat and my claws are very sharp."

Sean tore at the buttons on her shirt. "I'll take my chances." The need was burning inside him.

"And tomorrow when you are working on the deck with your shirt off, everyone will see your shoulders and raise their eyebrows. This thing between us will no longer be a secret." Hands shaking, she ripped at his shirt and buttons flew. "*Merde,* that was Jackson's shirt—"

"I'll buy him another—" The moonlight shone down on the dip and swell of her breasts, partially revealed by a pretty lace bra, and he wasn't thinking of the shirt or his brother. He couldn't remember ever wanting another woman the way he wanted Élise. "You're so beautiful." His fingers slid under the lace and he heard her moan.

"You are clever with your hands."

He decided lace was overrated and unhooked her bra. Her breasts were small and high and he wondered if the bra had any purpose other than to add another layer and drive a man mad. He slid his mouth down to her shoulder and lower, sucking her nipple into his mouth.

Her fingers dug hard into his shoulders. "Sean—"

Her nipple hardened against the slow flick of his tongue and he heard her breathing change.

Desire ripped at him, tearing through control, and he brought his mouth down on hers again, feeling her press against him. He was tired of pressure and complication. Tired of trying to second-guess his family and tired of feeling guilty. He wanted to blot it out. He wanted this. He wanted *her.*

And he wanted her now.

Her arms were around his neck. Her body pressed against his.

He decided if he was going to prolong his stay at Snow Crystal, he deserved to do whatever he could to preserve his sanity. And sex with Élise was deliciously uncomplicated.

Or was it?

He eased away from her at the same moment that she pulled back from him.

They stared at each other for a moment and then she curled her fingers into the front of his shirt and gave a crooked smile.

"You're a very sexy man, Sean."

"Glad I have something going for me given that my brain is so small and insignificant."

The dimple appeared in the corner of her mouth. "I like your sense of humor. And I like your body. But we should not do this again."

He thought about how complicated his life was. "You're probably right."

"But you must do one thing for me." Her voice was husky, her hand still on his chest. "You must fix this thing with your grandfather. You have to talk to him."

"You're probably right about that, too."

"Go to bed." She reached up and kissed him on the cheek, her lips brushing gently over his jaw. "Good night, Sean."

He opened his mouth to try and form a coherent sentence, but she'd slipped into the dark of the forest leaving him standing alone on the half-finished deck.

CHAPTER SEVEN

"So Sean isn't leaving. Bad news for Tyler because he'll lose his bet with Jackson." Kayla ran with her phone in her hand, slowing occasionally as she checked her emails. "And bad news for Jackson, because Sean keeps borrowing his clothes."

And bad news for me, Élise thought, *because Sean would be right under my nose until the party.*

Their encounter the night before had tested her willpower to its limits.

With him, it was almost impossible to keep her emotions under control. First, there had been the anger and frustration that he'd misunderstood Walter so badly, then real sympathy as he'd reluctantly confessed to the row.

He'd accused her of not understanding.

She understood everything.

More than he could possibly know.

She stopped running for a moment, emotion slamming into her and driving her breath from her body.

It had been years, but still the feelings would rush at her out of nowhere. Guilt and grief could still cut her off at the knees. It was because she'd never resolved it. Never been given the opportunity to resolve it.

And of course, it was her fault. All of it. Everything

that had happened was because she'd made bad decisions.

Ahead of her, Kayla stopped and pulled her earbuds from her ears. "Are you all right? Did Walter upset you last night? He was in a feisty mood."

"He didn't upset me. I was relieved to see him home."

"Sean got the brunt of it. As always." Kayla put her earbuds back in and carried on running.

Élise followed, wondering about the argument between Sean and his grandfather. If it had been on the day of the funeral then presumably it was something to do with his father.

And it had obviously been significant.

Because of it, he hardly came home and because he hardly came home his grandfather grew more and more upset with him.

She understood all too well how that cycle could occur.

Sometimes it was easier to let an argument simmer than resolve it. Sometimes the emotions were so thick, you couldn't cut through them. You told yourself you'd solve it later. That you'd wait for a better time. But sometimes, that time didn't come.

She knew. It had happened to her.

Her pace slowed.

Despite the exercise, she felt cold.

All she'd thought about through the winter months was finishing the boathouse and contributing to Snow Crystal. It was vitally important to her. But now all she could think about was the rift between Sean and his grandfather.

They needed to mend whatever had broken between

them. If that meant having Sean around for a little longer, she'd cope with that.

She increased her pace, overtaking both of her friends as they headed around the lake and ended up at the boathouse just as the sun rose above the trees.

There was no sign of Sean. She told herself that the sudden lift in her pulse rate was due to the exercise, not the thought of him working on the deck.

"Is Tyler bringing anyone to the party?" Kayla caught up with her and pulled the top off her water bottle. "Because if he has a plus one, I need to know. Bren? You work with him."

"I don't know anything about his sex life, if that's what you're asking me, but knowing Tyler it's probably pretty active," Brenna said flatly. "I need to get on. I'll see you later."

Élise watched as Brenna sprinted across the deck, sprang over a pile of planks and disappeared down the forest trail.

Kayla took a mouthful of her water. "I've never seen myself as cupid, but if I had an arrow I'd shoot Tyler in that perfectly formed butt of his—or *derrière* as you probably say."

"Butt works for me. Perhaps the party will help. The two of them will be together in the same place at the same time and we can let nature do the rest."

"From what people say she and Tyler have been in the same place at the same time for most of their lives." Kayla finished her water. "Nature's been pretty idle so far."

"So she needs a bit of a push. What's Brenna wearing?"

"Knowing Brenna, probably ski pants," Kayla said

dryly. "And anyway, I think it may be Tyler that needs the push. I'll find out if he's bringing anyone. He's been behaving himself since Jess came to live with him. Six months of behaving like a monk. The guy must be going crazy." She bent to adjust her running shoe and paused. "Well, well."

"Well what?"

"This is a button from one of Jackson's shirts." Picking it up, she turned it over in her fingers and glanced pointedly at Élise who felt heat streak across her cheeks.

Hoping her friend would blame her high color on the exercise, she shrugged. "So? Sean has been working hard on the deck."

"So hard he tore the buttons from his shirt? From what I've heard, he wasn't wearing a shirt for most of the time. According to Poppy the view from the boathouse has improved considerably in the last couple of days. She's going to start selling tickets."

"I wouldn't know. I have been too busy to look. And talking of busy—" She started to walk toward the boathouse but Kayla caught her arm.

"Sean is gorgeous. Clever, sophisticated, seriously sexy—why not have a fling?"

Because one night was all she ever allowed herself.

"We had one. It was over last summer."

"Are you sure?" Kayla turned the button in her fingers. "Because it doesn't look over to me."

"So you're not leaving?" Jackson had a mug of coffee in one hand and a slice of toast in the other. "Does Gramps know?"

"Not yet. I'm just on my way to undo the work on the deck so I can start again."

Jackson raised his eyebrows. "I'm sure that makes sense to someone."

"I need an excuse to stay here. Gramps is sending me away because he's feeling vulnerable." And he should have been the one to see that. Instead, he'd been blinded by his own complex emotions. "Helping with the deck is the only thing I could come up with. I have to try and make it seem like it's a massive job for me."

"Maybe that won't be so hard given how long it is since you did any manual labour."

"What do you think I do in the operating room?"

"No idea. Make eyes at Venus?"

"She's a neurologist. She doesn't work in the operating room." Sean helped himself to an apple from the bowl. "If I'm going to be staying, you need to get more fruit in your house. And vegetables. There are no vegetables in your fridge. Whatever happened to your five a day?"

"If you want to find vegetables when you open the fridge then you can put them there yourself. And if you're staying you need to go home and pack some clothes. I'm sick of you stealing my shirts." Jackson finished his toast and topped up his coffee. "So you're staying for Gramps."

"That and the view."

His brother sent him a look. "Just as long as the reason you're hanging around here has nothing to do with my chef."

"It's because of her I agreed to help with the damn Boathouse in the first place. She's obsessed with opening on time so she doesn't let you down. What's that about? Have you suddenly started beating the staff?"

Sean finished the apple. "Or is this intense loyalty more personal than that?"

"It's the way she is. She cares deeply about her work. She's loyal. She knows our financial situation is far from stable and she values her job."

"We both know that with Chez Laroche on her résumé, she could get a job anywhere. You're lucky to have her."

"She's worked for me for a long time." Jackson's expression revealed nothing. "We've been friends for years."

"Just friends? You first met her in Paris. So did you...?"

"No." His brother's voice hardened. "We didn't. And you're not going to, either. This is her home. I won't let you threaten that."

"Why would I threaten it?"

"Because you mess with women's heads," Jackson said irritably. "For some reason I've never managed to understand, they fall in love with you and go a little crazy when you don't love them back. I cleared up that mess plenty growing up, I'm not doing it again."

"I don't create mess. You're mixing me up with Tyler."

"No, I'm not. Tyler is like a bear. You see him coming. A smart woman will step out of the way. But you? You're different. You're all smooth charm and slick words. I see their eyes cross and then they start walking funny and the next moment they're crying on my shoulder because you're too focused on your work to notice them. I don't have enough shirts left to take it."

"I still don't understand why you describe this as Élise's home. Sure, she's living and working here now but she's talented. One day she'll move on. That's inevitable."

"If she moves on it will be because she's made that choice, not because she was left with no alternative because my twin brother fucked it up and made it awkward for her to stay."

She'd been in some sort of trouble.

It was the only thing that could explain such a fierce response from his protector brother.

"Maybe you don't need to worry about her." He thought about the night before. She'd shown more control than him. And then she'd walked away. "She doesn't strike me as the sort of woman who falls in love easily. She's very independent. Similar to me in many ways."

"There isn't a single way in which she's similar to you." Jackson thumped his empty mug onto the counter.

Yes, there was.

Sean thought of the way her hands had slid up his back, the way her mouth had burned against his. "Maybe I'm exactly what she needs."

"No woman in her right mind needs you. And I've grown out of comforting girls who thought they were in love with you."

"Did you really do that?"

"All the time. They were lining up from eighth grade. I was the good twin, you were the bad twin. My shirt was permanently wet from all the tears." Jackson picked up the milk and put it back in the fridge. "I don't care how you run your love life, but stay away from Élise."

Sean decided not to mention they were well past that.

Instead, he made his way to the Boathouse to start undoing the work he'd done the day before.

His grandfather arrived at midday, driven by Tyler who was on his way to take a family of six on a guided hike on one of the trails.

Before Sean could stand up and offer help, Élise was there, helping Walter to a table in the shade by the water on the side of the deck that was finished.

Sean watched her, his head full of questions. He wanted to know why Jackson acted like a guard dog around her. And he wanted to know what the hell she was doing in a place like Snow Crystal when she could have been working in Paris. He knew she was talented. He'd eaten her food and seen her passion. She could have worked anywhere, and yet she'd worked for his brother for eight years.

He watched as she slid her hand over his grandfather's and squeezed. Saw his grandfather return the gesture, his weathered face softening.

Sean tried to think of a time he'd seen his grandfather's face soften before.

Only with his grandmother, and occasionally his mother and Jess.

Even with Jackson he was blunt and direct.

"I will bring you a drink to enjoy and then one of the new staff will take your order." Élise rested her hand lightly on his shoulder. "You will tell me what you think of the menu and together we will refine it so that it is perfect. Does it feel good to be home?"

Walter's hand trembled. "It feels good."

Sean realized he never thought of his grandfather as frail. Even in the hospital he'd been feisty, barking out orders and refusing to let people make a fuss. But watching him with Élise he saw frailty.

He knew he ought to say something.

They needed to talk about that day of the funeral.

This was as good a time as any, and as good a place. The fact that there were other people around might stop his grandfather from exploding.

Élise walked off and Sean stood up and straightened his shoulders. "Gramps—"

Walter's gaze met his. "You're still here? If you're waiting for me to drop dead you're going to be here a long time."

If there was frailty, it was hidden again. Hidden behind layers of fear and fierce determination. Without Élise forcing him to look beneath the surface, he would have missed it.

"Glad to hear it, because I'm off duty. I'm here to finish the deck so that this place can open on time. Seems a shame to cancel a good party. We don't have that many around here."

"You wouldn't have come to the party. You would have been busy. With you, work always comes before everything. Even your family."

Sean's gut settled into a tight knot. The impulse to talk about the row vanished. "I'm here, aren't I?"

Walter looked around him. "Not much progress since I left."

Sean thought of all the work he'd undone and almost laughed. "Yeah. Going slowly."

"It's because you're out of practice. If you spent more time here, you'd be better at it."

And that, Sean thought, was how not to mend a row.

Gritting his teeth, he got on with the job, his mind occupied with the task of making the work last four days.

He told himself it was worth swallowing his pride and enduring the digs and comments to watch over his grandfather. Worth it to see his grandmother more relaxed.

And worth it to watch Élise.

She arrived back at the table with a tray of drinks and freshly baked pastries and Sean saw his grandfather smile at her.

The smile tugged at him.

Hell, was he really so desperate for his grandfather's approval?

Was he six years old?

Exasperated with himself, Sean turned away and focused his attention on the work that needed to be done, working at a snail's pace on the unfinished deck as the sun burned his shoulders.

The doctors in the hospital had told him his grandfather hadn't been eating much but Élise tempted him with tiny portions of his favorite food and sat with him while he ate it. She coaxed him, mouthful by mouthful, encouraging him to tell her stories about growing up at Snow Crystal. Sean worked with only half an eye on what he was doing, distracted by the tantalizing swing of that mahogany hair so close to that curving mouth.

The dimple was back, dancing in the corner of her mouth, and humor lit up her eyes.

Watching her with his grandfather, Sean saw a different side of her. With him she was always on her guard. With his grandfather she was softer and more open. It was clear she adored him.

And it made him realize even more how little of herself she'd given to him.

Sex, he thought. That was what she'd given him.

And that suited him just fine. That was all he wanted, wasn't it?

He swore as he almost removed the tip of his finger and caught his grandfather's eye.

"Don't worry," he muttered. "A sawn-off finger is something I can fix, remember?"

The café was a hive of activity as everyone worked to get the place ready for opening.

Poppy walked past carrying a stack of boxes and sent him a dazzling smile. "Good morning, Sean."

Remembering Jackson's comments about breaking hearts and wet shirts, Sean kept his response suitably neutral.

After a morning working in the sun he was thirsty and hungry. He was about to offer to drive his grandfather the short distance back to his house, when Tyler turned up to do it.

Fed up with working at a snail's pace under his grandfather's scorching glare, Sean sat down in a chair by the water's edge.

A moment later Élise put a tray in front of him. "Grilled panini, Green Mountain ham and local cheddar. Enjoy."

He'd expected her to go straight back to work but she sat down opposite him and poured them both glasses of iced water.

"Is Walter always like that with you or is it because of the row?"

He bit into the panini, wondering what had possessed him to mention the row to her when he hadn't even told

Jackson. "Friendly, you mean? Yeah. He adores me, can't you tell?" He chewed and decided it was worth putting up with a month of his grandfather griping at him to eat Élise's food.

"He does adore you. When you're not here, he talks about you constantly." She was frowning as she tried to work it out. "But for some reason he doesn't show it. He isn't a man who shows his affections easily, but still—"

Affection?

Sean almost laughed. "He has expectations. I don't fit them. Every time he sees me he remembers what a disappointment I am." He took another bite of the panini. "And the fight didn't help."

"So instead of fixing it, you stay away? What sort of twisted logic is that? It makes no sense."

"It makes perfect sense to me. It's easier on everyone if I keep my distance. I thought it might calm things down."

Her gaze slid to his. "For a while I was worried the reason you stayed away was because of last summer." Her tone was ultra casual. "I was afraid it might have made you feel awkward."

"It didn't."

"You so rarely came home."

"What about you?" Why hadn't that possibility occurred to him? "Did it make you feel awkward?"

"Not at the time, but afterward?" She turned her head and stared across the lake. "Afterward I wondered if it was a mistake. I wouldn't want to come between you and your family. If I thought that was the case, I would leave right now."

The remark was so typical of her. All or nothing.

He couldn't help smiling. "Before the Boathouse opens? Wouldn't that be letting Jackson down?"

"Yes, but nothing is more important than family. Nothing. I could not ever come between you." Her voice was fierce and he saw her knuckles whiten as she gripped the glass in her hand.

"Relax. The reason I don't come home often has nothing to do with you. It's mostly work pressure."

"Mostly, but not all." She thumped the glass down on the table. "When are you going to fix things with your grandfather?"

He didn't tell her he'd been about to do exactly that when Walter had laid into him. "I'll do it when the time is right."

"That time should be now." Something shimmered in her eyes and she blinked, stood up and reached for his empty plate. "Do you want more?"

He caught her hand. "Why should I do it now?"

"Because a conversation as important as that should never be postponed." Her voice was husky and he wondered why she cared so much about his relationship with his grandfather.

"I'll wait until he's stronger."

She pulled her hand away impatiently and cleared the table. "The problem is that you are both so alike and neither of you can see it."

"Alike?" He was genuinely astonished at the suggestion. "We're not alike. I am nothing like my grandfather."

"You both have a passion about something and that is all you see. With him it is Snow Crystal, for you it is your job."

"That's different."

"How is it different? You are both single-minded in the pursuit of what you want. You both find it hard to compromise. It is perhaps not so surprising that you clash."

He'd only ever thought about the differences. Never about the similarities.

"We clash because families always clash." How could she think he was like his grandfather? It was ridiculous of her to suggest it. "All families are complicated."

"Are they?"

"Isn't yours? You don't have warring uncles or disapproving grandparents? Come on—there has to be someone you avoid at family gatherings."

"There are no gatherings."

Sean lowered his glass, watching her hair shimmer in the sunlight. "You're not close to your family?"

"I don't have a family." Reaching out, she took the empty glass from his fingers. "I'll take that if you've finished."

"You talked about your mother. You told me she was your inspiration."

"She was. She died when I was eighteen." She balanced the glasses on the plates. "I need to get back to work. There's still lots to do here."

"Wait a minute." He tried to imagine a life that wasn't crowded with siblings, parents, aunts, uncles, cousins, grandparents. True, they drove him crazy half the time but he couldn't imagine a life without them. "There's no one?"

"That's right. Just me. But I'm very happy so you don't need to wear your concerned doctor face. I am surrounded by people I care about and who care about

me. And I borrow your family. I love them very much."
She gave a faint smile. "You should fix this thing with
your grandfather. Whatever it is that keeps you away
from Snow Crystal, you should mend it."

"What keeps you away from Paris?"

"I have no reason to go back. My life is here. This
is my home."

He noticed she didn't describe it as her job. "There's
a difference between not going back and staying away."

Her eyes met his. He saw shock there and something
else he couldn't interpret and then it was gone.

"Are you really going to lecture me on going home
when you can hardly remember the last time you were
here? Fix things with your grandfather. Don't wait."

Without giving him the chance to extend the conversation, she quietly picked up the empty jug and the
glasses and walked back across the deck toward the
kitchen.

SHE'D LIED.

She told him she had no family and strictly speaking that wasn't true, was it?

There was someone.

Someone she had cut out of her life.

Someone she tried not to think about.

Feeling sick and shaky, Élise removed a tray of perfectly cooked blueberry muffins from the oven and put
them to cool alongside the croissants and the *pains au
chocolate*.

Why was he suddenly asking questions?

Their relationship was supposed to be fun and flirty.
Casual. She hadn't expected him to shift the conversation to personal. Sean was well-known for not taking

his relationships to another level. It was one of the reasons she'd felt comfortable with him.

"Mmm, they look delicious." Poppy appeared next to her, stocking cupboards with ingredients. "I love this kitchen so much. It's so much more cozy than the one in the restaurant."

The kitchen in the Boathouse was on a smaller scale than the main restaurant, but Élise had made sure it was sufficiently equipped to ensure they could run the café from there.

"I'm testing the ovens." She broke open a croissant, examined the texture and then sniffed it and tasted it, thinking of Walter and Sean rather than herself.

They were trapped in a cycle that neither would break because neither would take that first step forward. And she understood that all too well because she'd done the same thing herself.

She'd assumed there would be time to fix things.

She'd been wrong.

Pain shot through her and for a moment she stood there, trying to shift the darkness of her past.

It depressed her that talking about Paris did that to her, even after all this time.

"Is something wrong?" Poppy was still unpacking boxes. "You look stressed out, but it's all going smoothly, isn't it? We're on track?"

"Nothing's wrong. I'm not stressed out."

At least, she shouldn't be.

She hadn't been back to Paris in eight years. There were days when she didn't even think about it. *About him.*

It was in her past and that was where it was staying. At one time it had dominated her life. Now, she didn't allow it that much importance. Which was why she never discussed it with anyone.

But Sean had noticed.

Just a little slip on her part, but he'd picked up on it.

Poppy cast her a worried glance. "You're probably stressed out by the last-minute rush to finish the deck. It's brilliant that he's helping out, of course, but if Dr. Scorching Hot is going to spend the whole week with his shirt off, I'm telling you now I'm going to have to take a swim in that lake." She pushed tins and containers neatly into the cupboard and closed the door. "How about you, Chef? Does it affect your concentration having him out there?"

"No. As long as he finishes the work, I don't care what he's wearing."

Poppy stared at her in amazement and Élise realized it would have been wiser to laugh, joke and admit that yes, Sean O'Neil was a sexy guy.

Pretending otherwise had simply drawn attention to herself when she'd been hoping to deflect it.

"I suppose I'm just too busy to notice."

"Right." Poppy turned her incredulous gaze back to unpacking boxes and Élise knew she'd been about as convincing as she'd been when she'd told Sean she didn't think of Paris.

CHAPTER EIGHT

SEAN HAD FORGOTTEN HOW it felt to spend a whole day outdoors. Used to dehydrating under the artificial lights of the operating room, it was a pleasant change to feel the sun scorch his back and breathe in the scent of summer rain.

What surprised him most was the discovery that he'd missed certain aspects of being home. He'd missed the lake and the forest, the feel of the wood against his hands, the rush of satisfaction that came from a job well done.

Nothing gave him the same satisfaction as operating, but he had to admit that over the past few days there had been moments when working on the deck had come close. After days of watching life go by, he could see how much Jackson had done to boost the fortunes of Snow Crystal.

Every morning, Brenna had taken a group of children out onto the lake in kayaks as part of her Outdoor Discovery week. Jess, Tyler's daughter, had joined them and Sean had been watching their progress.

Among the children he recognized Sam Stephens, who had been coming to Snow Crystal for the last five years with his parents. This year there was a new baby in the family so Sam had been enrolled in one of their kids' programs and if the smile on his face was anything to go by, he was loving it.

"Hi, Dr. O'Neil!" Sam waved madly and the kayak rocked.

"Hi, yourself." Deciding that a break was as good a way of slowing things down as any, Sean leaned over the railings. "Looking good, Sam."

"Brenna's been teaching us how not to capsize. You have to use your paddle and your body. A few of us fell in." He lowered his voice. "One of the boys cried, but I thought it was really cool."

Sean thought about the temperature of the water and decided "cool" probably didn't begin to describe it. "How's that sister of yours?"

"She cries a lot and she's too small to be any fun, but Dad says maybe in two years she can go on a bike or something." Sam almost smacked himself in the face with the paddle. "I'm going to be nine next week. I'm getting a bike for my birthday. Dad's going to take me out on one of the trails. Have you saved any lives today, Dr. O'Neil?"

"Not today. But it's only eleven o'clock." He'd lost his audience because the boy was peering past him, the kayak rocking as he craned his neck.

"Élise! Élise, look at me." He waved an arm, almost dropping the paddle. "I know the French word for lake. *Lac*."

"*Très bien!* You are very clever." Light on her feet, Élise crossed the deck and waved back. "Soon you will be fluent."

Sean glanced at her and saw that telltale dimple in the corner of her mouth. Her gaze was warm as she leaned over the railings and spoke to the boy, speaking slowly in French.

Sam was paddling and talking. "I like French but science is my best subject. I want to be a doctor. I want to be a surgeon like Dr. O'Neil. He fixes bones and things. Isn't that right, Dr. O'Neil?"

Sean dragged his eyes away from that dimple. "Yeah." Aware that he sounded croaky, he cleared his throat. "That's right."

"I guess if you're going to be a surgeon, you have to be okay with blood. I'm fine with blood. I don't faint or anything." Sam paddled away, kayak rocking in the water. "See you later, alligator!"

Élise grinned at Sean. "You said you wanted hero worship. I think you've got it."

"He's the one and only paid-up member of my fan club."

She straightened. "Finish my deck in time for the opening, and I'll be your second member."

"I'll finish your deck." He couldn't decide what to look at—the swing of her hair or the curve of her mouth, but he knew he wanted more time with both. He also knew she'd been avoiding him since their conversation a few days earlier. "Sit down for five minutes. You've been working all morning. You never stop."

"There is still too much to do and we're full in the restaurant tonight. Fortunately Elizabeth is working so that makes things easier. Having your mother helping out in the kitchen has changed my life."

"It's changed her life, too." He remembered how his mother had been after his father's death and compared it to the way she was now. "There was a time when I didn't know how she was going to cope without Dad. She always loved cooking for the family but none of us thought about her working in the business. You saved her."

"She saved herself. It just took a little time and that is not surprising. She lost someone she loved. You all did. You were close to your father."

"Yes." He saw no reason to deny it. "Of the three of us, I was probably the closest to him."

There was a brief silence and then she covered her hand with his. "Losing someone you love is very hard." She was about to say something else, but then she saw Sam waving and waved back. "I need to get on."

He wanted to ask about her mother, about her life in Paris, but he knew it was the wrong time. And the wrong place. "You work too hard."

"This, coming from you?" She tilted her head. "How many hours do you work a day, Dr. O'Neil?"

"I don't keep count but there are times when I think the daily average comes to more than twenty-four."

She smiled and then she was gone, striding across the deck with a bounce in her step, remarkable given the fact she had to be running on adrenaline and not much else.

He watched as she disappeared inside the Boathouse and then turned to find his grandfather standing next to him.

Sean tensed. The past few days the atmosphere had improved, but still there had been no opportunity to bring up the issue both of them were avoiding.

"That boy has been coming here since he was three. I lent him a pair of Tyler's old skis on the family's first winter trip." His grandfather watched as Brenna taught Sam to handle the kayak. "Look how he loves it. When he's grown he'll bring his children back here and they'll enjoy doing the things he did as a child. It's how things work around here."

Here we go, Sean thought, and braced himself for the inevitable lecture about tradition and family.

Hadn't his father had to listen to the same lecture from his cradle to his grave?

Grief punched him hard and along with the guilt came the frustration and anger.

"Maybe they'll want to do something different as the kids get older. Maybe they'll want to try other things or travel to—" He broke off as Sam gave a yell of delight, the boy's laughter so infectious that Sean found himself smiling, too.

His grandfather grunted. "Maybe they will. Because I'm pretty sure he's having a horrible time out there and he's never going to want to do it again."

Sean sighed. "It will be good for the business if they come back."

"It's not just about business. Not everything can be measured in dollars and cents. Your great-grandfather didn't set up the resort because he wanted the money. He believed Snow Crystal was too special to keep it just for the family. It's the air, the scenery, the local food—he thought somewhere like this should be shared and appreciated with people who felt the way he did."

"I know the story, Gramps."

"He loved this place. He and your great-grandmother started by letting out a few rooms. Bed-and-breakfast. Then they built the main lodge. He taught me all of it so that I'd be able to take over. By the time I was sixteen there wasn't a single job in the place that I didn't know how to do." Pride rang in his voice. "By the age of eighteen I was running the place."

It was a story they'd all heard a thousand times, gathered around the kitchen table while their mother cooked.

"What about you?" Sean turned to look at his grandfather. "Was there ever a time when you thought you might want to do something different?"

"This place was my dream." Walter's voice was gruff. "Living here was all I ever wanted. I knew it was a privilege. I'd been given this piece of land to tend and nurture and she was my responsibility. I used to wake up in the morning, eager to get to work. When a man feels like that, he knows he's doing the right thing with his life."

It was the first time Sean had ever felt he and his grandfather were speaking the same language. "That's how I feel about being a surgeon." He'd never tried to explain himself before and he was cautious about doing it now because he knew his grandfather had tunnel vision when it came to Snow Crystal. "People come to me broken and I do my best to fix them. Finding different ways, better ways, is what I love doing. It's all I've ever wanted to do."

"I know. I watched you grow up. Knew you were going to be a doctor when Tyler fell out of that tree. Jackson was as white as the snow. You? You just handled it." His grandfather watched as Sam's kayak rocked in the water. "It's just a shame you have to be doing the job so far away. Your brothers could use your help around here. If you were closer, you could come back more often."

Sean felt sweat prick the back of his neck because

he knew the reason he didn't come home had nothing to do with distance. "I'm busy." That, at least was the truth. "Working long hours."

"Don't know how you can bear to live in a city. Too many people and not enough space. I wouldn't be able to stand it, having to fight for my own patch of air to breathe." Walter waved again at Sam. "So are you going to finish in time for the party or are you still going to be fixing this place at Christmas?"

Sean glanced sideways, relieved to see his grandfather had more color. "I'll finish in time for the party." He could have finished days ago. Could have been back in Boston, enjoying his life, thinking only about himself instead of having to juggle a schedule that would have made a grown man cry. "I'm out of practice. Slow."

His grandfather was still watching little Sam. "You worked so hard *not* to finish this damn deck your brain almost burst with the effort. But it was fun to watch. How long did it take you to undo what you'd already done?"

Sean stared at him. "You—" *Shit.* "I don't know what you mean."

"I may not be a doctor, but that doesn't make me stupid."

Sean rubbed his hand over his jaw. "Was it that obvious?"

"I was the one who taught you to work with wood. You were good. If I'd really thought the deck was taking you that long I would have dropped you in the lake myself."

Sean shook his head, realizing how badly he'd underestimated his grandfather. "If you knew, then why the hell didn't you say something before now?"

SARAH MORGAN   143

"Because for once in your life you were putting something ahead of your work."

Sean breathed deeply. "Gramps—"

"And you were home. Your family likes having you home from time to time. It doesn't happen enough. It's done you good to slow down a bit and spend time at Snow Crystal. I've been watching you. You've been enjoying the lake and the forest."

Sean gave a disbelieving laugh. "You didn't really have a heart attack, did you? The whole thing was an excuse so you could sit on the deck with your feet up sipping Élise's lemonade while I work my butt off."

His grandfather sent him a look. "You can finish up here at the proper pace, put those tools back where Zach can find them and see what you can do to help Élise before she runs herself into the ground being in two places at once. That girl does the work of ten."

That was something he wasn't going to argue about. And her dedication still puzzled him. "She's obsessed with making sure the Boathouse opens on time. She's worried about letting Jackson down so she wants everything perfect. She puts a lot of pressure on herself. He's damn lucky to have her. She could get a job in any restaurant she wanted. Or open her own place." Seeing Sam paddle his way into the weeds at the edge of the lake, Sean eased himself upright, ready to intervene, and noticed his grandfather was watching, too.

"The boy is fine. Brenna is there. She's got him." He glanced over his shoulder to the Boathouse. "Élise wouldn't leave. She loves it here. This is her home. The Boathouse was her idea, did you know that?"

"Yes." He remembered the conversation they'd had on the first night, when they'd walked together and she'd told him about growing up. She'd talked about her mother. "But it's still a job. Staff move on. It's a fact of life. Why would someone with her talent stay in one place? Experience is valuable. Every hospital I've worked in has taught me something different."

His grandfather kept his eyes on Sam. "I guess sometimes a person needs more out of life than just a job."

"That's rich, Gramps, coming from you."

"This place is more than my job. It's my home. Maybe Élise feels the same way."

"It's not the same. You were born here."

"You're a man who likes fixing things, so tell me this—" Thoughtful, his grandfather ran his hand over the smooth surface of the railing Sean had finished the day before. "When someone comes into the hospital after an accident, can you tell just by looking that some part of them is badly broken?"

Sean wondered why he was changing the subject. "Sometimes, not always." It seemed a strange question to him, especially from his grandfather who was skilled at first aid. "You can't assess the extent of internal injuries by just looking, you know that."

"So it's possible for someone to look perfect on the outside, but have a lot of damage under the surface? Damage you can't see just at a glance?"

"It wouldn't be a glance. We'd do a thorough examination and there might be signs. Sometimes the nature of the accident would make us suspect there might be internal damage. We'd do a bunch of tests, use X-rays or other types of imaging to—" He broke off and stared at his grandfather. Then he glanced over his shoulder and looked at Élise who was still finishing off work inside the Boathouse.

It's possible for someone to look perfect on the outside but have a lot of damage under the surface.

His grandfather eased away from the railing and reached for the walking stick Alice had insisted he keep with him. "Good thing you moved around all those hospitals and picked up all those skills. It would be easy to miss something like that unless you were very skilled. That fancy hospital in Boston is lucky to have you. Now I need to get back. If I don't lie down, your grandmother worries about me. I do it to please her."

"No, wait a minute—" Sean was still looking at Élise. "Hell, Gramps—what are you saying?"

"You're the one with the medical degree and after the hours you've spent in that hospital since you left home, you should be good at what you do." He rapped his stick on the deck. "Figure it out."

ÉLISE HAD HER head full of a million different things and the moment she looked up and saw Sean leaning against the door frame, all of them vanished.

She'd spent the past few days trying to pretend he wasn't working half-naked on her deck. It had taken almost superhuman effort.

"Can I do something for you?" Oh, God, she shouldn't have said that. Of course, there was something she could do for him. And there was plenty he could do for her. If she'd let him. Which she wasn't going to.

"I'm finished." He put Zach's toolbox down at her feet, giving her a perfect view of wide shoulders.

"I thought you were going to try and make it last another day."

"Not much point. Turns out my grandfather was on to me right from the start. We talked."

"You mean you fixed things?"

"No." He rubbed his hand over his jaw. "We didn't talk about that. But other things."

She felt a pang of disappointment. "So you still haven't tackled it?"

"We just managed to be in each other's company for ten minutes without killing each other. I figured that was a good start. And now we can give up pretending, I've finished the deck."

Delight mingled with another far more dangerous emotion. Disappointment. If he'd finished the deck then he'd be leaving. He'd be going back to Boston and without a reason to come home, they were unlikely to see each other again before Christmas.

It appalled her how much she minded.

"So we can go ahead with the party." A few days ago she'd thought it was hopeless. She'd been depressed and dejected at her own failure to complete the task. Now that she knew it was going to be on time, she should have been bouncing with joy. So why wasn't she? "I am very pleased. Today you are truly my hero."

"I'm glad you feel that way, because it's time to talk about payment." He folded his arms and leaned against the door frame, that lazy blue gaze fixed on her face.

"Payment?"

His skin was glistening with the sweat of hard labor and she took a step backward. It was too reminiscent of that night last summer when they'd driven each other wild. She knew how those shoulders felt. She'd had her hands on them. And her mouth. And he'd had hands and mouth on her, too. She couldn't stop thinking about it and clearly he couldn't, either, because his eyes were fixed on her lips as if she were a meal he wanted to eat.

"Yeah, we haven't talked terms. But I'm ready to do that."

"What do you want?"

He smiled. "We'll start with dinner. I'm hungry." His gaze lowered to her mouth. "And given that you haven't stopped working all week, you must be hungry, too."

Merde. "Sean—"

"Eight o'clock suit you or do you want to make it later?"

"No, it doesn't suit me! There is no time for dinner. I have a party for more than one 'undred people in less than two days."

"You're nervous." His voice was soft and there was a gentle gleam in his eyes. "You always drop your *h*'s when you are stressed."

"Yes, I am nervous! This opening is really important to me."

He raised his eyebrows. "So it's the Boathouse that is making you nervous?"

"Yes! And as I was saying, I *have*—" she put special emphasis on the *h,* huffing the word at him "—nothing for the guests to eat. And I need to look at the deck. I don't want anyone falling through it."

He smiled, a slow sexy smile that slid into her bones and cut her off at the knees. "You want to take a closer look at my work? I can assure you it's the prettiest deck in Vermont and no one will be falling through it. Of course, if they do then I can fix whatever they break." He was so damn sure of himself and she ground her teeth.

"We don't eat dinner together. We don't do that."

"Well, this time we're going to. We've both had a long week." He hadn't bothered shaving that morning and his jaw was hazy with dark shadow, his eyes a lazy blue under thick eyelashes.

She wanted to eat dinner with him so badly it terrified her. There was no way, no way, it was going to happen.

"If you are hungry I will book you a table in the restaurant. The specials tonight are *coquilles Saint Jacques* and *confit de canard*. You'll enjoy it."

"I'm not dressed for the restaurant."

"You're not dressed at all." Her gaze slid to the sleek, pumped-up muscles of his shoulders. "That is the problem."

"It's a problem?" His husky voice told her he didn't see it as a problem at all, and Élise ground her teeth.

"Not a problem for me, but it will bother the other diners, so you can shower and change and turn up looking like Sean and not like—like—"

"Like?"

"Like you do." Gorgeous. Dangerous.

He leaned closer to her. "Nine o'clock, Élise. That gives you time to finish whatever it is you need to finish and still be awake. I'll cook. We'll have dinner on the deck."

She forced herself to breathe.

He'd been under her nose for days and it was slowly driving her crazy and now he wanted to spend the evening with her, too? And nine o'clock would mean eating dinner by moonlight and that was far too romantic.

She didn't do romantic.

"You've done a great job on the deck but it's teeming with people getting ready for Saturday and frankly—"

"I didn't mean this deck. I've had enough of staring at this deck. I meant your deck. At Heron Lodge."

Her deck?

Her territory. That was even more dangerous.

He was killing her excuses one by one, cutting them down as if they were trees in the forest blocking his path. And he did it with a smiling charm that assaulted her willpower and left her mind reeling.

Because she knew people were listening, she stepped out onto the deck so that there was no chance they could be overheard. "That's kind of you, but I really don't think—"

"Nine o'clock." He turned and walked away from her, treating her to a glorious full-on view of those wide muscular shoulders.

"Holy crap, that man is smoking-hot." Poppy breathed from behind her. "I think I need a doctor."

PUCCINI BLARING FROM the speakers, Sean drove into the village and picked up the food he wanted, along with a bunch of flowers for his grandmother. Traffic was heavy on the way back to Snow Crystal and he sat in a queue for a while, watching tourists take photographs of the pretty covered bridge with the forest and mountains in the background.

He couldn't get his grandfather's words out of his head.

It's possible for someone to look perfect on the outside but have a lot of damage under the surface.

Back home he found Jackson hunched over a laptop, staring at a spreadsheet. Maple was curled up asleep at his feet.

Sean glanced at him on the way to the fridge. "Does it add up?"

"Nothing ever adds up in this place."

"But it's getting better. You've still got the regulars coming back. Brenna's outdoor program seems popular. I can't believe how much little Sam has grown."

"Yeah, he's a great kid. I remember the year Gramps gave him those little skis Tyler had when he was three. His face was a picture." Jackson adjusted a couple of numbers. "So how is the deck going? Banged a nail through your finger yet?"

"It's done."

Jackson looked up. "I thought you were making it last."

"Gramps was onto me."

Jackson leaned back with a grin. "Good to know his brain isn't damaged. So I bet that was a lively conversation. Did he tell you to leave?"

"No. I got the usual lecture. I should spend more time here. The place is about tradition and families. You know how he is. Puts on the pressure. He did the same thing to Dad all the time."

Jackson's smile was replaced with a frown. "Sean—"

Before he could finish speaking the door opened and Kayla walked in. "Honey, I'm home." Her singsong voice was loaded with suggestive humor. "The interview went well. Prepare yourself for— Oh—" She broke off, embarrassed, as she noticed Sean. "Hi. I didn't know you were here. Sorry."

Relieved she'd interrupted because the last thing he wanted was to have a conversation about his father, Sean smiled at her. "Don't mind me."

Her blond hair was fastened in a clip on top of her head and she was wearing heels and a pencil skirt. She looked sleek and professional.

New York, Sean thought. Not Snow Crystal.

How the hell was she going to adapt to living in this place? At the moment she had the best of both worlds. She was living two lives, the only compromise being her energy levels. Like him, she'd been totally committed to her job. Until she'd met Jackson.

What would happen when she'd been here awhile? One day she'd wake up and realize what she'd sacrificed and then the resentment would start. Slowly at first, but then building into a dangerous ball of regret and bitterness.

Jackson flipped the lid of the laptop shut. "Goodbye, Sean, great seeing you. Drop by again sometime. Preferably Christmas."

"I could join you for dinner."

"Dinner is going to be takeout pizza in bed. You're not invited." Jackson walked across to Kayla, hauled her against him and kissed her soundly.

"Pizza?" Sean shuddered. "That's the best you can do when you're trying to impress a woman in bed?"

"We're carb loading to give us energy."

Sean decided to have some fun. "I could do with some carb loading after all the energy I expended on your deck. Want me to order?"

Jackson lifted his mouth from Kayla's long enough to shoot him a threatening glance. "I thought pizza was beneath you?"

"Suddenly I feel like eating dinner with you. Brotherly bonding."

Kayla eased out of Jackson's arms. "What a perfect idea."

Jackson scowled. "What's perfect about it?"

"Sean is welcome to stay for dinner." Kayla walked over to Sean, a mischievous smile on her face. "I'd like you to, really. Forget pizza, I'll cook something special. Something you'll never forget. I insist. It's been a while since I spent any time in a kitchen but I think I can remember where it is."

The two brothers exchanged glances.

Jackson grinned and folded his arms. "Great idea. Stay for dinner, Sean. Kayla will cook."

It was an ongoing joke that Kayla's significant abilities didn't extend to the kitchen and Sean backed toward the stairs, hands raised.

"Hey, my specialty is orthopedics, not toxicology."

"Are you insulting my wife-to-be?"

"No. I'm insulting her cooking."

"I'm wounded—" Kayla batted her eyelids. "And I was going to cook you something extra special. An experiment."

"All right, you win. I'll leave the two of you alone. Watching you together puts me off my food, anyway."

Leaving them to focus on each other he showered, borrowed another shirt from Jackson's room and then pulled out the bags of food he'd bought earlier, along with a bottle of chilled wine.

Kayla looked at the wine and the bags of food. "Where are you taking those?"

Sean paused. If he told them he was planning on seeing Élise they'd turn it into something more. "Thought I'd have a picnic." It sounded as ridiculous to him as it obviously did to his brother.

"Yeah," Jackson drawled, "because we all know what a 'picnic' person you are. Nothing you like more than ants in your food and mud on your pants."

"I never said anything about ants or mud. I'll see you both later." Ignoring the sarcasm, Sean strolled to the door. He opened it, thinking he'd got away with it when Kayla's voice stopped him.

"Why don't you just call Élise and book a table in the restaurant? She'd be happy to cook you something, I'm sure." The words were innocent enough but something in her tone made him glance over his shoulder at the woman who would soon be his sister-in-law.

Jackson frowned. "He can't do that. It's Élise's night off."

Sean's eyes met Kayla's.

She smiled.

She knew.

Jackson's phone rang and as he turned away to answer it Kayla's smile widened.

"Have a nice evening, Sean. Enjoy your—er—picnic."

CHAPTER NINE

WHAT DID A woman wear for a casual evening with a man she was trying to keep at a distance?

It had taken her an hour to decide. She'd discarded her little black dress—too formal—and her blue sundress—too pretty?

In the end she'd pulled out a pair of jeans she hadn't worn for at least four years. The weather was too warm for jeans but at least it wouldn't look as if she'd tried too hard.

Hot and uncomfortable, Élise paced across her tiny kitchen.

She met attractive men all the time. Some of them were even interesting enough to warrant further attention. But never, ever, had she been tempted to take a relationship further. She'd give her company, her food, her laughter and conversation, occasionally her body— but her heart? Just that one time. Never since.

Sean had promised to do the cooking, but to distract herself she'd made an appetizer of *grissini* infused with rosemary and dusted with Parmesan cheese that she was thinking of offering with drinks at the Boathouse.

The scent of baking filled Heron Lodge and soothed her. It reminded her of her childhood. Of her mother.

She felt a pang and wished for a moment that she

could turn the clock back. That she could have her time again and make different decisions.

She wanted to grab the rebellious, wild, eighteen-year-old version of herself and shake her.

Because she occasionally liked to remind herself of what was important, she reached for the photograph she kept on the window in the kitchen.

A beautiful woman smiled down at the toddler who stood on a stool next to her, whisking ingredients in a bowl, smiling back.

The photo gave no hint of what was to follow.

Pain and guilt clawed at her but then she heard Sean call her name and put the photograph back carefully so it was in its place when he appeared at her door.

"I thought I'd make plenty of noise this time so you couldn't accuse me of trying to scare you. Something smells good. You weren't supposed to be cooking. Not that I'm complaining." He strolled into the kitchen, two bags in his arms. He sent her a lazy, sexy glance that sent her tummy spinning and her pulse pumping.

The suit he'd worn on his mad dash from the hospital had been replaced by a pair of worn jeans and another of Jackson's shirts. She decided he looked equally good in both.

"This is just an appetizer. You can tell me what you think."

"I think I'm going to move in here." He put the bags on the counter and helped himself to the freshly baked *grissini*. "They look like the ones I ate in Milan. Another experiment?"

"It's just something simple. I love working with dough."

"You work too hard."

"Cooking never feels like work. It clears my head and helps me relax." And right now, with Sean standing in her kitchen, she needed all the help she could get with that.

He snapped the breadstick, tasted it and gave a moan of masculine appreciation that connected with her insides. "This is better than anything I tasted in Italy."

"It's the quality of the ingredients. Local flour and rosemary grown outside your mother's kitchen window."

She wasn't used to seeing a man in her home. In her kitchen. This was her space and she treasured it, protected it and, most important of all, felt safe in it.

Right now she didn't feel safe at all.

His hair was slick and damp from the shower, his jaw freshly shaven.

Jackson and Sean were identical twins and yet to her there were obvious differences. Sean's face was a little leaner and he wore his hair shorter. She suspected some might find him a little more intimidating, his smile a little less ready. He was certainly more complicated.

Or maybe it was her feelings that were more complicated.

Deciding that she didn't want to examine that idea too closely, Élise pulled a couple of plates from the cupboard.

"It's a beautiful evening. Let's go out on the deck." It would feel less crowded. Less intimate.

"First I need to cook the steak and prepare the salad." Sean opened a bottle of wine and poured her a glass. "Try this. It's Californian."

She sipped and gave a nod of approval. "It's good."

"I picked it up in the village when I was buying a

few things for Grams. She sent her thanks to you for filling their freezer, by the way. That was kind of you. You didn't have to do that."

"Why? Because I'm not family?" The rush of emotion knocked her off-balance like a gust of wind and she knew it was because she'd been looking at that photo. "To me they are like family. And nothing is more important than caring for people you love."

He reached for a skillet. "I wasn't questioning your affection for them or your relationship. Simply observing that between the restaurant and the café you already have more than enough to do."

And she'd overreacted. She could see it in his eyes.

She wondered what it was about this man that brought out the worst in her. She'd tried to tame that part of herself and had thought she'd succeeded.

Until Sean.

Miserably aware that where he was concerned her emotions were all over the place, she walked across the kitchen and found him a bowl for the salad. Her insides churned like an ice-cream maker. "I'll make a dressing."

"I already made one. You can relax."

Relaxing wasn't an option so she drank her wine and watched as he unwrapped two steaks and heated oil. It was a simple enough meal but still it was all too domestic and for a moment Élise stood there, frozen by her own memories.

Which made no sense because her one tarnished experience of domesticity had looked nothing like this.

He flipped the steaks expertly and threw her a glance. "What am I doing wrong?"

"Nothing. I didn't know you could cook."

"I don't think you'd describe this as cooking, would you?" His mouth was a sensual curve. "I live alone and despite what I tell my grandfather I don't always want to eat in the hospital, in restaurants or get takeout so I taught myself the basics. And, of course, it's useful for impressing women."

"And does it work?"

"Taste it and tell me." He plated up the steaks and salad. "I bought most of this from the farm shop on my way back from the hospital. There's a fresh loaf in the bag."

She placed the bread on a wooden board and cut through it, examining the texture with a nod of approval. "They have wonderful stuff. We serve their jams in the restaurant, although Elizabeth is working on a new Snow Crystal recipe. It's going to be spectacular."

"You serve jam and not just our own maple syrup? That's close to heresy."

"The maple syrup is available, too, of course. And not just because removing it from the breakfast menu would ensure your grandfather fired me."

"My grandfather would never let you go. And neither would Jackson. You're safe." He handed her a plate, his fingers brushing against hers. "It must have been a big risk for you, leaving a restaurant like Chez Laroche and joining Jackson's organization." The question was casual enough, even reasonable, but it put her on edge.

She walked across her little kitchen and picked up napkins and cutlery with her free hand. "Why? Jackson had a very successful company before he came back to Snow Crystal. It was very early in my career and I had more freedom working with him at Snowdrift Leisure than I ever did working for Pascal."

She'd practiced saying his name frequently so that she could be confident of pronouncing it without faltering or wanting to stick a knife through something.

"What was it like, working for someone as famous as Laroche? Did he have an ego?"

There was no reason not to tell the truth about this part, was there?

"He was complex. Charismatic, demanding, often unreasonable in his quest for perfection. A genius in the kitchen. Everyone wanted to work with him but for every person who came out able to get a job in any restaurant in the world, there were eight who he broke. Some never cooked again after working with him."

"But he didn't break you."

Élise stayed silent.

He had broken her, but not because of their working relationship. That, she'd survived.

"I was eighteen years old and all I wanted to do was cook. He was a legend in Paris." She shrugged. "Not just in Paris. There were no women working in his kitchen. He didn't believe women could make great chefs. He believed we didn't have the temperament, the stamina, the 'balls.' I told him I would take any job he would give me and do it better than a man."

"And?"

"The first day he made me scrub the toilets." It surprised her to discover she could talk about it so easily. "When I came back the next day he laughed and gave me the floor of the restaurant to clean. He used to say that running a successful business was about so much more than food and he was right, of course, although his way of making his point left a lot to be desired."

"How long before he let you inside the kitchen?"

"One month exactly. It was a Saturday night and he was angry with everyone, screaming if a plate of food didn't look exactly the way he'd envisioned it. Three of his staff were off sick with stress and then two of the young trainee chefs walked out. They'd had enough. I told him I could do the work of two. He told me I wouldn't last a night working in the pressure of a busy kitchen."

Sean leaned against the counter listening, the food forgotten. "I'm assuming you lasted a lot longer than that."

"I was the only girl in a kitchen of twenty-two men. I had long hair then and I tied it back in a ponytail." She remembered her mother brushing it when she was a child, long rhythmic strokes that had soothed her. "He used to drag me around the kitchen by that pony-tail. He wanted me to cry. He wanted me to walk out so that he could prove once and for all that women are too soft for a kitchen."

"Knowing you, you didn't cry or walk out."

"I cut off my hair." And then she'd cried, silent tears as she hacked at her glossy hair with kitchen scissors while locked in the cramped toilet used only by staff.

His gaze slid to her hair. "You've worn your hair short ever since?"

"Yes. And finally he accepted that I wasn't going to be scared away easily. He started to teach me. He was a genius, but that sort of temperament isn't easy to handle. Often the recipe was in his head and he'd lose his temper if one of his team got it wrong."

"He sounds half-crazy."

"He was." And dangerously charismatic. That temper could turn to charm in the blink of an eye and it was that charm and skill that made everyone dream of working with him.

She remembered the first time he'd smiled at her.

And she remembered the first time he'd kissed her.

She'd been dizzy with it, her longing for him so powerful it was almost physical pain. It had drugged her. Blinded her.

She hadn't allowed herself to feel that way since.

Until now.

Her gaze slid to Sean's. "The food is getting cold. We should eat."

He carried the plates out to the deck. "So you stuck it out, got a world-class training and then left the bastard."

Élise blinked and then realized he was still talking about the job. "Yes." She put the bread down on the table. "That's exactly what I did. Fortunately I met Jackson. He gave me the freedom to take what I'd learned with Pascal and develop my own style of cooking."

"Are you still in touch with him?"

"Pascal?" She picked up the knife and sliced the bread. "No. He wasn't the sentimental type. And neither am I."

Not anymore. He'd killed that side of her.

"And you don't yearn to go back to Paris? I'm still surprised you don't miss the city."

"I love mountains. When I was a little girl my mother used to take winter work in the Alps, cooking. I went with her. It was magical. Working for Jackson was more of the same."

"You're not tempted to go back to city life one day? I thought every chef dreamed of opening their own restaurant."

"Why would I want to do that when I have freedom

to do whatever I wish here? And I am opening a restaurant. The Boathouse will be built up from scratch and the Inn is already fully booked months in advance. And I would never leave Jackson." She sliced into her steak. It was perfectly cooked and she tilted her head to one side and nodded. "It's good."

"You're very loyal to my brother."

"Of course. I love my job."

"With Chez Laroche on your résumé you could walk into any job."

Do you think I'll let you go, Élise? Do you think anyone in Paris will give you a job now?

She put her knife down, her appetite suddenly gone.

"I have the job I want." It upset her that thinking of it could still have such an effect on her. She felt murky and dirty and she turned her face to the setting sun briefly in an attempt to burn out dark memories with brightness. "What about you? Will you stay in Boston?"

"It's where my work is and, like you, I love my work."

"And this week we've kept you from it."

He reached for his wine. "I confess I've enjoyed working on the deck more than I thought I would. And watching the kids on the lake has been entertaining."

"Brenna is so good with them. What did you love most about this place when you were growing up?"

"The skiing." He didn't hesitate. "First fall of snow and we'd be out there on the mountain. Gramps used to take Jackson and me but Tyler didn't want to be left behind so he came, too. He was bombing down those slopes before most of his peers had learned to walk."

"It must have been hard for him giving up competitive skiing. It was the most important thing in his life, like cooking is for me. I would die if I could no longer cook."

"Now that's a cause of death I've never come across." Smiling, he leaned across and topped up her wine. "Is everyone in France like you? Are the intensive care units packed full of people dying because they can't cook?"

"It is good to have passion."

"I'm not disagreeing with you. In fact, I rate passion above almost every other quality." His eyes met hers and the atmosphere shifted. The force of the connection shook her.

Putting her fork down, she told herself that physical compatibility had nothing to do with emotional engagement.

"It is not always good. When I love something I love it totally. I've never been good at half measures."

And that, she thought, was her problem.

His gaze lingered on hers for a moment. "You sound like Tyler. He said much the same thing when he threw himself off vertical cliffs at the age of six without first checking his landing." With that simple revelation he steered the conversation back onto comfortable ground.

"You have a passion for surgery."

"I wouldn't describe it that way." He helped himself to more salad. "I have an intellectual interest in being able to fix something that is broken."

"Including my deck?"

"That, too." He piled more salad on her plate and she shook her head.

"No more. I'm not hungry."

"You should eat and this salad is homegrown."

"You don't need to lecture me on nutrition."

"Good. Then eat."

"This place is your grandfather's passion."

"I'd call it an obsession. It makes it impossible for him to understand that other people might not feel the same way."

"Did your father?"

He stilled. "He loved Snow Crystal, but he hated the work. The irony was that working here stopped him from enjoying the place. He was too busy keeping it going to make the most of what it offered. He and Gramps clashed over it constantly when we were growing up."

"Walter loves it with every piece of himself. I understand that because I feel the same way and I have only lived here for two years."

"I admit I don't get it." Sean picked up his glass. "You're a sexy, clever, confident woman. Why are you burying yourself in a sleepy resort in Vermont when you could be in Paris?"

"Why do the guests of Snow Crystal deserve less than the inhabitants of Paris? In Paris you can find good restaurants on every corner. Here, that is not true. Should people here not eat well?" Her anger flashed fast and intense. "I do not feel buried, and if you keep making stupid statements like that you will be the one who is buried. I will hide your body under the deck and no one will ever know."

Sean sat still, watching her across the table with eyes that saw too much. "I didn't mean to make you angry."

She forced herself to breathe, knowing it was the mention of Paris that had triggered the anger. "If you don't want to see me angry then don't ever criticize something or someone I love."

"Was it a criticism? I described the place as sleepy. In comparison to Paris, Snow Crystal is sleepy, Élise. That's a fact."

"If that is the case then I will sleep for the rest of my life." She put her fork down with a clatter. "You are making me boil inside so now we must talk about something else. Something normal, that doesn't make me want to kill you. Tell me something else you like about this place apart from the skiing."

"Swimming in the lake. It was always fun pushing Tyler under water. What about you?" His voice softened. "Tell me more about your mother. She taught you to cook?"

The anger left her in a rush.

"Some mothers don't let their children in the kitchen because of the mess, but my mother believed the mess was part of creativity. She used to stand me on a chair next to her and let me put my hands in the bowl and mix just like her. It fascinated me, that butter and flour rubbed together could turn into a fine powder. That an egg broken into flour and mixed with milk could make a thick batter. I loved the idea that two different things mixed together like that could produce something that didn't resemble the original."

"You said she was a pastry chef?"

"She worked in a bakery. And at home we baked together. There is nothing as comforting as baking. And she taught me to trust my instincts. She never used a recipe book. She cooked by feel and instinct, using her senses. She was very talented. She was the one who taught me that fresh is best. We grew herbs in tubs on our windows and salad in pots in the kitchen. It is one of the things I love about this area. People love using locally grown foods. Here we have farmers and chefs working together and we never had that in Paris. In Paris I could not go to the farm and meet the people and see the food. It is very exciting."

"Did your mother know you got a job with Pascal Laroche?"

"Yes." Emotion twisted deep in her gut and she felt her throat thicken. "She knew that."

The rest of it, she hadn't known. And that was a relief. Her mother had witnessed plenty of her mistakes, but she hadn't known about the biggest mistake of all.

"I visited Paris once."

Grateful for the change of subject, she wondered if he'd guessed how close to the edge she was. "When?"

"I was eighteen. Before medical school. I did a trip to Europe. I spent a month in England with my mother's family and then traveled around a bit. Florence, Rome, Seville and Paris. I saw the Eiffel Tower."

"That is for tourists. If you'd come to Paris with me I would not have taken you there."

"So where would you take me?"

She wouldn't, because she had no intention of going back to Paris, but this was hypothetical, not reality. "I love the *Jardin des Tuileries* first thing in the morning before the city wakes up. I love watching the sun rise over the Louvre, and I love the little backstreets in the Marais district." She thought of the elegance of the buildings, of window boxes stuffed full of tumbling color. "I like to walk around the out-of-the-way streets of Paris and find a little bakery making fresh perfect bread. I love to go to the *Musée de l'Orangerie* to see Monet. What is your favorite place in Snow Crystal?"

"I don't have a favorite place."

"Of course you do. For me it is the lake and the forest. I like to sleep with the windows open so that I can hear the sounds and smell the air."

"Do I have a favorite place?" He drummed the table with his fingers, thinking. "I suppose it would be the mountains. Have you ever climbed to the top of the ridge? Takes about four hours from here. When we were kids Gramps used to make us pack up a tent, walk up to the ridge and camp overnight. In the morning we'd watch the sun rise over the mountains, wash in the stream and find our way home."

"You camped?" Thinking about Sean camping made her laugh, sadness and anger forgotten.

"Don't look so surprised. I could light a fire with nothing more than a hot look." He was laughing, too. "I admit I haven't done it for a couple of decades. I might need matches now. And a sprung mattress would be nice. And hot and cold running water and possibly room service."

"That sounds more like a five-star hotel than camping."

"Great idea. Let's do that." His voice changed and his eyes were locked on hers. "You, me, king-size bed and room service. I know a wonderful hotel near Burlington. Lake view. Four-poster bed. Goose-down pillows. All-night sex, no strings attached."

She was tempted, oh, so tempted.

And because she was tempted, she stood up. "You should try camping again. Sometimes it's good to go back and do the things you did when you were young."

"What, lie on hard, stony ground while Jackson snores next to me? I'm not sure the appeal was that great first time around, let alone going for a repeat."

He stood up, too. "So I guess that's a 'no' to a night in a four-poster bed with goose-down pillows? Just for the record is it because you're allergic to feathers? Because I can request hypoallergenic."

Trying to resist that charm, she stacked the plates. "Thank you for dinner. It was delicious. Good night, Sean." Without looking at him she walked into her kitchen, but he was right behind her.

"Dinner was on me. I should clear up."

"You cooked, which means I clear up. It's an equitable arrangement."

"Here's another equitable arrangement." He waited for her to put the plates down and then pressed her back against the counter, blue eyes locked on hers. "I kiss you and you kiss me back."

Their mouths collided. He had one hand in her hair, the other low on her back as he held her trapped between his thighs and kissed her until the world around her ceased to exist. His mouth was skilled and clever, driving thought from her head and replacing it with hunger and heat. She slid her hands over his shoulders, feeling strength and the swell of muscle under her seeking fingers.

She was the one who pulled away, even though it took all her willpower to do it.

Not because she didn't want this, but because she needed to prove to herself she was still capable of using her brain to make decisions.

When he would have kissed her again she flattened her palm to his chest. "Good night, Sean."

"I want you." His voice was raw and honest. "And you want me. It's simple."

But she knew it wasn't simple. Relationships had a way of becoming complicated really fast.

"Not everything we want is good for us."

"I'll make it good for you." His mouth slid from her jaw to her neck and she closed her eyes and tried to resist temptation.

"That wasn't what I meant."

"Then what did you mean?" His mouth was close to hers, his tone intimate, and she kept her hand planted firmly in the center of his chest.

"I don't want complications."

"Neither do I. It's yet another reason why we're perfect together."

"We had an agreement."

"I don't remember any agreement." His eyes were on her mouth. "There wasn't one."

"It was unspoken."

"Yeah," he said, his voice a deep, sexy rasp. "I remember every moment of our not speaking session, but I don't remember agreeing never to mention it again."

She hadn't factored this in. Hadn't thought that he might push for something more. It had been a year.

"Good night, Sean."

"You're sending me away like this? You have no heart."

She had a heart. Once she'd given it freely without question, but not any longer. Now she protected it with everything she had and that wasn't going to change.

CHAPTER TEN

PREPARATIONS FOR THE party took precedence over everything.

Tyler was responsible for the lighting and he had Jess helping him, holding ladders and directing him while he twisted lights into trees and along the overhanging roof of the renovated boathouse. He turned the air blue as he fiddled with bulbs, but he arranged everything as Élise instructed.

Guests using the trails around the lake stopped to watch and offer congratulations, all caught up in the excitement of the official opening. Everyone staying at the resort was invited and Élise felt a buzz of triumph that finally her dream would become reality.

The Boathouse Café would be good for Snow Crystal. Good for business.

She hadn't let Jackson down. She hadn't let the O'Neils down.

The newly laid deck was now home to stylish tables and chairs and she'd added large earthenware pots crammed full of colorful blooms she'd been nurturing herself.

Tables inside had been moved together to form a buffet table while still leaving room for a small dance floor.

"It's going to be great." Taking a quick break with Élise, Kayla watched Tyler work. "Subtle, perfect romantic lighting. You've done an amazing job, Élise. You've thought of everything. Don't forget to think of yourself and leave yourself time to change."

"I have half an hour at six. It will have to be enough." She couldn't afford more than that. She'd spent her morning moving backward and forward between the large kitchens in the main restaurant and the Boathouse. Almost all her team were focused on preparations for the party and she was more than happy with the way things were working out. Elizabeth had been wonderful as always. "I need to ask Sean to drop those tools back to Zach. I can't store them any longer."

"Sean's gone back to Boston. He left before dawn. I can ask Jackson to do it. He has to go out later, anyway."

Sean had gone back to Boston?

He'd left?

Happiness drained out of her, leaving her feeling shockingly empty.

She didn't know what upset her most. The fact he'd left without telling her, or the depth of her disappointment. And mingled in with those disturbing emotions was frustration that Sean had left without sorting things out with his grandfather.

Kayla glanced at her watch. "Brenna is coming to our place at six to get ready so that she doesn't have to go back to the village. I'm going to try and persuade her to wear my red dress, otherwise she'll turn up in the same black one she always wears when she's forced to dress up."

"Black is very elegant. I am wearing black."

"Nothing wrong with black, but Tyler has seen her in that dress a hundred times and I thought I'd shake

things up a bit, just to make sure he notices her. Why
don't you join us? We can all get ready together."

They'd want to talk about Sean and she couldn't
face it.

"I can't, but thank you. I need to be back here to supervise the last-minute preparations. The timing of the
food has to be just right. We have a mixture of hot and
cold appetizers and a choice of cocktails."

She'd been planning this party for months and not
once had she expected Sean to be there, so why did
she suddenly feel as if the evening had lost its gloss?

She was tired, that was all. The buildup to the opening had exhausted her.

She'd be fine once it was over and running the Boathouse became part of her routine.

"The band are setting up at seven, I can deal with
them. Guests arrive from seven-thirty." Kayla frowned
up at the sky. "The sky looks a bit ominous. Do you
think it's going to rain?"

"I really hope not, but if it does we'll just have to
move the whole thing indoors. We'll be tight for space,
but it will be fine."

She tried to push Sean out of her mind, for once
grateful she was busy.

BY THE TIME Élise stripped off her clothes and stepped
under a cooling shower in Heron Lodge, she was wishing she could just lie down and go to bed, but she still
had to supervise final preparations for the food as well
as making polite conversation.

Normally, she enjoyed that part. She loved talking
to guests in the restaurant, discovering their likes and
dislikes and who they were.

Tonight, she wasn't in the mood for making polite small talk.

Irritated with herself, Élise dried her hair quickly, applied her makeup and pulled on a black dress she'd bought on a trip to New York to visit Kayla. It was high at the neck and low at the back and the skirt swung to midthigh. Knowing she'd be on her feet all night and walking a lot, she slid her feet into a pair of ballet flats and pulled a single silver bangle onto her wrist.

She paused on her deck and allowed herself a moment to breathe in the peace and solitude, and then walked along the lake trail toward the Boathouse.

Her team were poised and ready and she delivered a final briefing, making sure they understood every dish and all the ingredients.

By the time the first guests arrived, everything was in place.

The band was local and sufficiently versatile to keep the growing crowd entertained as they stood on the newly completed deck, drank Élise's special cocktails and enjoyed the breathtaking view of the lake.

Élise circulated, dutifully chatting to the people Kayla introduced to her, discussing her plans for the Boathouse and the Inn at Snow Crystal, smiling until the muscles in her face ached and her head started to throb. Sounds mingled, music tangled with threads of conversation and laughter.

A bright point of the evening was when little Sam arrived with his family. He looked uncomfortable in a clean shirt with all the mud scrubbed from his face.

Élise made a point of locating the pizza bites she'd added to the menu especially for the younger guests.

"Yum." He helped himself to four and then caught

his mother's eye and put one back on the plate. "Kayaking was wicked fun. Brenna is awesome."

"Hey, you were a champ." Brenna ruffled his hair as she walked past. "You're going to put up a fight in that race tomorrow."

"I'm gonna win." Sam spoke with his mouth full of pizza and his mother rolled her eyes, switching the baby onto the other hip.

"Talk or eat honey, you know the rules. Not both together."

"It's a week until my birthday." He was almost jumping on the spot. "I'm getting a red mountain bike. So cool to be here for my birthday. I'm spending the whole day with Dad."

"A red bike?" Élise made a mental note to bake him a cake. "That sounds like a great present." She noticed that Brenna was wearing her usual black dress and assumed Kayla had lost the argument.

"I've waited three years." Sam's fingers hovered hopefully over another slice of pizza and Élise helped him out and put two slices on his napkin.

"Three years is a long time. You must be very excited."

"Dad promised I could have one on my ninth birthday. I've got a bike at home, but it's a baby's bike." He all but drooled over the pizza. "Can we have this same pizza for my birthday?"

"I'll speak to the kitchen."

Brenna stole a piece of pizza and winked at Sam. "When you're with me tomorrow I'll give you a map of the mountain bike trails. Be sure and start with the beginner one." Her smile dimmed fractionally and Élise glanced over her shoulder to see what had caught her friend's attention. Across the room, Tyler was laughing with a pretty blonde in a tight silver dress.

Élise ground her teeth and turned back to Brenna to suggest she ask him to dance, but the other girl had vanished.

Worried, Élise searched the crowded deck for a moment and then spotted her in a quiet corner talking to Josh, the chief of police.

She liked Josh. She'd had to put in a call to him once when a group of drunk tourists had descended on the restaurant on a Saturday night and he'd handled the situation skillfully and tactfully. In fact, she was fairly sure that half the people dining there that night hadn't even realized there was a problem.

And despite the small scar under his eye and the uneven ridge of his nose, both earned in the line of duty, he was handsome.

Maybe Brenna should give up on Tyler.

If they hadn't got it together after all this time, maybe they never would.

Sliding a final pizza bite onto Sam's napkin, she wished the family a fun evening, then turned around and bumped into Kayla who was looking worried.

"I can't find Brenna."

"She's hiding in a corner with Josh. I thought you were lending her a dress?"

"I tried. She thought my red one was too low."

"How low was it?"

"Low enough to catch a man's attention, not low enough to get her arrested."

Élise sighed. "Brenna is always pretty but tonight she looks as if she doesn't want to be noticed."

"She's never comfortable in this sort of social situation. She'd rather be sitting in the bar chatting to guests."

"I like Josh. I think they make a nice couple."

"Yes. There's only one thing that spoils it and that's the fact that she's in love with Tyler. If I get a moment I'm going to bash him over the head with something hard." Kayla walked off to greet another arrival and Élise intercepted Poppy who was circulating with plates of food.

"How is it going?" She tasted one of the delicate mushroom pastries she'd perfected days earlier, this time in miniature version.

"It's a hit," Poppy said happily. "This is my fifth trip to the kitchen. And they love the corn cakes, the goat's cheese with pine nuts and the calamari. I'm about to bring out the duck and the chicken wings with the maple glaze and I've called over to the Inn for more pizza for the kids. Most of it is in Sam's stomach."

Élise gave a nod of approval and was about to circulate again and judge for herself the reaction to the food when she saw Sean.

He was standing at the top of the steps, watching her.

Her heart lifted and swooped. Joy spread through her and she smiled before she could help herself, before she realized that her reaction should have been something different.

He smiled back and the smile was just for her, the curve of his lips slow and intimate. And with that smile came the panic.

She didn't want to feel this way. She really didn't.

If he asked her to dance, she was going to say no.

But he didn't. Instead, he was swallowed up by the crowd and the connection was broken.

So was her concentration.

She couldn't breathe. She felt dizzy.

"Élise?" Kayla was by her side, introducing her to various journalists and food writers she'd invited in the hope that the new Boathouse Café would receive positive media attention.

Somehow she managed to respond, answer their questions, enthuse about food and the importance of partnering with local farmers, all the time wondering where Sean was and whom he was dancing with.

Darkness fell, the setting sun hovering over the mountaintops like a child peeping over the bedcovers desperate to squeeze every last moment from a perfect day, and finally she glimpsed him across the deck, dancing with Brenna.

"Dance?" Walter stood beside her. He was looking better by the day but she still ached with worry for him and she knew today had been a long one for him.

"I'm a little tired. Shall we sit down together for a minute?"

"What you mean is that you're worried *I'm* tired." He gave a grunt. "Stop protecting me."

"*Je t'adore,* Walter. You are very special to me."

His expression softened. "Then would you do me a favor?"

"*Bien sûr.* For you, anything. Just name it."

"When my grandson asks you to dance, don't refuse."

"Tyler is too busy with his harem to even notice me."

"I'm not talking about Tyler."

Her heart pumped a little harder. "Me, I am not a very good dancer."

"You're a liar. I know you love dancing but you never do it. Tonight, you're going to dance."

"You should not meddle. Sean is too busy for a relationship and so am I."

"Which is why a dance is perfect. If you want to make an old man happy, you'll say yes."

"That's blackmail, Walter."

"At my age you do whatever works. How was dinner? Did he poison you?"

"You know about dinner?"

"I don't know why everyone around here assumes there's something wrong with my eyesight. He brought his grandmother flowers. I happened to see food and wine in the back of the car and I'm sure he wasn't cooking for his brothers."

"He bought flowers for Alice?" Her heart squeezed. Strong, inscrutable Sean had bought flowers for his grandmother.

"Yes. And talking of Alice, I've left her alone long enough." Walter's eyes were fixed at a point over her shoulder and then he squeezed her shoulder and stepped back. "You promised."

"Walter—"

But he'd already walked away from her, making his way back to the table to join Alice.

And Élise knew the reason he'd walked away was because Sean was standing behind her. Anticipation curled in her stomach and when she felt his hand on her back, she closed her eyes briefly.

Her insides churned with a mixture of delicious thrill and trepidation.

"I thought I was going to have to wrench you away from my grandfather."

She turned, smile at the ready. "He is doing well, I think."

"Very well." He raised his glass in a silent toast. "Your party is a success."

"So far no one has fallen through your deck so yes, I'd agree it's a success. I didn't think you were coming tonight. I thought you'd gone back to Boston." Up close he looked impossibly handsome. Showered, shaven and dressed impeccably.

"I did. Had a call first thing this morning from a colleague about a patient he was worried about. I agreed to drive up and help out. Given that he's been covering for me all week it was the least I could do. While I was there, I caught up with a few jobs and picked up some clothes. I've had enough of wearing my brother's shirts."

"I suspect that sentiment is mutual."

"Definitely." He removed her glass from her hand and put it down on the edge of the deck with his own. "Since I ruined a good pair of jeans on that deck, there is no way I would have missed the party."

"Walter is pleased you made it. Jackson will be, too."

"And how about you?" He spoke softly, those blue eyes sharp and perceptive as they lingered on her face. "How do you feel about it?"

That was a question she didn't want to ask herself. "I'm pleased to see you back with your family on an evening that is important to them. And it's always good to have a friendly face at a party."

Smiling, he pulled her into his arms. "I have to dance with you. My grandfather's orders."

She melted against him. "This must be the first time in your life you've followed his orders. And I shouldn't dance. I'm working."

"The work is done. People are having a good time." They were dancing in a quiet corner of the deck instead of on the dance floor inside the Boathouse. "People are fed and happy and the Boathouse will get rave reviews. I'd say you're officially off duty."

"I won't be off duty until the last person leaves."

"At this point in the evening most people are too drunk to notice or care what you're up to, and anyway, you deserve to enjoy yourself, too." His cheek brushed against her hair. "You smell delicious. And I love the dress. Especially the bits of it that don't exist." His hand rested on her bare back, his thumb stroking seductively over her spine. "You're beautiful."

The words and the tone made her head spin. She had to remind herself that he was smooth. That charm was as much a part of him as his smile. "Sean—"

"Relax. My grandfather is watching. If you walk away now he'll blame me. You don't want to make things worse between us, do you?"

There was no way she could relax while his hand was on her bare skin.

Her pulse was pumping.

"Your grandfather is matchmaking."

"Yes." But he didn't sound annoyed. "He has good taste, I'll say that for him. His choice in women is probably the one thing we agree on." He pressed her closer and she felt the hardness of his thighs against hers.

Her hand rested on his chest and she could feel the steady thump of his heart through his shirt. And then she looked up at him and was almost scorched by the humor and heat in those blue eyes.

He gave a crooked smile. "When are these people leaving?"

"Party finishes at one." Unsettled by the way he made her feel, she glanced up at the sky. "Do you think it's going to rain?"

"I don't know and I don't care. I can't wait until one."

"Wait for what?" She tried to ease away from him but he clamped her close.

"You can't move. Not right now."

"But—"

"Unless you want to embarrass me in front of all these important people, you need to stay exactly where you are. Right now you're protecting more than my reputation. I thought dancing was a good idea. Turns out it wasn't."

Pressed hard against him she could feel the heat and thickness of him through the fabric of his suit.

The chemistry was so intense it almost stifled her. She wanted him with a desperation that terrified her.

"There are plenty of women anxious for you to dance with them." She'd seen them, watching him across the deck, hope in their eyes.

"I'm dancing with the only woman who interests me."

More smooth words. "Perhaps I am not interested in you."

"I'm a doctor. Do you want me to explain all the reasons I know that to be a lie?"

"You're talking about the physical."

"Physical works for me. Last summer it worked for you, too."

She should walk away, but the slow, sure stroke of his hand on her back was driving her crazy. How could she end something that felt so good? And what was wrong with physical?

Because she no longer trusted her legs, she sank her fingers into his shoulder, feeling strength and muscle. He drew her closer, flattening her against him so that their bodies were touching from chest to ankle. Her thigh was trapped between his and when she looked up the humor in his eyes had gone, leaving only the heat.

"Enough. Let's go."

WITHOUT SPARING A glance for the people around them, Sean took her hand and drew her toward the steps that led to the forest trail. Without releasing her, he scooped up a bottle of champagne from a passing waiter.

Élise almost stumbled. "Where are we going?"

"Paradise." He slid his arm around her shoulders and hauled her against him. "Somewhere I'm less likely to be arrested for what I'm about to do to you."

He normally prided himself on his control. Tonight that control was nowhere to be found.

He could feel the race of Élise's pulse under his fingers, hear the shallow rush of her breath.

"We can't walk down the trail dressed like this. You'll ruin your shoes."

"Some sacrifices are worth it." *She was worth it.*

"These are my most comfortable shoes."

"In that case, hold this—" He handed her the champagne and scooped her into his arms while she gasped and tried not to spill any liquid.

"You're going to ruin my shoes *and* my dress."

"Bill me."

"And this is my favorite dress!" But she was laughing as he picked his way along the trail, muttering and cursing under his breath as twigs snapped and occasionally his feet sank.

"Normally when I try and charm a woman out of her underwear I pick a more glossy venue. Candlelit dinner. Maybe some dancing. I have some serious moves. Shit." He cursed again as his foot hit something soft. "My brother should build a proper path. Whenever I walk along here I step in something I don't want to identify."

"Is that one of your moves?"

"Very funny." He could feel her breath on his cheek and breathed in the scent she wore. He could feel her hair brushing against his jaw, feel her curves in his arms. The need to have his hands on her eclipsed everything else and he lowered her to the ground, keeping his arms around her. "The ground may not be firm underfoot but at least we have champagne. Never let it be said I don't know how to show a woman a good time." There was a roll of thunder in the distance and he winced as he felt the first drops of rain hit his shoulders. "Great. Please tell me you think rain is romantic."

"I think you know exactly how to show a woman a good time. Vermont is probably littered with broken hearts."

"Not just Vermont. I once kissed a girl from New Hampshire. If you're keeping count, you need to include her."

"And I mustn't forget all the broken hearts in Massachusetts."

"Those definitely weren't my fault. I warn women my work comes first. It's not my fault if they all want to reform me." He was about to kiss her when the rain suddenly increased and she gasped as raindrops splashed her face.

"Thank goodness the party is almost over! We should get indoors."

"I've got a better idea." He pulled her under the nearest tree, pushing her back against the gnarled bark, taking advantage of the leafy shelter. "You're shivering. Are you cold?" He shrugged out of his jacket and draped it around her shoulders, somehow managing to not drop the champagne. "Body warmth is best for that. Trust me, I'm a doctor." He brought his mouth down on hers, groaning as her lips parted under his. She was sweet, willing and as desperate as he was.

"Sean—"

"God, you taste good. It's been torture watching you walking around the deck with those long bare legs of yours—" The kiss was raw, desperate, lust clawing at him like a wild animal, urging him to take, and take. And she was equally demanding.

She locked her hand in the front of his shirt. "How do you think it has been for me with you half-naked on the deck for the past week?" Above them rain drenched the trees, filling the air with the scent of damp forest, the gentle patter of raindrops blocking out all other sounds. Protected by the dense canopy, they stayed dry. Oblivious.

She covered him with the flat of her hand and Sean groaned as he felt her fingers on his zip.

The champagne almost crashed to the ground.

Why the hell had he waited so long to do this again?

Sex with Élise had to be the most perfect, uncomplicated, sublime experience of his life.

In the distance, through the trees, they could see the lights from the party spilling onto the water, sending flashes of gold across the darkened surface. They heard the occasional strain of laughter as people scurried indoors out of the rain, but here in the forest they were alone. Tall white pine, sugar maple, white ash and red oak trees surrounded them and protected them from prying eyes and from the shift in the weather, silent witnesses to the building chemistry.

He lifted his mouth from hers and held out the bottle of champagne. "Drink?"

She took the bottle, her hand still cupping him intimately.

Her eyes holding his, she took a mouthful of champagne and gave a slow smile.

Still smiling, she freed him and then slid seductively down his body and took him in her mouth.

Wet warmth enveloped him and stars exploded in his head. Sean slammed his palm against the tree and closed his eyes, trying to steady himself, trying not to explode like a teenager. Her mouth was soft and skilled and she licked her way along his shaft and then drew him in deep until the pleasure blinded him.

Right on the edge, he dragged her up to him and the champagne fell to the ground with a thud, spilling liquid over their shoes.

The tension had been building for so long neither of them could pull it back.

They came together at the same moment, mouths colliding, bodies meshed, hands tearing at clothes.

Her fingers were jammed in his hair and she moaned as he powered her back against the tree. At the last minute he remembered her bare back and turned, so that he was the one against the rough bark. It scraped his shoulders and dug into his flesh.

He didn't care.

Nor did he care when the rain grew heavier and started to drip through the leaves onto their heads. Excitement ripped through him, raw, primal need drove every move he made. Dimly aware that he was stepping over a line he was careful not to cross, he reached into his pocket for the condom he always carried and she took it from him, fumbling in her haste, her mouth locked against his.

The feel of her hands on him almost tipped him over the edge.

His hands slid her dress up to her thighs and he lifted her. As she wrapped her legs around him, one of her shoes fell onto the forest floor and her fingers dug hard into his shoulders.

Her forehead touched his, her hair slid forward, her dense eyelashes shadowing eyes glittering with passion.

Sean slid his fingers between her legs, felt her wet and ready and saw those beautiful eyes darken.

She said something in French but he was past communicating in any language. He wanted to bury himself in that slippery heat and lose his mind. It was all about sex and electric chemistry. It saturated the air around them. It permeated everything, every breath, every look, every taste.

He clamped his hands on her shifting thighs, positioned her and thrust into that welcoming warmth with a throaty groan. Her body tightened around him, hot, wet, tight.

Christ.

His mind blanked.

All around him were the sounds of the forest and they were part of it, part of nature, stripped of sophistication, as they slaked their lust with mutual desperation. Heat shimmered, his shoulders were damp with rain as she moved with him, matching him, driving him on, and he felt the first ripples of her orgasm all the way down his rigid, sensitized shaft. She was lost and so was he. Knowing there was no way he was going to regain control he surrendered to it, taking her mouth with his and sharing every cry, every gasp, every breath as she pulsed around him, her body driving his to the same place. His own orgasm blinded him. His vision went dark, the intensity of it squeezing every last drop of energy from him. They kissed all the way through it, each of them inhaling and tasting every moan and gasp the other made.

It was like being run over by a truck.

"Holy shit." Sean felt dazed, unsteady on his feet, but he managed to lower her carefully, checking she could stand before he released her. It gave him some satisfaction that she kept her hands locked on his biceps.

So it wasn't just him, then.

Her dress was soaked, clinging to her body. Her hair was sleek against her head, her long dark eyelashes clumped together.

"Élise—"

Usually he knew what to say. Using words to his advantage was one of his skills, but right now he had no words at all, least of all slick ones.

His brain had blown.

The passion of it, the intensity and the insane chemistry was something he hadn't experienced before.

He was struggling to say something, anything, when she finally released his arms.

Without saying anything, she slid her dress back into place, stooped and retrieved her shoe, sliding it onto her foot.

Like an erotic version of Cinderella...

It seemed impossible to comprehend, but he wanted her again. Immediately. Desperately.

And he knew she felt the same way.

"Good night, Sean." She reached up and kissed his cheek briefly and he was so stunned by that unexpected dismissal it took him a moment to compute what she'd just said.

"'Good night, Sean'? What the hell is that supposed to mean?"

"It means I'm wishing you a good night."

"But—" His brain and body were so aroused he couldn't form thoughts or words. Both were broken into pieces, swirling around his dazed brain. "You're right. We can't stay here. You're soaking wet and cold. We'll go back to your place."

"No."

"No?" Nothing made sense to him. "What the hell just happened here?"

"Sex," she said shakily. "Incredible sex. You're very good."

It was a compliment smoothly blended with a rejection.

"No, wait! Just—" He swore and raked his fingers through his hair. "Just wait a minute while I think." But he couldn't think. His brain wasn't working. All he could think of was the contrast between the heat of her mouth and the cool champagne. The way she'd felt when he was buried deep inside her. The need to touch her was so strong he pulled her back to him but she extricated herself gently.

"It's been a long day. A long few months to be honest. I need to get some sleep. Good night, Sean. Be careful where you step walking home. The ground is wet and you don't want to ruin those shoes." With that, she flashed him a smile and ran into the darkness and the falling rain, leaving him dazed and staring and wondering what had hit him.

CHAPTER ELEVEN

BY THE TIME Élise let herself into Heron Lodge she was soaked and shivering. The rain poured down on the roof and thunder rolled in the distance.

Despite the rain, the party had been a success. The Boathouse would open on time. She should have been elated.

She wasn't.

It was no good telling herself that what had happened had been inevitable. That it had been building for months. The truth was, she'd lost control.

But it was still just sex, wasn't it? Still just sex. Not a relationship. Not feelings. She didn't do that. Would never again allow herself to feel because every emotion she felt was exaggerated, stronger, deeper than other people's.

She'd done it once before and it had ended in disaster.

She'd lost everything that had mattered to her.

There was no way she would ever risk that happening again.

Sick with the memory, palms sweaty, she pushed her hand through her soaking-wet hair and then heard the door open behind her.

She turned and saw Sean standing in the doorway, black hair sleek from the rain, those blue eyes fixed on her face. His shirt was plastered to his body, still half-undone and revealing hard muscle and a shadow of dark hair. Even with bits of the forest clinging to his trousers and his clothes wet and stuck to his body, he still looked insanely attractive.

Her tummy tightened and panic sank its claws into her flesh. "What do you want?"

"Are you seriously asking me that? You used me and abandoned me alone in the forest with no protection. Do you have no conscience?" His eyes gleamed with humor but that sexy smile simply spelled danger to her and she shook her head.

"Go away, Sean."

He didn't budge. "Call me old-fashioned, but when I've had a date with a woman I like to see her home safely."

"You can see I'm safe." But she didn't feel safe. She didn't feel safe at all with those powerful shoulders wedged in her doorway and those blue eyes fixed on her. "You're letting in the rain."

His response to that was to close the door with himself on the inside. "Tell me what's wrong."

"What makes you think something is wrong?"

He raked his fingers through his hair, sending droplets of water flying. "We had sex. You walked away."

"And women don't usually walk away from you, is that it?" The look in his eyes told her that she was right and she gave a tired smile. "You don't want a relationship and neither do I. It shouldn't matter which one of us walks away."

"It's true I don't have time for relationships. I've never made any secret of the fact. Right now work is my priority and I'm not prepared to compromise. Work comes before everything, including coming home to Snow Crystal, which makes me a selfish son-of-a-bitch or a dedicated doctor, depending on which way you look at it. If you're my grandfather, it's the first. Most of the women I've known would probably agree with him. And now you know just about everything there is to know about me and I know nothing about you." He swiped his palm over his jaw, removing droplets of water. "Do you want to give me some clues?"

She'd expected him to walk away. She hadn't expected him to come after her and she certainly hadn't expected him to still be standing here.

And she hadn't expected him to ask questions.

"I don't want a relationship. The reason for that doesn't matter." She didn't talk about it. Not with anyone. She'd buried it deep and she never, ever wanted to dig it up again. She'd left that part of her life behind and she wasn't ever going there again.

"If you don't want to talk about it that's fine with me, but do you have a towel I could borrow? I'm dripping on your floor."

"If you left, you wouldn't be dripping on my floor."

"I'm not leaving until I'm sure you're all right."

"Why wouldn't I be all right?"

"Sweetheart, you ran through that forest like little Red Riding Hood with the wolf behind her. I know you don't want a relationship and I don't have a problem with that. If I'm honest, it's a relief. You didn't need to freak out in the forest. You didn't need to run from me." His voice gentled. "You don't ever need to run from me."

"I did not freak out."

"Yeah, you did. And so did I. It was pretty intense.

Wild. Did I hurt you?" His tone was rough and she felt her tummy clench and emotion jam in her throat.

"No. You didn't hurt me." But the fact that he'd ask, *that he'd care,* unraveled a few more strands of the protection she'd wrapped around herself.

"So maybe I got the wrong fairy story. Is your middle name Cinderella by any chance? You lost your shoe back there so I guess you could have been running for a pumpkin pulled by mice."

Only then did she see that he was holding her shoe. She'd run through the forest without a shoe and hadn't even noticed. "I hate rodents."

"Right, so I won't buy you a pet rat for Christmas." A faint smile touched his mouth. "So was it the spiders? There are quite a few of those in the forest."

"That's it. That's the reason."

"Really?" The smile had gone and suddenly those eyes seemed darker than usual as they lingered on her face. "Because I figured it had to be that you were afraid. What happened between us scared you."

"I'm not afraid. It didn't scare me."

"Are you sure? Because it sure scared the shit out of me. I'm used to being able to walk away after sex but it's hard to walk anywhere when your brain is blown."

She stepped back and the edge of the counter dug hard into her hip. "I want you to leave now."

"I'll leave when I'm ready. You need to take off those wet things and get into a hot shower before you freeze. Is your foot all right? You could have stepped on something sharp." His gaze slid down her body and she felt as if she were on fire. She didn't need the shower to warm up, she just needed to look into those blue eyes.

"I'll shower when you've gone. And I didn't step on anything."

"Do you always ignore what the doctor tells you?" He pulled a face and glanced down at himself. "The problem is that if I turn up at Jackson's looking like this there will be questions I'm not sure I want to answer. I was hoping to use your shower and your clothes dryer."

The last thing she wanted was Jackson asking questions. He was very protective of her and she didn't want to come between the two brothers or be the cause of disagreement.

She would never, ever do anything that might damage a family, especially not this family. She loved them too much. This was the closest thing to a home she'd had for a long time and she wasn't going to put that at risk.

"You can use my bathroom."

"You use it first. And while you do that, I'll make us both a hot drink. Hot chocolate?"

She was shivering but she didn't know if it was because of the rain or because he was standing in her kitchen. "Chocolate is fine."

He reached into a cupboard and took out two mugs and then paused. He put the mugs down and picked up the photo of her with her mother. "Is this you?"

Her mouth was dry. "Yes."

"You were seriously cute as a child. And your mother is beautiful. You look like her. And she clearly adored you."

Her mouth was dry. "What makes you say that?"

"The way she's looking at you."

Élise looked at the photo, wishing she could rewind time and do everything differently.

"Sean—"

"Go and have that shower before you freeze." He put the photograph back carefully and pulled milk from the fridge. "Don't use all the hot water."

SEAN HEATED MILK and spooned chocolate into mugs. Then he stood and drank his, looking at the photograph.

The faint sound of the shower came from above his head. Because he knew she was going to be a few more minutes, he picked up the photo again.

His house was full of photos. His mother put them everywhere. Not just pictures of Tyler on the podium with medals around his neck, but family snaps—the three boys dusted with snow after a snowball fight, all of them grinning on a sled, the family dogs, pictures of his grandparents in their twenties, Snow Crystal before the lodges were built. A visual record of the passage of time. The whole house was plastered with memories. Jackson joked that their entire family history was right up there on the walls. And it wasn't just the photos. His mother still kept pottery the boys had made in school, wonky, shapeless, unidentifiable lumps of clay that for some reason she refused to part with. She kept drawings they'd done as children, a medal Jackson had won for being young entrepreneur in tenth grade. Hell, she even kept a certificate Sean had won in Science.

He stared down at the photo in his hand, seeing the dimple in the corner of young Élise's mouth.

Lifting his head, he glanced around Heron Lodge. Apart from the photo in his hand, there was nothing else that told him anything about her past. No clues as to who she was or where she came from. No more photographs. No objects. Nothing. It was as if her past didn't exist. Of course, it could have been argued that Heron Lodge was too small to house too many sentimental objects, but still he would have expected to see something.

This was the only possession of hers. This one photograph.

Mother and child.

The mother she'd lost.

Guilt stabbed him. More often than not, he saw family as stifling, whereas in fact it was a cocoon. Not a straitjacket, but a protection. He'd always had that, it had always been there, even when he hadn't noticed, or wanted it. Staying away didn't change the fact his family was always there for him.

And he took it all for granted.

The sound of water stopped suddenly and Sean put the photo back quietly and finished his chocolate.

A moment later Élise appeared in the kitchen, her cheeks flushed from the hairdryer.

Her face was scrubbed clean of makeup and the sexy black dress had been exchanged for a simple strap top and a pair of cozy lounge pants tied at the waist with a cream ribbon.

He fought the urge to carry her straight to bed and instead handed her the mug. "I made you chocolate."

"Thanks. If you leave your clothes outside the shower, I'll put them in the dryer." She took the mug and sat down on her sofa, curling her legs under her.

He took the stairs to the upper floor, remembering when he and his brothers had built the place. He'd banged his head a million times on the beam at the top of the stairs. So had Tyler.

The bathroom was off the bedroom and he had another glimpse of her personal space.

The bedcover was white and piled with small cushions. On the table by the bed was her phone, a small bottle of mineral water, various tubes of makeup and a notepad. There were no photographs. The only photograph he'd seen was the one downstairs.

The smell of her perfume was everywhere.

Feeling as if he was intruding, he walked into the shower room and blinked as he saw the number of bottles and potions lined up on the shelves. This, he thought, was another reason why he never invited a woman to stay at his place. He'd have to build an extension.

Smiling, he stripped off, dropped his clothes outside the door and showered. The shampoo smelled of flowers, smelled of her, and it was impossible not to remember that night they'd spent together last summer. Leading up to it, they'd been flirting. Still in the raw stages of his grief, his anger with his grandfather white-hot, he'd been so relieved to talk to someone who wasn't family, he'd sought her out. They'd talked about everything from wine to European politics.

Still, he'd kept his distance, knowing he had nothing to offer, not wanting to do anything that might destabilize the work Jackson was doing at Snow Crystal.

But then he'd taken a walk through the forest to the meadow behind the house and she'd followed him.

Remembering it, Sean cursed softly and switched the shower to cold.

They'd barely spoken. Barely exchanged a word, but what had followed had been the most intensely erotic night of his life.

And afterward, when he was afraid it might be awkward, she'd simply smiled and walked away.

At the time he'd thought he was the luckiest guy on the planet.

He'd found someone exactly like him. Her working day was almost as long as his, she was a perfectionist, a talented chef and devoted to doing everything she could to help grow the business at Snow Crystal. A workaholic who wasn't interested in a relationship.

He hadn't looked deeper. Her wild, passionate nature had stopped him seeing how guarded she was.

Stepping out of the shower, he knotted a towel around his hips and opened the door.

There, exactly as he'd left them, were his wet clothes.

Assuming she'd forgotten, he picked them up and carried them downstairs only to see her fast asleep on the sofa, the mug of chocolate cooling on the floor beside her, untouched.

Frowning, Sean walked across and studied her for a moment. Considering how hard she'd worked, the hours she put in, it was hardly surprising she'd fallen asleep, was it?

She was obviously completely exhausted.

Her dark lashes were the only smudge of color on her pale face.

Deciding that if he left her there she'd wake up with backache, Sean scooped her up in his arms.

She barely stirred.

Wishing it had occurred to him when he'd built the lodge that one day he might one day need to maneuver up the narrow staircase with a woman in his arms, Sean carried her carefully and lowered her onto the bed.

Then he pulled the white cover over her, switched off the lamp and walked away.

CHAPTER TWELVE

"IT'S BEEN SO long since we managed Sunday breakfast together. We love it when you girls find time to join us, don't we, Alice?" Elizabeth, the boys' mother, slid a stack of freshly cooked pancakes onto a plate and put them in the center of the scrubbed kitchen table. "Sit down, the three of you. What a wonderful party. I haven't enjoyed myself that much for years. Élise, you did us proud, sweetheart. You must be exhausted after all that work and excitement. Did you sleep at all last night?"

"Yes." And she'd woken in her own bed even though she knew that wasn't where she'd fallen asleep.

Sean must have carried her.

If she hadn't been so stressed about it she would have smiled because she knew he would have struggled to do it without banging his head.

Why had he bothered to come to her lodge when he could have just walked away?

And why had he asked all those questions? All he'd needed to know was that she didn't want a relationship. He didn't need to know the reasons why.

"It was a great party." Kayla had brought Maple with her and she cuddled the dog as she sat down at the table. "I talked to a million people and my face hurts from smiling. It's going to be great for the business. Is there anything I can do to help with breakfast, Elizabeth? Can I cook something?"

Brenna pulled a face and Elizabeth smiled nervously. "You just sit there, dear. I love cooking and we all know it's not your favorite thing."

"What she means is you are truly terrible at cooking." Élise poured coffee into mugs and set them on the table. "What? Why are you all looking at me?"

Brenna grinned. "Because you don't know the meaning of the word tact."

"I speak the truth so none of us is poisoned. At cooking, Kayla is truly terrible but at organization and marketing—" She lifted her mug in a toast. "She is a genius. To Kayla."

"To Kayla," Brenna said and Kayla grinned as she lifted her mug.

"To us and to teamwork. The summer hasn't been awful. We're still in business. Here's to a brilliant winter with masses of snow and more bookings than we can handle."

"Talking of winter, I spent some time with Josh last night." Brenna added maple syrup to her pancakes, missing the look Kayla sent Élise.

"He's a nice boy," Alice murmured. "His grandmother is in my knitting group."

"He's thirty-something, Alice." Brenna smiled. "Not exactly a boy."

"A man." Elizabeth topped up the pancakes. "A very handsome man. I've always liked him, even though his father once arrested Tyler for skiing off Mitch Sommerville's garage roof. What were you talking about, dear?"

"We're thinking about doing a course on winter safety." Brenna picked up her fork. If the mention of

Tyler had unsettled her, she wasn't showing it. "We're both members of the Mountain Rescue Team so it makes sense."

"Tyler's a member of the Mountain Rescue Team." Alice reached across and stroked Maple's soft, springy fur. "You could do it with him."

Élise winced. "Alice—"

"I just think the two of them would work well together, that's all. Isn't Maple looking well, Elizabeth? I remember when Jackson found her in the forest—she was skin and bone. It's done her so much good living with the family. She loves it here."

Élise felt a lump in her throat. She loved it here, too. Who wouldn't? Who wouldn't love living here, with the O'Neils?

Aware that Kayla was watching her, she helped herself to a pancake.

Merde, she was losing it. Now she was empathizing with Maple and what she should be doing was thinking of Brenna's feelings.

"I think it would be good for Brenna to work with Josh." For one thing it might be the wake-up call Tyler needed. "I like him."

The door opened and Jackson walked in. Maple sprang from Kayla's lap, hurtled across the room like a bullet and jumped up like a spring, deliriously happy to see him.

He scooped her up. "Any of those pancakes left?"

"Of course." Elizabeth slid pancakes onto a plate and placed it on the table. "Sit down. Are Tyler and Sean coming, too?"

"Tyler is on his way." Jackson sat down and slid his

hand over Kayla's knee. "Sean has gone back to Boston. He texted me."

"He dropped in to say goodbye." Alice picked up her knitting. "He said he'd be back next week to take Walter to his hospital appointment."

Élise kept her eyes on her plate.

She should be relieved he'd gone. It was what she'd wanted, wasn't it?

The intensity of what had happened the night before had shocked her.

It had shocked him, too.

She wondered if he'd spoken to his grandfather before he'd left, or whether he'd just left the topic of the row simmering between them.

"More to eat, Élise?" Elizabeth hovered, the pan in her hand. Élise shook her head.

"*Non, merci.* I am not hungry."

"I ate so much last night I may never eat again." Jackson gave her a smile as he reached for the maple syrup. "The food was incredible. Everyone was talking about it. You're a genius and we're lucky to have you. I probably don't tell you that enough."

"I am the one who is lucky." Living here. With them.

She looked up and met his gaze.

He was the best friend she'd ever had.

Without him…

She swallowed. She didn't even want to think about where she would have been without him.

Jackson stuck his fork into a pancake. "So is this a good moment to ask you another favor? Kayla and I have had a new business idea. We're going to offer corporate team-building events. We need help with the food."

"*Pas de problème,* I will book them a table in the restaurant." It was a relief to think about work again. "Just tell me how many."

"Not the restaurant. They're going to hike and camp overnight on the Long Trail. If that doesn't help them bond, nothing will."

"You are taking a group of senior executives *camping?*"

"Genius, don't you think?" Kayla sneaked some food to Maple who was still nestled on Jackson's lap. "It will be a real test for them. You're responsible for providing them with delicious food to take their mind off blisters and insect bites."

"Who is going to put the tent up?"

"They are. With a little help from Tyler. He's going to add in the whole gold-medallist-elite-sportsman-motivational-talk thing he does. All part of our unique offering."

"Tyler will be driven mad spending two days trapped with office types. How did you persuade him to do it?"

"Two of the first group are women. I showed him photographs. So could you design a menu? Something they can cook with limited equipment."

"Of course." Élise pondered the options. "It will have to be light to carry and easy to cook. You need to give me the equipment they will have and I will see what I can cook on it."

"I can go one better than that." Jackson helped himself to more pancakes. "You can do the trip yourself. Tyler is going to plan the route and pick the best camping spot. You can go together. There's the O'Neil Cabin high up on the trail but he thinks that's too far for just two days of hiking with city folk who usually just walk to a cab or a subway so he's going to find somewhere closer. Keep next weekend free."

"I have to be in the restaurant."

"Poppy and I can cope." Elizabeth wiped her hands on her apron. "And Antony, the boy who's just joined, is turning out very well. He's a hard worker. He just needs a little more confidence. We'll be fine. It will be good for us to manage without you. You can't carry on working this hard."

"I love working hard and it is important for the business that we bring in as many guests as possible."

She owed Jackson a debt. A debt she was determined to repay in full.

And now that Sean had gone and Walter was improving by the day, life could get back to normal.

"THEY'RE PLEASED WITH your progress, Gramps." Sean drove out of the hospital car park, determined that this time he was going to find a moment to bring up the topic of their row. He didn't know what he was going to say, but maybe they could clear the air a little. "I checked the results myself. You're a walking miracle. They want to know what your secret is."

"No secret. All it takes is Snow Crystal air and having your family around you. You were looking better yourself after spending time at home. Now after a week in the city you're back to wearing the stress along with the suit."

Sean knew his stress had nothing to do with his week in Boston and everything to do with what had happened the night of the party.

Élise had wanted him to leave, so he'd left. That should have been it. With his grandfather recovering, he'd expected to return to his life in Boston and pick up where he left off.

Instead, he found himself missing certain things. He missed the long days working on the deck. He missed the smell of summer rain on the trees and the slap of water against the deck as he worked. He missed exchanging banter with his brothers.

But most of all he missed her. The smile. The dimple. That mouth.

Shit.

He tightened his grip on the wheel. What the hell was wrong with him?

All right, so it had been good sex, but good sex didn't usually affect his concentration. And the fact she hadn't wanted to make any of it personal shouldn't worry him, either. No one understood that better than him.

"I'm not stressed, Gramps."

"Of course you are and that's hardly surprising with the life you lead, cooped up in that box under artificial lights."

"You mean the operating room?"

"That's what I mean. Unhealthy. You need air. And people. A job is all well and good but it's marriage to a good woman that makes a man happy and content." Walter stared straight ahead. "You should try it."

Sean almost drove the car into the ditch. *Marriage?* "I can tell you now that isn't going to happen so you can let that drop right now."

"A man can't fool around forever."

"I'm not fooling around. I love my work. I'm not prepared to compromise that for a relationship and no sane, self-respecting woman would put up with my hours."

His grandfather ignored him. "I worked long hours.

Your grandmother was very understanding. We're a team. Always have been, right from day one."

"Grams is a saint, we all know that."

"It was a good party. Shame you had to leave so early the next day. Still, at least you came. Élise is a good dancer, isn't she?"

Sean gritted his teeth.

His grandfather knew. Somehow, his grandfather knew.

Sweat pricked the back of his neck. He thought of Élise, her legs tangled with his, her mouth on his as the rain dripped through the canopy of the trees. "I had to leave. I'd fixed the deck and it was time to fix some patients."

"If you're fixing them on a Sunday morning I hope you're charging them a lot. I guess you are or you wouldn't be driving a car like this one." His grandfather stroked his hand over the seat. "It's not big enough for a family."

"I don't have a family."

"Yet. When you do, you're going to need to buy something bigger."

"I don't need anything bigger." Remembering why he'd chosen to live in Boston, Sean punched the gas and headed toward Snow Crystal. "So the hospital doesn't want to see you for another six weeks. That's great news."

It meant he had no reason to come back for six weeks. Six weeks was plenty of time to get back into the rhythm of his life.

"The doctors here are good. As good as any you'll find in Boston. You should work here. Then you'd be closer to home. Maybe the hours wouldn't be so long."

It never ended. No matter how old he was, the pressure was always there. It was like being trapped under someone's boot.

It had been like this for his father and he'd had it all the time with no respite.

His stomach felt hollow.

The desire to bring up the topic of the row fled. How could he talk about it when he was still angry inside? When the resentment was still there?

Instead, he kept to the subject of work. "You don't understand anything about what I do."

"So tell me."

Sean was thrown because his grandfather so rarely asked for details about his life. The conversation was only ever about Snow Crystal. The business. The family. What he wasn't doing.

He decided that anything was better than a conversation about marriage. "My department is at the forefront of innovation in ACL surgery." Knowing that his grandfather, an experienced skier, would understand exactly what that meant, he didn't bother simplifying it. Instead, he explained his research, his interests, what excited him. And his grandfather listened.

"So you're stabilizing the knee and getting the patient active again. That's good. Rewarding work."

Sean relaxed slightly. "Yes."

"So if you're the one running it, you could run it from here." His grandfather's tone was innocent. "I don't see why Boston should benefit from your skills. There are plenty of folks around here that would be happy to have you fix them when they've broken something and we have more skiing injuries than people in

Boston. Last time I looked they didn't have mountains there."

They'd come full circle. "I deal with top athletes. They travel from all over to see me."

"No reason why they couldn't travel here. And they'd have the views, good food and fresh mountain air thrown in for nothing. If you worked here, you'd be able to live at Snow Crystal, help your brothers and see plenty of Élise."

"Jesus, Gramps—" Sean slammed on the brakes and pulled the car into the entrance of the Carpenters' apple farm, narrowly avoiding a deep rut in the road.

"Don't use bad language. It upsets your grand-mother."

"Grams isn't here. And I'll use whatever language I choose to use, just as I'll live where I want to live and do the job I want to do."

"And kiss the girl you want to kiss."

"Yes." Sean narrowed his eyes, wondering just how much his eagle-eyed grandfather had seen the night of the party. "That, too."

"Just make sure you're not so busy kissing every pretty girl you meet, you lose the one you'd like to kiss for the rest of your life."

Suddenly all he could think of was the generous curve of Élise's mouth, *that dimple,* and he gritted his teeth.

"My focus is my job."

"A job doesn't keep you warm at night. I loved my job, too, but the moment I met your grandmother, I knew. So did she. Maybe you have to get to a certain age to know what's important in life. Health and people you love around you. That's it."

Sean leaned his head back against the seat. "Are you about done with the lecture?"

"Not lecturing. Just passing on my wisdom. It's been easier on your brothers, you being home more the last few weeks. It's because of you the Boathouse is opening. If you were closer, you could do more of that. And you could use some of that expertise people pay good money for to help Brenna develop a pre-conditioning program before the ski season. Now get out of here. The Carpenters aren't my favorite people and I don't want to be parked on their land."

Afraid that if he answered he'd say something he regretted, Sean was about to pull back onto the road when he saw a flash of long red hair far in the distance. Someone was walking in the Carpenters' apple orchards.

He squinted, trying to get a clearer look but whoever it was vanished out of sight.

Feeling uneasy, Sean turned his head to see if his grandfather had noticed anything but Walter was concentrating on the road.

"This car is too low down."

Sean glanced back at the farm but there was no one in sight.

Telling himself that there were plenty of women with long red hair, he pulled back onto the road and flattened his foot to the floor, deciding that the sooner he dropped his grandfather back, the better.

"I'll be back to take you to your next hospital appointment, not before."

Churned up inside, he dropped off his grandfather, reassured his grandmother that Walter was making miraculous progress and went to find his brothers.

He found Tyler outside the Outdoor Center, sprawled in the dirt, fixing a mountain bike.

His brother took one look at his face and sat up. "You look happy. Gramps is obviously back on form. Don't tell me, he wants you to move back home and run a private clinic right here at Snow Crystal."

"Something like that."

Tyler wiped his forearm over his forehead. "Haven't seen you since the party. I noticed you disappeared early."

"I was tired."

"Yeah, right. So tired you had to lie down in a nice big bed. I've been that tired a few times in my life."

Irritated by the conversation with his grandfather, Sean sent his brother a look. "Why is everyone suddenly so interested in my love life? What about you? Did you dance with Brenna at the party?"

"No, but I noticed you did." Tyler's expression darkened. "So what was that about? One woman isn't enough for you?"

"For your information I can't imagine kissing one woman for the rest of my life."

"You kissed her?" Tyler jumped to his feet and the bike crashed to the ground. "You kissed Brenna?"

Sean, who had been thinking about Élise, was startled to find himself pinned against the fence. "Hey, this is my favorite suit. What the hell is wrong with you?"

"You have to ask me that? You kissed Brenna!"

"I did not kiss Brenna."

Tyler's hold relaxed slightly. "You just said you did."

"I did not. I said my idea of a nightmare was kissing the same woman for the rest of my life. I did not say I kissed Brenna." Sean shoved his brother and smoothed his creased shirt, battling sibling irritation and other emotions he didn't want to examine more closely. "I've known her since she was four years old. She's like a sister to me."

"Right. Good." Tyler's shoulders relaxed slightly. "Your shirt needs ironing. Your standards are slipping since you arrived home."

Sean decided revenge didn't have to involve ruining a perfectly good set of clothing. "Of course, just because I've known her since she was four years old doesn't stop me from noticing that she's looking good." His shirt was already creased so he decided he might as well go for it. "Now you mention it, maybe I should kiss her. Why not?" He decided to stir a bit harder. "Although I might have competition."

"Competition?"

"Yeah. I saw her talking to Josh. Judging from the look on his face, he definitely doesn't think she's four years old. Women love Josh."

"They're friends." From the way Tyler spoke through his teeth it was obvious the relationship didn't thrill him.

"He sat next to me in biology and English, which means he's known her as long as I have. I don't see you creasing his shirt."

"If I creased his shirt I could end up in handcuffs for assaulting an officer of the law."

"So it doesn't bother you that she's with him?"

"She isn't with him. They're just friends. And sure it bothers me. But not as much as the thought of you and her together."

"Thanks. I love you, too. You always were my favorite brother."

Tyler didn't even raise a smile. "Brenna is straight-forward and uncomplicated."

"She's a woman," Sean drawled. "No woman is ever straightforward and uncomplicated."

"She is not your type. You'd break her."

Sean frowned. "I don't seem to recall you being exactly careful with female hearts."

"I never laid a finger on Brenna."

And that, Sean thought wearily, was his brother's main problem. "Why not?"

"I don't think of her like that." Tyler's scowl deepened. "And you're not going to think of her like that, either."

"But if you're not interested—"

"I've been looking for you, Tyler." Suddenly Jackson was between them, calm and solid. "Should have guessed you'd be hiding out here. I've got a problem."

"So have I." Tyler was glaring at Sean. "It shares your DNA and I'm going to break a bone in its body in a moment."

Sean rubbed at a smudge on his jacket. "Broken bones are my specialty, remember?"

Jackson ignored both of them. "Kayla has arranged a corporate team-building event. Overnight hike on the Long Trail."

"I know. You told me about it." Looking grumpy, Tyler lifted the bike out of the dust. "I have to take a bunch of out-of-condition office types hiking. It will be the highlight of my life."

"I need you to do a trial run next weekend."

"I don't need to do a trial run. I know that trail like the back of my hand. I could walk it in the dark in my sleep with both legs tied together and still be back in half the time you're giving them."

"It's not for your benefit. It's for Élise."

Stirred out of thoughts of his conversation with his grandfather, Sean frowned. "What does Élise have to do with it? She's not doing a trip with Tyler."

"Élise is preparing the food and she wants to be sure her menu will work with the equipment out in the wild. She's arranged cover in the restaurant next weekend."

"You want me to camp overnight with Élise? That sounds cozy." Tyler glanced at Sean and his scowl turned to a smile.

Sean ground his teeth. "Is that supposed to bother me?"

"I don't know. Does it?"

It did, but there was no way he was going to admit it. "Poor Élise," he said smoothly. "Someone had better warn her you snore."

"We probably won't sleep much. We'll be too busy keeping each other warm and staring into each other's eyes."

Jackson glanced between them in exasperation. "Are you two ever going to grow out of this?"

"Grow out of what?" Sean resisted the temptation to grab his younger brother by the throat. "If he wants to jump on Élise he can go right ahead. I hope he has fun. While he's eating boil-in-the-bag food and being bitten by bugs, I just might take Brenna to dinner. She's been working her butt off and deserves a little relaxation."

Seeing Tyler's expression blacken, Jackson swore under his breath. "I've got enough to do without pulling you two apart every two minutes."

Tyler had his eyes fixed on Sean. "Brenna has more sense than to say yes to dinner with you."

"Why? She went out to dinner with Jackson a few times last winter."

"That's different. Jackson doesn't try and sleep with every woman he takes to dinner."

Jackson rolled his eyes. "Are you about done?"

"I'm done." Tyler flashed a furious look at Sean and strode into the Outdoor Center, hauling the bike with him.

Jackson watched him go. "What the hell are you playing at?"

"Just conducting an experiment. Seeing how things are."

"We both know how things are and I'm happy for them to stay that way." Jackson glanced at the group of children cycling behind Brenna toward the Outdoor Center. "Tyler and Brenna are both essential to the running of this place. I don't want anything messing with that. Running this place is still a balance between swimming and drowning. It won't take much to push us under."

Sean glanced down at his shirt. "He wrecked a perfectly good shirt."

"Makes a change that it wasn't one of mine."

"He's crazy about her."

"Maybe." Jackson lifted a hand and acknowledged Brenna. "But he's also very protective of her. You should probably keep that in mind next time you're trying to goad him. And for God's sake don't take her to dinner. We had fireworks on the Fourth of July. We don't need any more right now."

"You took her to dinner."

"It was just dinner."

"I'm sure he loves Brenna."

"Yeah, well maybe he does, but we all know that business with Janet Carpenter messed with his head."

Sean hesitated, wondering whether to say something or not. "I pulled into the Carpenters' place a little while ago."

Jackson's eyes narrowed. "Why would you do that?"

"I was considering killing Gramps and I needed both hands. The thing is—" he paused "—I thought I saw Janet."

"You're kidding me. That isn't possible. She's in Chicago."

"It was from a distance. I could have been wrong."

"You were wrong." Jackson's mouth tightened. "Whatever she thinks of Tyler, she's Jess's mother. She wouldn't come back to see her folks and not tell her own daughter."

"Wouldn't she?" Sean wiped dust from his sleeve. "Last Christmas she sent that same daughter here to live permanently without giving a single thought to what was right for Jess. Didn't seem to bother her much. Think we should mention it to Tyler?"

"No. Because you could have been wrong. *Shit.*" Jackson dragged his hand over the back of his neck. "I hope you are wrong. The last thing we need around here is Janet Carpenter mixing things up. Jess is settled and happy. Tyler is steadier than he's been in years."

"I'm probably wrong. There are plenty of women with long red hair. And why would she be here? She fell out with her folks and she hates Snow Crystal almost as much as she hates Tyler."

"And Jess is stuck in the middle of that. From what

I can gather they don't even speak that often, but it doesn't seem to bother Jess much. Since that incident at Christmas, everything has calmed down. She adores Tyler, so whatever Janet has tried to do to kill that hasn't worked. Let's just forget it and if it is her and she's come back without telling her own daughter, all the more reason not to mention it. Jess doesn't need the hurt and Tyler doesn't need the hassle."

"Yeah, you're probably right. And talking of causing Tyler hassle, about this camping trip—" Sean bent and brushed dust from his shoe. "I'll do it."

"You?" Jackson looked at him in astonishment. "You'll be in Boston."

"I was planning to come home next weekend, anyway. Just to check on Gramps." The six weeks away from Snow Crystal he'd been planning suddenly felt like too long. "I'll be here so I'll do it."

"So not only are you planning on coming home again, you want to go camping?" Jackson didn't even bother to try and hide the smile. "Has someone suddenly invented a five-star tent with private facilities that I don't know about?"

"I was brought up here, same as you. I know those trails as well as you. My wilderness survival techniques are as good as yours."

"Since when did wilderness survival equipment include walking in handmade Italian shoes?" Jackson's gaze slid from his shirt to his feet. "They're going to look good after a day hiking on the trail. Is that your idea of dressing casually? Because you wouldn't look out of place in a box at the opera."

"That shows how many times you've taken a box at

the opera. And for your information I just took Gramps to the hospital."

"Right. That explains why your mood is so cozy and warm. That hike is tough. That's why we've chosen it."

"I can do tough. Try standing on your feet for twelve hours operating and then get up in the night for an emergency, then you'll know tough."

"You want to give up two days of your time to nurse-maid a load of quarreling businessmen?"

"No. Tyler can do that part. I want to do the practice session."

Jackson swatted a fly. "You're really willing to go to these lengths just so Tyler doesn't get to spend a night in a tent with Élise?"

"It's got nothing to do with Élise. I'm doing my bit to help with the family business. It will get Gramps off my back. I just thought I could help out, that's all. Visitor numbers are up. You can't employ more staff until the numbers are healthier so I'm guessing you're all stretched to the limit."

"We are. But we've been stretched to the limit before and I didn't see you throwing down your scalpel and running to our rescue. Which is fine, because you're doing what you're trained to do and we're all proud of you." Jackson's gaze was steady. "So do us both a favor, cut the bullshit and tell me what the hell is going on."

"Like I said, I'm helping out."

Jackson sighed. "Fine, do it. As you say, we're short of staff. It will free up Tyler to take that family on a mountain bike trip. But you do anything to Élise, you bring even one tiny tear to her eye, and I'll be the one breaking your bones, not Tyler."

CHAPTER THIRTEEN

ÉLISE BURIED HERSELF in work in the hope that it would stop her thinking about Sean.

She knew he'd taken Walter to the hospital. The fact that he hadn't stopped by to see her bothered her more than it should have.

And now he was back in Boston, getting on with his life and she was getting on with hers.

Which was exactly the way it should be.

She cooked every night in the Inn serving award-winning food in elegant surroundings and spent the rest of the time supervising and working in the new Boathouse Café. She experimented with menus, removed dishes that didn't seem popular, and added a few others. It pleased her to see the newly completed deck crowded with families, old and young alike.

And in the few spare hours she had, she designed a menu for the team-building event Kayla had arranged. The food had to be light to carry and easy to cook.

Tyler had given her the little outdoor stove they'd be using and she reproduced all the dishes using only the equipment she'd have on the trail.

On the morning of the trek, she met him at the Outdoor Center.

"For goodness' sake take bug repellent." Tyler handed her a bag. "And wear long sleeves and long pants the whole time. It's the middle of summer so there are a whole load of biting bugs out there. Luckily you've mostly missed blackfly season. That's a real joy."

"You can walk ahead of me." Élise pushed the food into her backpack. "That way they can take a mouthful of you and maybe they won't be so hungry."

"I'm not going." He helped her with the backpack. "Family of six want to explore the mountain bike trails and I'm their guide. We can't turn down that sort of money."

"No, of course you can't. So is Jackson going to—?"

"Sean." Tyler pulled the backpack closed and fastened it. "Shocking though it may sound, my lightweight, city-loving brother is going to do it."

Her mouth dried. "Sean?"

Tyler gave her a sympathetic look. "Scary, I know, but believe it or not he used to know this trail really well. And look at it this way—if he can't save you from being attacked by a bear because he's worried about protecting his shoes and his suit, he can at least put you back together afterward. Don't look so terrified." He misinterpreted the look on her face. "You're not likely to see a bear. They're pretty nervous of humans, although once they get a whiff of your cooking that might change. Just kidding."

Sean was coming with her?

She hadn't seen him since that night when she'd fallen asleep on the sofa and woken to find he'd carried her upstairs.

"I thought he was in Boston."

"According to Jackson he's suddenly been filled with a brotherly urge to help out." Tyler shrugged. "We're pretty busy around here so none of us are about to argue. You two are going to check the route, cook that food, camp overnight and then let me know if we need to make any changes to the plan before these soft city folk arrive here."

"I gather two of them are women."

"That's right." Tyler grinned. "I'm planning to arrange a bear encounter so they decide to snuggle in my tent."

Despite the feelings churning around inside her, Élise laughed. "Is Brenna going with you?"

"She is." Tyler reached out and adjusted the straps on her backpack. "It's important that the weight is in the right place or you'll be uncomfortable. And if it gets too heavy give it to my big brother to carry, it will do him good."

"So you'll be sleeping with the women, which means that Brenna will be sleeping with the men? And one of them owns the company, no? So he is probably very rich." The humor in Tyler's face faded.

"Brenna will be in her own tent."

"Aren't you worried she'll be afraid of the bears?"

"Brenna isn't afraid of anything. You should have seen her as a kid. She climbed everything we climbed, skied everything we skied. Wherever we were, she was right there, too."

And still is, Élise thought. *But you don't notice her.*

She wondered if the camping trip would change that.

But she didn't have time to dwell on that idea because she saw a flash of red and heard the throaty roar of the engine, announcing Sean's arrival.

Tyler put his hand on her shoulder and squeezed. "Are you all right with this plan?"

She was touched that he'd asked.

Touched that he cared.

It was yet another reason to love this place and the people in it.

"I'm fine with it. Why wouldn't I be?"

"Because my brother has his eyes on your sexy ass. If he tries anything, just punch him. He's a soft city boy. No muscle or backbone."

She knew that wasn't true. She'd seen those muscles.

It wasn't nerves that fluttered in her stomach, it was something else altogether.

But what was she afraid of?

Just because he'd carried her to bed, tucked her in and left her didn't change the way she felt about him. She was attracted, that was true, but it didn't go deeper than that.

She didn't want that and neither did he.

"I need to go. I'm already late for a meeting with a rep from a ski company. Good luck. If you need anything, call me."

He lifted a hand to Sean and strode off toward the outdoor store attached to the Center.

Sean parked the car and strode over to her carrying a large backpack.

"Hey, Dr. O'Neil—" Sam Stephens was circling on his new bike and Sean paused to talk to him, a smile on his face.

"Hey, yourself. Is that the birthday bike?"

"Sure is. I got the red one." He beamed with pride and rode it closer to Sean, who duly admired it.

"How's your vacation?"

"Awesome. Except we only have two days left. Today my dad and I are cycling on the forest trail. Mom is staying here with my baby sister."

"Sounds good. You be careful. Keep that helmet on. If you come off that bike you don't want to bang your head."

"I saw your car. Did you just come from Boston? Did you save any lives today, Dr. O'Neil?" The boy's eyes were big, round and full of admiration.

"Not yet." Smiling, Sean fastened the backpack. "But the day is young. Who knows what will happen."

Élise felt her throat close

He was so good with the child.

Sam pushed his bike closer to his hero. "Did you know he saved a man's life, Élise?"

"No." She was relieved her voice sounded normal. "No, I didn't know that, Sam. But he's a doctor, so I suppose that's his job."

"This wasn't his job. It didn't happen at the hospital. It happened on the mountains up there—" Sam waved an arm and the bike wobbled. "A man fell skiing. Broke every bone in his body." The boy described it with a ghoulish delight that made Élise wince.

"It wasn't quite every bone," Sean said mildly, but there was no deflecting Sam who was determined to tell Élise the whole story with as much embellishment as possible.

"There was blood all over the snow and people were screaming. The man was screaming. My dad was nearby and he saw it all. He said Dr. O'Neil skied over, cool as a Popsicle and he just took over. And he fixed him." Drunk on hero worship, Sam let his concentration lapse and his bike wobbled again. With lightning reflexes, Sean shot out a hand and steadied him before the boy could crash into the dirt.

"I didn't exactly 'fix' him. I stabilized him enough

to get him down the mountain to hospital so the doctors there could fix him."

"But if you hadn't done that, he would have died. Right there on the mountain."

"Maybe. Now put your feet down before you fall over." Sean was patient. "That's it. And be careful on that trail. It's rough in places."

"I'm fine." But the boy put his feet down. "What's the French word for blood, Élise?"

"Sang," she said. "But I hope you don't ever need that word."

"I might. When I grow up I'm going to be a surgeon like Dr. O'Neil. I'm going to save people. That would be really cool."

Checking that the boy was steady, Sean let go of the bike. "You'll be a great doctor, but that's enough talk of blood for one day. You're making my stomach turn."

Sam hovered, unwilling to let his hero go. "You see blood all the time."

"Just one more reason why I don't want to see it on my day off. You have a good day, Sam. Say hi to your mom and dad for me."

Sam cycled off, wobbling a little while Sean watched.

"I hope they're careful on that trail. He isn't that stable."

"He's adorable. And he adores you."

"He's been coming here for years and he's easily impressed. Are you okay with your backpack or is it too heavy?" He swung his own backpack onto his broad shoulders and secured the straps. Élise watched those muscles flex and ripple under his shirt.

For a moment she felt a little of Sam's admiration and then pushed it away. Physically Sean O'Neil was as close to masculine perfection as it was possible to get. That was a fact. It wasn't something to get emotional about.

And then she met his gaze and saw the heat in his eyes.

Raw chemistry slammed into her and she steadied herself, telling herself it was the backpack that was making her legs unstable.

"I'm fine. Let's walk."

"Tyler gave me the route he's planning to take. We'll follow it exactly and break where they are going to break."

"*Bien.* It sounds good to me."

"So did you ever do this in France? Hiking?"

"*Oui,* of course. In the mountains, with my mother." The memory squeezed her heart. "She used to cook in the winter for skiers. Occasionally we would go to Chamonix in the summer and she would cook for hikers and climbers. Chamonix has some of the best climbing and skiing in the Alps."

Sean led the way onto the trail that led from Snow Crystal up onto the Long Trail.

"We walked here all the time when we were kids. Gramps used to take us out camping and then leave us to find our own way home."

"That didn't worry your mother?"

"Probably. She worried about Tyler. He was the daredevil, always breaking something, so there was more reason to worry. Jackson and I looked out for each other. But Mom didn't have much say in it. Gramps ruled. Still does."

"He is looking much better. I hear the hospital appointment went well?"

"Yes."

"So did you clear the air? Did you have that conversation?"

"Not yet."

She felt a rush of frustration. "Why do you keep putting it off?"

"I was going to, but then he started going on about—"

"About what?"

"Nothing. Shit." He swore fluently as he sank ankle-deep in mud. "How the hell did I miss that?" They were in the heart of Vermont's backwoods, surrounded by tall trees and the scent of the forest. And they had the trail to themselves.

"City boy." Smiling, Élise stepped past him, sprang over the mud and landed on solid ground.

"You've been talking to Tyler." Still muttering, Sean scraped the worst of the mud off his boots. "Great. You're going to love sharing a tent with me tonight."

"We have two tents."

"One tent. Two people. Two tents is unnecessary weight."

"I thought there were two tents."

"Just the one. Is that a problem?"

"I prefer my own space."

"You can have your own space. The left-hand side of the tent is yours. Right-hand side is mine." The corner of his mouth flickered into a smile. "Relax. We're not moving in together. This is strictly a temporary arrangement."

And there was nothing she could do about it, was there? To make a fuss would give the situation too much weight and importance, so she forced herself to shrug and carry on up the trail.

The forest grew dense, the light dimmed and then finally the trail opened out, revealing incredible views of the Green Mountains.

"C'est incroyable." Élise stopped dead, drinking in the view, feeling the cooler air on her heated skin. "It's truly beautiful."

"Yeah, it really is." Sean eased the pack off her shoulders and put it down next to a rock. "Let's take a break and cook up some of that food you brought with you. What's for lunch? *Langoustines à la greque?* Coquilles Saint Jacques?"

"You are in the mountains."

"Nothing in the Green Mountain code book tells me I have to compromise my standards of eating just because I'm in the wild. Look—" he pointed as a bird soared above them "—red-tailed hawk."

She stared up at the sky. "You know this, how?"

"Gramps. He knows everything there is to know about the birds and wildlife around here. You want to know which mushrooms are safe to eat? He's the one to ask. And talking of eating, I'm starving." He reached into his pocket and removed a pair of sunglasses.

With the sunglasses catching the light, she could no longer see his eyes.

"I don't have mushrooms." Élise opened her backpack and removed the first pack from the cool bag. "Lunch is a picnic. Local Green Mountain ham served with my sourdough bread and fresh olives."

"If I found you mushrooms you could make some of those delicious pastries we ate the night of the party."

"And how would I cook it? You think I am carrying

around an oven? A simple life calls for simple food. But 'simple' does not mean poor quality." She handed him a neatly wrapped pack and he picked out a spot on a rock and sat down.

"When we did these trips as kids, Gramps didn't let us carry food. We had to eat what the forest provided." He tucked ham inside thick chunks of fresh bread. "We knew which berries were safe to pick and which ones would poison us. We knew how to catch fish from the river and how to light a fire to cook it that didn't burn the forest down. Jackson and Tyler used to do the foraging for food while I found the wood for the fire. In reality I found a quiet spot in the forest and sat down to read the book I'd sneaked into my backpack. The ham is good. Is there any more?"

She wondered if he realized how much he talked about his grandfather.

"Did your father go, too?" Élise handed him another slab of bread and slice of ham.

"He was usually working."

"You were very close to your father."

"Yes." He tore off a chunk of the bread. "I was."

She wondered if that had something to do with the row he'd had with his grandfather, but she didn't pursue it. If he wanted to talk about it, he'd talk and if he didn't—well, she understood more than most the need to keep some things close.

When they'd both finished eating they carried on up the trail, walking along the ridge with views of Lake Champlain.

"It is the prettiest view I've ever seen. Why haven't I been up here before?"

"Because my brother works you to the bone." He

shielded his eyes. "We're lucky it's a clear day. Often the visibility is poor up here. See the lake? That was discovered by your countryman, Samuel de Champlain. He was a French explorer and he sailed inland from the Atlantic Ocean and found this large freshwater lake."

"It is the most beautiful place. Where are we supposed to camp?"

"Walter's Ridge. We camped there all the time as kids. If you drop down the other side you can follow the river back home. It's the reason we never got lost."

They walked a little farther and then reached an open area with boulders and a spectacular view.

Sean eased the pack off his back and glanced around him. "This is good."

"So camping is allowed?"

"In some places. Part of the Long Trail crosses our land but we allow public access and camping in designated areas. No campfires. Campfires have the worst ecological impact of all camping practices. And we stay off the trails during mud season in late fall and early spring when the ground is saturated."

"So you own this land?"

"Yeah, it's part of Snow Crystal." He grinned. "I'm trying to impress you."

He did impress her. Not because they owned the land, but because he knew so much about it. Despite complaining when he stepped in something soft and smacking insects with his hand every few minutes, he'd proved himself to be tough and competent in the outdoors. He was skilled and efficient and in no time they had food cooking on the camping stove and the tent erected.

Élise sprinkled freshly grated Parmesan over a bowl

of pasta and handed it to him, trying not to think about the two sleeping bags laid side by side inside the two-man tent.

"Tomorrow you are catching fresh fish for our lunch."

"No way." He shuddered dramatically. "I am not wading in a stream and catching my own food. That's too primal. When I choose fish I prefer it to already be dead and on a restaurant menu, not swimming around my feet."

"Fresh is best."

"There is fresh and then there is still alive." He forked up the pasta and tasted it. "Mmm. This is spectacular, and not just because I didn't have to gut it before I ate it."

Laughing, she ate, too. "*Bien.* I think even the most inept corporate person will be able to manage this. It is good, no?"

"Far too good for them. I thought the idea was that we made them suffer a little so that they bonded together in the face of adversity."

"Is that what you and your brothers did when your grandfather left you out here to find your way home?"

Sean finished his food and helped himself to more. "It didn't feel like adversity to Tyler and Jackson. And not to me, either, I guess, although I would rather have been left in peace to read."

"You always liked books?"

"It was a way of escaping."

"Escaping from what?"

For a moment she thought he was going to make his usual glib, dismissive comment but he didn't.

Instead, he put his bowl down and stared off into space. "The pressure."

The atmosphere shifted. There was a serious note to his voice she hadn't heard before.

"What pressure?"

"For my grandfather the world begins and ends at Snow Crystal. He's never been able to figure out why not everyone feels the same way. It was the reason he put so much pressure on my father. The atmosphere was pretty tense when we were growing up."

"But your father loved it here?"

"He loved the place. He was an excellent skier. There are people around here who think he was almost as good as Tyler when he was in his teens. What he didn't love was the work. He wasn't built to be trapped behind a desk being nice to tourists. He just wanted to ski."

Exactly like Tyler, she thought. "Then why did he stay? Why not do a different job?"

"Love. Isn't that why most people end up compromising their dreams?"

"Do they?"

"Sure. It's logic if you think about it. How can two people possibly have the same goals? They can't, so it's obvious that at some point one of them is going to have to give up on their own ambitions to satisfy someone else. In my father's case, he was torn between his own wishes and the responsibility of running the family business. I guess the fact that my mother loved this place tipped the scales for him. A career in competitive skiing would have meant leaving her alone much of the time, traveling, living a life that was insecure and nomadic. It's not great for a marriage."

Élise thought about Tyler's reputation. "No."

"And it would have meant Snow Crystal being run by someone outside the family. He couldn't do that to Gramps, so he stayed and did a job he didn't want to do. And the resentment ate him up."

"He talked to you about it?"

"All the damn time." Sean leaned forward and turned off the stove. "He used to call me, mostly late at night, when Mom had gone to bed and he was on his own drinking in the kitchen, staring at a mountain of debts and paperwork he had no idea how to handle. He'd call me and he'd say the same thing every time, 'Stay away from this place. Never give up on your dream.'"

"Does Jackson know he used to call you?"

"There was no reason to tell him." He reached into his bag and pulled out water. "His business was going well in Europe, he was having a blast, making money, living the dream. It was all blue skies for him and I didn't see any reason to put a cloud in that sky."

He'd been protecting his brother. Carrying the weight by himself. "You didn't tell anyone?"

"No. And then Dad was killed and I wished I had. If I'd said something sooner maybe we could have done something."

"His car spun on the ice. How could you have prevented that?"

He turned the water bottle in his hands. "Dad was traveling because he couldn't stand to be at home. He wanted to be where the snow was so he went to New Zealand. Gramps wouldn't leave him alone. He pressured him to spend more time here, and the more he put the pressure on, the less Dad wanted to be here. He was already giving it everything he could." His voice was raw. "At the funeral, I lost it."

"This was the row you had? It was because of your father?"

"I blamed Gramps." He rubbed his fingers over his forehead and pulled a face. "I accused him of putting too much pressure on Dad. I said it was his fault. He lost it, too, and told me I should have been at home helping. He said if I'd been here, there wouldn't have been so much pressure. He told me I didn't have a clue what was really going on. Neither of us has mentioned it since."

Two men, both too stubborn to say they were sorry.

But it explained a lot. It explained the tension between the two men. It explained why Walter was so defensive with Sean and why Sean still hadn't dealt with it.

"You still blame him. You're still angry."

"Yeah, I guess part of me is and I hate that. That isn't the way I want to feel." He stared at his hands. "I need to apologize because obviously Gramps wasn't responsible for Dad's death and I should never have said that, not even in the black misery of grief, but that doesn't change the fact I'm still angry at the pressure he puts on everyone."

She swallowed. "And your brothers don't know why you stopped coming home?"

"They didn't notice much of a difference. Work has pretty much kept me away for the past few years and when we were together it was usually around the holidays and there were so many of us the rift wasn't so obvious. When Jackson called to tell me about Gramps I knew I had to come home, but I was pretty sure he wouldn't want to see me. And I was right. The moment I showed my face at the hospital he told me to go back to Boston."

"But not because he didn't want you there." Her heart ached for him. For both of them. "It's been two years. You must talk to him."

"Maybe." He stood up, his mouth a grim line. "But he isn't easy to talk to and I don't trust myself not to say the wrong thing and make it worse. Being home just brings it all back. The pressure. The anger. The guilt. It's all there in a great churning mess."

She stood up, too. "It's grief," she said quietly. "Grief is a messy, horrible thing. Guilt and anger are all part of it. You think the emotions should be clean and straightforward, but they're not. Believe me, I know. I felt it all when my mother died. You should talk to him. I don't think it matters if you say the 'wrong' thing. What matters is that you're talking."

"What do I say? The truth is he did put pressure on my father. There's no getting around that. But I shouldn't have lost my temper and I definitely shouldn't have blamed him. And yeah, I regret it. There isn't a day when I don't wish I could pull those words back." He rubbed his hand over his jaw and gave her a lopsided smile. "I've never told anyone that before. Here I am, baring my soul. I guess that's what happens when you're out in the wilderness."

The air was still, the sun dropping down behind the mountaintops sending a rosy glow over the peaks and the forest.

"We all have things we regret in life. Things we wish we hadn't done. Things we wish we hadn't said. Your grandfather loves you, Sean. He really loves you. You have to try and fix it."

"So do you have things you regret?"

Her heart thudded a little faster. A little harder. "Of course."

"Name one."

She pulled the pan away from the camping stove, thinking of Pascal and wishing she wasn't. She'd erased him from her life. It was just a shame she couldn't erase him from her thoughts.

"My mother taught me to think of mistakes as a lesson. She used to say *'If there is a lesson to be learned learn it and move on. Everything else is just experience.'*"

"So what was your biggest lesson?"

Élise stared into the stove for a long moment, feeling vulnerable and exposed. "We should probably go inside the tent before the insects start biting."

"They've already bitten. Hey—" He closed his fingers over her arm, his hand strong and comforting. "You know all my innermost secrets. At least give me one of yours. What was your biggest lesson, sweetheart? I want to know."

The endearment, so unexpected, knocked the breath from her lungs.

"My biggest lesson?" She felt his touch through layers of clothing and the softness of his tone penetrated the layers of defenses she'd wrapped around herself. "There are two. The first is never to delay saying sorry to someone you love because you may lose the chance, and the second is that for me, love is not possible. And now we need to get some sleep."

SEAN PACKED AWAY the evidence of their meal, wondering what was wrong with him.

He wasn't the type to talk about his feelings. Hell,

most of the time he didn't even *think* about his feelings. He was too busy to dwell on should have, would have and what if. But tonight, sitting outside with Élise, it had all spilled out. He'd said far more than he'd intended to and she'd listened quietly, allowing him to talk.

But still she'd said nothing about herself.

Just enough to tell him she'd been hurt. Badly hurt. *For me, love isn't possible.*

She hadn't said "I don't believe in love" or even "I don't want love."

He stood, staring at the mountains, analyzing the facts at his disposal.

He'd assumed her lack of interest in a relationship had been linked to her career goals and ambition. He worked with plenty of women who were unwilling to compromise their careers for a family so it hadn't occurred to him to question it.

What was it Jackson had said?

You have no idea what you're dealing with.

Swearing softly, Sean dropped to his haunches and finished removing all evidence of their presence.

Leave no trace. Wasn't that what his grandfather had taught them?

You're a guest in the forest, Sean, and guests don't leave a mess behind when they leave.

Life, unfortunately, wasn't so clean and tidy. It left plenty of traces. Plenty of mess. And clearly life hadn't just left a trace on Élise. It had left deep scars.

He glanced across at the tent, but there was no movement. No words encouraging him to join her.

Once he'd cleared the site to his satisfaction he strode to the tent, pulled off his boots and ducked inside.

Élise was already in her sleeping bag, curled up in

a ball. Her body language sent a clear message that the conversation was over.

"Is this the penthouse? Room service? Air-conditioning, infinity pool and 360-degree views?" He tried to remove his jacket, a task hampered by the width of his shoulders and the small tent. "There is no way this is a two-man tent. Tyler always did have a sick sense of humor. Still, at least we won't be cold."

Something about the way she lay, huddled down and hiding, tugged at his heart. He wanted to comfort her and he didn't understand it because comforting women definitely wasn't on his list of skills. Comfort was Jackson's domain.

Aware that he was stepping over a line he didn't usually cross, Sean stripped off his shirt and trousers and stretched out next to her. "I'm feeling naked here."

"Then keep your clothes on." Her voice was muffled and she didn't lift her head.

"Not that sort of naked. The sort of naked where I just spilled my soul and you gave me nothing in return." He shifted closer to her. "Why isn't love possible for you?"

"Good night, Sean."

"I hate it when you do that. You did it to me the night of the party. You just shut down a conversation when you don't want to talk. It's the verbal equivalent of slamming a door in someone's face."

"I'm tired."

"You're not tired. You just don't want to talk about your feelings. But I wish you would. You listened to me. I'd like to listen to you." He saw her shoulders tense and took a gamble. "At least give me his name and address. Then I can send Tyler to punch him. I'd go myself, but I don't want to ruin another shirt. And if I use my fists, it messes up my operating schedule, I'm sure you understand. Lives to save and all that."

"Are you ever going to go to sleep?" But this time there was laughter in her voice and he felt a rush of relief.

"First we have to have the whole wilderness-bonding thing. Am I doing it the wrong way? I've never done this before so I'm bound to make some mistakes."

She rolled over to face him. "Let me get this straight. You, Sean O'Neil, master of the superficial, want me to spill my innermost feelings?"

He knew a brief moment of panic and then reminded himself he dealt with blood and guts on a daily basis. He could handle emotions if he had to. He just had to tread carefully, and not do or say the wrong thing. "Yes. I want to know why you don't want a relationship. You told me you learned a lesson." He softened his voice. "What lesson did you learn, Élise? Why is love not possible for you?"

He thought she wasn't going to respond but then she sat up, the sleeping bag still snuggled around her middle. She was wearing a loose T-shirt and it drifted down over her arm, exposing her shoulder. There was something about the curve between her neck and that bare, slender shoulder that made her seem even more vulnerable.

"I am not a good judge of character. I am very emotional. It blinds me." She hauled the T-shirt up and it immediately slid down again. "Sometimes I make very, very big mistakes. I have too much passion."

After their encounter in the forest he was ready to disagree with that.

But it was obvious to him now that she'd loved some-one and he'd let her down.

It explained the contrast between heat and cool. "Is there any such thing as too much passion?"

"The problem with passion," she said softly, "is that it is all too easy to mistake it for love. It blinds you to lies. You believe what you want to believe and you give your all. And the risk of giving your all, is that you lose everything."

"It was him, wasn't it? Pascal Laroche." He wondered why it had taken him so long to work it out. "He was the one."

"I was eighteen. He was thirty-two. Older. Very attractive. I'd been working for him for four months when he kissed me for the first time. At first I didn't think he could possibly be interested in me. I was so naive. So unlike the women he usually dated. I said no, without realizing that for him 'no' was the incentive he needed to start the chase. Pascal was the most competitive person I have ever met. In the kitchen he was a genius, admired by everyone. That admiration was his fuel. It drove him. He pursued me relentlessly and I fell in love. You are wondering why, but he could be so charming and I suppose I was flattered. I loved him with every part of myself and I truly believed he loved me back. That was when I learned that wanting something doesn't make it happen. My mother was worried, but I wouldn't listen. She was always overprotective and usually I tolerated that, but this time I reacted in a bad way. Rebelled."

"Every teenager rebels. You should talk to my mother about some of the stuff Tyler did. He got a girl pregnant. That was a pretty rough time, I can tell you.

The Carpenter family wanted to kill Tyler. Gramps still can't drive past their apple farm without growling. He never liked Janet."

"But your family stuck together. When my mother became pregnant, her parents refused to have anything more to do with her. My grandparents never even wanted to see me. As a result my mother and I were very close. I was her only family and she mine." She paused for a moment and then carried on. "When I got the job at Chez Laroche she was very proud of me. And then when she met Pascal and saw how things were, how he was, she was frightened. She could see instantly what sort of man he was. She tried to warn me but I wouldn't listen."

"That sounds like a fairly typical teenage response to me."

"It was the first time in our lives that we argued. She would yell at me and threaten me and I would yell back. I can see now she was at her wits' end, not knowing how to control me but to me it made me want to go home even less."

It was all too easy to see parallels with his own situation and Sean shifted uncomfortably.

Hadn't he felt exactly the same way after the row with his grandfather?

"You were being pulled in two directions."

"I stayed out at night and wouldn't tell her where I was because I knew she would try and stop me going. All I cared about was Pascal. I was blinded. Dizzy with it. I was in love and I was dismissive of all her warnings. What could she possibly know about love? She got pregnant with me when she was eighteen and she admitted she was crazy in love with the man who was my father. She told me that loving like that blinds you to how a person really is. You see what you want to see, and believe what you want to believe. She told me I had to end the relationship and get another job."

"You didn't."

"No. I was in love with him. I didn't want it to end and I certainly wasn't about to listen to my mother. We had a horrible, screaming row and I told her I was moving in with Pascal." Her hand gripped the edge of the sleeping bag, her knuckles white. "She was on her way to the restaurant to reason with me when she was hit by a cab. I had a call from the hospital. She was—how do you call it?—dead on arrival."

Sean closed his eyes and then shifted across the tent and pulled her into his arms.

Suddenly it all made sense to him. The reason she was so desperate for him to fix things with his grandfather. The emphasis she placed on family. Her reluctance to ever allow herself to fall in love again.

"That wasn't your fault. None of it was your fault."

"If I hadn't moved in with Pascal she wouldn't have been crossing the *Boulevard Saint Germain* at that moment." Her voice was muffled against his chest and she sat rigid in his arms. Inflexible. "I never had a chance to say goodbye. I never had a chance to say I was sorry. Nothing. The last words we both spoke were angry ones and I have to live with that for the rest of my life."

"But she loved you and she knew you loved her."

"Perhaps. I do not know. Back then I was such a mess maybe she didn't love me. And I didn't say that I loved her, so perhaps she didn't know that, either. I will never know. And afterward, I fell apart. I didn't know what to do. I had no one. No one except Pascal.

He took care of everything, including me. I leaned on him. I took his kindness as evidence that my mother had been wrong about him, but of course, she wasn't." She pulled away a little and pushed her hair away from her face. "This story has a horrible inevitability to it, doesn't it? Are you sure you want me to carry on?"

Part of him didn't. He sensed what might be coming and it sickened him. "Yes."

"The first time I caught him with another woman was the day after our wedding."

"You married him?" That he hadn't expected and he struggled to hide his shock. Listening was like watching a runaway train, knowing that disaster was imminent but having no way of stopping it.

"I was in love with him, so for me that was the obvious conclusion. I dreamed of building a family with him, of having children together and maybe buying a place in the countryside outside Paris. It is funny, no? You are thinking I watched too much Disney growing up."

"Sweetheart—"

"The signs were there, but I ignored them. I saw only the parts of him I wanted to see. His genius. His charm. I told myself his temper was natural because he was so brilliant it was understandable he would be frustrated with those less brilliant. And he was very attentive after my mother died. Coping with that loss was terrifying. Without him I think I might have died, too. I was so heartbroken, so lonely, that when he proposed to me I didn't think twice. It was like being swept down a raging river and suddenly being offered a stick to hold on to. It was grab it or drown. Looking back, I can see my neediness fed his ego. I made him feel important and feeling important was essential to him. It was another type of adulation and he fed on that. He was not interested in a relationship of equals. Always, he had to be the superior one."

His gut clenched.

A lonely, grieving girl at the mercy of a narcissistic bastard. "You don't have to talk about this. I'm sorry I pushed you to tell me."

"On the day after the wedding, when I caught him with the other woman he told me it was a mistake. A mistake! As if two people could slip on a wet floor and land like that." She rolled her eyes and even managed a laugh but Sean wasn't close to laughing.

"You forgave him?"

"Yes, because the alternative was too brutal to confront." She shook her head. "It shames me to admit that I gave him another chance, but I was very vulnerable and admitting that my mother might have been right was just too painful at that time. Of course, it didn't end there. It never does, does it? He was famous. There were always women. The fact that he was married to me made no difference. He had a continuous string of affairs, sometimes more than one at the same time. And always the endless lies. Everything he said was a lie. One night in the middle of a terrible row I told him I wanted a divorce. That was the first time he hit me."

"Christ, no." Sickness mingled with the anger. "Oh, baby—"

Why the hell hadn't he guessed?

He didn't know what to say. *What was he supposed to say to that?*

"Afterward he was sorry. He said he was so desperate at the thought of losing me, he'd flipped a little bit.

Just as his affairs were all accidents, so this was an accident, too. It was my fault for provoking him. Pascal never took responsibility for anything he did. Everything was always someone else's fault." Her voice was flat. Matter-of-fact. "He told me it would never happen again. He was just stressed. It had been a very bad night in the restaurant, three members of staff off sick and lots of pressure. I was shocked, of course. No one had ever hit me before. My mother never hit me. You read about these things, but when it happens to you it's scarily easy to listen to the excuses. And I told myself everyone makes mistakes. I'd made plenty myself so I was very tolerant of mistakes in others. And I knew that if I'd left him, I would have lost not just my home but my job. And I actually did love my job. Some of the customers were regulars. Pascal worked long hours, I was lonely and they were the closest thing I had to family."

Diners in her restaurant, family?

He thought of his own family. Tight-knit. Infuriating. Always there. Always.

"It wasn't just that one time. He hit you again?" He forced the question through clenched teeth. Thinking about her coping with it alone made him ache.

"Yes. And that time I did walk out."

He wanted to cheer but he could tell from the look on her face that the story wasn't finished. "Where did you go?"

"I got a job in a tiny little place on the Left Bank. It was low-profile. Under the radar. I thought Pascal would be relieved I had gone and wouldn't bother following. I was wrong. Turned out that me leaving him was the ultimate humiliation. As punishment for taking me on, he put the owner of the restaurant out of business. And when he came to break the good news, he told me that I would never get a job in Paris again and I would be forced to come back to him. And then he hit me again. And I'm forever grateful that he did because Jackson was in the restaurant that night."

"Jackson?"

She gave a soft smile. "He'd come in three times that week because he liked my cooking. He'd been telling me about his business, about the hotels and the skiing. He was the one who found me in the street outside, bleeding and in a state. He took me to the hospital, reported Pascal to the police and then took me back to his hotel. I slept in his bed and he slept in the chair."

"Was Pascal arrested?"

"Yes. But he hired a lawyer and his PR people hushed it up. Told some story that the media believed. The next morning Jackson offered me a job, cooking for him. To begin with I said no, because I didn't want to risk bringing trouble to him after all he had done, but he refused to leave Paris without me."

"Good." Not for the first time in his life, Sean had reason to admire his twin brother. "So you went to Switzerland."

"Yes. Jackson gave me that opportunity. He saved me. I owe him everything. And I have not been back to Paris since, even though the apartment I shared with my mother is still there. And sometimes it makes me sad because once I loved the city so much, but after my mother and Pascal—" She shrugged. "For me the place is poisoned. I can never go back. It would be too painful. I can only think how much I let my mother down."

Finally everything made sense. All of it. Her devotion to his brother. Her loyalty. Her unwavering love for his family.

And her reason for not wanting a relationship.

It wasn't that she didn't want love. She was desperate for a relationship and a family of her own, but she was too scared of getting it wrong to trust her judgment again.

She was too scared of losing everything.

She'd made his family her own because that way she could have all that without risking her heart.

And he understood why Jackson had wanted him to stay clear of her.

His brother was right. He was entirely the wrong sort of man for a woman like her.

"Pascal Laroche might be a brilliant chef but he's obviously a pathetic excuse for a human being. I want to operate on him without an anesthetic." With a supreme effort of will, he let her go. "Have you had any relationships since him?"

"You know I have."

"I'm not talking about sex. I'm talking about intimacy."

There was just enough light left for him to see the color streak across her cheeks. "I don't want that."

"What about just having some fun? Dinner in a restaurant? A night at the opera?"

"People do that when they're dating and want to get to know someone. I don't want that. I can't have that. Love blinded me. I saw what I wanted to see. I gave all of myself, everything. I won't do it again."

But she'd done it with his family. She'd taken that love that she was too afraid to give to a man, and she'd given it unreservedly to the O'Neils. She'd found somewhere she felt safe and she'd hidden herself there, wrapped in the warmth of his family.

He ached for her. "It's the reason you walked away after the party."

"I don't usually spend two nights with a man. It shook me."

It had shaken him, too.

The desire to haul her back into his arms was overwhelming but he knew that would be the wrong thing to do. Exercising willpower he didn't know he possessed, he slid down inside his sleeping bag. She did the same and the wriggling treated him to a glimpse of shoulder, a hint of breast and a smile, complete with dimple.

"It is a good job it was you on this trip and not Tyler. If I'd said all that to him I would have killed him dead. He would rather wrestle a bear than listen to a woman unload her emotions."

But they both knew she never would have said any of that to Tyler. She'd never said it to anyone before.

For some reason, knowing that warmed him. "Get some sleep. You need to rest. If a bear comes in the night I expect you to protect me so you need energy."

"You're still trying to persuade me you don't know how to survive in the wilderness? It's too late for that. I know the truth."

"Maybe you don't. Aren't you scared the tent will collapse on you in the night?"

"You already know what scares me. I just told you." She lay facing him, snuggled inside the sleeping bag. "What about you? What scares you, Dr. O'Neil?"

The thought of hurting her.

She was lying there, her gaze fixed on his face, waiting for his answer.

"What scares me? The thought of ruining my favorite suit. Get some rest." He closed his eyes even though he knew he wouldn't sleep. Not now. His head was full of what she'd told him and he lay there in silence, thinking about how her life must have been and wondering how she'd managed to come through it so strong and whole.

CHAPTER FOURTEEN

ÉLISE WOKE WRAPPED in her sleeping bag with the feeling of exhaustion that followed an outpouring of emotion. She hadn't cried, and that was good, but still she felt drained and empty.

And vulnerable.

What had possessed her to tell Sean so much? She'd never told anyone the whole story before, not even Jackson.

Merde, she'd shared her innermost secrets. Her feelings. Her emotions. *Her life.*

All of it.

She'd held nothing back, not one single thing and he hadn't done anything to stop her talking.

There had been a moment when she'd thought he was going to kiss her. Right after she'd finished talking there had been a look in those lazy blue eyes that had made her wish her rule was three nights, not one. If he'd reached for her then, she wasn't sure her willpower would have held out. Instead, he'd slid into his own sleeping bag and hadn't touched her.

Knowing his sex drive as she did, that could only mean one thing.

She'd scared him off. He'd thought she was like him, more interested in work than relationships. Now she knew the truth he'd be keeping his distance. She should be relieved about that, because the alternative would have her breaking even more of her rules.

She sat up, pushed her hair away from her face and breathed.

Shaken by her own feelings and confused about his, she pulled on her clothes and emerged from the tent to find him cooking breakfast on the lightweight stove.

"I found breakfast in your magic bag. Homemade English muffins and bacon. Good choice." He flipped the bacon, defusing any tension in the atmosphere with an easy smile. His hair shone blue-black in the early morning light and his jaw was dark with stubble. Despite appearances, he was as comfortable out here in the wilds as he was in an expensive restaurant.

Her stomach was knotted so tightly she doubted she could eat a thing. The confidences of the night before had unsettled her in a way sex never had. Ridiculous though it seemed, that conversation was the most intimate thing they'd shared.

She knelt by the stove and watched the sun rise over the mountaintops. "What time is it? Are we in a hurry?"

"We're on Tyler's schedule and he's a slave driver. His instructions were that breakfast had to be cooked at sunrise. It also means we do the toughest part of the hike before it gets warm and muggy. He thinks his group of unfit businessmen will be whining by lunchtime so the aim is to get down to the frozen waterfall by then. That's our next picnic spot."

He was speaking as if nothing had happened. As if nothing had changed.

"Frozen waterfall?"

"That's what we call it because you can climb it in the winter." He tipped the toasted muffins onto a plate, added bacon and handed it to her. "Obviously it's not frozen now."

"It is where your father proposed to your mother. She told me about it once."

"Yeah, that's the place." He stared at his own plate for a moment and then started eating. "This was a good choice. Even Brenna can cook bacon."

They ate, cleared up, packed away all their food so that they didn't attract wildlife and hiked at a steady pace, following the river back toward Snow Crystal. They stopped at the waterfall, now in full flow, ate lunch and then continued on to the point where their path intersected one of the resort's mountain bike trails.

They'd barely started down the trail when they heard shouts.

"Qu'est-ce que c'est?" Élise wrinkled her nose and listened.

"Kids." Sean paused, head tilted to one side. "Someone having fun?"

"It didn't sound like a child."

Even as she said it, a man appeared farther down the path, waving his arms.

Élise squinted. "Isn't that Sam's dad?"

"Yes. Something is wrong." Without bothering to take the backpack off his back, Sean sprinted down the trail toward the man and Élise followed as quickly as she could with the backpack weighing her down.

As she caught up with them she saw little Sam lying still on the ground, blood staining his trousers and soaking into the path, the wheel of his new red bike buckled and lying at a strange angle.

She felt a moment of pure panic. He looked so small and defenseless.

"Oh, mon dieu—"

"His bike hit a rock and he came off. He's hurt his leg." His father was pressing ineffectually on the leg but blood seeped around his fingers. "I can't stop the bleeding. It's spurting everywhere. I shouldn't have left him but I needed to get help. Christ, make it stop. *Make it stop.*"

"It's an artery." Cool and calm, Sean swung his backpack off his shoulders and squatted down next to Sam.

The boy's lips were blue. Mud streaked his cheeks and his hair was matted where he'd fallen. "I broke my new bike. I broke it."

"We're going to fix your bike so it's good as new." Sean took over from the father who was shaking so badly he couldn't maintain pressure on the wound. "And we're going to fix you, too."

The boy's eyes fluttered closed. "I feel weird. Swimmy."

"That's nothing to worry about. You're going to be just fine." Sean placed his hands above the wound and pressed, steady and reassuring. "Élise?"

"Yes." She wanted to do something, but she felt helpless. Useless. Just as she had when Walter had had his heart attack. Every part of her was shaking, her hands, her knees— "What can I do? Tell me and I will do it." *Just don't let him die, don't let him die.*

"There's a first-aid kit in the top of my pack. I need it. And then call Jackson."

"There's no signal." The boy's father was frantic, his face gray. "I've already tried."

Fumbling, Élise found the first-aid kit and pulled it out.

"Is that my blood on the ground?" Sam's voice was wobbly and faint. "It looks like a lot."

Élise was silently in agreement with Sam. It was a whole lot of blood. More than she'd ever seen in her life.

"It's nothing." Sean's voice was steady and reassuring. "A small amount of blood can make a whole lot of mess. Haven't you ever got blood on your T-shirt? Man, that stuff spreads everywhere." He gestured for Élise to open the pack. "There's plenty more where that came from, don't you worry."

"Mom will be mad at me for getting it on my jacket."

"She's not going to be mad. She's just going to be pleased you're okay."

Sam's eyes were wide and desperate. "I feel sort of numb and everything is far away."

"I'm right here, Sam, and you're going to be fine. I'm right here with you and I'm not going anywhere."

"Cool." His voice was faint. "You save lives all the time, right?"

Sean's expression didn't change. "All the time. All in a day's work. You don't need to worry."

"I didn't see the rock."

"Happens to the best of us, buddy. Get Tyler to take his shirt off for you one day. There's a story to go with every scar. It's going to give you something to boast about when you're back at school. Impress the girls." His fingers were slippery with Sam's blood but he didn't release his grip. "Élise, use those scissors to cut off his trousers."

She picked up the scissors and worked through the soaked fabric, cutting through the mud and leaves that had stuck to the boy's clothes, all the time aware of the father's anguish as he tried again and again to get a signal.

"The phone is useless." He held it above his head and waved it around desperately. "Nothing. Christ, don't let him die, don't let him die—"

Élise saw fear flare in the little boy's eyes and knew he'd heard.

"No one is going to die." Icy-calm, Sean gestured with his head. "Try farther down the path, toward the waterfall. It's patchy, but I've been lucky there before. Go."

Sam's father hesitated, clearly torn between leaving his son and making that all-important phone call.

"I don't want to leave him."

"We're fine here. Trust me."

Élise swallowed. She trusted him. Right at that moment if he'd told her to jump off a cliff, she would have jumped without question. And Sam's dad clearly felt the same way because he seemed to pull himself together.

Responding to the authority in Sean's voice, he nodded. "I'll—I'll be back in just a minute, Sam. You just hang in there. Dr. O'Neil has you safe. He's going to fix you up. You're going to be fine, son. Just fine." It was obvious he didn't believe it and looking at the volume of blood and the blue tinge to the little boy's lips, Élise wasn't sure she believed it, either. But she believed Sean was doing everything that could be done, and if he had any doubts, he wasn't showing them.

"Open the sterile pads. All of them. And then give me your scarf." His instructions were clear and concise but she stared at him, panic clouding her thinking. All she could concentrate on was how there was so much blood for a very little boy. How could he possibly survive it?

"My scarf?"

"I'm going to need a bandage. Maybe a tourniquet." His tone cut through her panic. "Do it."

She followed instructions because her own brain wasn't working and somehow, despite fumbling and shaking, she opened the pads and gave him her scarf.

"Right, let's see what we're dealing with here. So how was the trail before you hit the rock? Were you having fun on your new bike? I wish I had a bike like that." He kept talking to the boy, keeping it light as he worked, cleaning away blood so that he could get a close-up view of the damage. For a brief second blood spurted upward like a fountain but then he took the sterile pads and pressed down hard, bound it in place with a firm pressure bandage and secured it with Élise's scarf. His fingers were slippery with blood, his shirt stained with it. But the man who complained when he got mud on his shoes and dust on his trousers didn't seem to notice the mess. All his attention was on the child who seemed to be fading under his hands. "Élise, get me a knife or a fork from our pack."

Her hands were shaking as much as her knees. "Which? Knife or fork?"

"Either. I just need something to tighten this. Pressure isn't enough."

"Am I going to die?" Sam's eyes were fixed on Sean's face. "My dad said I'm going to die."

"You're not going to die, Sam. You're going to feel pretty rough for a few days, but you're going to be just fine."

"Why would he say that if it isn't true?"

"Because he was panicking. You're his boy. He loves you." He moved the scarf and tightened it. "It's hard to see someone you love in pain."

"But you're not panicking, right?"

"Nothing to panic about." Sean looked almost bored. "You've cut your leg, that's all. No big drama."

Élise looked at the blood and the child and decided she never wanted to witness Sean's idea of drama.

Sam clutched Sean's arm. "I heard you say it's an artery. That's bad, right?"

"Well, if we leave it, it's bad. But we're not leaving it. We've stopped it bleeding and now we're going to get you to a hospital and the doctors there will fix it."

"Will you fix it? I want you to be the one to fix it."

"There are doctors who are better trained at this sort of thing than I am. If you'd broken your leg, that would be different. Then I'd be your man."

Élise would want him to be her man. If she were in trouble, she'd want that.

Suddenly she understood his total commitment to his work. He was gifted. Focused. When he went to work in the morning he saved lives. What did she do? She cooked pastry. No wonder he hadn't understood that she was stressed about a delay to the opening of the Boathouse. What did the café matter compared to the life of a child? What did anything matter compared to that?

He did something few other people could do. He had skills few other people had. It was right that he put them to good use.

Sam's eyes closed and then he forced them open again. "Will you come to the hospital with me, Dr. O'Neil?"

"I'll be there."

"Will you stay with me the whole time, even when I'm asleep?"

"I'll stay with you the whole time." Sean didn't hesitate. "I'll be there when you go to sleep and I'll be there when you wake up."

"Do you promise? Pinky swear?"

"I don't know what pinky swear is, but I won't leave you. That's a promise."

"Cool." Sam finally allowed his eyes to close, his eyelashes the only color in his ashen face.

Élise swallowed down the lump in her throat.

She'd never seen this side of Sean before. Or maybe she had. Hadn't he been the same with his grandfather? Cool and calm while everyone else was panicking? And last night, when she'd spilled all her secrets, he'd been cool and calm then, too.

And after the party, when he could easily have walked away, he'd cared enough to come after her. Cared enough to carry her to bed and tuck the covers around her.

"I got a signal." Sam's father arrived back, red in the face from running. "They're coming. They're coming right now. They reckon five minutes. Is that too long? How long do we have before— Oh, God, is he unconscious? That's bad, right?" He was shaking with fear and shock, sobbing with it, and Sean's gaze flickered to Élise and she understood his meaning immediately.

He couldn't deal with the father and the boy.

He wanted Sam's father away so that he couldn't make things worse.

"We'll walk down the trail and meet them." Almost stumbling because her own legs were wobbly, she took his arm and steered him gently away. "It will speed things up if they see us. Sean has this under control. Come with me."

This time Sean didn't look up and she didn't expect him to.

He was trying to save the boy and nothing, *nothing* was more important than that.

And Élise knew that if the child died it wouldn't be because Sean O'Neil hadn't done everything he could.

"BOTH HIS PARENTS are here now. The surgeon is just talking to them and they'll be able to see Sam real soon. I guess you can go, Dr. O'Neil. You're the hero of the hour." The nurse was pretty, her smile interested.

Sean didn't even notice. His eyes were on the child who lay pale and still in the bed. It had been the longest six hours of his life. "I'll stay until he wakes up."

"You don't have to." The nurse eyed him. "Do you want to change? Your clothes are covered in blood. I could put them in a bag and lend you some scrubs."

"I'm fine." What the hell did it matter what he was wearing? The boy had almost died and she was worrying about a few bloodstains on his clothes?

"I have a place near here if you want somewhere private to wash and change."

As invitations went, it couldn't have been more blatant.

If he'd had more energy he would have laughed.

Who did she think he was? A superhero?

After the emotional pressure of the past six hours, the crazy ambulance ride, the life-or-death rush to the operating room, if someone showed him a bed he'd fall asleep instantly. The whole of the Boston ballet could have danced naked across the room and he wouldn't have noticed.

He was wrecked.

And then he saw Élise standing in the doorway and his heart lifted.

But instead of the warm look that should have followed the night they'd spent together and the drama they'd shared, her eyes were blank. The expression on her pretty face was frozen. Those green eyes that could start a fire with just a look, as cold as ice.

"I came to tell you that Sam's parents are here." Her tone was as cool as her eyes. "I drove them. They weren't safe behind the wheel. His mother is naturally very anxious. The doctor is talking to them now."

"Right." What the hell was wrong with her? She must be in shock. This whole business with Sam had probably scared her to death. It had certainly terrified him.

"I have to go back now. The restaurant is full this evening and I can't leave them without help."

"I'd offer to pitch in but I'm going to be tied up here for a while."

"Of course you are." Her smile was thin. "I don't suppose you'll be able to get away for quite some time."

He assumed she was referring to Sam. "Yeah. Well, I might see you later."

"I doubt it. I'll be working and then you'll be back in Boston. Good night, Sean."

She took a last long look at Sam and for a moment her gaze softened. Then she turned and walked out, closing the door quietly behind her.

He had a feeling he was missing something, but he was too tired to work out what it was.

ÉLISE COOKED, SMILED, served almost a hundred people and tried not to think of Sean tangled up with the pretty nurse.

She'd seen the smile.

Heard the invitation.

The invitation he hadn't refused.

A week ago it wouldn't have bothered her. Now?

"Merde." She tugged a pan out of one of the cupboards, sending others crashing.

It didn't bother her now, either. He was a free agent and he could sleep with whomever he wanted. So what if he'd pretended to be all kind and sensitive and it had all been a sham? That wasn't what upset her. No, what really upset her was that he'd broken his solemn promise to Sam.

He'd promised Sam he'd stay until he woke up but it was obvious that promise had come with conditions and one of those had been not getting a better offer from a sexy-looking blonde nurse who had no sense of timing or appropriate behaviour.

So he lied when it suited him. Why was she surprised? She'd spent long enough with a man who had done just that to know what people were capable of.

She slammed a pan onto the burner and saw Poppy jump.

"Everything okay, Chef?"

"Everything is just fine." She poured in oil and waited for it to heat before adding garlic and ginger. "Couldn't be better."

She didn't care about herself. She had no interest in whether Sean O'Neil slept with the whole damn female staff in the hospital, all she cared about was that he'd broken his promise to little Sam.

How could he do that?

How could he lie to a child?

That was the lowest of the low. There was no excuse.

"Are you *sure* you're all right?" Poppy was by her shoulder, looking anxious. "It's just that you're burning the garlic, Chef."

Élise glanced down at the pan.

It was true. The garlic was dark and had that bitter aroma that offended her sense of smell.

She'd burned it, like an amateur. It was years since she'd done that.

With an exclamation of disgust she pulled the pan off the heat and stepped away, hands raised. "I should not be cooking tonight, I am too upset."

"Of course you're upset." Her voice soothing, Poppy reached across and switched off the burner. "You've had a traumatic day. We're all worried about Sam. I've been asked a million times how he is. Sometimes you think people are only interested in whether their steak is perfectly cooked, but then something like this happens and you realize they do care. Restores your faith in human nature to be honest."

Did it? Her faith in human nature had been shattered years before and nothing she'd seen today had done anything to restore it.

It was like Pascal all over again.

Poppy nudged her out of the way and started with a fresh pan. "Go and talk to the guests, Chef. We're fine here. I've got everything in hand."

Talk to the guests.

Élise blinked. Breathed. Yes, she'd do that.

And she'd stop thinking about Sean.

If anything she should be pleased he'd shown his true

colors. For a moment when he'd saved Sam's life she'd been ready to lay down her own life for him. She'd been in awe. Totally overwhelmed by how amazing he was.

But she had no admiration for a man who broke promises to a child.

She wandered between the tables, a smile fixed on her face, her mind elsewhere.

"Any news on little Sam, Élise?" A family staying in one of the lodges looked at her with somber faces as she walked into the elegant dining room.

"The doctors are very pleased with him." It always surprised her how quickly bad news spread, but perhaps that wasn't so surprising given the size of the resort and the fact that some of the guests had been coming to Snow Crystal for years.

"I saw him on that new bike of his with his dad. Looked so pleased with himself. Such a shame."

"His poor mother. They're saying if it hadn't been for Dr. O'Neil the boy would have died. He's a real hero."

"Is he doing all right, Chef?" Even Tally, the head waitress whose customer service was second to none, left the table she was serving to get an update.

Élise murmured words of reassurance, expressed a hope that everyone was enjoying their meal despite the events of the day, and moved around the room.

At every table she faced the same questions. The same exclamations. The same talk of Sean's heroics until in the end she took refuge back in the kitchen.

"All anyone can talk about is Sam and Sean."

"How is the little guy, Chef?" Antony, her newest re-cruit, and the most junior member of her kitchen staff, looked up from dicing vegetables. "He was in here last night eating his favorite pizza. And he told me he loved his chocolate birthday cake. Great kid. Good job Dr. O'Neil was there."

Élise ground her teeth and forced herself not to pounce.

"Sam is doing well. But it's important that we don't all lose focus. Our guests will still expect to eat good food. They don't want the staff to fall apart."

"Yes, Chef. I mean no, Chef." Antony looked nervous and she felt a flash of guilt.

She was a perfectionist, that was true. People were paying good money to eat her food and they deserved it to be just right. But she wasn't a bully.

And she knew that in this case her temper didn't originate from a fall in standards, but the fact that she kept imagining Sam waking up alone and wondering where Sean was.

I won't leave you, that's a promise.

Poor Sam. He was about to learn at an early age that people made promises when it suited them and then broke them without a second thought.

She kept imagining Sean's long, strong limbs entangled with those of the nurse.

But mixed up with those thoughts was an entirely different vision of him, this time with his hands sure and steady as he worked to save Sam. She kept hearing his voice, reassuring and kind as he'd calmed the panicking child. And then she kept seeing him, sitting by the boy's bed and smiling at the nurse.

"Merde."

Antony jumped. "Chef?"

"Nothing. You are doing well. I'm lucky to have you on my team." She forced herself to get on with her job, furious that she'd allowed herself to be so distracted.

By the time she'd finished her shift, she'd worked herself into such an angry state that she walked the distance to Heron Lodge in half her usual time.

She took the steps to the deck two at a time and stopped dead when she saw Sean sprawled on the chair on her deck.

He was the last person she'd expected to see.

Her heart lifted and then a breath hissed through her teeth and all the anger she'd kept contained throughout her shift burst to the surface. There was no question of reining it in.

"What are you doing here? Get off my deck you 'orrible lying piece of—" She used a French word and saw his expression shift from warm to wary.

"Sorry?"

"You expect me to greet you with open arms after what happened? How do you think I feel?"

He was very still. "I should imagine it was upsetting to witness."

"Upsetting? That is an understatement. For a while I thought you were a hero but now I know there is nothing heroic about you, Sean O'Neil." The emotion of the day spilled out unrestrained. "Nothing."

"I agree. I was just doing my job." Mouth tight, he rose to his feet. "Look, it must have been pretty shocking for you, I understand that. Why don't we—"

"Stay away from me." Furious, incensed, she lifted her hand in a stop sign. "If you know what's good for you, you'll stay away from me. Don't come any closer."

Of course, he ignored her. "If you're half as tired as I am you need to lie down. Let's go inside."

"You think I would lie down with you? After what you did? Because you save a life and behave like a hero and buy your grandmother flowers, you think you are this great big gift to women, no?" She was so angry she stumbled over the words, switching from English to French and back again. "You think you're so irresistible." He was just like Pascal. Exactly like Pascal.

"Wait a minute, just rewind—" he frowned "—a moment ago you called me a lying piece of— What did I lie about? And what does buying Grams flowers have to do with anything?"

"Go away!"

"Not until you tell me what you think I lied about."

The fact that he needed to ask tipped her over the edge. "Why are you here, anyway? Did she kick you out? Or did the great Sean O'Neil break his own speed record for leaving a woman's bed?"

"Did who kick me out?"

She curled her fingers into fists, the misery a solid lump in her throat. "You can't even remember her name. You *disgust* me."

"Honey, I'm so tired I can barely remember my own name." But amusement had been replaced by irritation. "Do you want to tell me what's going on here? Because I'm coming up blank."

She'd backed along the lake path but still he kept coming, across the deck and down the steps until he was standing right in front of her. "I want you to leave. Now."

"I'm not leaving until you tell me what's made you so mad."

"You broke a promise! You say—said—" she fell over the words in her temper "—you said things but you didn't mean any of them. It was all lies." Furious with him and with herself for believing him, she gave him a massive shove just as he stepped toward her and he lost his balance and toppled into the lake.

There was a huge splash and Élise was showered first with water droplets and then with male cursing.

"What the hell is *wrong* with you? I only put these clothes on half an hour ago. That's two sets I've ruined today. I go through more clothes in Snow Crystal than I ever do in Boston." Swearing, he hauled himself out of the water, dripping all over the path and a million miles from his usually sophisticated self.

"I want you to go away."

"Yeah, I got that message." He wiped the water from his eyes and glanced down at the shirt now plastered to his chest. "Before I do that you're going to tell me what promise I supposedly broke."

"You don't even remember! You break promises so often you don't even care." She ran up the steps, picked up a glass candleholder that was on the table and hurled it at him. "You promised Sam you wouldn't leave him."

He ducked and there was a splash as the candleholder landed in the water. "That's the promise?" He stared at her through eyelashes clumped together with water. "We're talking about Sam?"

"Yes. He was terrified and you took his hand and you were so cool and calm and you *promised* him, Sean. You said those words as if you meant them and then you—then you—" Her normal fluency deserted her and she switched to French, abusing him with words that any taxi driver in Paris would have admired.

His bemused expression told her that his education hadn't included listening to many French taxi drivers.

"I've lost you. If you're going to insult me, do it in English or at least textbook French."

"You promised him, and then you left 'im to go and 'ave sex with that nurse with lascivious eyes and a too-red mouth that pouted like so—" She pushed her lips out in an exaggerated imitation of the other woman and saw his brows lift in astonishment.

"That's what this is about? The nurse?" Water dripped down his face and he cursed again and wiped it away with his palm. "All this throwing and screaming and pushing me in the lake is because you're jealous?"

"I am not jealous! This is not about me! It is about Sam."

"Sam told you to drown me and hurl a candleholder at me? I don't think so. This isn't about Sam, it's about you, sweetheart."

"I am *not* your sweetheart."

"You're jealous." He said it slowly, like a revelation, and his sudden smile made her want to push him straight back in the lake and hold his head under.

"Why would I be jealous? I do not *at all* care who you sleep with, *tu me comprends?*"

"I do understand you," he said calmly, "but the correct sentence structure should be 'I do not care at all.' You split the infinitive, baby."

"I am not your baby. And I will split as many infinitives as I want to split, right along with your skull! I am not jealous. I do not care that you slept with her. I do not care that you saved Sam's life or that you bought flowers for your grandmother. I do not care about you at all!" She was yelling now. "I only care that you broke your promise to a child. You have no standards! Because of you he 'as learned never to trust people."

"Are you about done yelling?" Sean swiped his fingers through his sleek dark hair, sending more droplets showering his shirt. "Because if so, I'd like to say something."

"I don't want to hear it! I don't want to hear that she was pretty, that it didn't mean anything or that you slipped and fell on her or any of that shit men say when they're making excuses for bad behavior."

"How about the fact that I didn't sleep with her. Do you want to hear that?"

"I am not listening to your lies!" She clamped her hands over her ears. "And I don't care, anyway."

"Sure you care, but you're so damned scared you won't let yourself listen. And after what you told me last night I understand that. But I'm not him, Élise. I won't let you transfer your feelings for him onto me."

She paused, her breathing shallow.

Remembering just how much she'd told him made her squirm. "It is not for myself that I care. We have no relationship. We are not together and you don't owe me anything. It is not at all the same thing as with Pascal because my feelings, they are not engaged." She stumbled, groping for words, frustrated when they poured out in the wrong order. "I am angry only for little Sam. I don't care what you do."

"You don't care?" Sending her a meaningful look, he squeezed water from his shirt. "Are you sure? You seem pretty wound up for someone who doesn't care. And because I can see you're very upset, I'll say it one more time. I didn't touch her. I wasn't with her."

"I was there, Sean. I was there when she made you that offer and gave you that smile. *Merde,* I'm surprised she didn't just drag you into Sam's bed to save time! *I was there.*"

"But judging from the fact you just pushed me in the lake and almost dented my skull with a candleholder, you weren't there when I turned her down."

"I—" *Turned her down?*

Her temper, unleashed on full throttle, suddenly screeched to a halt like his sports car at a stop sign. "You turned her down?"

"Yes. And next time you're wondering where I am, you could pick up the phone or just send me a text. I gave you my number, remember?"

"I would never call you. Or text you. You—you—" Relief mingled with the realization that she'd made a giant fool of herself and Élise subsided. The relief terrified her most of all. She shouldn't care, should she? *She shouldn't care this much who he kissed or what he did?* She shouldn't care that he hadn't stayed with Sam. He'd said it to reassure Sam and reassurance was important in a situation like that.

As usual she'd overreacted.

She was tired, that was all.

Stressed after the terrible events of the day and the outpouring of emotions the night before.

"*Je suis desolée.* I have this terrible temper and I thought, I thought—" her breath caught "—please could you go now."

He frowned. "Élise—"

"Go. You are right. I am very tired. I need to lie down."

"We should—"

"No, we shouldn't." Even if he hadn't gone off with the nurse, it didn't change the fact that he'd broken his promise to Sam. It was the wake-up call she needed. Exactly the wake-up call she needed. "Go. Please. Go right now."

CHAPTER FIFTEEN

"I SAW AN interesting sight last night on my way back from town." Tyler was crouched in the dirt with Jackson, fixing a new wheel onto Sam's bike. "Nothing wrong with this as far as I can see. Kid was just unlucky. And unstable. He shouldn't have been on that trail. It's clearly marked, so stop beating yourself up and blaming yourself. Hand me that wheel, will you? This is going to be good as new when I'm done."

The buckled wheel lay on the ground, a distorted reminder of the horror of the day before.

"So this interesting sight—" Jackson focused on the conversation, grateful for anything that stopped him thinking about blood and hospitals. "Blonde or brunette?" He hoped it wasn't a redhead.

He hoped it wasn't Janet Carpenter.

"It wasn't a woman."

Jackson breathed again. "You notice stuff that isn't female?"

"I noticed this." Tyler pushed the new wheel down into the frame. "This was our brother. Dr. Cool. He was walking along the lake trail from Heron Lodge."

Absorbing the implications, Jackson straightened, Janet Carpenter forgotten. "I'll kill him."

"Judging from his somewhat rumpled appearance, I'd say someone already tried to do that. He'd taken a

swim in the lake and I'm guessing it wasn't voluntary."
Tyler caught his finger in the spokes and cursed.

"He is spending far too much time with Élise. Shit,
you're bleeding. After yesterday, I never want to see
blood again. Clean it up."

"Your sympathy overwhelms me." Tyler dealt with
the blood and then reattached the brakes, his fingers
swift and skillful. "That's what I find interesting. Every
time I turn around, he's right there panting over her.
When has he ever spent time with one woman before?"

"I don't care who he pants over as long as it isn't
Élise. You know what Sean is like. When it comes to
women, he's trouble."

"Maybe. Maybe that's why she pushed him in the
lake." Tyler wiped his brow with his forearm. "But
looking at his face, I'd say he was the one in trouble
this time. Knowing the way Élise feels about relationships, he might be about to be served a spoonful of his
own medicine."

Jackson frowned. "You really think it's serious?"

"No idea." Tyler spun the wheel, checking it. "But
he's spent more time here in the last few weeks than
he has in the last few years. Of course, that could be
because of Gramps, but seeing as Gramps is looking
healthier than you, I doubt it."

Jackson muttered under his breath. "You're still
bleeding."

"I'm done here." Tyler turned the bike the right way
up, spun the wheel and nodded with satisfaction. Then
he swung his leg over the bike and rode it in a circle,
testing the brakes.

"You are four times too tall for that bike. You look
like something out of a circus."

"Not letting the kid back on it until I'm sure everything works." Tyler gave the brakes a final squeeze and sprang off. "Good as new."

"I wish the same could be said for Sam. Every time I think of it I break out in a sweat."

"He'll be all right thanks to Dr. Cool."

"Yeah. Shit. How the hell can I be angry when he does something like that?" Jackson rubbed his hand over his face, thinking of the alternatives. "If Sean hadn't been passing—"

"He was and that's the end of it. And he does stuff like that because he's trained to do it. Don't look impressed or he'll be unbearable and then I'll be forced to dunk him in the lake. We don't want to be accused of pollution. You know what an eco warrior Gramps is. Come to think of it, you're the same."

Jackson stared at the mountains, remembering how calm Sean had always been in every crisis they'd had growing up. "Maybe he is trained, but he's still damned good at it."

"I'm not arguing with that. I'm going to wash this bike and then deliver it back to Sam's family. Not that Sam will be riding it for a while from what I've heard. Weren't they due to go home tomorrow?"

"We've given them the cabin for another week. Sam isn't well enough to travel. First time I've been grateful we're half-empty."

"When he's up and about I might give him a few lessons," Tyler said casually and Jackson stared at him.

"You? Teach kids mountain biking? You'd die of boredom before you left the resort."

His brother shrugged. "Exceptions can be made. It

would be a shame if the fall put him off mountain biking."

Jackson thought about what it would mean to Sam
to get a chance to go mountain biking with his gold-
medal-winning brother. "That's good of you."

Tyler looked alarmed. "Maybe don't mention it to
anyone. It's not going to be a habit."

"Fine." Hiding a smile, Jackson stooped and cleared
up the tools. He glanced at the bike, which looked as
good as new. "And Tyler, thanks."

"No problem. I can't fix the kid, but I can fix the
bike and one out of two isn't so bad."

ÉLISE BARELY SLEPT. Instead, she lay awake, reliving the
events of the day before, blood merging with red lipstick in her aching head until dawn sent beams of light
through her bedroom.

To take her mind off Sean, she busied herself making a large chocolate cake, icing it and then carrying it
over to Sam's family's lodge.

The door was answered by Sam's father. Judging
from his white face he was suffering the same what-if
flashbacks that tormented her.

"Hi." The buttons on his shirt were unevenly fastened, as if he'd dressed in a hurry and hadn't bothered
looking in the mirror. He opened the door wider. "I was
going to find you later to thank you."

"Is that Élise?" Sam's voice came from the living
room. "Can I see her?"

Receiving a nod from the boy's father, Élise stepped
over a pile of toys in the hallway and found Sam tucked
up on the sofa with a blanket over him watching car-
toons. He was pale, but smiling.

"How are you doing, *mon petit chou?*" She bent down to kiss him on the forehead. "I brought you a cake. It's chocolate. Your favorite. I made it myself."

"Oh, wow, that's *enormous.* Mom! Come and see my cake. It's the same one I had for my birthday."

Élise was relieved to see him so energetic. "So how are you feeling?"

"A bit weird, but Sean says that's normal. He's not worried." Sam stretched his hand out toward the cake just as his mother walked into the room with the baby in her arms.

"Sam, no! You can't have cake before you eat your breakfast. And it's Dr. O'Neil to you, not 'Sean.'" Her face was pale, the dark circles under her eyes announcing that she'd had no sleep the night before.

Sam's eyes went huge. "He told me to call him Sean."

"I'm more comfortable with Dr. O'Neil."

"I'll let you be guardian of the cake." Smiling, Élise handed the cake over to Sam's mother and sat down next to the boy. "So you must be so tired after your night in the hospital. Did you come home this morning?"

"No. I didn't stay in. Sean—I mean Dr. O'Neil—drove me home last night."

Élise hid her surprise. "You mean he drove back to the hospital to pick you up?"

How had she not known that?

Why hadn't he mentioned it?

Because she'd pushed him in the lake and thrown a candleholder at him.

"He never left," Sam said proudly. "He stayed with me the whole time, just like he promised. When they told him to go home, he refused. And one of the doctors tried arguing but Sean, I mean Dr. O'Neil—" He grinned sheepishly at his mother. "But he just stood there with a funny smile on his face saying he'd leave when I left and not before. It was so cool. Like he was my personal doctor or something. And the man who fixed my leg said that Sean saved my life."

His mother turned a shade paler and this time she didn't correct him. "We owe him everything."

"I'm going to be like him one day. I want to save lives." Sam peered at the cake. "Is it chocolate frosting?"

"*Oui.* Yes."

"You can speak in French," Sam said generously. "I'm learning it at school. *Je m'appelle Sam.* And I know *sang* because you taught me that."

Remembering, her stomach turned. She never wanted to see *sang* again. "*Super,* you have a very good accent! So you are saying Dr. O'Neil never left the hospital?"

"Not once. And then he gave me his private phone number and he said I could call it anytime I felt weird. Isn't that right, Dad?"

"We owe him a great deal, that's for sure." Sam's father looked exhausted. "Can I get you a drink, Élise? Something cold? Coffee?"

"No. Thank you. I have to get to work." Still absorbing the fact that Sean hadn't broken his promise at all and had, in fact, stayed with the child not only until he woke up from the anesthetic but until he'd been discharged and safely driven home to his cabin at Snow Crystal, Élise stood up. "I'm going to send over lunch so that you don't have to leave your lodge this morning. Are you tired of pizza?"

"No!" Sam's face lit up. "Cheese and tomato, but not

with slices of tomato. That's yucky. They do it like that in the village. I like the way you always do it with that thin sauce. It's better than back home."

"Pizza it is, and no slices of yucky tomato in sight. And chocolate cake for dessert." She walked to the door, her head spinning. Sean hadn't left. He hadn't broken his promise. *How could she have gotten it so wrong?* "I'll put together a few extra bits for the adults."

"We appreciate that." Sam's father walked with her to the door and once they were outside he caught her arm. "I wanted to say thank you for yesterday. I was panicking so hard I don't know what would have happened if you two hadn't shown up when you did."

Élise covered his hand with hers. "Sean is the one you should be thanking."

"Yeah. And I intend to do that next time I see him. I can't stop shaking," he confessed, rubbing his fingers across his forehead. "Couldn't sleep last night. Kept imagining what would have happened if you both hadn't come along right at that moment."

Élise didn't say she'd been imagining the same thing. "Let's not think about that. I have to get to the Boathouse. If you need anything, just call Reception and they'll get a message to me."

What time had she arrived back at Heron Lodge? Midnight.

When she'd seen Sean sitting on her deck she'd assumed he'd been with the pretty nurse.

Instead, he'd been driving the family home from the hospital. Sticking close by Sam's side the whole time, refusing to leave even when they'd asked him to.

And his reward for that sacrifice and for keeping his

promise to a small boy was being on the receiving end of her furious temper and taking a dunking in the lake.

Sᴇᴀɴ ᴡᴀs sɪᴛᴛɪɴɢ on the deck of the Boathouse, drinking a coffee provided by Poppy.

The place was packed, inside and out, and he thought about what a tremendous job Élise had done, building the café up so fast. There was no sign of her and he assumed she was over at the restaurant.

His grandfather sat opposite him, talking about something.

Sean had no idea what. He wasn't listening. His mind was fully occupied by thoughts of Élise. He remembered the look on her face just before she'd pushed him in the lake. He remembered her hair, slick against her beautiful face as rain dripped through the forest canopy onto their bodies. He remembered that bare shoulder and her faltering voice as she'd revealed the truth about her past.

Realizing that his grandfather was waiting for a response to a question he hadn't even heard, Sean picked up his coffee and made an effort to concentrate.

"What were you saying, Gramps?"

"I said, I've been hearing things about you."

Things?

Braced for a comment about Élise, Sean gave what he hoped was a casual shrug. "You don't want to believe everything you hear."

"I'm happy enough to believe this."

Which meant he was matchmaking again.

Sean sighed and put his cup down.

One night with a woman and suddenly everyone around him was booking the church.

"I don't know what you've heard, but it's probably exaggerated."

"Really?" His grandfather's gaze was sharp. "Because what I'm hearing is that you saved the boy's life."

Sam. He was talking about Sam, not Élise.

Realizing he'd almost given himself away, Sean breathed deeply.

"He was bleeding. I stopped it. It was basic first aid."

"Didn't sound that basic to me. Word is, you're a hero." His grandfather picked at one of the little almond cookies Poppy had baked fresh that morning. "Everyone is talking about it."

"The kid's doing well. That's all that matters."

"But he's doing well because of you." His grandfather's tone was gruff and Sean gave a faint smile.

"Hell, Gramps, is that praise? Because it sounded almost like it."

His grandfather bit into the almond cookie. "All I'm saying is that I'm glad you've put those hours of training and reading to good use. You didn't waste your brain, which is good because I hate waste. I'm proud of you."

It had been a week of shocks. First the revelations from Élise, then the near tragedy with Sam and now this.

Sean felt his throat thicken. "Gramps—"

He didn't know what to say and it didn't help that Élise chose that moment to walk onto the deck of the Boathouse. Her hair shone like polished oak and curved around her pretty face. For a moment he saw her with long hair and imagined her being dragged across a stark, gleaming kitchen by her ponytail.

His gut clamped in a tight knot.

Emotion slammed into him and all he could think was *not now*.

He couldn't handle his feelings for her now, not when his grandfather was saying things he'd never said before.

"I didn't save him." He forced himself to concentrate. "The surgeons did that."

"From what I've heard the only reason they had someone to save was because you'd saved him first. Of course, just because you're a hotshot doctor doesn't mean you couldn't come home more often. It wouldn't kill you to show up for family night once in a while."

Family night? He squirmed. "You still do that?"

"Yes, as you'd know if you were here a bit more. Your grandmother would love to see you there."

Élise was walking toward him, her eyes on his.

Her heels tapped on the deck.

His heart tapped against his chest.

He wondered if she was about to push him in the lake again. At this rate he was going to have to buy himself a whole new wardrobe.

"Good morning, Sean." She gave him a cool look and then bent to give his grandfather a hug. "Walter. You are looking so much better. You have some color. How are you feeling?"

"I'm good. But I can't walk five steps around this place without someone telling me my grandson is a hero." Walter gave a grunt. "Load of fuss about nothing, I say. If he can't save a boy after all that training, what is the point of it all I ask?" But he stood up and closed his hand over Sean's shoulder. The strength in that wrinkled, weathered hand made it difficult for Sean to speak.

"It was lucky we arrived when we did."

"Lucky you were home. You see? You don't need to go back to Boston to save a life, you can do it right here at Snow Crystal."

Sean laughed, relieved to have that hint of normality. "You never give up, do you?"

"Never. And neither do you. Which is why that boy is alive." Walter turned away and kissed Élise on the cheek. "I'm going to leave the two of you. I can't stomach all this medical talk."

"I love you, Walter."

Sean paused with his hand halfway to his coffee cup because now he understood. He understood why she lost no opportunity to say those words to the people who mattered in her life.

He reached for his cup and finished his coffee, noticing the way Élise's hair curved around her jaw, drawing attention to her mouth.

The mouth he wanted to kiss again. And again.

He waited until his grandfather had moved away to talk to Poppy before meeting Élise's gaze. "So did you come here so that you can push me in the lake again? Because if so I should probably move a little closer. I don't want to splash that family of four over there."

"I came to say I'm sorry." She sat down in the seat vacated by Walter. "I accused you of breaking your promises. You should have told me I was wrong."

"I tried. You weren't listening and then I was inhaling lake water and after that—" he dropped his gaze to her mouth "—you wanted me to leave."

"I was very angry with you. And now I'm angry with me. And you should be angry with me, too."

Angry?

He was feeling all manner of emotions he didn't recognize, but anger wasn't one of them. And it was starting to terrify him. For him, women slotted neatly into a clearly identified part of his life labeled entertainment. They provided company, someone with whom to share dinner, enjoy the opera and, yes, sex. They were part of his life without ever influencing it. They came into his life and when they left he rarely gave them more than a passing thought. He was the master of the superficial, an expert in the art of keeping himself detached. Until now. Now, his head was full of Élise. She intrigued him. She excited him. He thought about her. All the time.

Shit.

Part of him wanted to run but his feet were nailed to the deck. "I'm not angry. You were upset about Sam. So was I."

"I thought you'd told him a lie. You didn't. I shouldn't have yelled at you. I was wrong to lose my temper."

"I'm not afraid of your temper. And besides, you weren't really yelling at me, were you?" He spoke softly, wishing they'd started this conversation somewhere other than the crowded Boathouse. A swift glance told him that no one was near enough to overhear what was being said. "You were yelling at him."

Her breathing grew shallow. "Him?"

"Pascal. The guy who stomped all over that heart of yours. The guy who broke his promises and made you afraid to risk falling in love again. The guy who lied." He lifted his cup and finished his coffee, thinking that from the outside it probably looked as if they were talking about the food or the weather. "The one who makes you keep your relationships to one night, no more. That's the guy you were yelling at, and I don't blame you. If I met him, I'd probably yell at him, too. I might even lob a candleholder at him and push him in the lake, too."

She was staring at him, those green eyes wide and wary. "He can't swim."

"All the more reason to push him in. There's a deep part about a hundred yards up the lake path. That should do it."

"You gave Sam your phone number in case he needed you in the night."

"Yeah, well, I figured he was unlikely to call me twenty times a day to tell me he loved me."

"He might. He has a serious case of hero worship."

"He had a scary experience."

"So did I. I can't forget it." She lifted her hand to her face and breathed deeply. "All night I saw him bleeding. I kept thinking about what would have happened if we'd stayed to look at the view for another five minutes, or if we'd stopped just two minutes longer on the path."

"We didn't. And thinking like that will drive you crazy."

"I think I'm already a little crazy." Her hand dropped. "You really were a hero. You were so calm."

"You didn't see the size of the whiskey I poured myself when I got back to Jackson's."

"But that was afterward. At the time—you didn't even shake. And—" she swallowed "—I was thinking of other things, too."

His gaze met hers. "What things?"

"Camping." She licked her lips. "I told you so much. Things I haven't told anyone."

He wondered why knowing that made him feel good

when in reality it should have made him panic. "I'm glad."

"Are you?"

"When someone tries to knock you unconscious with a hard object it always helps to understand why."

"I really *am* sorry. I accused you of sleeping with that nurse. And you're not at all that guy."

He wanted to agree with her, to reassure her and tell her he would never do a thing like that, but he couldn't, could he?

"Maybe I am that guy. Maybe our reasons are different, but I don't do relationships any more than you do. For me, work always comes first." Or at least it always had. Now? He wasn't sure. He wasn't sure of anything anymore and it was starting to unsettle him because he'd always known exactly what he wanted. Always been clear about his goal.

Hell, any moment now he'd be building a house and putting up a white picket fence.

And as for Élise—he'd thought they were the same, but he knew now that they weren't.

She wanted a relationship and a family. She wanted it all. But she'd been hurt and she didn't trust. That put her in a different place to him.

When he dated a woman he never talked about the past or the future. He lived in the present. For both their sakes he ought to go back to Boston and stay away until Christmas.

"I have to go back to Boston tonight."

Something flickered in her eyes. "Of course you do."

That was it. So now he should stand up and get the hell out of there before he did something that was going to end in trouble.

I'll see you around, Élise.

"There's a new restaurant about an hour from here I've been meaning to try. If you could persuade my brother to give you a night off next Saturday, you could come and give your professional opinion."

She stared at him. "You mean go out together?"

"As opposed to having crazy sex in the forest?" His tone was dry. "Yeah, I mean go out together. Spend an evening together where I don't ruin my shoes. Share food and conversation. It's not hard to do." But he guessed for her, it was.

"So—you mean like a date?"

He'd chosen not to give it a name. "Well, I'm planning on getting through the evening with our clothes on, if that's what you mean. If we're in public, we might even manage it. So what do you say?"

"I don't date."

"Neither do I. So I guess that makes both of us clueless about that part, but we both eat so we could just focus on that and see how it goes. We have fun together. It doesn't need to be any more complicated than that." He enjoyed her company. She enjoyed his. That was all it was. Two people spending time together.

"All right." She said it slowly, as if she wasn't sure. Then the dimple flickered in the corner of her mouth. "But I'm only saying yes because it means you'll be coming back here again next weekend and that will please Walter."

"You could just cut me out and have dinner with Gramps if you prefer."

"No, because then you wouldn't have a reason to come home. But we could take him with us. If we're keeping our clothes on, it wouldn't make any difference."

"I might have been lying about that. I might have been planning on getting you naked after dinner."

She laughed. "Maybe I was planning on getting *you* naked. Can you really take the time off?"

"Yes." More juggling. More favors. "Can you?"

"I'll need to check with Poppy and Elizabeth. I should be able to. We have a strong team now. And anyway, this is research. It's important."

"Research?"

"I'm a chef. It's good to sample other people's food occasionally." She stood up. "I'll see you on Saturday."

CHAPTER SIXTEEN

SEAN FOUND JACKSON up a ladder, fixing the roof of one of the lodges. "You get all the glamorous jobs."

"That's me. Living the life of a tycoon." Jackson finished the job and climbed down the ladder. "I assume you're getting your butt back to Boston?"

"Soon. I just checked on Sam. He's doing all right."

"Thanks to you." Jackson put his tools down. "So when will we see you next? Christmas?"

"Gramps invited me to family night."

His brother smiled. "I wish I'd been there to see your face. I presume you won't be there?"

"No, but I'll be here next weekend. I'm taking Élise out to dinner so if you want to put dents in me, you should probably do it now."

Jackson wiped his hands on his jeans. "From what I heard, she's perfectly capable of putting dents in you herself. What did you do to her?"

"Nothing! Not that it's any of your damn business." Sean swore under his breath. "Is anything secret around here?"

"Not when you're living in my house, trailing lake water into my kitchen and distracting my staff."

"As it happens I didn't do anything, but there was a time I probably did deserve it and didn't get it so we'll call it even. Can the restaurant survive without her on Saturday night?"

"If she says it can, then it can. She's the one in charge of that side of the business. She's been careful to put in a good staff so that the place doesn't fall apart if she isn't there. And she deserves five minutes off. I'm just surprised she wants to spend it with you."

Sean gave a short laugh. "Thanks. I love you, too."

He never said it, he realized. *He never said those words to his family.*

They all just took it for granted.

"So is this going to be a regular thing? You coming home more often? Because over the past couple of years I got the impression you'd rather be just about anywhere but here."

It was the first time they'd addressed the truth so bluntly.

Sean felt tension ripple across his shoulders. "I've been busy."

"Yeah, I get that. But we both know that isn't what's keeping you away." Jackson kicked a stone with the toe of his boot. "You're not the only one who misses him, you know. We all miss him. And Gramps probably misses him most of all."

Sean felt a stab of guilt because he knew he'd been so focused on getting through his own grief he'd barely thought about anyone else. His strategy for survival had been work and absence. "We had a row. At the funeral."

Jackson nodded. "I guessed there was something."

"I said things—" The memory ripped through him, bringing with it the pain and the feeling of helplessness. "I was out of line."

"It was a bad time for all of us."

"I blamed him." Sean pressed his fingers to the bridge of his nose. "I said it was his fault. If Dad hadn't hated being here so much, he wouldn't have gone to New Zealand. Wouldn't have been in that damn car and wouldn't have hit the ice."

"You know that's bullshit, right?"

"Is it?" He couldn't quite let go of it. It had played on his mind over and over again. Every time he was on the edge of bringing up the subject with his grandfather, that fact got in the way. "Gramps heaped pressure on Dad right from the start. All he ever cared about was this place."

"Yeah, he cares about this place, but he was protecting the family home and business." Jackson pulled the ladder away from the roof and lowered it to the ground. "Which is more than Dad did."

Sean felt the anger spark. "He did his best."

"Did he?"

"He didn't want to be here. He didn't want to spend his life doing this."

"Then he should have stood up and said so. He should have had the courage to make that choice." Jackson's knuckles were white on the ladder. "Instead, he ran Snow Crystal into the ground. He should have told someone he couldn't handle it, but he hid the figures from everyone, including Gramps. Gramps suspected, which is why he kept putting pressure on Dad to tell him the truth. Gramps was panicking."

"Because he thought they'd lose the business—"

"Because he thought they'd lose their home! Everything! For fuck's sake, Sean, think about Grams and Mom and all the people we employ. The truth is Dad had a responsibility and he ignored it. He took charge of the ship and then he stood there and let it sail onto the rocks."

"That isn't what happened."

"Isn't it? Were you here? Did you look at the books? Did you talk to Gramps about what was going on or did you just listen to Dad? Yeah, you two were close— I know that and I never had any problem with it, but it blinded you. You're supposed to be a doctor. You're supposed to be analytical and make judgments based on evidence, not emotion. Maybe it's time you did that."

Sean's mouth felt as if he'd swallowed sand. The image in his head, once so clear, was blurry and distorted. "I had evidence. Dad used to call me late at night to offload. He told me Gramps was on his back the whole time. That he was doing his best but it was never good enough."

"He called you? I didn't know that." Jackson closed his eyes briefly and shook his head. "Why didn't you tell me?"

"Your business in Europe was expanding. You had your own problems. I didn't think you needed to know." He breathed. "I should have known there was more than one side to the story. I should have asked more questions. I knew Dad hated running the business. He'd always hated it so I didn't see anything new there. I didn't know he was hiding things. I didn't know he was struggling. Gramps never said anything."

"He didn't want to tarnish the memory we had of him." Jackson gave a short laugh. "The irony was, I was doing the same thing. Once I discovered the mess, I tried to unravel it without revealing the extent of it. I thought it would upset Gramps. Turned out he knew all along."

"When did you find out the truth?"

"After Dad died and I came home. By then Gramps was so terrified of trusting someone else, so guilty about giving Dad Snow Crystal when he didn't want it, he was pretty difficult to handle. Wouldn't let me pick up a pinecone without checking with him first." Jackson picked up a bottle of water that was piled on his tools. "We got through it."

Sensing the depth of that understatement, Sean felt a new respect for his brother. "You didn't tell me any of that."

"I didn't want to tarnish Dad's memory for you, either."

"He resented this place. He felt as if it was trapping him. I guess he passed a little of that onto me."

"He shouldn't have dumped all over you the way he did. You should have said something."

"Didn't want to burden you with that." He gave a humorless laugh. "So everyone was protecting everyone."

"Seems that way." Jackson drank. "And I was handling it. I thought the detail was something you didn't need to know. If I'd known you were getting those calls, I might have thought differently."

"It was always late at night. Must have been after Mom went to bed."

"He unloaded onto you." Jackson gripped the bottle of water in his hand. "You should have told me. And I should have told you about the mess he'd left. It would have stopped you nurturing your anger at Gramps for the past couple of years. Is that why you haven't been coming home?"

"That and the guilt."

"Guilt?"

Sean kicked a loose stone. "You gave up everything to come home and run this place. It dropped from Dad's shoulders onto yours. And I left you to get on with it."

Jackson frowned. "What else would you do? You may be a damn good doctor but you know nothing about profit margins and getting heads on beds. And there's the fact that running this place isn't what you want to do."

"That's true, but—"

"Running this place *is* what I want to do. It's what I do best. You're doing what you do best and we're all proud of you." Jackson screwed the top back on the bottle. "And that includes Gramps."

Sean thought about the conversation they'd had earlier. "Maybe."

"It's not a maybe."

"There's something else. About Dad." He licked his lips. He'd never said the words out loud before. Just thought them. "Do you think it really was an accident or do you think he—"

"No, I don't. I'm not saying the thought didn't enter my head at the time it happened because it did, but it only hung around for a second." Jackson reached out and closed his hand over Sean's shoulder. "Dad was a lousy businessman but he loved his family. And he loved this place. He just didn't know how to run it and he didn't want to learn. He crashed the car because he hit ice. The accident report was clear on that. Nothing else. He wouldn't have done that to Mom. To Grams. To all of us."

"I need to talk to Gramps. We've both been putting it off. Talked about everything but what happened. I owe him an apology."

Jackson dropped his hand and grinned. "You could show up to family night. That should do it."

THE RESTAURANT WAS pretty, with views over Lake Champlain to the mountains beyond.

"It's charming." Élise slid into her chair and glanced around her, taking in flickering candles and silverware. "Not as cozy as the Boathouse and less formal than the Inn. A blend of both."

"Taking someone who can cook like you out to dinner is a daunting prospect." But Sean didn't look daunted as he spoke briefly to their waiter and shrugged off his jacket. She shouldn't have looked, but she did. At his shoulders, broad and powerful under the tailored shirt, at his jaw, freshly shaved but already showing a suggestion of shadow. Tonight he was pure sophistication, but for a moment she had a vision of him stripped to the waist, working on her deck and then that vision morphed into another one of him, this time with his shoulders slammed against the tree, shirt half ripped where she'd torn it from his body.

Her heart beat just a little faster. It didn't matter whether he was half-naked on her deck or dressed in a suit, he always had the same effect on her.

She was relieved he couldn't read her mind and then she lifted her gaze to his face and realized that he could.

It was there in his eyes. The heat. The wry gleam that told her he was feeling the same way.

She looked away. "You shouldn't feel daunted. I'm just pleased not to have to cook my own food."

"You look pretty in that dress. Blue suits you."

Her pulse danced. Her life didn't include dinner with men and compliments. "It's teal."

"Is it? Then teal suits you. This place is supposed to be the best place to eat around here. The chef is new." He relaxed in his chair, glancing around him and she wondered if he'd sensed her tension.

"I can't wait to see the menu."

"You're not looking at the menu. I'm ordering."

"You think I've lost my powers of speech?"

"No, but if we give you a menu you'll be studying every dish and every ingredient instead of paying attention to me. We'll have the chowder followed by the maple glazed duck." Smiling, he handed the menu and the wine list back to the arriving server and ordered a bottle of Pinot Noir. "Are you going to tell me off for ordering red wine with fish?"

"No. I love Pinot Noir, as you well know. It is an excellent wine for food."

"And a really tricky grape to grow. André Tchelistcheff said 'God made Cabernet Sauvignon whereas the Devil made Pinot Noir.'" He waited until the wine was poured and lifted his glass. "One day I'll take you on a Pinot Noir tasting trip to California. We'll start in Yorkville and end up on the coast at Albion. Forty miles of glorious scenery. Redwood forests that have been there for centuries and acres of vineyards. We could even drive to San Francisco and spend a few days tasting sourdough bread and seafood."

He was talking as if they had a future. As if this were a relationship, not a night out.

Or maybe he was just trying to keep the conversation light and general to make her comfortable.

She studied the color of the wine, a light ruby-red, thinking that what he described sounded wonderful. "That would be like a dream."

"It doesn't have to be a dream. Now that the Boathouse is up and running you can employ more staff, have more time off."

"We can't afford to employ more staff. Things are better, but not that good. I know Jackson is still worried. He worries that if the winter season is not good, if there is not enough snow—" She shrugged. "It is very hard for him."

"No one knows more about getting heads on beds than my brother. He ran a successful hotel business before he took over Snow Crystal. And of course, now he has Kayla and she has serious skills when it comes to spreading the word about something."

Their food arrived and she admired the presentation and then savored the flavors. "It's good. You chose well. It is the first time anyone has chosen food for me since I was about four years old. My mother used to save hard and once a month we would go to a restaurant. She would let me choose what we ate. She wanted me to study the ingredients and decide what sounded good together."

"That sounds like a perfect mother-daughter trip."

"She thought it was important. A good way to spend money. If I am honest I was just as happy cooking with her at home."

"You said your earliest memory was cooking madeleines. That's what you were doing in that photograph in Heron Lodge?"

Emotion settled in her chest. "Yes. For me, my whole childhood is in that one picture."

"I've never tasted your madeleines. In fact, I don't think I've ever eaten one."

"I don't make them anymore. I haven't because they

remind me—" She shrugged. "There are other delicious things to make."

"Would you like to have your own restaurant?"

She was grateful for the change of subject. "The Boathouse feels like mine. And living at Snow Crystal is my dream. I wouldn't want anything else."

"My family is lucky to have you."

"I'm the lucky one." She glanced up. Candlelight flickered across his features, softening hard lines and sending a shimmer of light over glossy dark hair.

She decided that with this man as her date ambiance was irrelevant because no woman in her right mind would be focusing on anything but him. And it wasn't just his looks that drew her, he was sharp and clever and talking to him gave her a rush she could never remember having with anyone else.

She barely remembered what she and Pascal had talked about. It had been a relationship based around food. Their job. And he'd never shown any interest in what she wanted. Never asked her about her dreams. Never paid her the attention Sean did.

She thought about the night they'd spent in the tent. The night he'd spent just listening while she'd spilled all her secrets.

And he was listening now, his gaze warm and attentive. "You've done a good job with the Boathouse. It will give Snow Crystal a real boost."

"Without you it would not have been finished, but it all had a happy ending. And talking of happy endings, little Sam went home yesterday. He seemed none the worse for his scary experience and they've already rebooked for Christmas and next summer." It unsettled her less to talk about work, to keep the conversation neutral, and perhaps he realized that because he did the same thing.

"That will keep Jackson and Kayla happy. How about you? Still having flashbacks?"

She shuddered and put her fork down. "I do not allow myself to think about it." That was one topic she wasn't prepared to use for distraction purposes.

She glanced across at him, ignoring the uneven thud of her heart.

His shirt was open at the neck, showing just a hint of his throat, but all she needed was a hint. She was more than able to fill in the blanks.

She noticed the woman at the table nearby sneak a glance in his direction and was torn between annoyance and sympathy. If you were female it would have been a waste not to look at Sean and to be fair to him the only person he'd looked at since entering the room was her. "He told me that you texted him. That was kind."

"He had a fright. I'm glad to hear it hasn't put them off coming back. So is the Boathouse busy?"

"Full every day, breakfast, lunch and dinner. Locals are using it for Sunday brunch. Jackson is pleased."

He paused. "I spoke to him last week. I told him about Dad."

"About the phone calls? I'm glad. You shouldn't have had to carry that burden by yourself."

"Turned out I should have told him a lot sooner." His mouth tightened. "I was wrong about a lot of things."

"About your father?" Élise put her glass down slowly. "Do you want to talk about it?"

He gave a tired smile. "We both know the person I should be talking to is Gramps. You were right about that. And pretty much everything else. I think he's coming around a bit. For a moment last week I thought he was going to bring the subject up."

"He didn't?"

"No. Just told me he was proud of me." A faint smile pulled at the corners of his mouth. "Which was unusual."

"I think seeing what you did for Sam made him realize how good you are at what you do. How medicine is the right thing for you."

"I don't suppose that will stop him nagging me to get a job closer to home."

"No. And it won't stop him nagging you to show up for family night."

Sean laughed. "Tyler calls it Fright Night."

They were talking, but every glance was filled with the promise of something more. The atmosphere snapped tight. Heat pulsed between them. It was almost impossible to conduct a conversation, but she was determined to try.

"I think it's a lovely tradition. Not so different from my mother taking me out to dinner once a month. It was a time for us. A time we talked about things without distraction. Your family night is the same thing except there are lots of you and it's very noisy. You're lucky. So when are you planning to talk to your grandfather?"

"Tomorrow."

"You're staying the night at Snow Crystal."

"That's the plan." His gaze was focused on her. "Of course, my brother is sick of having me as a house guest so I might end up driving back to Boston unless I can find somewhere else to sleep."

Neither of them noticed as the waiter removed their plates.

"Sean—"

"I know what you're going to say. You're going to say you've never spent a whole night with a man, you don't do that. But we already spent a whole night together, Élise. Last summer was the whole night. I'm just suggesting we do the same thing but without the butt-biting insects and the showers of rain."

She laughed, as he'd intended her to. "I loved the rain. The whole thing was magical. Special." But she knew it hadn't been the rain or the scent of summer clinging to the forest leaves that had made it special, it had been the chemistry. The connection between them.

"I loved the rain, too." The glint in his eyes suggested his memory of that night was as fresh as hers. "Let's go."

He paid, and they walked from the restaurant to the car, shoulders brushing.

"Thank you. I enjoyed myself tonight."

"So did I. Next time I'll take you to Boston. We'll go to the opera."

Next time? She felt as if she were on a runaway train with no brakes. "I've never been to the opera. My mother took me to the ballet once. It was incredible."

"You'll love it. Tyler calls it caterwauling."

They drove home through darkness, along winding roads hugged by forests, through valleys and villages, past pretty churches and covered bridges.

She was aware only of him. Of his hands on the wheel, of his strength, his control.

Of her own feelings.

She couldn't stop thinking, looking, wanting to touch until she thought she'd go mad with it. She thought it was just her, but then he stopped at a set of lights, reached across and slid his fingers over hers and her heart stopped.

Neither of them said anything and then she curled her hand into his, so aroused she could feel the delicious curl of anticipation unravel inside her.

He stared straight ahead and then finally, for one brief moment, turned his head to look at her. He pressed her hand down onto her leg so the tips of his fingers brushed against her bare thigh.

The look in his eyes robbed her of breath and by the time he turned into the road leading to the resort she was ready to throw herself from the moving car and head for the protective covering of the forest.

He killed the engine and they came together like two wild creatures. His mouth collided with hers. She locked her hands in the front of his shirt. She felt the bite of his fingers in her hair, the erotic slide of his tongue against hers, the heat of his mouth and the sizzle of the blood in her veins. It was a heart-pounding, blood-pumping kiss and she slid her arms around his neck, trying to get closer.

With an effort he dragged his mouth from hers, but only long enough to mutter the words *"not here."*

They disentangled from each other long enough to stumble out of the car, then he grabbed her hand and they ran along the narrow trail that led to the lake and Heron Lodge.

Too far, she thought, and caught his shoulder with her hand.

"Kiss me—"

With a soft curse he slowed, lowered his mouth to hers and then groaned as she slid her arms around his neck. "Not here—not—" He clamped his arm around her waist, still kissing her, and she was scorched by the heat of it, drowned by the tide of sensation that threatened to knock her off her feet.

Dizzy from the skill in his kiss, she tugged at his shirt, desperate to touch, to have her hands on his body. "I want you—"

"Jesus, Élise—" He trapped her up against a tree, his hands on her hips, holding her against the hard throb of his erection as she dragged her hands over his shoulders. His muscles were rock-solid under her fingers and she closed her eyes as she felt the roughness of his jaw scrape the soft skin of her neck.

"Now—please now—" she couldn't wait any longer and she heard him stifle an oath and then sweep her into his arms. "Sean—"

"Don't say a word." His teeth were gritted, his jaw clenched as he carried her the short distance to her lodge. "Just don't say a word. And definitely don't kiss me. I'm trying to walk."

"I want—"

"Yeah, me, too." He took the steps in two strides. "But this time I want to see what we can do with a bed and a locked door."

The air was still, the water quiet and serene, the forest sleeping in the warmth of the summer night. Barn swallows swooped with the ruffle and quiver of wings as Sean crossed the deck but tonight she wasn't interested in her surroundings, only in the man.

She trailed her mouth across his jaw and heard the breath hiss through his teeth. "Have I told you you're sexy?"

"Don't tell me," he said, as he shouldered the door open, "not yet. Hold that thought."

"You're sexy—"

"Holy shit—" He kicked the door shut and then gave up the fight and took her mouth. He was out of control and she was, too, and they stumbled toward the stairs, losing clothes, kissing, touching, greedy and desperate.

She tore off his shirt. He stripped off her dress. Her bra hit the floor next and then the tiny scrap of matching silk that was all that was left of her clothing. And then they were both naked and he pushed her back onto the bed, his mouth on hers, his kiss hotly sexual and explicit.

Moonlight streamed through the open windows, spotlighting naked limbs, powerful shoulders, the gleam of black hair, the glimmer of blue eyes.

The heat they generated was ferocious, the need a ravenous beast inside her and she shifted her hips, wanting him so badly it drove everything she did.

His hand slid between her legs, the intimate stroke of his fingers sending a dart of agonizing excitement through her body. His mouth moved lower, fastening on her breast, teasing, driving her wild until her moans turned into a sob and he slid lower and spread her legs. She felt naked, exposed and just for a moment something in her faltered, but he trapped her there, anchoring her hips with strong hands while he tortured her with his mouth and his tongue, each skilled flick driving her higher and higher.

Finally, when she was right on the edge, almost blind with it, he shifted her under him and entered her with a single thrust that made her cry out. Hard, hot, powerful he surged into her and she dug her fingers into the sleek muscle of his shoulders, holding on, afraid to let go because she'd never experienced anything so out of control, so wild. And deep down a part of her knew this wasn't just sex, that the connection was different this time, and briefly she struggled to regain her emotional balance, to find the level of control that had been her protection for almost a decade, but it was out of her grasp. The armor, the walls she constructed around herself for protection, came tumbling down, or maybe he smashed them down because the way he was looking at her, the way he held her gaze with each driving thrust, left her nowhere to hide. And she realized that *this* was exposed, not being naked, but sharing this moment of exquisite intimacy with this man.

"Come for me—" he growled the words against her mouth "—don't hold back. I want all of it. All of you."

"Sean—" she had no choice but to give him everything he demanded. She was lost, possessed, out of control and she felt sensation erupt and shower them both, dimly heard him groan as her body tightened around his and then she was tumbling, spinning, unable to stop herself, holding on to the strong shoulders, gasping his name against his lips as they crashed over the edge together.

It took a while for either of them to move or speak.

She was aware of the solid weight of him, of the strength of him as he held her, of the uneven rasp of his breathing as he struggled for control. And as for her—

She lay stunned, staring up at the ceiling of her little bedroom, trying not to panic.

What had happened?

"Holy hell—" He dropped his head onto her shoulder and then eased away from her, rolling onto his back and dragging her with him. "I'm proud of us."

"Sorry?"

"We made it to the bed. For us, that's a major achievement."

Even in bed he made her smile. The panic faded. "The top of the bed. We didn't manage to pull back the covers. I hope you didn't drop bits of forest on my white bedcover. It's very precious to me." After the intensity of what they'd shared, it calmed her to keep the conversation light.

He lifted himself onto his elbow and eyed the pretty bed piled with soft cushions. "Who the hell has a white bedcover?"

"I do. It's silk. It belonged to my mother."

"Fine—next time we'll just stay in the forest. Anywhere. I'll give up the pretense of being a modern, sophisticated man. With you I'm right back in the cave, ready to spear something for you to cook."

Laughing, flattered, she slid her hand over his jaw, feeling the rough scrape of stubble over her palm. "You'd ruin your shoes."

"Damn, I knew there'd be a catch." He leaned forward and kissed her mouth. "For you it would be worth it. So are you going to come and live in my cave?"

She knew he was joking but her heart beat a little faster. "Does your cave have silk sheets?"

"Not yet, but it will once you move in."

"I'll think about it. Or maybe we could just live in the forest. I love the forest." She slid her hand to his shoulder, feeling pumped-up muscle and hard strength. He was more powerfully built than Pascal but she knew this man would never use his strength to hurt someone. That was a weakness and Sean was strong right to the core. "I liked being with you in the rain."

His eyes darkened. "Great. The one thing I can't

fix for you. Maybe I should go outside and do my rain dance. Or we could use the shower. Would that count?"

"I like that idea. Shower and then sex on my silk sheets."

"Sorry? All I got from that was the word *sex*. After that I zoned out." His hand slid into her hair. "The shower is a great idea in theory, but I'm six-two and I'm not sure there's room in there for both of us. I built that shower, remember? Tyler grumbled nonstop for three days because he kept banging his head when he was tiling. The sloping roof was a bitch to work around."

"I think it's charming. And I think it's time to test its possibilities, don't you?"

"Yes. No. Christ, I don't know— Don't ask me to think. I can't think while you're lying there naked." His mouth found hers, rough, seeking as he plundered her lips. "You taste like heaven. I could kiss you all night."

"I hope you will. It would be a shame to waste the time. You don't come home often enough for that."

"I'm thinking of moving back."

Smiling, she slid out of bed and walked to the shower, knowing he was watching every movement.

In two strides he was behind her, ducking into the shower, cursing about the size of the room.

Although the space was small it was cleverly designed, a stylish wet room with Italian tiles and glass. The O'Neils had taste and the finish was perfect.

The room always gave her pleasure, but tonight it gave her more than that. It gave her heat and possibilities. And Sean. Here, in this confined space, she was even more aware of the raw power of the man.

Lifting her gaze to his, she saw desire burning in his eyes and knew he was seeing the same in hers.

"Rainfall. But presumably not cold." He adjusted the controls so that the water flowed at the right temperature. Every movement he made was purposeful and she felt her stomach squirm and her blood heat as he gave a wicked smile and reached for the soap. His hands were large and strong and he stroked every inch of her, leaving no part untouched until she was gasping and pliant under the fall of water, her fingers digging into his shoulders.

He was as physical as she was. As passionate and unrestrained.

Slow foreplay was never going to work for them. Once again the meeting of their mouths was more of a collision than a kiss, the stroke of his tongue hot and sensual, the nip of his teeth adding a ferocity she found deeply thrilling.

She breathed in the scent of him, stroked her hands over hard muscle and glistening male flesh, listened to the harsh sound of his breathing. When he lifted her and fastened his mouth over her breast, she let her head fall back, lost in the excitement, the sensations, the pleasure that burst around her with each slow flick of his skilled tongue. She wrapped her legs around him, feeling the smoothness of him brush against her but he held her high, for once denying her what she wanted and needed.

"No—" he growled the words against her throat "—not yet."

"Yes, now." She drove her hands into his hair, brought her mouth down on his and moved her hips, but he was stronger and he held her tightly, trapping her movements against him so that she could do nothing to alleviate the growing ache in her pelvis.

"I want you. Again and again—" He pressed her

back against the wall, kissing her long and hard as he reached out and killed the flow of water. Without the rush of water the only sounds were the jagged rush of their breathing. "How do I stop feeling this? Tell me, because at this rate I'm not going to be able to go to work on Monday." With those words he peeled away another layer of her protection but before she could try and snatch it back he grabbed a towel from the rail and wrapped her in it, still kissing her. His movements were rough and uncoordinated but that made it all the hotter. The fact that this normally sophisticated, controlled man was thoroughly out of control around her, escalated her own excitement to fever pitch and she told herself that self-protection could wait. That this was still just sex. *Just sex.*

His hair gleamed dark with droplets of water and he picked her up and deposited her on the bed, naked and slightly damp.

"Do your sheets mind a little water?" He didn't stop kissing her, trailing his mouth and tongue down her body. The heat was intense. The chemistry so powerful her belly cramped with it. When he raised himself over her she grabbed his shoulders, dragging him down to her. She felt him, thick and hard against her and then he rolled onto his back and pulled her onto him so she straddled him.

They were both so aroused there was no question of taking it slow or holding back. She dug her nails into the sleek, hard muscle of his shoulders and sank down onto him, taking him deep.

"God, Élise." He groaned deep in his throat, thrust his hands in her hair and drew her head down to his. She sank her teeth into his lower lip and he retaliated in kind, his eyes locked on hers as he drove into her. His eyes were dark with heat and raw desire, his jaw clenched in a face so handsome it almost hurt to look at him. But she did. She looked and so did he. There was no hiding, no pretending, just the same honesty with which their whole relationship had been conducted. She felt herself start to fall, felt her own spasms grip his straining shaft and heard his agonized groan as he lost his own struggle to hold on to control. Sensation swamped her, crashed over her in brutal waves and he smothered her cry with his mouth as he thrust deep and emptied himself.

Recovery took a while.

Drained, shattered, she lay on his chest, aware of the warmth of his hand against her back, the protective curve of his arm. As her heart rate slowly approached normality, she tried to move but he held her trapped and shifted slightly so that he could drag the duvet over them both.

It was the final intimacy. An intimacy she hadn't allowed herself since Pascal.

Frowning, she was about to slide out of his arms and make noises about him going home when he turned his head, hauled her against him and kissed her again.

He was a master kisser. He knew just how to use that clever mouth of his to rob a woman of willpower and he'd done it to her on numerous occasions, but not this time. This time his intent wasn't seduction, it was tenderness and the slow gentle nature of the kiss rocked her world.

Shaken by feelings she couldn't identify, she stared into those seductive blue eyes and felt everything inside her melt.

He clearly intended to spend the night and she wasn't sure how she felt about that.

"Do you honestly think that sleeping in the same bed is any more intimate than what we just shared?" The fact that he could read her so easily scared her.

"I don't do this. And neither do you. You don't ever spend the night with a woman." She knew Sean had broken as many hearts as he'd mended bones. "You walk away. Every time."

"Sweetheart, I can tell you there is no way I am capable of walking anywhere." His eyes closed and a hint of a smile touched his firm mouth. "My body has ceased to function."

Panic unfurled inside her.

"I need to use the bathroom."

"Fine, but come straight back."

Extracting herself from his grip, she rose from the bed and walked to the bathroom, wondering if he'd take the opportunity to leave once she was no longer in the room.

Churned up and confused, she took her time in the bathroom.

Ten minutes later she opened the door.

And saw Sean asleep on the bed.

He lay sprawled, long strong limbs stretched out, his left arm flung above his head. Those thick dark lashes that normally took second place to those blue eyes fanned bronzed skin and a strong bone structure.

Élise stood for a moment, locked in indecision. She could join him, but that would mean waking together and that would put their relationship on a whole other level and she didn't want that.

She could wake him now and ask him to go and

sleep at Jackson's but he already slept the deep sleep of exhaustion. She knew his work was punishing and the events of the past few weeks had placed extra demands on his stamina. He showed nothing, absorbed stress and pressure like blotting paper, but still the effects were there.

There was no way she could wake him. She wasn't that selfish.

With a sigh, she accepted that she wasn't going to move him, which gave her two choices.

This time, she allowed her brain to make the choice, easing the covers over him so he didn't get cold in the night.

Then she picked up a couple of pillows, pulled out a blanket from the white wicker basket at the bottom of her bed and resigned herself to a night on the couch.

CHAPTER SEVENTEEN

Sᴇᴀɴ ᴡᴏᴋᴇ ᴛᴏ the call of birds and the sounds of the lake and lay for a minute, his brain still shrouded in sleep, his limbs heavy. It took him a moment to ease into the day and remember where he was.

Heron Lodge.

In Élise's bed.

But there was no sign of Élise. A single glance told him she hadn't spent any part of the night in her own bed.

He'd crashed out and she'd slept—where?

"Shit." He groped for his watch, saw that it was past eight o'clock and knew it was already too late to avoid awkward questions from his twin brother. Unable to remember the last time he'd slept this late, he rose and went in search of Élise but Heron Lodge was empty. Fresh coffee sat on the counter, cold, evidence that she'd left a while ago.

She hadn't hung around for slow morning sex, or even morning-after conversation.

He probably should have been relieved. It surprised him to discover that he wasn't.

He bit into one of the pastries she'd left on the plate, took a moment to admire her skill as a chef and then heated the coffee. It was only when he lifted the mug to his lips that he noticed the blanket folded neatly on the couch.

He lowered the coffee.

She'd slept on the couch?

Guilt, sharp and unfamiliar, stabbed him along with other emotions that were unfamiliar and unrecognizable.

Hearing footsteps behind him, he turned to find her standing in the doorway wearing the shortest pair of running shorts he'd seen. Her dark hair was held back from her face by a band and her cheeks were pink.

Lust punched right through his body. It didn't matter what she was wearing, he wanted her.

"Why did you sleep on the couch?"

"Because you were in the bed."

Given that they'd spent half the night locked together it seemed like flawed logic to him.

"The bed was big enough for both of us. I didn't intend to kick you out. You've made me feel guilty."

"Why would you feel guilty over something that was my decision?" She walked into the kitchen, opened the fridge and poured herself a long glass of ice water.

Sean wondered whether pouring it over himself would solve his problem.

The tension in the atmosphere was enough to give a person heatstroke.

His pulse was thrumming. He was hard as rock. He wanted to power her back against the kitchen counter and remove those shorts. He wanted to spread her legs, taste her, bury himself in her. He wanted to feel her bite down on his lip, feel her tongue in his mouth and her hands on his skin. He wanted to feel the fire again, be burned up by it. But he also wanted to see her laugh, see that dimple, listen to her spill secrets and feel the rush that came from knowing she'd begun to trust him at least a little bit. That he was the one who had broken through those barriers. He wanted to protect her and reassure her that not all men were like Pascal. He wanted to tell her that they were good together.

But how could he do that?

When had he ever been anything but bad news for any woman?

His history was littered with relationships that had ended. When the hospital called, when his patients needed him, he dropped everything and he wasn't prepared to change that. He wasn't prepared to make the sacrifice that needed to be made for a relationship to work.

So why was he still standing here?

Apparently unaware of his turmoil, Élise drank deeply, rinsed the glass and put it down. Cool. Calm. "I have to shower and then get over to the restaurant. Thanks for a lovely evening, Sean. It was fun."

Fun? That was it? That was all she was going to say?

It was like trying to open a door with a key you'd used and suddenly that same key didn't fit.

And what had the evening been to him? He'd invited her on impulse but not once in the hours they'd spent together had that impulse felt like a mistake. They were friends, that was all. What was wrong with friends spending time together?

"I know you're scared—"

"I'm not scared. Why would I be scared? We're not in a relationship. We both know this was just sex. Admittedly sex in a bed for a change—" she smiled "—but still just sex. You're worrying for no reason. Have a good week, Sean. Perhaps I'll see you at family night."

"THE TOMATOES ARE wonderful this year." Élise picked one from the vine, sniffed, and put it in the basket on her arm. "We'll put them on the menu at the Inn tonight. It's a shame the season is so short."

"Thank goodness for Tom Anderson and his greenhouses."

"Oui." Élise glanced at Elizabeth, wondering how much she dare ask. "He is a very nice man, I think, Tom. And it was kind of him to find the time to help out in our garden this summer. You have known him a long time?"

"He and his wife used to come here for dinner on their anniversary. She died about eight years ago. It's been a lonely time for him. Of course, the local community here is wonderful, but it isn't the same as having that one special someone. I'm sure that's why he has been spending so much time growing his vegetables."

"We must support him." Élise picked another tomato, hoping her instinct hadn't been wrong. "If the Boathouse stays as busy as this, we should be able to double our order for salad and vegetables."

Elizabeth looked pleased. "I'll mention it next time he's here. Oh, look—the flat leaf parsley is looking good, and the mint. Shall we put tabouleh on the menu this week?" She picked a sprig and sniffed. "Michael always preferred the winter because of the snow, but I love summer in Vermont."

"I love summer, too. And yes to tabouleh. Good idea."

"So how was dinner with Sean?"

"The surroundings were lovely. The food was good. The wine, delicious."

"And the company?"

Her heart skipped in her chest. "The company was good, too, of course. Sean is always entertaining."

"He's been coming home more often." Elizabeth heaped mint into her basket. "Walter is pleased and it's been a real help to Jackson. Thank you."

"Why are you thanking me? I am not the reason he is here."

Elizabeth looked at her. "After Michael died he stopped coming home. I know he was hurting badly, we all were, but of course, Sean wouldn't talk about it. He has never been one to show his feelings easily. He doesn't talk about personal things."

He'd talked to her.

And she'd talked to him. About everything. It was the first time she'd ever done that.

"Losing someone you love is always hard."

"Yes." Elizabeth pushed a leaf aside and found another cluster of tomatoes, shining like rubies in the sunlight. "I don't know how we ever got through those days. It was like walking through a dark fog. We were all stumbling around, trying to find our way, holding onto each other."

"Yes." The lump wedged in her throat. "I love that you do that. Being able to hold together is what makes you a family. If you fall there is someone to catch you." Until she'd arrived at Snow Crystal, she hadn't had that.

"Last Christmas everything changed. Kayla came and I started working with you in the kitchen." Elizabeth picked the tomatoes carefully. "I honestly think that was what saved me. You saved me."

A sting of tears added to the lump in her throat. "It was Kayla's idea."

"But you took me into the kitchen and made me one of the team."

"And that was lucky for me. You are very talented. Because of that I am now able to take time off!"

"What you've done for Snow Crystal—first the Inn and now the Boathouse—it's fantastic. It's because of you the Inn has been named best restaurant again. For a while I really did think we might lose the business. But between Jackson, Tyler, Kayla and you, you've dragged it back from the edge."

Élise didn't point out that it was still a bit too close to the edge for any of them to sleep properly at night. "It is certainly better. Much will depend on the winter, I think. We need a good season."

"It isn't just the business you've helped. You've brought the whole family together. Helping you on the deck has forced Sean to spend more time here. It's been good for everyone. I feel as if the whole family is finally healing. I saw his car parked outside Alice and Walter's this morning and I know he's arranged a gift for his grandfather so hopefully that will be well received."

"A gift?"

"Something to help Walter. I know Sean worries about him, although he doesn't show it. He was always the same. Tyler would explode with whatever was bothering him, Jackson would think about it and then talk about whatever it was, but Sean—he always kept it to himself. He was always the brooding type. I'm glad he stayed the night. I worry about him driving back to Boston when he's tired." Elizabeth hesitated and cast her a look. "Élise, this may not be my business—"

"You can say anything to me!"

"I love my sons very much, but that doesn't stop me seeing who they really are. Sean has always been single-minded when it comes to his job. He only ever wanted to be a doctor. I saw it in him when he was young. And I'm proud of him but yes, sometimes I worry because I'd like to see him with more in his life than just a career to be proud of. A life needs balance. He doesn't have it. I'm not sure he ever will."

"And you're telling me this because…?"

"Because over the past two years you have become as much a daughter to me as he is a son and I don't want to see you hurt."

Her breath caught. Tears clung to her lashes. "Elizabeth—"

"Maybe I'm wrong and there's nothing going on, but if there *is* something going on then—well, I don't want him to hurt you."

"Oh, *bah,* now you will make me cry." Élise put her basket down and hugged her tightly, squeezing her eyes to kill the tears that threatened to fall. "I love you very much, too. And Alice and Walter and dear Jackson, Kayla, Brenna and even Tyler although I wish sometimes he would open his eyes. I am the one who is lucky, living and working here. And I will not be hurt." That wasn't possible. She protected herself too carefully. "Sean and I, we laugh together, we talk and yes perhaps some other things I will not discuss with his mother, but you do not need to be worried. However, I am touched that you care. And I am glad Sean is coming home more, too. It is right that he should. He has a very special family."

And she was part of that family. No one could take that away.

She wondered if Sean was talking to Walter. If he was finally mending the rift that had kept him away from the place for the past couple of years.

She truly hoped so. And if he'd taken a gift, maybe that would be the beginning of a whole new phase in their relationship.

"WHAT THE HELL is that?" Walter stared at the machine in the middle of the yard.

"It's a log splitter." Sean studied it, pleased with his choice. It had taken him ages to think of exactly the right thing to buy, and hours of research to finally come up with this particular model. "I arranged to have it delivered here."

"Why? Who is it for?"

"It's for you." The phone in his pocket vibrated but for once he ignored it. Whoever it was could wait. This conversation was more important than any phone call. "It's a gift, Gramps. So you don't spend your time and energy hefting an ax."

"Are you saying I'm not capable of hefting an ax? Do you think I'm a wimp?"

"No." Sean frowned. "I think you just need to be careful, that's all."

"I'll decide what I do and what I don't do." Walter prowled around it suspiciously. "How much did this thing cost you?"

"It's a gift so the cost is irrelevant. And this thing can split logs like they're nothing."

"So can I." His grandfather's gaze was fierce. "I've been doing it since before you were born."

"So maybe it's time to take it easy."

"I don't want to take it easy. I don't need to take it easy, so you can just send it back where it came from and get your money back."

Sean stood in silence, absorbing the blow. Not for a moment had it occurred to him that the gift might not be welcome.

He could send it back, of course. He could arrange for the damn thing to be transported right back where it came from and let his stubborn, muleheaded grandfather carry on swinging his ax until it finally killed him.

All it would take was one phone call.

He'd done his best. He'd tried. If his grandfather didn't want it, then there was nothing else he could do.

He closed his fingers around his phone, and then had an image of Walter lying still and pale in the hospital, with Alice at his side, refusing to leave. He thought of his mother, of Jackson and most of all he thought of Élise.

Élise, who had been with his grandfather when he'd collapsed.

Élise, who treated his family like her own.

I love you, Walter.

Unable to get her voice out of his head, he pulled his hand out of his pocket and squared his shoulders.

"I'm not going to do that. I'm not going to send it back."

"Then it can sit there and rust because there is no damn way I'll use it. I'll be using my ax, same as I always have."

"You haven't even tried it."

"I don't need to try something I know I don't have a use for."

Sean stood still for a moment, searching for a persuasive argument and coming up blank. "Please, Gramps—" he struggled to keep the emotion under control "—just use it. Just for once, please do this."

"Give me one good reason why I should."

"Because you frightened the shit out of us!" It wasn't what he'd intended to say, but he'd said it, anyway. Anger and frustration, held back for too long, rose to the surface. "Hell, Gramps, the whole of last winter I was nagging you to get yourself checked out, and did you do it? No. You're so damn stubborn, so—" He pressed his fingers to the bridge of his nose, forcing himself to breathe, trying to calm himself sufficiently to articulate his feelings. "Do you know how I felt when I got that phone call from Jackson telling me you'd collapsed? It was like getting that phone call about Dad all over again. I don't remember a single thing about the drive from Boston to the hospital. All I remember is that my legs were like jelly and I kept thinking that if you died, if you died, then I'd—" His voice cracked and he broke off, his hands curled into fists and his feelings right there for the whole world to see.

His grandfather stared at him in silence. Then he cleared his throat. "You shouldn't have driven in that sort of state in a car like yours. You could have had an accident."

Sean gave a disbelieving laugh. "Is that why you told me to get back to Boston?"

"No. I said that because I thought you didn't want to be here." Walter stared at the ground and let out a long breath. "I know you haven't exactly liked coming home since your father's accident and I didn't want to put that pressure on you. And I didn't want to pull you away from your work when it's so important to you."

"Well, of course my work is important, but not more important than being with my family when they're in trouble. Did you think I'd carry on working while you were in the hospital? You frightened us all half to death. That's why I bought you the log splitter, in the hope you'd take better care of yourself. And I'm not going to send it back. You're going to use it if I have to chain you to the damn thing."

He was braced for a long drawn-out battle. An argument that would no doubt put a few more dents in their already bruised relationship.

Instead, his grandfather stirred. "I didn't know you felt that way. I didn't know you were worried about me."

"Yeah, well, you do now." Sean dragged his fingers through his hair, furious with himself for losing his temper. "I'm sorry I yelled. Believe it or not, I actually came here to apologize to you."   .

"Apologize? For what?"

The words were stuck in his mouth. The emotion was stuck in his chest. "For all the things I said to you at Dad's funeral. I was out of line. I was so far out of line."

His grandfather straightened slightly. "You were upset."

"That is no excuse. You should have told me to shut up. You should have yelled back or something. Why didn't you?"

For a moment his grandfather didn't respond.

Then he sank down onto the bench, his hands on his knees. "Because you were crushed by grief." His voice trembled. "We all were. You wanted to blame someone, and I understood that because I was doing a whole lot of blaming myself. That happens when you lose someone. You only said what I was thinking. It *was* my fault."

"No. No, it wasn't."

"Maybe not all of it, but some of it."

"That isn't true." Sean's voice was raw. "I was wrong about that. I was wrong about so many things. And I shouldn't have said what I did."

"You lost a father."

"And you lost a son."

"Yes." Walter stared ahead at the mountains. "My earliest memory was playing by the lake with my own father. This place was everything to him and it was everything to me. It never occurred to me to do anything different. I lived it, breathed it, dreamed it. Then I met your grandmother and she felt the same way. It wasn't just a way of life, it *was* life. It didn't occur to me that my son wouldn't want that life."

"Dad loved the place."

"He loved the place, but not the business. Michael wanted no part of that side of things."

Sean thought of the conversation he'd had with Jackson. "But he didn't tell you that. He never said that."

"He was trying to be what I wanted him to be. He didn't want to let me down." Walter's voice was husky. "I should have known. I was so focused on what *I* wanted I never asked what *he* wanted."

"It's good to be focused. Good to be passionate about something."

"Not when passion makes you blind."

"He could have said something. He should have."

"Possibly. But would I have listened? I like to think I would have, but I can't be sure. This place isn't an easy weight to carry, I know that."

"Jackson loves it."

"Yes. And I sleep easier, knowing that."

Sean sat down next to his grandfather, shoulders brushing. "I'm going to come home more."

"Your grandmother would like that."

Sean turned his head and looked at his grandfather. "And how would you feel about it?"

Walter cleared his throat. "I guess I'd like that, too. But only if it's what you want."

"It's what I want. I should have apologized to you sooner instead of staying away. And I should have said— I mean, I probably should have told you— I love you, Gramps— Shit—" He ran his hand over his face. "I can't believe I said that. Thank God Tyler's not here."

"Thank God your grandmother isn't here, with you swearing." There was a long silence and then his grandfather gave a laugh that was decidedly unsteady. "I love you, too. I thought you knew that."

Sean thought of Élise. "Sometimes it's good to say these things aloud, just so everyone is clear. But it's not easy."

"You've never found it easy to talk about your feelings. I don't, either."

"Funny you should say that. Élise thinks you and I are alike."

His grandfather smiled. "Clever girl, that one. Strong. And Kayla, too. She and Jackson are breathing new life into this place and that's good. Now she's going to be living here full-time things will be even better."

"I worry about Kayla. She's giving up a lot, quitting her job to come and live and work here."

"You think so?" Walter watched as a flock of birds

flew overhead. "I'd say she's gaining more than she's giving up."

"She worked for a top New York PR company. She had a career."

"And now she's working with the man she loves, planning a future. A happy life needs more than work. It needs balance. I'm lucky. For me, work, home, family are intertwined. I have it all in one place. You have a great career, no question, but it's a hell of a price you're paying. One hell of a sacrifice. Be sure it's worth it."

"Sacrifice?" Sean was astonished. "I'm not the one making the sacrifice. I don't have to think about anyone but myself. I can spend as much time as I like at the hospital without anyone asking what time I'll be home."

His grandfather stared at the forest, framed by blue sky. "Sound like a lonely life to me."

"I'm surrounded by people."

"But do those people give a damn about you? Would they care if you collapsed on your deck and couldn't get yourself back up again? Do they laugh with you and keep you warm at night? Do they sit with you when you're lying in a hospital bed and hold your hand the whole time? Are they still going to be by your side in sixty years?" His grandfather's voice shook. "Do those people do that?"

Sean stared at him, stunned. "Gramps—"

"Love isn't sacrifice, it's a gift. But you're afraid, and I understand that. It takes a brave man to admit he's in love."

"I'm not in love." Sean frowned. "Why would you even suggest that? For a start, I don't have time to date. There's no one I—" He broke off and clenched his jaw. "If you're suggesting—"

"I'm not suggesting anything. I know better than to suggest anything to you."

It wasn't love.

"Élise and I have been working alongside each other, that's all."

"Good." Walter eased himself to his feet and strolled over to his new machine. He stood looking at it while Sean stared at him in exasperation.

"I fixed the deck because I wanted to be around for you and Grams. It had nothing to do with Élise."

"Thoughtful of you. We all appreciate it. And it was thoughtful of you to take her camping."

Sean clenched his jaw. "Tyler was busy."

He thought he saw his grandfather smile but when he looked again Walter was staring intently at his new toy. "Does this thing come with a manual?"

It wasn't love.

There was *no way* this was love. It was a serious case of lust with a whole lot of like and laughter thrown in.

"She doesn't want a relationship. Neither do I."

"Sounds like you're perfectly matched."

Perfectly matched?

Sweat bathed the back of his neck. He thought about Élise breathless and laughing in the rain. Hugging his grandfather. Dancing on the deck. Ripping his shirt off. He thought of her legs, her passion, her kindness, her dimple, her mouth. *Oh, God, that mouth.* The mouth he could happily kiss every day for the rest of his life.

No!

It wasn't love. No way. *No way.*

His heart was pounding. He couldn't breathe. His chest felt tight.

He stared down at his shaking hands and realized

he'd never felt panic like this before. Not even knowing he had someone's life in his hands. His job was something he'd trained long and hard to do, but this? Nothing had trained him for this.

He forced himself to breathe slowly and think calmly and analytically.

"I'm not in love, Gramps. And I won't pretend I am just to please you. I have to get back to Boston." He stood up and dug his keys out of his pocket. Dropped them. Cursed under his breath as his grandfather's brows rose.

"Are you all right? Because normally you have the steadiest pair of hands I've seen."

"I'm fine. But I have a busy week. I'm making up time." And at least back in Boston people wouldn't be making ridiculous suggestions.

"Drive carefully. Your grandmother worries about you." Walter stood up, rubbing the base of his back. "Sometimes you think you don't want something, and then it turns out you were wrong. Has that ever happened to you?"

"No, it has not." Sean ground his teeth. "I do not love her."

"I was talking about my log splitter." His grandfather glanced over to his new toy. "What were you talking about?"

Sean felt as if he were being strangled. "I have to go."

CHAPTER EIGHTEEN

ÉLISE SMILED AS she wound a scarf around her neck and added discreet jewelry.

It was family night, and Sean was coming home.

If anyone had told her at the beginning of summer that he'd be joining them for family night she wouldn't have believed it, but now that he'd healed the rift with his grandfather it was a natural next step to spend a little more time at Snow Crystal.

"*Et donc,* even two very stubborn men can eventually be persuaded to talk to each other." She beamed at herself in the mirror and swept lip gloss over her mouth, relieved that the O'Neil family were sailing in smoother waters. The Boathouse was a success, the resort itself wasn't exactly booming but it was stable, Walter was relaxed, Alice was her old self and Elizabeth had a new bounce in her stride.

And as for her—

Her heart pumped a little bit faster.

It had been a week since dinner and Sean hadn't been in touch but that didn't worry her. She hadn't been in touch with him, either. They didn't have that sort of relationship. She enjoyed his company—*what woman wouldn't?*—and it was true their friendship had grown over the summer into something she would never have predicted, but that was simply because they'd spent so much time together.

She was pleased for Walter's sake that he was coming to family night. For herself, it didn't bother her either way.

Convinced of that, she took the stairs down to the kitchen and then stopped when she saw him standing in the open doorway. His shirt was unbuttoned at the neck and his eyes were tired.

"Sean! I wasn't expecting you. I was on my way over to the house. How was your drive?"

"Long. Hot. Can I come inside?" Without waiting for an answer, obviously tense, he walked into her kitchen and closed the door. "How are things here? Gramps all right?"

"He is doing well! And things here are good, I think. A little busier than usual. The Inn is fully booked for the next three weeks, the café is doing well, Jackson says bookings are up for the winter." She wondered why he was standing so far away from her and then realized she was being ridiculous. He'd come home for family night, not to indulge in hot sex in the forest. "Kayla has been really happy with the media coverage and she's negotiating for me to do a guest cookery slot on local TV."

"That's great."

"Yes, I must try not to say *merde* on camera or Kayla says she will kill me." She had a feeling he wasn't listening. "Walter is so pleased with his log cutting machine. It was a good choice. You are very clever, I think. And Tom has been helping us out in the garden so that's been a real help for Elizabeth." She wondered how Sean would react to the news but he didn't seem to be listening. Instead, he stared out of the window at the lake.

"That's good."

She studied his profile, admiring the straight sweep of his nose, the strong lines of his jaw. "Is something wrong?"

"No. Yes." He turned and his gaze collided with hers. "Let's go outside."

Her gaze slid from him to the door. "I thought you wanted to be inside."

"I've changed my mind. I want to do this outside."

"Do what?"

But he was already striding through the door.

She followed him, baffled. "What's wrong? Is this to do with family night? Are you feeling pressure? Did you have a bad day at work?"

"No and no." He paced to the edge of the deck and locked his hands over the smooth wood of the railings. For a moment he stared down at the water and then he drew a deep breath. "I told myself this couldn't happen to me. I've always believed that."

"What couldn't happen to you?"

"I refused to look at the truth because looking at it scared me."

"What truth? What scared you?" Frustration mingled with exasperation and a deeper concern that his relationship with his grandfather, still fragile, was about to be shattered again. "I do not understand what you are saying. *Merde,* in a minute I will push you in the lake again if you do not tell me."

"I didn't think I wanted this."

"*What didn't you want?* You are making no sense at all and I am the foreigner here."

"I didn't want to fall in love. I never wanted that. I didn't think it would happen to me."

The air was still. The only sound was the occasional faint splash as birds skimmed the water. "You—?"

"I love you." Everything about him was tense. Jaw. Shoulders. "Christ, before this summer I'd never said those words before in my life and suddenly I'm saying them all the time."

"What do you mean, you are saying them all the time?"

"I said them to Gramps."

The breath left her in a rush. "Of course you did." Relief flooded her. "That is good. You love him. For a moment I thought you were saying the words to me."

"I was. I am."

She stared at him stunned, wondering if she'd misunderstood. If this was a language thing.

"You *love* me? No, you don't."

"I do." His eyes met hers and his voice was soft. "I love you, Élise."

"What? *C'est pas vrai.* You're wrong." Panic simmered below the surface. "Sean, you're freaking me out."

He gave a short laugh. "Believe me, I've been freaking out all week."

"All *week?*"

"Since Gramps suggested it."

"Your grandfather—?"

"He knew. He knows."

Some of the tension left her. Finally there was an explanation for his strange behavior. "Thank goodness. It is just Walter playing his games, interfering. He has been pressuring you again and it has confused you."

"No. Not this time. He just made me think about a few things, that's all. And I'm not confused. I'm very clear about my feelings."

The panic was back, this time increasing in intensity. "It is pressure, just subtle pressure. It is what he does best, you know that. You have to ignore him just as you have for the past three decades."

"This isn't about him. It's about me. And you." His gaze was steady. "I know I love you. And I think you love me."

Oh, God. "I don't! Of course I don't."

She couldn't. She wouldn't. That wasn't going to happen to her ever again.

His eyes locked on hers. "Are you sure?"

"Of course I am sure! And what arrogance is this to assume I don't know my own mind? You're so used to being able to have your pick of women, you can't imagine that one might not feel the same way about you as you do about her." Her hands were shaking and she wrapped her arms around herself, wondering why she suddenly felt so cold.

Love? No way. No *way* was that ever going to happen to her again.

"Élise, you were so jealous when you thought I'd slept with that nurse you almost drowned me and knocked me unconscious."

"Because I thought you'd let Sam down. I may have overreacted. Just a little. And if you're really in love with me, which I doubt, then I'm sorry for it, but I never gave you reason to think this relationship would go anywhere." She was talking so fast the words tumbled over each other. "For me it has only ever been a casual summer fling. I thought it was the same for you."

"A casual summer fling? Sweetheart, we left casual behind weeks ago. In fact, if we're honest, we left casual behind last summer when we spent the whole night together."

"That was just sex."

"Maybe it was, but what we have now is a hell of a lot more than that and you know it."

"No, I don't. To me, it isn't more." Her heart was pounding. Her mouth was dry.

"The best parts of this summer have been the time I spent with you."

"Yes, because the sex is fantastic and it has blown your brain." She backed away. "I think perhaps you should not operate for a few days. You are not yourself. Why are you saying all this? We are the same. Neither of us wanted this. It's the reason we get on so well."

"Has it occurred to you that the reason we get on so well is because we like each other? We make each other laugh. We can't share the same space without wanting to rip each other's clothes off."

"That is just chemistry."

"Just?" He lifted an eyebrow. "I think about you all the time."

"That is very normal. Men think of sex every six seconds."

"In that case I'm in trouble because I'm down to about two seconds. And I'm not talking about sex. I'm talking about *you*. I think about *you* every two seconds. The way you laugh, the way you talk, the way you walk. All of it."

"So we will go indoors and have sex and then we will go to family night and you will forget it."

"I'm not going to forget it, Élise. This isn't going to

go away. The way I feel isn't going to change. I love being with you. I love who you are. I love your passion. I love that you're so loyal and that you love my family so much. I even love the side of you that would push me in the lake." He breathed. "I love you and I really do think you love me, too."

"I don't! I will never fall in love again, *ever.* I told you that. You knew that. I can't."

"I know you don't want to and I understand that you're scared." His voice was gentle. "I know you went through hell and your life fell apart. I understand that has left you feeling vulnerable and determined to protect yourself, but are you really going to let Pascal ruin the rest of your life?"

"Ruin? My life is happy! I have never been happier!"

"So you'd rather live on the edges of my family than in the center of your own?"

A lump wedged itself in her throat. "I love your family."

"And they love you. But every night you go home to your own house and sleep alone. You deserve to live life to the full, experience everything it has to offer, not hide away here so that you don't get hurt."

She couldn't breathe.

She felt as if all the oxygen had been sucked from the air.

"To tell you this is the hardest thing because I do not want to hurt you, and I know how hard it must have been to say those things to me, but I don't love you. I don't love you and I won't lie to you about that."

"What about lying to yourself?" His voice was raw. "Are you willing to do that?"

"I am not lying! I have been honest about my feelings. You are the one who has changed."

"Yeah, I've changed. But I recognize that and I'm trying to deal with it. What you're doing is hiding. When you're ready to admit that, come and find me." He turned to walk away and she took a step toward him.

"Wait! You can't just— Where are you going? It's family night." She couldn't believe that an evening she'd been looking forward to had ended before it had even started.

"Suddenly I'm not in the mood for family night."

"But Alice is looking forward to it. Everyone will be there—your grandfather, Tyler, Jess, your mother and—I'll be there, too."

There was a brief pause and then he turned his head and looked at her. "Do you think this was easy for me? That it meant nothing? Do you really think I can tell you I love you and then sit across the kitchen table and act as if nothing happened?"

"I wish it hadn't happened. I didn't want it to happen." Tears wedged in her throat and stung her eyes. "I didn't ask you to say that. I didn't *want* you to say that. We had an agreement—"

"Yeah." He gave a crooked smile. "And I broke it."

"Please don't leave. You just arrived and—" her voice broke "—you *can't* leave. Everyone is expecting to see you. Alice is so excited. Your mother—even Walter. They've talked of nothing else all week. The whole family is together for the first time in ages."

"I hope they have a nice evening." He turned and strode away from her, leaving Élise standing staring after him feeling as if she'd been run over by a truck.

For the first time in months he'd been intending to

join them for family night, and now she'd ruined it. And *he'd* ruined it. He'd ruined everything.

Her phone buzzed and she saw a text from Kayla.

Where are you? Put your clothes on and get over here :)

Kayla thought she and Sean were—

Feeling sick, she slumped on the chair on her deck.

She didn't want to go to family night now, either, but someone had to tell them that Sean wasn't coming.

They'd be so disappointed.

And it was her fault. *All her fault.*

Knowing she had to get it over with, she stood up and walked slowly toward the house. There was a roar of an engine and she saw a flash of red as Sean's sports car sped out of Snow Crystal toward Boston.

Gone.

Part of her wanted to chase after him, wave her arms and yell at him to turn around but her feet were welded to the ground and her mouth was too dry to make a sound.

How could he love her?

Sean didn't fall in love. He didn't want that. And he knew she didn't want that.

Shaken, she opened the door to the kitchen and was engulfed by laughter and delicious smells of cooking. Walter was in his usual place at the head of the table, Alice was knitting, Tyler was arguing with Jackson and Kayla was checking her emails under the table. Jess was helping Elizabeth with the cooking.

Maple jumped up and down like a spring, barking a welcome.

They were all there, the whole O'Neil family around

the table. Only one member was missing and that was her fault. She was the reason he wasn't here.

Her legs trembled. She felt sick.

"Come in, dear, we were wondering where you were." Elizabeth placed a large blue casserole dish in the center of the table. "Sean is late, but I suppose that's not a surprise to anyone."

Élise tried to speak but her voice wouldn't work. She stooped and picked Maple up, needing the comfort. Then she tried again.

"I— He isn't coming." It was such a faint croak that for a moment she thought no one had heard, but then Alice patted the chair next to her.

"Of course he's coming, honey. He promised he'd be here. We saw his car just half an hour ago. We're all so excited. It's the first time Sean has been here for family night since Christmas. I just love having the whole family together."

Elizabeth tipped crisp roast potatoes into a dish. "He's probably taking a phone call from the hospital. You know what he's like. Jess, I need another mat for the table, sweetheart. And some napkins."

Tyler pulled a face. "I never understood the point of napkins."

They weren't listening to her. They were all so excited at the prospect of Sean's arrival, they weren't paying any attention.

She tried again, and this time her voice was louder. "He isn't coming. He's driving back to Boston." She sank into the vacant chair, still holding Maple. The dog licked her palm and gazed up at her with warm caramel eyes, sensing her misery.

"But that just doesn't make sense." Alice looked

puzzled. "Why would he come home and then drive back again?"

Because of her.

She was the reason.

But what was she supposed to say? *He told me he loved me, but I don't love him?*

"I'm sorry."

There was a disappointed silence and then Elizabeth forced a smile. "Well, I don't know why you're apologizing. It's not your fault."

It *was* her fault.

This time it was *all* her fault.

She was the reason he wasn't here with his family.

She'd driven a wedge between them and she'd never, ever intended for that to happen. She should have stopped him from walking away. Instead of allowing him to leave, *she* should have left. She should have made an excuse about being too busy in the restaurant, and encouraged him to spend the time with his family.

She'd ruined everything.

"Do you think something bad has happened?" Alice was looking troubled. "Perhaps Jackson should call him. He said he was going to be here. He doesn't normally say that. We were all looking forward to it. Jackson, you should definitely call him. Something might be wrong."

Something was wrong, Élise thought. She'd hurt him.

Jackson pulled out his phone, dialed and then shrugged. "It's going to voice mail."

She felt like sliding under the table. Guilt showered her. This summer had finally mended the rift between Sean and his family. He should be here. He would have been here if it hadn't been for what had happened between them. He deserved the support of his family and instead she was the one sitting here, soaking up the O'Neil warmth in her hour of misery.

"Stop fussing." It was Walter who spoke, his voice firm. "He's probably just been called back to the hospital, and didn't have time to tell us. We all need to get on and eat. I'm starving."

"Me, too." Tyler reached for a plate. "I'm glad he's not here. I'll eat his portion. Just don't expect me to use two napkins."

Élise sat there, watching them all, these people who had taken her in and treated her like a member of the family. None of them had any idea that she was the reason Sean wasn't here.

Jackson handed Tyler a beer. "Did you take that family out on the mountain bike trail? How did they get on?"

"They were good and the whole party returned alive with their limbs attached which is good since our resident surgeon has left us." Tyler was about to put his feet up on the table when he caught his mother's eye and rethought it. "Jess came, too, didn't you, angel?"

Elizabeth's eyes softened as she glanced at her granddaughter. "How was it, sweetheart?"

"It was fun." Jess helped serve the food. "Except the mom couldn't stop looking at my dad. That was pretty gross."

"Understandable, not gross." Tyler heaped potatoes onto his plate. "Sooner or later you're going to have to get used to the fact that your dad is a sex symbol."

Alice sent him a disapproving look but Jess snorted with laughter.

"Dad, that is even more gross."

"Women just can't help themselves around me."

Jackson rolled his eyes. "Did you rebook them for next week?"

Jess was still giggling. "The mom rebooked. For two more sessions."

They chatted, shared news and stories, and Élise sat quietly, her hand resting on Maple's soft head.

Maybe they'd get through tonight, but what would happen next time? Not just family night but Christmas, celebrations, birthdays and anniversaries. Would he stay away then, too?

While she was here, he'd never be able to come home, would he?

She'd stolen this from him.

She'd stolen his family.

She looked at Jackson who was laughing at something Tyler had said. Dear Jackson, who had saved her when her life had hit rock bottom. From the first day she'd arrived at Snow Crystal, she'd known she wanted to live here forever, but how could she stay when staying meant sending an earthquake through the family?

She looked at Walter who was smiling at Alice and heaping his plate with vegetables grown in his own garden. He was improving by the day and with the winter ahead he'd be looking forward to skiing with his three grandsons.

And Elizabeth—dear Elizabeth who was like a mother to her.

They'd been so good to her.

"I wanted to thank you all." The words blurted out and she saw their surprise. "I just— I don't know if I have said this before but you are wonderful people and you have given me a home and a job and a life when

I needed it and I will always love you very much. I just wanted to say that while we are all together here because, well, it is important to sometimes say these things."

Elizabeth's expression softened. "We love you, too, dear. We're so lucky to have you."

"I'd have to agree with that." Walter grunted and gave her a wink. "Even if your idea of what makes a good pancake differs from mine."

"I love her pancakes," Alice said happily. "I'm knitting you a new scarf for Christmas, Élise. This one will be green. And I'm knitting you a sweater, Tyler."

Tyler's expression switched to one of alarm. "You don't have to do that, Grams. That's way too much work for you. You just knit Élise a scarf and I'll enjoy looking at it."

Alice beamed. "It's no trouble. And with winter coming I'll have plenty of time to knit."

Élise looked at the wool and thought of the previous Christmas when Alice had knitted everyone a red scarf. She'd been careful to wear it every time she'd visited them.

"Are you all right?" It was Jackson who asked her the question. Jackson who noticed that she wasn't herself.

"Me? I am fine." She switched on her most exaggerated smile. "But it's important sometimes to say these things so people know they are loved and appreciated." She hadn't done it with her mother and because of that she had to live with the fact that her mother had died not knowing how much she was loved. "You are all very special to me. The most important thing in my life."

"Are they all like you in France?" Tyler finished his

beer. "Because I don't have a problem being loved and appreciated. Maybe I should move there."

Everyone laughed and the attention moved away from Élise. She stroked Maple gently, drinking in their faces and their voices. And when Jackson asked her once again if she was sure she was all right, she smiled and nodded.

She was fine. She was going to be fine.

"DR. O'NEIL? Your brother wants to speak to you. He says it's an emergency."

Sean looked up from the MRI scan he was studying. Emergency? Was it his grandfather? His heart lurched. He hadn't been in touch all week. Not since the conversation with Élise. There had been a missed call from Jackson but no message and he hadn't returned the call. "Which phone?"

"He's not on the phone. He's waiting outside." She looked dazed. "I didn't know you had a twin brother."

"He's here?" Sean straightened. "I'll be back in a moment." Wondering what could possibly have brought Jackson to Boston without warning, he pushed through the doors. One glance at his normally calm brother's tense shoulders told him this wasn't a social call. "What's wrong? Is it Gramps?"

Jackson's mouth was tight. "Gramps is fine. But we need to talk. Is there somewhere we can go?"

Worried, Sean gestured toward the end of the corridor. "There's an office we can use just along here. So what's going on? You've never come to the hospital before."

As soon as the door closed, giving them privacy,

Jackson rounded on him. "Damn you, I warned you not to mess with her."

"I don't know what the hell you're talking about."

"Élise. She's gone. And it's your fault."

"Gone?" Sean felt his mouth go dry. "Gone where?"

"Back to Paris."

"Paris?" He thought about what she'd told him. Thought about what the place meant to her. "No. She wouldn't have done that."

Jackson thrust a piece of paper at him. "Read that."

Sean unfolded it and saw it was a printed copy of an email. Élise's name was on the top. "It's addressed to you."

"Read it."

Mon cher Jackson, I am so very sorry to let you down but I can no longer stay at Snow Crystal. It is very sad for me because I thought I would be here forever, but I see now that is not possible. I hope you will forgive me. I will never do anything to harm your family and staying will make it awkward for Sean to come home. Do not try and argue with me or come after me because I know I am right. I am supposed to give you notice, but I have trained Elizabeth and Poppy and they are both very good, and all the other staff, they are good, too. Snow Crystal has a strong team. Me, I shall go back to Paris. I should have done it a long time ago but I am a great big coward and it was easier to hide here with you where it was safe. I will miss you and Kayla, Brenna, Tyler, Jess, Elizabeth and dear Alice, and of course, Walter, more than I can say, but perhaps one day when you have forgiven me you will visit me and I will show you Paris. The nice parts, not the tourist parts. You saved me when my life was so very terrible and I will never forget that. Do not worry about me, I will be fine. And do not be angry with Sean. The fault is mine, not his. I didn't mean to steal his family. Again, I am so very sorry to let you down. Élise.

Sean scanned the email again. "I don't believe this. She wouldn't walk out on you. She just wouldn't."

"That's what I thought. Seems we were both wrong."

"She hero worships you."

"Which just goes to prove how bad she must be feeling to do this."

Sean swore under his breath. "I can't believe she'd choose to go back to Paris." He thought of her, alone and anxious in a city she'd vowed never to return to, and something knotted in his gut. "Why the hell would she do that?" He barely had time to finish the sentence before he was slammed back against the door and Jackson's fist was locked in the front of his shirt.

"Damn it, you *know* why she's doing that! She's doing it because of you! She says so in the email. I warned you to stay away from her but you just couldn't do it, could you?"

Staring into the furious eyes of his normally even-tempered brother, it took Sean a moment to gather himself. "Let go of me, you're wrinkling my shirt. And you don't know what you're talking about."

"She was happy at Snow Crystal. She had a home. We're family to her. And now you've gone and trampled the whole of that just so that you could burn up the sheets with her for five minutes."

"It was more than five minutes," Sean snapped, "and

she was hiding with you because she was too afraid to live her life."

"So you thought you'd help her live it?"

"It wasn't like that." Pushing his brother away, he paced to the center of the office.

Why would she do this, when Paris held nothing but bad memories for her? *Why?*

"You've got no end of women to pick from, but you just had to have Élise."

"I've told you, it wasn't like that."

"So you're going to pretend you didn't get involved with her?"

"No, I'm not!" Struggling with his own feelings, Sean backed away. Where would she have gone? Not to *him,* surely. Maybe this was his fault. He'd accused her of hiding, hadn't he? "She still owns an apartment in Paris. It belonged to her mother."

"She told you that?"

"She told me a lot of things. She hasn't been back there since she left. What if Pascal finds out she's back? Will he hurt her? What if he hasn't moved on?"

Jackson's eyes narrowed warily. "She told you about that, too?"

"Yeah, she told me."

"She's never told anyone else that. Not even Kayla and Brenna."

"Well, she told me. And she also told me she'd never go back to Paris. She was scared." And guilty that she'd let her mother down. Lonely. Frightened. Sweat pricked the back of his neck. "Do you have an address? Do you know where that apartment is?"

"No, and if I did, I wouldn't tell you. Seems like you didn't just rip up the sheets with her, you let her get close to you. You encouraged her to spill her secrets, something she has never done before by the way, and then you did your usual thing and told her you didn't love her." Jackson stood, legs spread, glaring at him. "You broke her heart."

Sean felt the ache in his chest throb. It was the same ache that had been there every day for a week. "That is not what happened."

"Really? Then why don't you tell me your version, and tell me fast because right now I feel like putting a few dents in you. If you didn't break her heart, why isn't she still at Snow Crystal?"

"Because she broke mine!" His tone raw, Sean paced to the other side of the room. "She broke mine, all right? And it fucking hurts, so don't come here and lecture me about causing her pain."

There was a stunned silence. "She broke yours?"

"Yeah. And now if you don't mind I need to be on my own to think this through."

"I drove here to find out what's going on and I'm not leaving until I find out."

Sean gritted his teeth. "I told her I loved her. She told me she didn't love me. Do you need more detail than that? And you're welcome to tell me I deserved it and that I finally got what was coming to me but I'd rather you waited until I've sorted this out." He saw the astonishment in his brother's face and gave a humorless laugh. "You're thinking this is justice. Well deserved for all those women who cried on your shirt because I wouldn't tell them I loved them. The first time I actually say those words to a woman it's to one who doesn't want to hear them."

"You actually told her you loved her? And she left?" Jackson's brows rose. "I'm confused."

"Then you don't know her as well as you think you do."

"I assumed she'd fallen in love with you and it wasn't mutual. I assumed she'd left so it wouldn't be awkward. If you're in love with her, why did she leave? That makes no sense."

"It makes perfect sense. We're her family. Or rather, you are." Sean gave a grim smile. "Family is the most important thing to her. She's spent the whole summer trying to get me to fix the damage with Gramps. Pushing me to talk to him, to heal things."

"And you did. So why would she leave?"

"Because she thinks if she's there, it will keep me away. She thinks I'll come home less. That the family will see me less."

"Because you didn't show up to family night?"

"That was probably what put the thought in her head. Having just been rejected I wasn't in the mood for family togetherness."

"And you're sure you said those words? You didn't just imply it, or assume she knew or—"

"I said those words! Those three words I never thought I'd say. First time ever, well apart from Gramps but I don't count that."

"Gramps?"

"Never mind. For the record, I said them more than once to Élise, just so that there could be no misunderstanding. And no, she didn't say them back, she didn't run into my arms and no, we're not going to live happily ever after. Can we stop talking about it now? Living through it the first time was hard enough. Reliving it isn't much fun, either."

Jackson ignored him. "I'm surprised, because I actually thought—" He shook his head. "Never mind. It explains why she was so quiet at family night. And why she kept saying it was her fault that you hadn't turned up."

"It wasn't her fault. It was mine. I wasn't in the mood for company, but I didn't for a moment think she'd blame herself for the fact I wasn't there, or that she'd decide she was a threat to our family."

"She was behaving very oddly. She told us all how much she loved us."

"Why is that odd? She tells everyone she loves them all the time. Everyone except me. Have you tried calling her?"

"Her phone is switched off."

"Why would she switch her phone off?" His concern deepened. He thought of her going back to a place she hadn't returned to since she'd left with Jackson. A place that held nothing for her except memories of violence and loss. The thought of her facing that alone made his chest ache. "I'll fly to Paris."

"How are you going to do that?"

"The same way everyone does it. I'm going to get on a plane."

"But you have work."

"This is more important. Élise hasn't been back there for—how long is it? Eight years? Someone should be with her." He pulled his phone out and searched for flights while Jackson gaped at him.

"You're going to take time off?"

"I did it when Gramps collapsed."

"Gramps is family."

"So is Élise. People will have to cover for me."
Again. He already owed more favors than he could
ever repay. "There's a direct flight to Paris leaving tonight. All I need is the address."

"I don't have an address. She's worked for me for
the past eight years."

"But you went to her apartment the night you res-
cued her. What do you remember about it?"

"It was eight years ago and I was dealing with an
abusive husband and a terrified woman. I wasn't exactly looking at the neighborhood."

Sean reined in his impatience. "Think!"

"All I remember is getting her out of there and trying not to break every bone in that man's body." Jackson spread his hands, clearly frustrated. "She lived near
the river, I know that. We were in her apartment for
less than half an hour. She just stuffed a few things in
a case while I kept watch in case he showed up. I could
just see the Louvre from her bathroom window. *Rue
de Lille,* yes that's it. She lived on the *Rue de Lille.*"

"Apartment number?"

"No idea."

Rolling his eyes, Sean booked himself a flight out of
Boston. "Let's just hope it isn't a long street."

"You're just going to turn up there and hope you
can find her?"

"If you don't have her address, I don't have much
choice."

"How do you know she's going to want to see you?"

"I don't. But I know that if she's back in that place
she's going to need a friend."

CHAPTER NINETEEN

THE APARTMENT WAS coated with thick dust and a deep layer of memories. They choked her, suffocated her, made her throat ache and her eyes sting. It hadn't changed. Nothing had changed and everywhere she looked she saw her mother. And mistakes.

The feelings she'd buried pushed their way to the surface. Picking up a pot she'd made in school when she was eight years old, she turned it over in her hand, remembering her mother's delight on the day she'd brought it home.

She'd just been kidding herself, hadn't she? When she'd thought she'd moved on, she'd been kidding herself. All she'd done was ignore the past, block it out, refuse to look at it like a child closing her eyes in a dark room so that she couldn't see what was there. But she hadn't really moved on. There was a big black hole in her life and instead of filling it in, she'd fenced it off and tiptoed around it, afraid to look at it, afraid that if she took one wrong step she'd fall back in.

Tired after the long flight and crushed by the memories, she collapsed on top of the bed, unable to sleep, and spent the night thinking of her mother, tortured by guilt, knowing she couldn't live here, sharing this tiny apartment with the ghosts of her past.

But she couldn't go back, either.

Sean didn't need another reason to stay away from Snow Crystal. The O'Neils didn't need someone disrupting their family.

In the morning she threw open the shutters and stood for a moment watching sunshine dance across the roofs of Paris. The apartment was tiny but the position perfect, just a few steps from the river Seine. If she stood on tiptoe and peeped out of the small bathroom window she could see the distinctive architecture of the Louvre.

With light and fresh air pouring into the apartment, she started clearing.

It took her two days.

She filled huge sacks with clothing and possessions. Some she threw away, some she took to a thrift store. She wanted no reminders of the past, no reminders of the bad choices she'd made, the consequences, the misery. The only exception to that were a few personal items of her mother's and a collection of photographs. She'd had no idea her mother had taken so many. A quick glance showed that they ranged from baby photos right through to a clipping of Élise being the only woman in the otherwise all-male kitchen of Chez Laroche. Finding an empty shoe box she stuffed them inside, promising herself that she'd look at them properly one day, hoping the time would come when she'd be able to go through them without feeling bad.

When she'd finished clearing, she vacuumed, polished and wiped until the place gleamed and not a speck of dust remained.

It helped her to keep busy, to occupy her mind and to not think.

She tried not to think about cooking with her mother,

about those dark days with Pascal. But the one thing she absolutely couldn't stop thinking about was the O'Neils.

What would they be doing now? She glanced at her phone and calculated the time difference. It would be morning in Vermont and they'd be serving breakfast in the Boathouse.

Kayla would be on her phone, checking emails. Tyler would be eyeing the female guests and grumbling about the work. Walter would be overdoing it. Alice would be knitting and worrying and Elizabeth would be busy in the kitchens with Poppy. And Jackson, dear Jackson, would be keeping everything going, steering the ship into deeper water so it didn't smash to pieces on the rocks.

Did they miss her? Did they think of her?

No, probably not.

She'd let Jackson down. After everything he'd done for her, she'd let him down.

To drive out the guilt and the misery she worked herself to the point of exhaustion but still she couldn't sleep and at night she lay awake in the bed listening to the scream of car engines, horns and sounds of the city finding it impossible not to think of Heron Lodge.

She missed the peace of the lake, the nights when the only sound was the hoot of an owl swooping overhead. She missed the smell of the water and the fresh scent of the forest.

She missed Sean.

Not that she loved him, because she absolutely didn't. She'd switched that part of herself off, refused to allow her emotions access to her decision-making or the way she lived her life. But they'd had a wonderful summer and she missed him. She missed the laughter, the flirting, his intelligence, his appreciation of food and wine and yes, she missed the sex. And she couldn't stop thinking about him.

Had he been home since that day he'd told her he loved her? Was he still staying away?

She hoped not.

She rose early and was sitting on the floor, sorting listlessly through yet another drawer full of photographs when she heard the unmistakable sound of male footsteps on the curving staircase that led to her top-floor apartment.

She'd barely left the apartment except for her few trips to the shops. It was unlikely that anyone she knew had spotted her. Even less likely that Pascal would take the trouble to pay her a visit.

All the same her heart stumbled as she heard the footsteps pause outside her door.

Had Pascal somehow found out she was back?

"Élise?"

Her heart stumbled as she recognized Sean's voice.

Sean was in Paris?

Scrambling to her feet, she pulled open the door. "What are you doing here? Has something happened to Walter? Or Jackson?"

"Why do you always assume that when I show up there has to be bad news?" He held up a bottle of wine. "I found this amazing bottle of Pinot Noir and I have no one to drink it with. It's wasted on Tyler and Jackson is too busy."

She gave a choked laugh. "So you flew to Paris?"

"I don't know anyone who appreciates wine and food like you do."

She stared at the wine, then at him. "What are you *doing* here? You should be in Boston, working."

"Some things are more important than work." He stepped inside without waiting for an invitation and dropped his bag on the floor. "I heard you were in Paris. I thought you might need a friend."

"A friend?"

"I don't blame you for looking surprised. I don't claim to be an experienced friend, but I have had plenty of experience of going back to a place that has bad memories so I figure I can learn the rest as I go along."

She was still dizzy from the shock of seeing him on her doorstep. "How did you find me?"

"I threatened Jackson until he revealed everything he could remember about the view from the window. I got here and worked it out. There aren't that many apartments that give a view of the river and the Louvre. I banged on a few doors and woke a few people up." He put the wine down on the counter and glanced around him. "Nice place."

"It's tiny." And it seemed even tinier now that Sean was standing in it. Broad and powerfully built, he filled the space but there was something so reassuring about his presence she felt the tension rush out of her. She should send him away but she couldn't bring herself to do it.

"If you're done cleaning, do you feel like showing me around? Taking me to your favorite parts of Paris? You should have phoned me to tell me you were thinking of coming, then we could have flown together."

"I wouldn't have done that."

"No. You're too scared that calling me will turn what we have into a relationship. I get that." He opened cupboards until he found wineglasses. "So, I'm starving and there's nothing to eat here. What's wrong? Your kitchen is usually crammed with food."

"I didn't feel like cooking." Because everything reminded her of her mother and remembering hurt too much. And perhaps he realized that because he watched her for a long moment and then nodded.

"Right. Well I'm doubly glad I came because if you don't feel like cooking then I know there's something wrong. So where is the best place for dinner?"

"Close by? There is only a local brasserie."

"That will do fine."

"Sean, what are you *doing* here?"

He poured wine into glasses and handed her one. "I never thanked you properly, did I?"

"Thanked me for what?"

"For being there this summer. For pushing me to fix things with Gramps. For listening while I talked about Dad. For all of it."

"I didn't do anything. You did it. You have nothing to thank me for." She sipped the wine and it was so good, for a moment she closed her eyes. It made her think of Snow Crystal, of summer, of *him*.

"Being with you got me through this summer. When I got the news that Gramps had collapsed—" he put his glass down slowly "—I felt as if I'd been kicked in the gut by a moose. And then when he told me to get back to Boston—I had no idea how to fix it—how to bridge that gulf."

"He loves you. He is so proud of you."

"I know. And I love him." He gave a faint smile. "Listen to me, getting all mushy, as Tyler would say."

"I'm glad things are better."

"They are. I've even promised to be there for family night next month and I'm talking to Brenna about helping put together a pre-conditioning program for the winter." He looked at the stack of shoe boxes on the floor. "What are those?"

"Photographs." She felt an ache in her chest. "My mother took a lot of photographs. I can't face looking at them yet but I can't bring myself to throw them away, either. I'm glad things are better at home for you, but that still doesn't tell me what you're doing here."

"So far you've done all the supporting in this friendship, so I figured it was my turn. I thought I'd hang around in case you need someone to carry heavy boxes or punch ex-husbands."

Her gaze met his. "You'd crumple your shirt."

"Some things are worth the sacrifice." He lifted his glass and drank. "So have you heard from him?"

"No. And I don't want to."

"Well, you don't need to worry about it now because I'm here so if he shows up, he and I can have a little conversation. And talking of conversations, it's your turn to tell me what *you're* doing here." He leaned against the counter, his broad shoulders dominating the narrow kitchen area. "What are you doing back in Paris when I know how much you love Snow Crystal? I know how much you love your job."

"I'm doing what I should have done a long time ago. I was a coward. I avoided coming back here because the place was full of bad memories."

"So put the apartment up for sale and then get yourself back to Snow Crystal. Winter is coming. Everyone is planning how to make the best of this season. You're an essential part of the team."

Something twisted inside her but she shook her head. "I can't do that."

"Fine. So don't sell it. Rent it."

"It isn't this place. I will sell it. I have someone coming around tomorrow to do a valuation. But I won't be coming back to Snow Crystal. I'll find somewhere else. Maybe not Paris. Maybe Bordeaux."

"Why? Because I told you I loved you and scared the hell out of you? That was a mistake." His voice was soft. "If I promise never to say it again, will you come back?"

"You think it was a mistake?"

"Yeah, that's right. Big mistake."

It was ridiculous to feel disappointed about something that she didn't want, anyway. It made no sense.

None of her feelings made any sense.

"You're right. We should go out." She grabbed her purse and her keys and ushered Sean out the door. "Tell me how everyone is. How is Walter? Is he using his new machine to cut logs? And Alice? How's her knitting coming along? Are Elizabeth and Poppy coping well in the kitchen?"

"I have no idea. You know I leave the running of Snow Crystal to my brother. You'll have to ask him when you see him."

She ignored that. "How did you know I had left?"

"Jackson came to the hospital ready to punch me. For the record, that's the first time I've seen my brother spoiling for a fight. Normally he's the one breaking them up." They reached the street and Sean caught her arm as a moped sped past, almost mowing her down.

She felt the strength of his fingers on her skin, breathed in the male scent and the desire to kiss him was almost overwhelming. Almost.

She pulled away. "He punched you? Jackson would never do that."

"No. But it was a close thing. That's how much he cares about you. He creased my shirt."

She couldn't help smiling. "I told him it wasn't your fault."

"He didn't believe you. If I come back without you my life won't be worth living."

It was a perfect late-summer evening and they ate in the little brasserie, sitting elbow to elbow with tourists and locals and drinking house wine and simple food. Then they walked along the river, watching the sun set over the Louvre.

Sean told her about his work at the hospital, about his research and then made her laugh with stories of Tyler's neck-breaking exploits growing up.

The only thing they didn't talk about was the fact he'd told her he loved her.

"Where are you staying tonight?"

"I've booked a hotel down the street. I wasn't sure you'd feel like company." He took the key from her and let them both into her apartment, watching her face as she paused by the door. "Bad memories?"

"Mostly guilt. I hate that my last words to my mother were angry and that she died without knowing how much I loved her. I can't stop thinking about it." Shaking it off, she walked to the little kitchen area. "Coffee?"

"Thanks." He sprawled on the sofa, next to the boxes of photos she'd stacked earlier. "I know you don't want to look at the photos, but do you mind if I look?"

"Go ahead." Maybe she should have thrown them

away. What was the point in keeping something that just made her feel worse?

She made coffee and placed a mug on the little table in front of him. "I miss my coffee machine."

"We all miss you making coffee with your coffee machine. Élise, you should look at these."

She kept her back to him. "I can't. Not yet. Maybe one day."

"You really should look at them."

"Sean—"

"You weren't sure if your mother knew you loved her and I can tell you for sure that she did."

"How do you know that?"

"Because I'm looking at the evidence, sweetheart. You should come take a look, too."

She turned and saw him leafing through photographs.

"Where was this taken?" He showed her a photo and she smiled, remembering.

"The top of the Arc De Triomphe. I was eight. I climbed to the top and was very proud of myself." Despite her reluctance, she sat down next to him.

"And this?" He went through the photos, asking when, why, how until she felt crowded by memories.

"Put them away, Sean."

He slid the photos back into the box and closed the lid. "I messed up with my grandfather but he forgave me because that's what families do. And even when I was angry with him, there wasn't a moment when I didn't love him. And he knew that."

"I know. The moment you heard he was in the hospital you dropped everything and came. But your family is different."

"Your mother knew you loved her. It's all here." He lowered the box gently onto her lap. "She knew you loved her and she loved you right back, which is why she wanted the best for you. It's what we always want for people we love. You can't switch that on and off. Cross words don't change that." He stood up. "I have to fly back tomorrow. Come with me."

She felt the tug of longing and ignored it. "I can't do that."

"Snow Crystal is your home. Everyone misses you. You should be there." He hesitated and for a moment she thought he was going to kiss her but then he walked to the door. "If you change your mind or if you need anything, call me."

"I won't. I've never called you."

His eyes gleamed. "I've never said 'I love you' before last week, which just proves anything can happen. My number is in your phone."

CHAPTER TWENTY

"So FINALLY THE whole family is together. It's like living in a fairy story, isn't it, Jess? We even have napkins. Civilization comes to Snow Crystal." Grinning, Tyler stood up and took the large casserole dish from his mother. "So that's my portion. Where is everyone else's?" He put it in the center of the table and glanced around. "I've never seen so many gloomy faces around a table. It's family night. You're all supposed to be laughing and enjoying one another's company. What the hell is wrong with everyone?"

Walter stirred. "Don't swear. It upsets your grandmother."

"That's not the reason I'm upset." Alice shook her head as Elizabeth tried to serve her some food. "I don't want much. I'm not hungry."

"I'm starving, I'll eat yours." Tyler reached forward and his napkin slid to the floor. "As I said, I've never seen the point of napkins."

Jess grinned. "It stops you getting food stains on your clothes."

"Stains add character. There's a story behind every mark on my jeans."

"We really don't want to know." Ignoring his brother, Jackson pushed the potatoes toward Alice. "You should eat, Grams."

Alice stared miserably at her plate. "I can't because it's pot roast. Pot roast is Élise's recipe. She's the one who taught Elizabeth how to cook it and I can't see it without thinking of her. It makes me feel sad that she's not here. Why wouldn't she come back with Sean when he flew all that way to see her? What did you say to her?"

Walter grunted. "It's probably more a question of what he didn't say to her."

Sean met Jackson's gaze across the table and reached for his wine. He was fairly sure there wasn't enough alcohol in the house to get him through the pressure of family night. Why had he agreed to come? "I said what I wanted to say."

"But did you tell her you loved her?" His grandmother's food lay untouched on the plate. "Women like to hear that and men don't say it often enough."

Tyler attacked his pot roast with no visible loss of appetite. "I love you, Grams."

Her eyes softened. "I know you do, honey. You've always been a wild one, but underneath you have a big strong heart and one day some woman is going to snap you up for the rest of your life."

Tyler choked on his food. "Not if I see her coming first."

Jess giggled. "You could hide under the napkin."

"That would be one use for it."

"What do you mean men don't say it enough?" Walter was looking at Alice. "I say it to you every day and have since the day we met."

"I know." Alice's gaze softened and she stretched out her hand. "I came to buy maple syrup—"

"Oh, please, no, not that—" Tyler dropped his fork

and pushed his plate away. "And please no kissing at the table. I am done with all this kissing at the table. If people want to gaze at each other then go book an evening in the restaurant and do the whole candles and wine thing. Don't bring it to family night."

"Talking of the restaurant, we need more help," Elizabeth said quietly. "Once the season starts we won't be able to cope without another member of staff. You'll need to recruit someone, Jackson."

Jackson reached for the salt. "I'll deal with it tomorrow."

"I'll do it." Kayla typed a note into her phone. "You have enough to do."

"You will not be recruiting anyone." Walter brought his fist down on the table with a thump that made cups and cutlery rattle. Maple dived for cover. "We already have the best chef there is. We don't need to go looking for another one."

Jackson put his fork down. "She's gone, Gramps. She's gone back to Paris."

"Because she had things to sort out there. And she'll be back when she's done. And in the meantime, we'll manage because that's what families do and she's family."

Jackson exchanged glances with Sean. "Gramps—"

"And her job will be here waiting for her when she's ready to return to it." Glaring, Walter reached for his glass but Sean noticed his hand was shaking.

"She's not coming back, Gramps." There was a heavy lump behind his chest. "Jackson has to make decisions about this place."

"She's been gone five minutes and already you want to give her job away?"

"She's gone, damn it!"

"I don't understand why everyone is shouting?" Alice pushed the food around her plate, too upset to complain about the language. "And I don't understand why she left. She loved it here. I know she loved it here. Last time we had family night she couldn't stop telling us how much she loved us."

"Because she was about to leave," Jackson said wearily. "It was her way of saying thank you but none of us understood it at the time."

Sean let out a breath. He understood it.

After what happened with her mother she would never, ever miss an opportunity to tell the people in her life that she loved them.

The irony was that she'd said it to everyone but him.

The ache behind his chest intensified.

"What does she have to thank us for?" Walter scowled. "We're the ones who should be thanking her for producing food that's the talk of Vermont, New Hampshire and most of the East Coast. We had people from California here last week who had read about her! So don't talk to me about finding a replacement because she's irreplaceable. And if Sean had spoken up, she might not have left."

Sean swore under his breath and thumped his glass down on the table. "I spoke up! I told her I loved her. Yeah, that's right—" He met his mother's astonished gaze. "I told her that. Several times, in fact, so there could be no misunderstanding. And now can we all talk about something else?"

Jackson sent him a concerned glance.

Tyler and Kayla were gaping at him and as for his mother—

"Oh, Sean." Tears shimmered in her eyes and she covered her mouth with her hand. "That's just— It's perfect. I couldn't be happier."

"You don't have any reason to be happy because she doesn't feel the same way, Mom. Now can we move on? We've talked about this for long enough."

"Doesn't—" Elizabeth exchanged glances with Alice, perplexed. "Well, of course she does."

Sean clenched his jaw, wondering what he had to do to move the conversation onto a different topic. "So how are bookings for the winter, Jackson?"

"Slightly up." His brother came to his rescue. "All we need now is plenty of snow, but overall I'm optimistic."

"I may not know anything about mending broken bones," Elizabeth said stoutly, "but I know when a woman is in love."

Alice smiled. "I knew straight away."

Sean breathed deeply, looking for an escape. "My phone is buzzing," he lied. "I've had it on silent." That was true, but when he pulled it out of his pocket and surreptitiously turned it on he saw that it really had been ringing.

He had twenty missed calls.

Exactly twenty. All from Élise.

"I have to—" *Shit.* Twenty? "I have to get this. I have to make a call."

Tyler sighed. "Of course you do. Lives to save, people to heal. Don't mind us. It means we can all talk about you behind your back."

Walter frowned. "Can't you tell them you'll call them back when you've finished your food? A man has a right to eat a meal."

Tyler reached across. "I'll eat his meal. Shame to let it get cold."

His grandfather slapped his hand. "He'll be coming back. Is there any problem that can't wait five minutes?"

Right on cue his phone started ringing again and Sean glanced down at the screen and saw Élise's name again. His heart lurched. She'd never called him before. Not once. And she'd been calling him and calling him and he'd had his phone switched off. What could have happened?

He told himself that twenty missed calls didn't mean anything except that something bad had happened.

Was it Pascal?

He never should have left her there alone.

The phone was still ringing but he didn't want to answer it in front of his family.

Sweating, he stood up quickly, knocked his wineglass over and sent wine flowing over the table. "I need to—"

"Go." Tyler stood up and threw his napkin on the table, watching as the cream fabric slowly turned red.

"Those napkins were a wedding present." His mother sighed as Tyler piled another one on top.

"Glad to have finally found a use for them."

Sean slammed the door behind him and answered the phone. "Élise? Are you all right?" His hand was shaking so badly he almost dropped the phone. "Where are you? Is something wrong?"

ÉLISE PACED ALONG the lake path, wondering if she'd misjudged. Wondering if he'd come. And then finally she saw him, sprinting through the rain, his shirt glued to his chest and his hair plastered to his head.

"I can't believe you're here! I thought you were in Paris." He grabbed her arms and pulled her under the shelter of the trees. "Why didn't you tell me you were coming back?"

"I didn't intend to, but then you left and I did a lot of thinking and, *merde,* why is it raining again?" She was shivering and he dragged her into his arms, holding her close.

"My phone was switched off and when I saw the missed calls from you I almost had a heart attack. I thought maybe Pascal had shown up at the apartment or something. You've never called me before. Never."

"I know." Her teeth were chattering but she knew it was nerves, not cold. "I needed to talk to you. I took a chance that you'd be here. It's family night."

"Why didn't you come straight to the house?"

"Because there are things I have to say. Just to you, not to everyone."

He eased away from her, his blue gaze suddenly sharp. "Do you want to go to Heron Lodge? We can dry off."

"No. This is fine." She gave a nervous laugh as water dripped through the trees onto her neck. "Most of our relationship has been conducted in this forest."

"Relationship?" His tone was guarded. Cautious. "I didn't think we had a relationship."

"Neither did I, but then I realized I was kidding myself. We've been in a relationship since the moment we first met. It was always there—the chemistry, the connection—all of it, but it frightened me so badly I wouldn't even consider it."

He breathed in deeply. "Élise—"

"Ever since Pascal I have never allowed my emotions

to be involved. I did not trust myself because with me everything is always exaggerated. I love with all of me, my whole heart, not just a little bit—" she clasped her fists to her chest "—and I could not risk that again so always now I make decisions with my head. And then suddenly last summer everything changed."

"It changed for me, too."

"I told myself it was nothing because you hardly ever came home so my feelings were easy to control, but I thought about you all the time."

"I thought about you, too. I thought you were like me. I couldn't understand why Jackson was so protective."

"So then you discovered I was not like you and you should have driven back to Boston at supersonic speed, but instead you kept coming back here and then you told me you loved me and it was a very big shock because I did not at all expect it."

"I was shocked, too, which is why I didn't handle that part well."

"The fault was not with you, it was with me. I was very afraid. I did not want to fall in love and I didn't want you to fall in love with me. I would not do anything that would harm your family or make things difficult. I love them so very much, but it's true that having them here for me made it easier for me to hide. I had love in my life, and that was enough for me. I told myself I didn't need romantic love."

"Élise—"

"I went back to Paris because I knew I had to face all the things I have been avoiding for so long. And then you came."

"I couldn't bear the thought of you facing that alone."

"It meant a lot to me that you came." She locked her hand in the front of his shirt, now soaked. "You were the one who made me look again at the photographs and think of everything differently. After you left I sat there and went through them all, every single one, and I could see that you were right. The evidence was right there for me to see. My mother loved me very much, and she knew I loved her. I will always regret that I didn't say those words to her more often, but I believe that you are right and she did know it. And I sat there after you left and I remembered how strong she was, living her life fearlessly even when it was hard, always finding fun in life, and I knew she would not be proud of me hiding away and being afraid all the time. She would not be pleased that one very bad decision stopped me from living my life fully."

"Sweetheart—"

"I spent a lot of time thinking about how it is between us, how amazing and how I feel when I am with you and I realized that I have been a great big idiot. So I got on a plane and came back here and I have just one question to ask you and you will answer me honestly because it is very important." Her heart was bumping and her hands were shaking. "In Paris you said that telling me you loved me was a mistake. Is that because you wish you hadn't told me, or because you don't love me? Because you also said that love wasn't something that could be switched on and off."

"The mistake wasn't loving you, it was telling you. I upset you. Scared you. Forced you to leave a place you see as home and people you think of as family. That's the reason it was a mistake. You had a life here you loved, and I shook that up."

"It needed to be shaken up. I did love it, but it wasn't a whole life. You were right when you said I was hiding."

"After what you went through no one would ever blame you for hiding."

"But I don't want to hide any longer. That's what I wanted to tell you. That's why I came back. To say I'm ready to start living properly and to say that—I love you." Saying it was so terrifying she almost choked on the words. "I really do love you, and if you still think you love me then maybe we could both try not to panic about this and perhaps see each other or something. Have a relationship that is as much indoors as outdoors. I can come to Boston sometimes and you can come here more often."

He didn't speak. Instead, he stared at her. Rain darkened his hair and clumped his lashes together and she waited, not breathing, the only sound the soft patter of rain on the trees around her.

Why didn't he say something?

Had she scared him to death?

She knew a moment of panic and then, just as she'd convinced herself she'd got it all wrong and misunderstood his feelings, he dragged her against him and brought his mouth down on hers.

"I don't think I love you, I *know*." He spoke the words against her mouth. "But I wasn't at all sure you loved me."

"Didn't you check your phone? You should have twenty missed calls. I called twenty times to tell you I love you but you didn't answer." Drenched in raindrops and happiness, she wrapped her arms around his neck.

"I love you. I love you with my whole self. I cannot switch it off. It is the worst thing about me, I think."

"I happen to think it's one of the best things about you. I love your passion and your loyalty to the people you love. I love that you called me twenty times to tell me you love me. I hope you do it every day." His voice was husky and he hauled her close and held her tightly. "I stayed away from this place because being here created so many conflicting emotions but over the summer I fell back in love with the place and you're the reason for that. I saw it through your eyes. You're the reason I managed to fix things with Gramps."

"You would have done it, anyway. I just pushed you a little because love should not be a quiet thing. It is important to tell people, every day. I learned that."

"You said it to everyone except me," Sean groaned, kissing her again. "You said it to my brothers, to my grandfather—to anyone and everyone except me. I'd given up ever hearing you say that to me."

"Because I was afraid of saying it. Saying it to you would have meant something very different. I always knew that. I was very scared. When you love with everything, you can lose everything."

"And you can also gain everything." He pulled her against him, trying to shelter her from the rain. "I always thought that relationships were all about sacrifice. It was Gramps who made me see that I was the one making the sacrifice."

"You should not have to make a sacrifice! Your work is important to you and I wouldn't want to change that. You are an amazing doctor. What you did for little Sam—" she shuddered "—you have such skill and you should use it."

"I will use it, but there's nothing to say I can't use it closer to here. Your job is here. Your life."

"Walter has been nagging you again. You need to make the decision that is right for you."

"This is the decision that is right for me and it has nothing to do with my grandfather, although it will feel good to be able to be more involved with the place and see more of my family. It's what I want for us. I've already talked to the local hospital about joining the orthopedic department. It's not going to be an instant thing, of course, but we can work something out in the meantime. My car has done the journey from Boston to Snow Crystal so often over the summer it can probably do it by itself now." He was kissing her again and she was kissing him, too, both of them pressed up against the tree.

She slid her hand under his shirt. "Perhaps we should go back to Heron Lodge."

"Yes. No. Wait—" With difficulty he dragged his mouth from hers. "There are still things I want to say."

"You can say them later."

"In my pocket—" The words were muffled against her neck and she closed her eyes.

"What about your pocket?"

"Put your hand in my pocket."

"I don't know what you—" Her fingers encountered a small square box and she stilled. "What is it?"

"It's for you. Open it." Those blue eyes burned into hers. "Open it."

Hands shaking, she flipped it open and blinked at the beautiful emerald that nestled on a bed of velvet. Her knees started shaking, too. "It's a ring. You are carrying a ring around with you?"

"I had it with me that day I told you I loved you and it flew to Paris with me. It's been with me the whole time. I couldn't bear to take it back to the jewelers because that would have meant coming to terms with the fact you'd turned me down."

"Sean—"

"Would you have preferred a diamond? It's just that when I saw it, it reminded me of the forest and the forest is our place."

"I love it." She lifted herself on tiptoe and crushed her mouth to his. "I love it so much. It's perfect."

"And will you wear it?"

"Always and forever. I love you. And I will phone you twenty times a day to tell you that."

"I can live with that." He took the ring from its box and slid it onto her finger. Then he kissed her and stroked her hair away from her face. "You're soaking wet."

"So are you."

"We could go to Heron Lodge or we could go to the house. It's family night." A smile touched the corners of his mouth. "And as you're about to officially become a member of our family, we should probably be there."

"Has Jackson already given away my job?"

"No, but he really didn't think you'd be back. He suggested that we might need to find help in the kitchen and Gramps almost bit his head off. Shall we make a run for it? We're already wet, anyway."

"I just need my suitcase—there's something in there." She grabbed it from under the tree where she'd left it and Sean took it from her and then drew her onto the path. They ran through the rain and arrived at the house, breathless and soaked. His hand tightened on hers. "Ready?"

"Of course."

She held tightly to his hand as Sean put the suitcase down, opened the door and pulled her inside.

"Look who I found outside in the rain."

Stunned silence fell across the table and then everyone started talking at once. Maple sprinted across to her, Jackson stood up and pulled her into a hug and Elizabeth exchanged a knowing smile with Alice.

"I told you she'd be back," Alice said. "Why do none of you ever listen to me?"

"I knew she'd be back, too." Elizabeth crossed the kitchen and gave her a hug. "You're soaking wet! Sean, you shouldn't have kept her out in the rain. We need to get you dry."

"I'm fine. I'm not cold. I am very pleased to see you all, and I have a present for you." She unzipped her case, now soaking wet, and pulled out a tin. "I made these for you and carried them all the way from Paris." She tipped them gently onto a plate and Kayla gave her an odd look.

"Cakes?"

"They're madeleines," Sean said gruffly, his eyes on Élise. "I'm glad you made them."

He understood the significance and she smiled. "It was time. Time you tried them. If you like them I will put them on the menu at the Boathouse and it will be a small piece of Paris."

A small piece of her past.

"I just hope they're better than those things you call pancakes," Walter muttered and she sped around the table and hugged him tightly.

"I love you, Walter. How are you feeling?"

"I don't know why everyone keeps asking me that because I'm just fine."

"That's good," Sean said, "because we have something to tell you." Even as he said the words Alice spotted Élise's finger and gasped.

"You've given her a ring. Oh, Sean!"

Elizabeth beamed. "I knew she loved you. A woman always knows."

Walter frowned. "I knew, too. I was the one who pointed out he was in love. For all that brain of his, he's very stupid about some things."

Rolling his eyes, Sean pulled Élise against him. "She said yes, so now you can all give us some peace."

"Did you go down on one knee?"

"It's pouring with rain out there. He'd ruin his trousers." Tyler stood up and wrapped her in a tight hug. "Welcome to the family. I'm glad it's official. Just don't start slobbering all over each other, that's all I ask. There's enough of that around here with Jackson and Kayla. I'd suggest we all have a drink to celebrate but Sean has already thrown most of it over the table. Thank God for napkins, I say."

"She's already family," Walter grunted, "and she would have stayed family whether she married Sean or not. And we should definitely have a drink. Champagne. Jackson? Is there any champagne?"

"I do not need champagne to celebrate. Being here, it is enough." Élise felt tears prick her eyes. "You are all very dear to me and I love you very much."

Tyler winced and retreated back to his seat at the table. "If you're going to get mushy, I'm going to need alcohol. Probably a crate of the stuff. Raid the cellar, Jackson."

Ignoring all of them, Élise tugged at Sean's hand and pulled him toward her. "I love you. I love you always and I tell you this in front of everyone and I will tell you every day."

Tyler groaned and slid down in his char. "I'm moving out."

"It is important to say how you feel."

"In that case, you should know I feel sick." Tyler shook his head and turned his back on them. "Tell me when it's safe to turn around."

Laughing, Jackson passed him a beer. "It's not champagne but it will numb the agony of witnessing true love. So now the excitement is over, can we get back to planning the winter? We have a ski season ahead and we need to do everything we can to make sure it's the best it can be."

Still holding Sean's hand, Élise slid into her chair, knowing that for her, life was already the very best it could be.

She helped herself to a madeleine, thinking of her mother. For the first time ever, the memory made her smile.

Sean sat down next to her and took one, too. He bit into it and smiled. "It's good."

"Yes."

His hand found hers under the table, his fingers strong and firm as he looked around at his family. "If you're planning the winter season then you can count me in. I might be around a bit more."

Jackson lifted an eyebrow. "Will you be providing your own shirts?"

"That depends. I quite like the ones Kayla buys for you. I might borrow those sometimes."

Alice picked up her knitting. "Have you noticed that the scarf I'm knitting is exactly the same color as Élise's ring?"

"These madeleines, or whatever you call them, are delicious." Kayla reached for a second one. "You should definitely put them on the menu."

Brenna smiled. "If you eat too many of those I'll have to double the length of our morning run."

The conversation bounced around the table, everyone talking at once, and Élise sat quietly, soaking it up.

The O'Neils. She loved each and every one of them. But most of all she loved the man sitting by her side, holding her hand, refusing to let her go. The man who had dropped everything and flown to Paris to be by her side. The man who had finished her deck so the Boathouse could open on time. The man who had made her see the truth about her mother and who had given her the courage to love again. And she knew love was a gift she would never, ever take for granted.

Unable to believe life could be this good, she turned her head to look at him, her heart overflowing, and then she reached for him and kissed him, ignoring their audience.

"I love you."

Sean smiled at her. "I love you, too. Shall we get out of here and go home?"

Home. Home to Heron Lodge. "It's family night."

Tyler choked. "Go! For God's sake, go and leave the rest of us to eat in peace. And don't come back until you can be together for five minutes without touching."

"In that case—" Élise stood up and Sean grabbed his coat and wrapped it around her.

"It's still raining. We'll make a run for it. Are you ready?"

"Yes." She was more than ready and she held his hand tightly as he opened the door, smiling as they stepped out into the rain together.

* * * * *

ACKNOWLEDGMENTS

PUBLISHING A BOOK is always a team effort and there are many people who deserve thanks. I'm always anxious I might miss someone so it sometimes takes me as long to write the acknowledgments as it would to write a whole chapter of a new story.

As always, my biggest thanks go to the readers who buy my books. I feel privileged that you choose to read my stories.

I'm grateful to my agent Susan Ginsburg, and to Susan Swinwood, Flo Nicoll and the team at Harlequin in the U.S. and U.K. who work so hard to make my book the best it can be and put it into the hands of readers across the globe.

I'm indebted to lovely Ele for helping with my French. Any mistakes are mine (blame it on the Pinot Noir consumed for research purposes).

Thanks to the fabulous Sharon Kendrick, who read the first sentence of this book over my shoulder on a flight and told me it was crap (thanks, Sharon, you'll be relieved to hear I rewrote it). She then read out the first sentence of hers in a loud voice and we were subsequently banned from flying with that airline ever again. Just kidding. Or maybe not. I won't know until I try and book my next flight.

As always, thanks to my family for their endless patience. Living with a writer isn't easy and no amount of pizza and chocolate can compensate for those times when a book is going badly and I'm pulling my hair out. You make me happy and I'm lucky to have you.

Read on for a sneak peek at

Maybe This Christmas,

*the final fabulous story in the O'Neil brothers
trilogy from Sarah Morgan.*

Available October 2014

Tyler O'Neil stomped the snow off his boots, pushed open the door of his lakeside home and tripped over a pair of boots and a jacket abandoned in the hallway.

Slamming his hand against the wall, he regained his balance and turned the air blue. 'Jess?'

There was no response from his daughter, but Ash and Luna, his two Siberian huskies, bounded out of the living room. Cursing under his breath, he watched in exasperation as both dogs cannoned towards him.

'Jess! You left the door to the living room open again. The dogs aren't supposed to be in there. Come down here right now and pick up your coat and boots! Do *not* jump up—*I'm warning you*.' He braced himself as Ash sprang. 'Why does no one listen to me around here?'

Luna, the more gentle of the two dogs, put her paws on his chest and tried to lick his face.

'Nice to know my word is law.' But Tyler rubbed her ears gently, burying his fingers in her thick fur as Jess emerged from the kitchen, a piece of toast in one hand and her phone in the other, head nodding in time to music as she pushed headphones away from her ears. She was wearing one of his sweaters and his Olympic medal dangled round her neck.

'Hi, Dad. How was your day?'

'I made it through alive until I stepped through my own front door. I've skied off cliffs safer than our hallway.' Glowering at her, Tyler pushed the ecstatic dogs away and nudged the abandoned snow boots to one side with his foot. 'Pick those up. And leave your boots in the porch from now on. You shouldn't be wearing them indoors.'

Still chewing, Jess stared at his feet. 'You're wearing *your* boots indoors.'

Not for the first time, Tyler reflected on the challenges of parenting. 'New rule. I'll leave mine outside, too. That way we don't get snow in the house. And hang your coat up instead of dropping it over any convenient surface.'

'You drop *yours*.'

Holy hell. 'I'm hanging it up. Watch me.' He shrugged out of his jacket and hung it up with exaggerated purpose. 'And turn the music down. That way you'll be able to hear me when I'm yelling at you.'

She grinned, unabashed. 'I turn it up so I can't hear you yelling at me. Grandma just sent me a text all in capitals. You need to teach her how to use her phone.'

'You're the teenager. You teach her.'

'She texted me in capitals all last week, and the week before that she kept dialling Jackson by accident.'

Tyler, entertained by the thought of his business-focused brother being driven insane by calls from their mother in the middle of his working day, grinned back. 'I bet he loved that. So what did she want?'

'She was inviting me over while you're at the team meeting at the Outdoor Centre. I'm going to help her cook.' She took another bite of toast. 'It's family night. Everyone is coming—even Uncle Sean. Had you forgotten?'

Tyler groaned. 'Team meeting and Fright Night? Whose idea was that?'

'Grandma's. She worries about me because I live with you and the only thing that never runs out in our fridge is beer. And you're not supposed to call it Fright Night. Can I come to the team meeting?'

'You would hate every moment.'

'I wouldn't! I love being part of a family business. The way you feel about meetings is the way I feel about school. Being trapped indoors is a waste of time when there's all that snow out there. But at least you get to ski all day. I'm stuck to a hard chair, trying to understand maths. Pity me.' She finished the toast and Tyler frowned as crumbs fell on the floor.

Ash pounced on them with enthusiasm.

'You're the reason the fridge is empty. You're always eating. If I'd known you were going to eat this much I never would have let you live with me. You're costing me a fortune.'

The fact his joke made her laugh told him how far they'd come in the year they'd been living together.

'Grandma says if I wasn't living with you, you'd drown in your own mess.'

'You're the one dropping the crumbs. You should use

a plate.'

'*You* never use a plate. You're always dropping crumbs on the floor.'

'You don't have to everything I do.'

'You're the grown up. I'm following your example.'

The thought was enough to bring him out in a cold sweat. 'Don't. You should do the opposite of everything I have ever done.' He watched as she bent to make a fuss of Luna and the medal around her neck swung forward, almost hitting the dog on the nose. 'Why are you wearing that?'

'It motivates me. And I like the example you set. You're the coolest dad on the planet. And you're fun to live with. Especially when you're trying to behave.'

'Trying to?' Tyler dragged his gaze from the medal that was a painful reminder of his old life. 'What's that supposed to mean?'

'I mean I like living here. You don't worry about the same stuff as most grown-ups.'

'I'm probably supposed to.' Tyler ran his hand over the back of his neck. 'I have a new respect for your grandmother. How did she raise three boys without strangling us?'

'Grandma would never strangle anyone. She's patient and kind.'

'Yeah, right. Unfortunately for you, I'm not—and I'm the one raising you now.'

The reality of that still terrified him more than anything he'd faced on the downhill ski circuit. If he messed this up, the consequences would be worse than a damaged leg and a shattered career. 'So, have you finished your assignment?'

'No. I started, but I got distracted watching the recording of your downhill in Beaver Creek. Come and watch it with me.'

He'd rather poke himself in the eye with a ski pole.

'Maybe later. I had a call from your teacher.' Casually, he changed the subject. 'You didn't hand in your assignment on Monday.'

'Luna ate it.'

'Yeah, right. You are allowed one late assignment in each trimester. You've already had two.'

'Weren't *you* ever late handing in assignments?'

All the time.

Wondering why anyone would choose to have more than one kid when being a parent was this hard, Tyler tried a different approach. 'If you have five late assignments you'll be staying late at homework club. That cuts into your skiing time.'

That wiped the smile from her face. 'I'll get it done.'

'Good decision. And next time finish your work before you watch TV.'

'I wasn't watching TV. I was watching you. I want to understand your technique. You were the best. I'm going to ski every spare minute this winter.' She closed her hand round the medal, making it sound like a vow. 'Will you be at race training tomorrow? You said you'd try to be there.'

Floored by that undiluted adoration, Tyler looked into his daughter's eyes and saw the same passion that burned in his own.

He thought of all the jobs that were piling up at

Snow Crystal. Jobs that needed his attention. Then he thought about the years he'd missed out on being with his daughter.

'I'll be there.' He strolled through to his recently renovated kitchen, cursing under his breath as cold seeped through his socks. 'Jess, you've been dripping snow through the whole house. It's like wading through a river.'

'That was Luna. She rolled in a snowdrift and then shook herself.'

'Next time she can shake herself outside our house.'

'I didn't want her to get cold.' Watching him, Jess pushed her hair behind her ear. 'You called it "our" house.'

'She's a dog, Jess! She has thick fur. She doesn't get cold. And of course I called it "our" house. What else would I call it? We both live here, and right now there's no chance of me forgetting that!' He stepped over another patch of water. 'I've spent the last couple of years renovating this place and I still feel as if I need to wear my boots indoors.'

'I love Ash and Luna. They're family. I never had a dog in Chicago. Mom hated mess. We never had a real Christmas tree, either. She hated those because she had to pick up the needles.'

Tension and irritation fled. The mention of Jess's mother made him feel as if someone had stuffed snow down his neck. Suddenly it wasn't only his feet that were cold.

Tyler clamped his mouth down on the comment that wanted to leave his lips. The truth was that Janet

Carpenter had hated just about everything. She'd hated Vermont. She'd hated living so far from a city. She'd hated skiing. Most of all she'd hated him. But his family had made it a rule not to say a bad word about Janet in front of Jess, and he stuck to that rule even when the strain of it brought him close to bursting.

'Yes, we'll have a real tree. We'll take a trip into the forest and choose one together.' Aware that he might be overcompensating, he reverted back to his normal self. 'And I'm glad you love the dogs, but that doesn't change the fact you should keep the damn living room door closed when they're in the house. This place is no longer a construction site. The new rule is no dogs on sofas or beds.'

'I think Luna prefers the old rules.' Her eyes sparkled with mischief. 'And you're not supposed to say damn. Grams hates it when you swear.'

Tyler kept his jaw clenched. 'Well, Grams isn't here, is she?' His grandmother and grandfather still lived at the resort, in the converted sugar house that had once been the hub of Snow Crystal's maple syrup production. 'And if you tell her I'll throw you on your butt in the snow and you'll be wetter than Luna. Now, go and finish your assignment or I'll get the Bad Parent award— and I'm not prepared to climb onto the podium to collect that one.'

Jess beamed. 'If I promise to hand in my assignment and not tell anyone you swear, can we watch skiing together in your den?'

'You should ask Brenna. She's a gifted teacher.' He was about to reach for a beer when he remembered he was supposed to be setting an example, so he poured himself a glass of milk instead. Since Jess had moved in he'd disciplined himself not to drink from the carton. 'She'll tell you what everyone is doing wrong.'

'She's already promised to help me now I've made the school ski team. Have you seen her in the gym? She has sick abs.'

'Yeah, I've seen her.' And he didn't let himself think about her abs.

He didn't let himself think about any part of her.

She was his best friend and she was staying that way.

To take his mind off the thought of Brenna's abs, he stuck his head back in the fridge. 'This fridge is empty.'

'Kayla's giving me a lift into the village so I'll pick something up. We're eating with Grandma tonight.' Her phone beeped and she dug it out of her pocket. 'Oh—'

Tyler pushed the door shut with his shoulder and then caught sight of her expression. 'What's wrong?'

'Kayla texted to say she's tied up at work, that's all.'

'Sounds painful. Never mind. I'll go to the store tomorrow.'

Jess stared at her phone. 'I need to go now.

'Why? We both hate shopping. It can wait.'

'This can't wait.' Her head was down but he saw colour streak across her cheekbones.

'Is this about Christmas? Because it's not for another couple of weeks. We still have plenty of time. Most of my shopping gets done at three o'clock on Christmas Eve.'

'It's not about Christmas! Dad, I need—' She broke off, her face scarlet. 'Some things from the store, that's all.'

'What can you possibly need that can't wait until tomorrow?'

'Girl stuff, OK? I need *girl stuff!*' Snapping at him, she spun on her heel and stalked out of the room, leaving Tyler staring after her, trying to understand the reason for her sudden mood explosion.

Girl stuff?

It took him a moment and then he closed his eyes briefly and swore under his breath.

Girl stuff.

Comprehension came along with a moment of pure panic. Nothing in his past life had prepared him to raise a teenager. Especially not a teenage girl.

When had she—?

He glanced towards the door, knowing he had to say something but clueless as to the most sensitive way to broach a topic that embarrassed the hell out of both of them.

Could he ignore it?

Tell her to look it up on the internet?

He ran his hand over his face and cursed under his breath, knowing he couldn't ignore it or leave something that important to a search engine.

It wasn't as if she had her mother to ask. He was the only parent in her life. And right now she was probably thinking that was a raw deal.

'Jess!' he yelled after her, and when there was no response he strode out of the kitchen and found her tugging on her boots in the hall. 'Get in the car. I'll take you to the store.'

'Forget it.' Her voice was muffled, her hair falling forward over her face. 'I'm going to walk over to the house and ask Grandma to drive me.'

'Grandma hates driving in the snow and the dark. I'll take you.' His voice was rougher than he'd intended and he stretched out a hand to touch her shoulder and then pulled it back. To hug or not to hug? He had no idea. 'I was going to the store anyway.'

'You were going tomorrow, not today.'

'Well, now I'm going today.' He grabbed his coat. 'Come on. We'll pick up some of that chocolate you like.'

Still not looking at him, she fiddled with her boots and he sighed, wishing for the hundredth time that teenage girls came with an operating manual.

'Jess, it's all good.'

'It's *not* good,' she muttered in a strangled tone. 'It's like a *massive* avalanche of awkward! You're thinking this is your worst nightmare.'

'I'm not thinking that.' He gripped the door handle. 'I'm thinking I'm messing it up. I'm saying the wrong things and making you feel uncomfortable—which is not my intention.'

She peeped at him through her hair. 'You're wishing I'd never come to live here.'

He'd thought they'd got past that. The insecurity. Those creeping, confidence-eroding doubts that had eaten her happiness. 'I'm not wishing that.'

'Mom told me she wished I'd never been born.'

Tyler zipped up his jacket viciously, almost removing a finger in the process. 'She didn't mean that.' He dragged open the door, grateful for the blast of freezing air to cool his temper.

'Yes, she did.' Jess mumbled the words. 'She told me I was the worst thing that ever happened to her.'

'Well, *I've* never thought that. Not once. Not even when my socks are wet because you've let the dogs drag snow into the house.'

'You didn't sign up for any of this.'

Her voice faltered and the uncertainty in her eyes made him want to punch a hole through something.

'I tried to. I asked your mom to marry me.'

'I know. She said no because she thought you'd be a useless father. I heard her telling my stepdad. She said you were irresponsible.'

Tyler felt emotion rush at him. 'Yeah, well, that may be true—but it doesn't change the fact that I wanted you, Jess, right from the start. And when she wouldn't agree to marry me I tried other ways of having you to live here with us. Why the hell are we talking about this *now*?'

'Because it's the truth. I *was* a mistake.'

Jess gave a tiny shrug, as if it didn't matter, and because he knew how much it did matter he hesitated, knowing that the way he responded was vitally important to the way she felt about this whole situation.

'We didn't exactly plan to have you, that's true. I'm not going to lie about that. But you can't plan every single thing that happens in life. People think they can. They think they can control things and then *whoosh*—something happens that proves you're not as in control as you think. And sometimes it's the things you don't plan that turn out best.'

'I wasn't one of those things. Mom also told me I was the biggest mistake of her life.'

His hands clenched into fists and he had to force himself to stay calm. 'She was probably upset or tired.'

'It *was* the time I snowboarded down the stairs...'

Tyler managed a smile. 'Right—well, there you go. That's why.' He dragged her against him and hugged her, feeling her skinny body and smelling the familiar scent of her hair. His daughter. *His child*. 'You're the best thing that ever happened to me. You're an O'Neil all the way, and sometimes that drives your mom a little crazy, that's all. She doesn't have that much love for us O'Neils. But she loves you—I know she does.'

He *didn't* know that, but he reined in his natural urge to speak the truth.

'Her family isn't close, like ours, and that makes her jealous.'

Her voice was muffled against his chest and he felt her arms tighten round him.

'You may skip classes, but you're not stupid.'

Jess pulled away, her cheeks streaked pink. 'Is that why you don't want to ever get married? Because of what happened with Mom?'

How was he supposed to answer that?

He'd learned that with Jess the questions came with no warning. She bottled stuff up and held them inside until she burst with containing them.

'Some people aren't the marrying type, and I'm one of those.'

'Why?'

Tyler decided he'd rather ski a vertical slope in the dark with his eyes closed than have this conversation. 'People are good at some things and bad at others. I'm bad at relationships. I don't make women happy.' *Just ask your mother.* 'Women who care about me often end up being hurt.'

'So you're never going to get involved with anyone again? Dad, that's really dumb.'

'You're telling me I'm dumb? What happened to respect?'

'All I'm saying is it's OK to make mistakes when you're young. Everyone messes up sometimes. It shouldn't stop you trying again when you're older.'

'Jess—'

'Maybe you'll be better at it now you've got me. If you want to know how the female mind works, you can ask,' she said generously, and Tyler opened his mouth and closed it again.

'Thanks, sweetheart. I appreciate that.' Deciding that the conversation was getting more awkward, not less, he dug out his car keys. 'Now, get in the car before both of us freeze in the doorway. We need to get to the store before it closes.'

'It would have been easier for you if I'd been a boy. Then we wouldn't have to have embarrassing conversations.'

'Don't you believe it. Teenage boys are the worst. I know. I *was* one. And I'm not embarrassed.' Tyler's tongue felt thick in his mouth. 'Why would I be embarrassed by something that's a normal part of growing up? If there's anything you want to ask—' *Please, God, don't let there be anything she wanted to ask* '—you come straight out and say it.'

She tugged on her boots. 'I'm good. But I need to get to the store.'

He grabbed her coat and thrust it at her. 'Wrap up. It's freezing out there.'

'Can Ash and Luna come?'

'On a trip to the store?' He was about to ask why he would want to take two hyperactive dogs on a trip to the village, but then he saw her hopeful expression and decided the dogs might be the best cure for awkwardness. And hopefully they'd take her mind off her mother and the complexity of human relationships. 'Sure. Great idea. Nothing I love more than two panting animals while I'm driving. But you'll have to keep them under control.'

Jess whistled for Ash and Luna, who came bounding, ecstatic at the promise of a trip.

Tyler drove out of Snow Crystal, slowing down for the guests who were returning from a day on the slopes.

The resort was half empty, but it was still early in the season and he knew visitor numbers would double once the Christmas break arrived.

And across the Atlantic in Europe the Alpine Ski World Cup was underway.

He tightened his grip on the wheel, grateful that Jess was chattering. Grateful for the distraction.

'Uncle Jackson told me the snowmaking is going really well. Loads of runs are open. Do you think we might have a big fall of snow? Uncle Sean is here.'

She talked non-stop as she stroked Luna.

'I saw his car earlier. Gramps said he was here for the meeting, but I don't get why. He's a surgeon. He doesn't get involved in running the business. Or is he going to be here to fix broken legs?'

'Uncle Sean is working up a pre-conditioning programme with Christy at the spa. They're trying to reduce skiing injuries. It was Brenna's idea.' Tyler slowed as they reached the main highway and turned towards the village. The snow was falling steadily, coating the windshield and the road ahead.

'How come Brenna is the one in charge of the outdoor programme when you're the one with the gold medals?'

'Because Uncle Jackson had already given her the job before I came home, and because I hate organisation almost as much as I hate shopping and cooking. I'm only interested in the skiing part. And Brenna is a brilliant teacher. She's patient and kind, whereas I want to dump people in a snowdrift if they don't get it right the first time.' He glanced briefly in his rearview mirror. 'Are you going to sleep over with Grandma tonight?'

'Do you want me to? Are you planning on having sex or something?'

Tyler almost swerved into the ditch. '*Jess—*'

'What? You said I could talk to you about anything.'

He steadied the car. Focused on the road. 'You can't ask me if I'm planning on having sex.'

'Why? I don't want to get in the way, that's all.'

'You don't get in the way.' He wondered why this conversation had to come up while he was driving in difficult conditions. 'You never get in the way.'

'Dad, I'm not stupid. You used to have a lot of sex. I know. I read about it on the internet. This one article said you got a woman in bed faster than you made it to the bottom of the slope in the downhill.'

Feeling as if he'd been hit by another avalanche of awkwardness, Tyler slowed right down as he approached the village. Lights twinkled in store windows and a large Christmas tree stood proud at the end of Main Street. 'You don't want to believe everything you read on the internet.'

'All I'm saying is, you don't have to give up sex because I'm living with you. You need to get out there again.'

Speechless, he pulled into a parking space by the village store. 'I'm *not* having this conversation with my thirteen-year-old daughter.'

'I'm nearly fourteen. You need to keep up.'

'Whatever. My sex-life is off-limits.'

'Did you ever have sex with Brenna? Was she one of the ones you had a relationship with?'

How was it possible to sweat when the air temperature was below freezing? 'That is personal, Jess.'

'So you *did* have sex with her?'

'No! I never had sex with Brenna.' Sex with Brenna was something he didn't allow himself to think about. *Ever.* He didn't think about those abs. He didn't think about those legs. 'And this conversation is over and done.'

'Because it would be fine with me. I think she really likes you. Do you like her?'

Realising he'd just been given permission to have sex

by his teenage daughter, Tyler raked his fingers through his hair. 'Yeah, of course I do. I've known her since we were kids. We've hung around together for most of our lives. She's a good friend.'

And he wasn't going to do anything to damage that. Nothing. Not a damn thing.

He'd messed up every relationship he'd had. His friendship with Brenna was the one thing that was still intact and he intended to keep it that way.

Jess unclipped her seat belt. 'I like Brenna. She's not all gooey-eyed about you like some women are. And she talks to me like a grown-up. If you could give me some money I'll go and buy what I need. I'll buy some stuff for the fridge too, so if Grandma drops by she'll be impressed by your housekeeping.'

'Gooey-eyed?' Tyler pulled his wallet out of his pocket. 'What is that supposed to mean?'

Jess shrugged. 'Like some of the moms at school. They all wear make-up and tight clothes in case you're picking me up. The other day when Kayla picked me up there was almost a riot. And sometimes the other girls want to know if you're coming or not. I guess their moms don't want to bother with the whole lipstick thing if you're not going to show up.'

Tyler stared at her. 'Are you serious?'

'Yeah, but it's OK.' Jess tugged her coat around her skinny frame. 'I'm cool with the fact my dad is a national sex symbol. But if you're going to pick someone I have to live with and call Mom I'd like you to pick someone like Brenna, that's all. She doesn't flick her hair all the time and look at you with a dopey smile.'

'No one is coming to live with us, you won't be calling anyone Mom and, for the final time, I'm *not* going to have sex with Brenna.' Tyler spoke through clenched teeth. 'Now, go buy whatever it is you need.'

Jess slid down in her seat. 'I can't.' Her voice was strangled. 'Mr Turner has just gone in there with his son, who is in my class. I want to *die*.'

Tyler breathed deeply and then rummaged in the mess in his car until he found an old restaurant bill and a pen. 'Make me a list.'

'I'll wait until they've gone.'

It was dark in the car, but he could see she was scarlet again.

'Jess, we need to do this before we both die of hypothermia.'

She hesitated, and then snatched the pen and scribbled.

'Wait here.' Tyler took it from her and walked into the store. If he could ski Austria's notorious Hahnenkamm at a speed of ninety miles per hour, he could buy 'girl stuff'.

* * * *

Ten minutes later Brenna walked into the store, relieved to be out of the bitter cold.

Ellen Kelly came out from the room behind the counter, carrying three large boxes. 'Brenna! Your mother was in here earlier today. Told me she hadn't seen you for a month.'

'I've been busy. Can I help you with those, Ellen?'

Brenna took them from her and stacked them on the floor. 'You shouldn't carry so many at once. The doctor told you to be careful lifting.'

'I'm careful. Storm's coming, and people like to stock up in case they're snowed in for a month. We're all hoping it's not going to be as bad as 2007. Remember Valentine's Day?'

'I was in Europe, Ellen.'

'That's right—you were. I forgot. No snow at all in January, and then three feet in twenty-four hours. Ned Morris lost some of his cows when the barn roof fell in.' Ellen rubbed her back. 'By the way, you just missed him.'

'Ned Morris?'

'Tyler.' Ellen bent and opened one of the boxes. 'And he had Jess with him. I swear she's grown a foot over the summer.'

'Tyler was here?' Brenna's heart pounded a little harder. 'We have a meeting back at the resort in an hour.'

'I'm guessing they had an emergency. Jess stayed in the car and he came in and bought everything she needed. And I do mean *everything*.' Ellen Kelly winked knowingly and started unpacking boxes and transferring the contents to the shelves. 'I never thought I'd see Tyler O'Neil in here shopping for a teenage girl. I remember people had nothing but bad to say about him when Janet Carpenter announced she was pregnant, but he's proved them all wrong. That Janet is cold as a Vermont winter, but Tyler...' She arranged cans on a shelf. 'He may be a bad boy with the women, but no one can say he hasn't done right by that child.'

'She's almost fourteen.'

'And looking like a different person from the one who arrived here last winter, all skinny and pale. Can you imagine? Sending a child away like that?' Ellen clucked her disapproval and bent to open another box, this one packed with Christmas decorations. 'Disgraceful.'

Brenna was careful to keep her opinion on that to herself. 'Janet had a new baby.'

'So she gave up the old one? All the more reason to keep Jess close, in my opinion.' Ellen hung long garlands of tinsel on hooks. 'She could have been scarred for life. Lucky she has Tyler and the rest of the O'Neils. Would you like any decorations, honey? I have a big selection this year.'

'No, thanks, Ellen. I don't decorate. And Jess isn't scarred. She's a lovely girl.' Loyal and discreet, Brenna tried to steer the conversation in a different direction. She didn't mention the insecurities or any of the problems she knew Jess had suffered settling in. 'Did you know she made the school ski team? She has real talent.'

'She's her father's daughter all right. I still remember that winter when Tyler skied down old Mitch Sommerville's roof.' Smiling, Ellen sat an oversized smiling Santa on a shelf. 'He was arrested, of course, but my George always said he'd never seen a person so fearless on the mountain. Except you, perhaps. The two of you were inseparable. Used to watch you sneaking out when you should have been in class.'

'Me? You've got the wrong person, Ellen.' Brenna grinned at her. 'I never sneaked out of school in my life.'

'Must be a real blow for Tyler, losing his career like that. Especially when he was right at the top.'

Brenna, who would rather jump naked into a freezing lake than talk about another person's private business, made a desperate attempt to change the subject. 'There's plenty to keep him busy up at Snow Crystal. Bookings are up. Looks like it might be a busy winter.'

'That's good to hear. They deserve it. No one was more shocked than me to hear the place was in trouble. The O'Neils have lived at Snow Crystal since before I was born. Still, Jackson seems to have turned it around. There were people round here who thought he'd made a mistake when he spent all that money building fancy log cabins with hot tubs, but turns out he knew what he was doing.'

'Yes.' Brenna picked up the few things she needed, wondering if there *was* such a thing as private business, living in a small town. 'He's a clever businessman.'

'He's always known his own mind. And that girl of his…'

'Kayla?'

'Her heart is in the right place, even if she *does* walk in here with those shiny shoes, looking all New York City.'

Brenna added milk to her basket. 'She's British.'

'You wouldn't know it until she opens her mouth. Take some of those chocolate cookies while you're there. They're delicious. Not that you're short of good things to eat at Snow Crystal, with Élise in charge of the kitchen. Now that Jackson and Sean are settled it will be Tyler's turn next.'

Brenna dropped the jar she was holding and it

smashed, spreading the contents across the floor. *Crap*. 'Oh, Ellen, I'm so sorry. I'll clean it up. Do you have a mop?'

Annoyed with herself, she stooped to pick up the pieces, but Ellen waved her aside.

'Leave it. I don't want you cutting your fingers. There was a time when I thought the two of you might end up together. You couldn't be separated.'

Double crap.

'We were friends, Ellen.' The last thing she needed was this conversation. 'And we're still friends.'

By the time she left the store she was exhausted from dodging gossip and thinking about Tyler.

She drove straight back to Snow Crystal and parked outside the Outdoor Center next to Sean's flashy red sports car. The snow was falling steadily, the path already covered with half a foot. The temperature had dropped and there was the promise of even more snow in the air—which was good news for Snow Crystal, because snow cover was directly related to the number of Christmas bookings.

And they needed those bookings.

Despite what she'd said to Ellen, she knew the resort was still struggling to stay afloat. The log cabins, each with its own hot tub and a private view of the lake and forest, had been expensive to build. For the past two years they'd had more cabins empty than occupied. Things were slowly improving, but they still had too many vacancies.

Brenna stamped the snow off her boots, pushed open the door and was enveloped by a welcome rush of warm air. She walked through to the peace and tranquillity of the spa. The lighting was muted, the walls a soothing shade of ocean-blue. Soft music played in the background and the air was filled with the scent of aromatherapy oils. It tickled her nose—but then she'd never been one to lie around and let someone she didn't know rub oil into her skin. It seemed intimate to her. Something a lover might do, not a stranger.

Not that lovers played much of a part in her life.

Christy, who had joined them in the summer to run the spa, glanced up from behind the desk. A mini Christmas tree twinkled from the corner. 'Still snowing out there?' She was a cool blonde, a qualified physiotherapist who had added massage and aromatherapy to her already impressive list of qualifications. 'You've had a long day. Is it always as crazy as this at the beginning of a winter season?'

'There's a lot of planning and preparation, that's for sure.' Brenna pulled her hat off her head, sending another flurry of snowflakes onto the floor. 'Is everyone here already?'

'We're still waiting for Élise and—'

'*Merde*, I am late.' Élise, the Head Chef, sped past her like a whirlwind. 'We are full in the restaurant tonight, and also there is a party of thirty who booked out the Boathouse for an anniversary dinner. I don't have time for this. I know already my plan for the winter season—which is to give people the best food they 'ave ever tasted. I will see you in the gym first thing tomorrow, Brenna. I'm sorry I missed this morning. It is the first time for months, but we were crazy in the kitchen.'

'It's Christmas, and your restaurant is the one part of this resort that has never been in trouble.' Brenna pushed her hat into her pocket. 'You're stressed. You only ever drop the "h" when you're stressed.'

'Of course I am stressed. I am doing the work of eight people and now I am expected to sit in a *meeting*.' Disgusted, Élise strode off, as light on her feet as a dancer, her shiny cap of dark hair swinging around her jaw.

Christy raised her eyebrows. 'Is she caffeinated?'

'No, she's French.' Brenna glanced out of the window. 'I saw Sean's car, so I guess that means everyone is here?'

'Everyone but Tyler. He's late. I texted him but he hasn't replied.'

'He's probably turned the ringer off on his phone. He does that a lot. He used to have to change his number once a month because women kept calling him.'

'I'm not surprised. The man is so insanely hot I disconnect the smoke alarm whenever he walks through that door. I saw him in the gym this morning—which was a special treat, given he usually uses the one in his house. The guy can bench-press the weight of a car.' Christy fanned herself with her fingers. 'I'm thinking of adding his name to the list of attractions at Snow Crystal.'

'He's already *on* the list. Kayla has talked him into doing a few motivational talks, and he occasionally acts as a guide for experienced skiers who are willing to pay a price to ski with Tyler O'Neil.'

And she knew he hated it. He wasn't interested in fame or adulation, just in skiing down a mountain as fast as possible. He didn't want to talk about what he did; he just wanted to do it. Other people didn't seem to understand that, but she did. She understood his love of the snow and the speed.

'He'll turn up when he's ready, as he always does. He operates in his own way, in his own time.'

'I love that about him. It's a very sexy trait. I guess you don't notice? You've known the O'Neils your whole life. They're probably like brothers to you.'

How was she supposed to answer that? Two out of the three O'Neils were like brothers—that was true. As for the third... She'd long since reconciled herself to the fact that Tyler O'Neil didn't return her feelings, and she'd learned the hard way that dreaming made things worse. As children they'd been inseparable. As adults— well, things hadn't turned out the way she'd once hoped they might, but she'd learned to live with it. She knew better than to wish for something that was never going to happen. She had her feet firmly on the ground, and if her brain ever wandered in that direction then she pulled it back fast.

'You're lucky,' Christy fed a fresh stack of paper into the printer. 'You get to work with the guy every day.'

And that probably should be hard. When she'd accepted Jackson's offer of a job running the Outdoor Programme for Snow Crystal Resort she hadn't known she'd be working with Tyler.

But it wasn't hard.

Working with Tyler was one of the things she loved most about her job. She got to spend most days with the man of her dreams.

She'd tried curing herself. She'd tried dating other men, and she'd even worked abroad, but Tyler was wedged in her heart and she'd long since accepted that wasn't going to change.

And if over the years it had hurt her to see him with women, she'd consoled herself with the fact that the women in his life came and went, whereas their friendship had lasted for ever.

'How is the spa doing? Are you going to be busy over Christmas?'

'It's looking that way.' Christy keyed something into the computer, her perfectly manicured nails tapping the keyboard, her shiny blonde hair curving around her smooth cheeks. 'I'm fully booked for the Christmas week.'

'You're doing a good job, Christy.'

Brenna wondered how many hours it took to look as polished as Christy. As a child, she'd barely sat still long enough for her mother to drag a brush through her hair. She'd hated ribbons and bows and shiny shoes, which had come as a disappointment to a woman who had longed for a little girl who would wear pink and play quietly with dolls. All Brenna had wanted to do was climb trees and play in the dirt along with the three O'Neil boys. She'd envied them the freedom of their lives and envied their close family, so accepting and supportive.

The O'Neil boys weren't expected to be a certain way or to satisfy a set of rules before they were loved.

She'd wanted to do everything they did—whether it had been climbing trees or skiing steep slopes. She hadn't cared how messy or dirty she'd got; she hadn't cared if she came home with scraped knees and torn clothes. With them she'd felt accepted in a way she never had been at home or at school.

'So, is Tyler seeing anyone at the moment?' Christy's voice was casual. 'I guess there's a queue?'

'He's not known for his long-term relationships.'

'Sounds like my type of guy.' Christy input some figures into the spreadsheet. 'I love them wild. All the more fun when you tame them.'

'I'm not sure Tyler *can* be tamed.' And she didn't want to tame him. She didn't want a different version of Tyler. She wanted Tyler the way he was.

'So what's a guy like him doing here? I mean, Snow Crystal is lovely, but it's more of a family resort than a hive for the rich and famous.'

'Tyler loves Snow Crystal. He grew up here. And this is a family business. He does what he can to help.' And she knew it half killed him to no longer be competing. 'If we get another fall of snow in the next few days it might tempt a few more people to book. I know Kayla is putting together some packages.'

'Yes, I've been working on a non-skier programme with her. And talking of Kayla…' Christy rummaged in the drawer of her desk. 'Can you give this to her? It came in this morning and I forgot to tell her. It's nail polish. The shade is Ice Crystal. She's going to use it in a promotion she's doing. Has she mentioned her plans for an Ice Party to you?'

'No.'

'She's planning a pre-Christmas event here, for locals

as well as guests. An Ice Party. Fire pit, ice sculpture, sled dogs, hot food, fireworks—it sounds fabulous.'

'I can't wait to hear more. Aren't you joining us for the meeting?'

'No. There are only two of us in today. Angie has flu, so I'm covering the phones, and anyway I'm not sure I can cope with all that O'Neil testosterone in one room. What do you think of the nail polish? It's pretty, don't you think? Perfect for the holiday party season.'

Brenna turned the bottle over in her hand, watching it sparkle in the light. 'I spend most of my day with my hands in thick mittens or else I'm chipping my nails hauling skis all over the resort, so I can't honestly say Ice Crystal nail polish is going to have much of a place in my life—but, yes, it's very sparkly.'

It was the sort of thing her mother would have liked her to wear.

'You should come in and have a spa morning before we get busy. My treat. I could massage away all those skiing aches. And you *must* tell me what you do to your hair. It's so shiny. I want a bottle of whatever you're using.'

Christy's expression changed from friendly to feline as the door opened, letting in a blast of cold air. She smoothed her already smooth sheet of blonde hair and smiled.

'Hi!'

Brenna didn't need to turn her head to see who had walked in. Any one of the three O'Neil brothers might have caused a woman to sit up straighter and moisten her lips but, given that two out of the three were already in the meeting room, she knew exactly who was standing behind her.

Her heart lifted along with her mood, as it always did when Tyler walked into a room. If she were a dog she would have wagged her tail and jumped all over him.

'Hi, Bren.' Tyler slapped her on the shoulder with the same casual affection he showed his brothers, his attention focused on Christy, whose eyelashes were working overtime.

'You're late, Tyler. Everyone else is here.'

'Saving the best until last.' Tyler winked at her. 'So, how's it going here in Beauty Central?'

Brenna watched as Christy's cheeks turned a little pinker. The same thing happened every time Tyler O'Neil smiled at a woman. He radiated energy, and the combination of dark good looks, masculine vitality and casual charm proved an irresistible combination.

'It's going great.' Christy leaned forward, giving him the full benefit of her green eyes and her cleavage. 'We're busier than last year, and Kayla and I have been working out some great ski/spa promotions. Any time you fancy a massage, let me know.'

She flirted easily, naturally—as most women did when they were around Tyler.

Brenna was hopeless at flirting. She didn't have that way of looking, that way of smiling—but most of all she didn't have the clever words.

Christy used words like a rope, throwing them out, using them to draw him in like a wild horse being broken.

Watching it, Brenna felt as if her heart were being

squeezed in someone's hands.

She was about to melt away quietly to the meeting room when Tyler caught her arm.

'Did you hear the forecast?' His eyes gleamed with anticipation and she nodded, reading his mind.

'Heavy snow. Good for business.'

'Powder day. Good for us. What about it? Deep snow, back country and just the two of us making tracks the way we used to when we were kids?'

His voice was a soft, sexy purr, and she felt her knees weaken as they always did when she was this close to him.

She consoled herself with the fact that this was something she shared with him that Christy couldn't. She might not be able to flirt, but she could ski. And she skied well. She was one of the few people who could almost keep up with him.

Ellen was right. They had skipped classes.

On one occasion her mother had been called down to the school, but the tense atmosphere at home in the aftermath of that confrontation had been worth it for those few blissful hours spent alone with Tyler, doing what they both loved best.

But there was no skipping anything now.

They both had responsibilities.

'I'll have to get in line. We have a waiting list of people willing to pay good money to ski powder with you.'

His smile faded. 'Lucky me.' He let his hand drop and turned back to Christy, who had somehow managed to apply another layer of gloss to her lips in the short time Tyler's head had been turned.

She smiled, giving him the full benefit of Chanel. 'I expect you're looking forward to skiing the hell out of those slopes? I watched a replay of your medal-winning run the other day on TV. You were unbelievably fast.'

Knowing it was a sensitive subject, Brenna glanced quickly at Tyler—but his expression didn't change. There was nothing in that wickedly handsome face to suggest this situation was difficult for him.

But she knew it was. It had to be, because Tyler O'Neil had lived to race.

From the moment he'd strapped on his first set of skis he'd been addicted to the speed and adrenaline of downhill. It had been a passion. Some might have said an addiction.

And then he'd fallen.

Thinking about that day made her stomach turn. She could remember the gut-wrenching terror of waiting to hear if he was dead or alive.

The whole family had been there to support him while he raced, and because she'd been working for Jackson in Europe she'd been there too. They'd stood in the grandstand, watching the skiers hurtle down at brutal speeds, waiting for Tyler. Instead of beating them all, and ending the season triumphant, he'd fallen and ended his downhill career for good. He'd spun, twisted and crashed heavily, before sliding down the near vertical run and slamming into the netting. Like all skiers, he'd had falls before—but this one had been different.

There had been screams from the crowd and then a murmur of anticipation—followed by the dreaded stillness and the breathless agony of waiting.

Trapped in the crowd, Brenna had been unable to do anything but watch helplessly as he'd been lifted, seriously injured, into a helicopter. There had been blood on the snow and she'd closed her eyes, breathed in the freezing air and begged whoever might be listening, *Please let him live*. And she'd promised herself that as long as he survived she'd stop wanting the impossible.

She'd stop wanting what she couldn't have.

She'd stop hoping he'd return her feelings.

She'd stop hoping he'd fall in love with her.

She'd never complain about anything ever again.

As she'd waited for news, along with his family, she'd told herself she didn't care who he was with as long as he was alive.

But of course that promise, made in the scalding heat of fear, hadn't been easy to keep. Even less so now, when they worked alongside each other every day.

She'd witnessed his frustration at being forced to give up the racing career he loved. He hid his feelings under layers of bad-boy attitude, but she knew it hurt him. She knew he ached to be back racing.

He was a gifted athlete, and it made her sad to see him standing on the sidelines or coaching a group of kids. It was like watching an injured racehorse trapped in a riding school when the only place he wanted to be was on the track, winning.

She hadn't made a sound, but he turned his head and looked at her.

He had the O'Neil eyes—that vivid, intense blue that reminded her of the sky on the most perfect skiing day.

A knot of tension formed in her stomach. A dangerous lethargy spread through her body. Neither Jackson nor Sean had this effect on her. Only Tyler. For a moment she thought she saw something flicker in those blue depths, and then he gave her a slow, lazy smile.

'You ready, Bren? If I'm going to die of boredom, I don't want to do it alone.'

No matter how bad the day, Tyler always made her laugh. She loved his wicked sense of humour and she loved his indifference to authority. If he did something, then it was because it made sense to him, because he believed in it—not because it was laid out in a rulebook.

As someone who had grown up with the rulebook stuck in her face, she envied his cool determination to live life on his terms. He had a wild streak, but his downhill skiing career had fed his desire to duel with danger and provided an outlet for that excess energy. How he would have used that wild streak had he *not* been a skier had been the subject of endless speculation, both in the village and on the World Cup circuit.

He threw a final smile in Christy's direction and strolled towards the meeting room: six foot two of raw sex appeal and lethal charm

Brenna followed more slowly, giving herself a lecture.

It was the beginning of the season. She had to start as she meant to go on—being realistic about her relationship with Tyler.

He saw her as 'one of the boys'. A ski buddy. Even on the rare occasion when she dressed up and wore heels and a tight dress he didn't look in her direction. Which might not have been quite so galling had it not been for the fact that he looked at almost every other female who crossed his path.

She had the distinction of being the one girl in Vermont Tyler O'Neil hadn't kissed.

In the background she heard the phone ring. Heard Christy pick it up and answer in her pitch-perfect professional voice. 'Snow Crystal Spa, Christy speaking, how may I help you?'

You can't, Brenna thought miserably. *No one can help me.*

She'd been in love with him her whole life, and nothing she did, or he did, had ever changed that. Not even when he'd got Janet Carpenter pregnant and she'd felt as if her heart had been sliced in two.

She'd taken a job on another continent in the hope of curing herself. She'd dated other men in the hope that one of them would cure her of Tyler. Before coming to the conclusion there was no cure. Her feelings were deep and permanent.

She was doomed to love Tyler O'Neil for ever.

WIN

A summer spa break!

To celebrate the launch of *Suddenly Last Summer*,
we're giving you the chance to enjoy that holiday
feeling this summer with an indulgent
one-night Champneys spa break.

Visit millsandboon.co.uk/spabreak
for your chance to win.

MILLS & BOON®

If you enjoyed **Suddenly Last Summer**,
why not share your thoughts with
hundreds of other Sarah Morgan
fans and post a review at:

amazon.co.uk   goodreads

Don't miss Sarah Morgan's first, irresistible O'Neil brothers story

Enjoy more sizzling summer stories from Sarah Morgan

**Discover more at
www.millsandboon.co.uk/sarah-morgan**